The Sweetest Fall

AUTUMN GREY

The Sweetest Fall
Copyright © 2015 Autumn Grey

Cover design: Rocking Book Covers
Edited by: Hot Tree Editing and Tricia Harden—Emerald Eyes Editing
Formatting: Champagne Book Design

All rights reserved including the right to reproduce, distribute, or transmit in any form or by any means.

This book is a work of fiction. Names, characters and incidents are a product of the author's imagination and are fictitious. Any resemblance to actual events, or persons living or dead, is coincidental.

Author's Note
The Sweetest Fall was previously titled *Havoc Series Box Set*. The story hasn't changed. It's still the same.

This book is dedicated to every person who has ever looked in the mirror and thought, "I look terrible".

You don't.

You're beautiful and perfect the way you are.
You are uniquely you.

Be Brave.

Be You.

Part One

Loving your curves is sexy. Wear your curves proudly.

Remington St. Germain

> The only way to get rid of temptation is to yield to it.
> Oscar Wilde

Prologue

Selene Michaels

Nineteen months ago …

When I woke up this morning, I had a feeling my life was about to change dramatically. I wish I would have known the extent of the damage.

I glanced around the living room, searching for something to take my mind off the envelope sitting on the kitchen counter.

Hopelessness and heartbreak swept through me like a hurricane, destroying everything in its path. My heart splintered a little more as I listened to my soon-to-be ex-husband, James's, heavy footsteps upstairs. Finally, unable to delay the inevitable, I opened the envelope and stared down at the papers.

The past few years had been filled with heartache for both of us, and I'd grown dependent on James. I wondered if my therapist had a cure for heartbreak because she sure as hell hadn't given me a solution to stop the never-ending ache of losing the only hope I had of saving this marriage.

I pressed my belly, the safe haven where only months ago a life had nestled, and the loss slammed into me all over again. All I wanted to do was lock myself in a room and take the medication that would sweep me away from this world for a few hours or days. Not that it would help. It never did.

God, what was I thinking? Just because life knocked me on my ass didn't mean I was going to curl up in a corner and die. I hadn't spent half my life fighting to be where I was today only to fail in the end. I wasn't going to admit defeat.

I straightened as James came down the stairs carrying a big, brown box. I studied the man who had been my first in everything. He had blond hair meticulously combed back, ice-blue eyes, and lips that, when touching mine, stoked an unquenchable need only he evoked.

James. Beautiful James.

There was no going back. He had made the decision.

I grabbed the pen on the table, and steeling my arm to stop it from shaking, signed my name across the dotted line.

"Is that all?" I asked him, forcing myself to meet his gaze, and pushed the envelope and papers toward him.

He nodded, his eyebrows scrunched up as if in thought. "I've arranged for a real estate agent to stop by to appraise the house." He looked like he wanted to say something else. Instead, he came around the table and took the papers before kissing my forehead.

"Good-bye, Selene."

He turned and walked out the front door without looking back, taking with him the end of six years of marriage.

I continued to stare at the door, praying that somehow,

this was a nightmare. That he'd appear again and tell me he was staying.

Nothing happened.

I had failed to make him stay. Everything was disintegrating around me, and the world was quickly shifting beneath my feet. Suddenly, rage like no other swept through me, settling deep in my bones. My body on fire, I swung my arm and knocked the bills off the counter. Then I stalked into the living room, snatched the silver-rimmed picture frame from on top of the cabinet next to the television, and stared at it through red-hot tears. There I was on my wedding day, dressed in white and staring lovingly into James's face, but his gaze wasn't focused on me. Not really. I hadn't noticed that tiny detail until now. If I remember correctly, my best friend, Gena, had been standing behind me. Gena, with her long, dark-brown hair and slim body, was the reason he'd left me; James confessed this when he walked in the house an hour ago. I flung the picture across the room and watched as the glass hit the wall and shattered on impact. I continued smashing everything in sight, angry with him, angry with myself, and angry with God for taking away my child. Angry at the whole fucking world.

I had thought I knew pain, but the past two years had proven me wrong. I felt it crush my chest until I couldn't breathe. Oh, my God, I couldn't breathe.

I need to breathe.

I need to breathe.

I shuffled blindly to the nearest couch and sat down, pulled my knees to my chest, dropped my chin on them, and took deep breaths the way the therapist had shown me. I could feel my heartbeat slowing down and air returning to my lungs.

Moments later, I lifted my head and wiped my cheeks with the sleeve of my sweater, feeling completely spent both emotionally and physically. I picked up the sonogram photo on the table where I'd left it earlier this morning and stared at it, running a finger along the tiny shape.

My sweet baby, Ines.

I could feel air leaving my lungs again. No, I wasn't going to panic. I shot up from the couch and headed upstairs, focusing my mind on the only thing that helped me keep my sanity in times like this.

I changed into my running shorts and shirt, but this time I didn't need my iPod to keep me company. I wanted the chaos raging inside my head out, scattered into the chilly evening, and I hoped the dark night would consume it.

As soon as the door slammed shut behind me, I hit the ground running, blinking the hot tears from my vision. I knew the route by heart, so I let my legs guide me, and right there I made a promise to myself.

This was life. When you stumble and fall, pick yourself up and dust yourself off. I had done it before, and I would do it again.

I was heartbroken, but I wasn't dead. In fact, I'd probably been given another chance. A do-over. There was no way I was going to let bitterness and rejection rule my life.

Chapter One

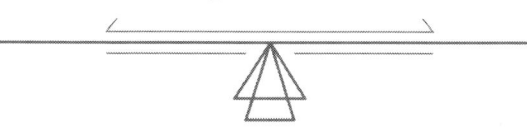

Selene

Present …

Ah, Paris. City of love, lights, and everything in between. I glanced around the lobby of the Hotel L'Arc, where I'd be spending the next three months, and smiled. I felt content; so far, considering where I was nineteen months ago, my life had turned out pretty good.

The months following my divorce had been a blur of tireless workouts to get into shape to return to modeling. If there was a city that'd make me forget the shit plaguing my life, Paris was it. I was here for work and pleasure, and I intended to take the pleasure part very seriously. Just because things hadn't worked between James and me didn't mean I had to give up on romance. Plus my therapist, my family, and I had worked hard to get me where I was today.

As my sister, Marley, had said, right after hugging me tightly and pushing me toward the boarding gate with tears in her eyes, "Follow that rainbow, Selene. You might find a pot of gold or a very hot leprechaun."

I smiled again at the memory, turning back to face the fidgety receptionist returning from the back office with a sober look on his face. The wave of bliss I'd been riding since my feet touched France's soil vanished. I'd conveniently forgotten the idiots had lost my reservation. In other words, I didn't have a place to sleep for tonight. I was still waiting for Andrew, my contact with Sara Arden Modeling agency here in Paris, to call me back after having left several voice messages on his phone.

I hoped to God there would be a no-show so I could get a room. Jet lag was starting to set in, and I had a busy morning tomorrow. I needed a good night's sleep.

"Any messages for me?" a deep voice said, pulling me from my thoughts.

My spine straightened as the timbre of his voice caressed my senses, making me gulp for air. I turned around and instantly forgot my current problem as my gaze locked with the tall man standing beside me, dressed in a black peacoat and jeans. His eyes widened slightly as if shocked to see me standing there. He quickly schooled his expression, but the intensity of his stare deepened. His brow furrowed as though he were trying to figure something out. Or was it confusion?

I couldn't take my eyes off him though. He was tall with dark, slightly wavy hair that curled at the nape of his neck, high cheekbones, and a chiseled jaw covered in a light scruff. Dark eyebrows and long, spiky lashes fringed his unreadable emerald-green eyes. Finally, his full lips. Sexy and kissable were the only things that came to mind as I stared at his mouth.

My gaze moved away from his to take in the way his coat framed his broad shoulders and his blue jeans hugged his muscular thighs.

God, he is hot.

Umm … why the hell was he still staring at me like that?

Like I was the next best thing since crème brûlée, yet he couldn't wait to get away from me. Weird. Crème brûlée was supposed to be devoured.

Oh hell! My heart was performing a crazy dance in my chest as I fought the urge to squirm under his scrutiny. As a size-twelve model, I was used to people staring at me appreciatively or sometimes in veiled disgust. I saw none of that on this man's face. Admittedly, not everyone was into women like me, women on the fuller side. Not knowing what was going on behind those green eyes was as disturbing as the weird pull I felt toward him. I've always heard people say how they met someone, and right there the earth shifted around them or some gravitational shit. This wasn't that kind of pull but a primal awareness of two souls.

Remington

I noticed her in one point five seconds.

She stood about five feet ten inches at most. Her jet-black hair fell in a riot of curls to her mid-back, and as if it were a beacon, my hands twitched at the thought of fisting locks of it in my fingers. She shifted her weight to her left foot, and my eyes slid down her curvy body.

Mon Dieu!

That right there was the reason God put women on Earth. She had lush curves and great legs that had my cock hardening shamelessly. Dangerously sexy with one hip jutted out. I bet the front view was as generous as the back.

"She is beautiful, no?" a voice on my right asked.

I followed the trail of that voice and found one of the students attending the Art Symposium, grinning as his twenty-something-year-old eyes seemed to undress the woman. He looked up at me and whatever he saw on my face wiped off the smile on his.

He cleared his throat, smiling nervously. "Great seminar, Monsieur St. Germain."

I gave him a curt nod and murmured, "Thank you."

He swiveled around and quickly darted through the crowd in the lobby. I returned my focus to the woman, who was now leaning on the counter in front of her, tapping her foot. Gripping the portfolio case in my hand, I strode toward the reception desk.

The receptionist shifted nervously when he noticed me and dashed toward me, looking relieved.

"Any messages for me?" I asked him, stealing a glance in the direction of the woman with curves that could make me commit all of the seven deadly sins. I was already lusting after her, even though she hadn't cast a glance my way.

Merde! This woman's incredible body reminded me that I had starved my body of sex for far too long.

"None, Monsieur St. Germain," he replied in French.

I nodded, finally focusing on her at the same time she lifted her head and turned around.

Everything in me froze as I took in her features. Wide, hazel eyes. High cheekbones. Straight nose with a slightly upturned tip. Her lips looked soft and plump, and even from where I stood, I knew they could drive a man insane.

I couldn't breathe as attraction and confusion warred within me.

Is this some kind of joke? Or maybe I'm just hallucinating? How is it possible for one person to look so similar to another?

I blinked and my vision cleared just as she straightened, scrutinizing every inch of me as I was her. I exhaled and shook off the confusion and forced myself to focus clearly. She was definitely not a ghost from my past. Her make-up-free, flawlessly rich, brown skin reminded me of warm caramel instead of the pale face that had haunted me for years. Her body was fuller, her face kinder, and her eyes more green than brown.

Besides, I didn't believe in ghosts. This woman was flesh and blood. The ghosts of my past had been buried five years ago.

This was ridiculous. My mind was once again playing tricks on me. I probably needed to get my brain examined.

As beautiful as her eyes were, an air of sadness dulled them, but then the faint lines bracketing her mouth indicated she smiled often. She was quite the conundrum.

She licked her lips. It was obvious my scrutiny made her nervous, yet I couldn't take my eyes off her.

"Can I help you?" she asked in French, frowning. Her voice was sultry and breathy, sending blood straight to my cock. The way she spoke told me she wasn't French. And damn it, I wanted to hear her voice again.

How could I feel this way, when only moments ago I thought she was someone from my past? A woman who had brought nothing but utter chaos into my life and had almost destroyed me?

I cleared my throat to get rid of the lump stuck there. "What's your name?" I asked, stepping closer.

"Selene," she said in that voice again. "Selene Michaels."

"Selene Michaels," I said, letting her name roll off my tongue. "I guess from your accent you're not French."

Is that all I could come up with? I shook my head in disgust and blamed it on the fact I hadn't dated a lot in the past year or two.

"American."

Merde! I had to calm down or I'd scare the shit out of her.

My gaze fell to her top full lip, the urge to touch, taste, and bite it forcing me to step an inch closer. Her eyes widened, briefly darting to my mouth before she quickly brought them back to my face.

Ah, yes. It seemed like we were both experiencing the same unexpected attraction if the flush creeping up her cheeks was any indication.

Selene

He exhaled deeply and opened his mouth to speak, but a group of young men and women stopped in front of him, interrupting whatever he'd wanted to say. His eyes shifted away from me for just a few seconds while he greeted the group before returning to me.

Monsieur St. Germain was a suitably mysterious name to match the man. Undeterred by his inattention, one of the women in the group launched into a conversation with him, her hands touching his arm to catch his interest. When he didn't show any sign of changing his focus, she stopped and glanced my way. The group eventually left, leaving me and Mr. Tall, Handsome, and Brooding in a battle to outstare each other.

Finally, he dropped his gaze to his black dress shoes and ran his long, strong fingers through his hair before turning around and striding away, his gait confident. He was almost arrogant in his impatience, commanding the people and the air around him. A few people stepped in his way, hands extended in greeting. He halted, but only for a few seconds to return the greeting.

Oh, wow! Someone hand me a paddle and bend that guy over. "Who's that man?" I asked the receptionist.

He smiled, relieved and eager to divulge the information, now that St. Germain's appearance seemed to have diverted my attention from the fact I didn't have a room to sleep in tonight.

"Monsieur St. Germain, no? He is a famous artist here in France." His eyes lit up in obvious admiration.

Well, okay. "So, have you checked with your boss about my reservation?"

"I'm sorry, Madame Michaels," the receptionist repeated, the words fast souring my optimistic mood. His eyes darted over his shoulder toward the back office, probably hoping his boss would materialize to rescue him. He sighed, then turned to face me. "He is still in a meeting."

Where the hell is Andrew? I had worked with him on my previous modeling jobs, and this was the first time something like this had happened.

I exhaled a breath of frustration. "Could you please call some hotels to check if they have a room for me for tonight?"

He nodded, quickly snatching up the phone at the same time it started to ring. He spoke into the phone for a minute or two before passing it over to me, a slight blush creeping up his cheeks.

"Monsieur Carmichael," he said, then shuffled to the end of the reception desk, sneaking glances at me as if I might bite him.

Smart guy. I was tired and cranky. I wasn't above biting, and not the good kind.

Even before I pressed the phone to my ear, I could hear Andrew cursing wildly in French. I waited until he paused his tirade then inhaled audibly.

"Selene?"

"Thank God, Andrew," I said, shifting around to face the

crowded lobby, noting most of the guests were carrying a portfolio similar to the one St. Germain had in his hand. "What's going on?"

Andrew blew out a breath. "Inefficient bastards. I got your messages. I'm held up in Lyon and won't be back until tomorrow morning. Are you okay? How was your flight?"

"Good. Just tired." I sighed wearily. After eight hours of travel, all I wanted to do was take a shower and collapse in bed.

"I'm so sorry about this, Selene. Look. Let me make some calls and call you back in five minutes, okay, babe?"

"At this point, I'd sleep under a truck. I'm too tired to be too choosy." Seconds later, I handed the telephone to the receptionist. "I'll be at the bar if Mr. Carmichael calls." I turned to leave, not in the mood to discuss anything.

After ordering a Manhattan, I leaned back on the stool, feeling the events of the last months bearing down hard on me: the divorce, selling the house James and I had owned, moving in with my parents because I was a complete mess, therapy sessions, and eventually this trip to Paris.

Shaking my head, I pushed back those thoughts, choosing to focus on the coming weeks. It might take a while to ease into modeling again after having been absent for so long. The time I spent getting back in shape had been the best I'd had in a long while. I had three months before I returned to New York. I wasn't going to spend them questioning everything. It was time I had some "me" time.

"A call for you, Madame Michaels."

I turned around to face the bartender who'd served me a few moments ago. He handed me a phone while his eyes wandered down my body in appraisal, boosting my self-confidence. Not that I needed any kind of validation, but it felt great to have a stranger look at me as if I mattered. Living in the shadow of someone who demeans you eventually takes a toll on you, leading you to believe you are worthless.

James was the master of demeaning insults, albeit veiled in words that anyone listening would think of as flattery. He had never raised a hand to me, but his words were just as effective as a well-aimed blow.

"Any luck, Andrew?" I asked, sliding my glass to the middle of the counter and leaning on my elbows.

"The city is flooded with trade shows and conventions at the moment. I haven't been able to locate one decent hotel for you."

"Surely, you couldn't find a room in a city this huge? There are so many hotels—"

"Of course I can find something. But it will not be classy or close to Sara Arden offices, unless you changed your mind …"

I pressed two fingers on my eyes, feeling the weariness return again. "Hey, what about your place?"

"No one's home. Wife and kids are visiting her mother in Calais. Hey, I have a place for you, though." He paused as if waiting to hear my response.

"If I didn't love you so much, I'd be demanding you bring your ass back to Paris to sort this out," I said jokingly. He chuckled. "Tell me."

"I spoke to a friend of mine. He won't be staying in his townhouse in Montmartre tonight. You could stay there if you're comfortable with it. I'll sort out your accommodations as soon as I get back to Paris tomorrow. Whatcha think, hon?"

Feeling panic coil inside my chest, I took deep breaths. The idea of spending the night in another man's personal space felt somewhat intimidating. I had avoided any romantic relationships since the divorce. I couldn't seem to get past the fact that the man who had been my best friend since high school, the man I'd loved and exchanged vows with, had easily left me for my former best friend. That in itself was a very bitter pill to swallow.

Bastard.

Come on, Selene. The guy isn't spending the night in his house. I'd just have to pull myself together. I was a twenty-six-year-old independent woman for crying out loud. On top of that, I needed to be well-rested for tomorrow. From my experience, the first day of work was very demanding.

"Selene?" Andrew's voice pulled me out of my thoughts.

"Sorry. Yes, that will do."

"Remington's driver will pick you up in a few minutes. You have my phone number. Call me if you need anything at all. I'll bring you a mobile tomorrow."

"Remington. That's your friend's name? Sounds posh."

He laughed. "Stay out of trouble. I'll see you tomorrow."

"You know me," I said, smiling. "Thanks for organizing this."

"See you soon, beautiful girl," Andrew said before disconnecting the call.

I handed the phone back to the bartender and went back to nursing my drink as pondered how far I had come, when I heard someone clear their throat behind me.

"Madame Michaels?"

I shifted around to face a tall woman, dressed in a mid-thigh, black suit skirt, a white shirt, and knee-length boots. Her blond hair coiled at the nape of her long, elegant neck, her blue eyes framed by long lashes.

"Yes?"

She stuck a hand toward me. "My name is Adele Dufort. I am to drive you to St. Germain's house, yes?" She spoke in clear, unaccented English.

My heart skipped several beats, remembering Mr. Tall, Hot,

and Brooding earlier at the reception counter. "St. Germain? Is Remington his first name by any chance?"

She paused, studying me curiously, and nodded. "Have you two met before?"

I shook my head, hopping down from the stool. "Not officially. He's proving to be quite popular tonight." I shook her hand.

She smiled briefly and looked around the lobby area. "Your luggage, madame?"

After retrieving my suitcases from the storeroom, courtesy of the nervous receptionist, I pulled a sweater from my carry-on bag, putting it on. I followed Adele out of the hotel and into the nippy autumn evening.

Chapter Two

Selene

The Peugeot pulled up in front of Remington's townhouse. I climbed out of the car before Adele could come around to open the door for me. I straightened and my mouth fell open as I stared ahead.

Holy wow!

Before me stood an impressive, stark white, brick and glass residence with tall windows, reflecting the light from the nearby houses. The only light burning was the porch light. Tiny lamps illuminated the path leading to the door from the parking area, which was designed to accommodate about five cars.

Slowly, as I turned around, my breath caught in my throat as I took in my surroundings. On my far right, Sacré Coeur Basilica stood in all its pristine, imposing majesty, bathed in floodlights from the ground. I'd been in this part of town only once, years ago, while attending an after-party hosted by The Curves Fashion House. That was before I took a break when I got married.

Grace Dresner was the head designer and owner of the

fashion house, as well as one of my closest friends. She had jokingly told me she didn't want me, her "Face of Curves Fashion line," looking like a zombie on the lingerie shoot the following day. What can I say? It was a party and wine flowed aplenty. It was the beginning of my career, and I was a young woman who thought she could take on the world, intoxicated or not, and believed that alone would protect me from a hangover. The next day, all I wanted to do was dig a hole and live in it so I wouldn't have to interact with anyone until my hangover had worn off. I had winced at any sound, no matter how small, and squinted at the strobe lights and camera flashes. Surprisingly, I'd pulled it off quite well. It was a nightmare, and a lesson well-learned.

Smiling at the memory, I continued to soak in the sight of Paris spread below a moonless sky.

"It's beautiful, isn't it?" Adele asked, her hoarse voice surprisingly close.

"It's breathtaking."

"Monsieur St. Germain has good taste." Her voice was almost… reverent. I glanced over my shoulder. Her face shone with adoration. She quickly schooled her features when she caught me staring. "He is traveling to Provence, so you have the house to yourself tonight."

Wow. Someone seemed to be in love with her boss.

"When will he return from Provence?" I walked back to the car to remove my suitcases from the trunk.

"In a week." She motioned at the luggage as I began to pull them out. "Leave them. I will bring everything in."

"There's no need—"

"It'll displease him." The words were spoken in the same tone of voice as before. Whoever this guy was, he sure was lucky to have such devotion.

"Fine." I took a step back, hitched the strap of my carry-on bag higher on my shoulder, and waited for her to lead the way.

Inside the house, I halted just beyond the doorway, yawning and waiting for Adele to drag the second piece of luggage from the car. She offered to make me a snack if I was hungry, but food was the last thing on my mind. After she pointed me to the guest bedrooms upstairs and explained to me the different amenities the rooms afforded, I thanked her for everything. She nodded once and said that she would pick me up in the morning and drive me to Sara Arden's offices. As soon as she left, I headed upstairs, abandoning the luggage downstairs as I'd be leaving the next day. During my modeling years, I'd quickly learned the benefits of packing extra clothing in my carry-on bag, especially if the luggage got delayed or lost somewhere in transit.

I stepped inside the first room in the hallway and flipped the light switch on. The room came into focus. The interior decor was simple and stylish, just as the glimpses of decor in the hallway. White walls with a black dresser standing right across from the bed. A square mirror above the dresser. The bed was decked in a black bedspread with hints of white sheets beneath it and two huge white pillowcases bracing the headboard. Nothing was out of place. Did every room resemble this one? Such a neat freak.

After dropping my bag on the bed, I headed to the bathroom, which was a masterpiece. The spacious retreat had white marble-tiled floors with a huge bathtub located near the floor-to-ceiling windows. The shower had four showerheads, two fixed on the ceiling and two on the wall. St. Germain seemed to value luxury with a passion.

I stepped out of the shower and grabbed the plush,

terrycloth towel from the mahogany rack to dry myself, then wrapped it around my body and used a smaller one for my hair. I returned to the room, combing my fingers through my semi-dry hair and dropped the towel on an armchair next to window before heading to bed in the middle of the room. My step faltered as a pair of feet came into focus at the door. I squealed and stumbled back in an attempt to grab the towel from the chair, but I caught air instead. I lunged forward, snatched the heavy, satin bedspread, and tugged. Nothing happened. I tried again. Nada. I gave up and turned around, feeling heat rise to my cheeks.

My gaze lifted from the bare feet to blue jeans-clad legs, lingering on the muscular thighs before proceeding. Toned arms were folded across an equally impressive chest with one shoulder braced on the doorframe. I swear my heart stopped beating when my eyes clashed with green ones.

"What are you doing here?" I blurted out, my mind too messed up to think clearly.

One dark eyebrow shot up. "I never thought I would be questioned about being in my own house, inside my own bedroom," he drawled in a deep voice laced with a trace of a British accent mingled with his French.

Crap, crap, crap! Wasn't he supposed to be on his way to Provence? And his room? I glanced around and groaned inwardly as I realized my mistake. I had failed to notice the simple, yet sheer masculinity surrounding me. I had taken up residence inside the lion's den.

I prided myself on being a strong woman, proud of my body, but whom was I kidding? The scorching look on his face made me want to hide under the bed. Before leaving the US, I'd made up my mind that pleasure was part of this three-month work and play trip. A flirt here and there, maybe a quick romp between the sheets to rejuvenate the nerves. My girly bits hadn't had any action for a while now, and I was ready to go back to the playing field, as scary as it was. By the look on his face and the way he was staring at me, playing and flirting were definitely not on his mind right now.

The floor did not open up to swallow me whole as I'd been hoping, so I stepped forward, my breasts jiggling a bit, and did the only thing a confident woman would do in a situation like this. Keep my head up and face an oncoming disaster. His gaze dropped to my chest for just a split second before moving back to my face, unimpressed. Heat crept up my face. Had I read him wrong? Oh, my God, this was so embarrassing.

What kind of man didn't like a free view of boobs? I probably sounded like a self-involved cow, but the longer I stood in this man's presence, the faster my confidence cracked around the edges.

I mentally smacked myself on the head. After James, I'd sworn no one would ever make me feel as though I were inferior.

I stuck out a hand to him in greeting. "Sorry for being rude. You caught me by surprise. I was under the impression I was alone for the night since Andrew and Adele told me you'd be in Provence."

His eyes widened for just a second before going neutral. Good. He had probably expected me to cower under his gaze.

"I postponed my trip." He unhitched his shoulder from the doorframe and strode forward, then wrapped those strong fingers around my hand. His handshake was firm, his palm rough against my skin. He leaned down so we were eye to eye, and immediately, the scent of earthiness slammed into me. "Remington St. Germain." He seemed to struggle to keep his eyes on my face though. I saw him sneak a peek down my body. Perhaps he wasn't as immune as I first thought. "Do you do that often? Walk around naked when you're alone?"

I couldn't tell if he was teasing me or being genuinely curious. Gah! This man was the epitome of frustrating.

"It's a free country." I shrugged, feigning nonchalance, like this was a nightly hobby of mine. I didn't want to show him that his scrutiny, the way his eyes kept lingering on me with such unconcealed lust, was affecting me. "You already know my name so…" I trailed off and then cleared my throat, trying not to wilt into a pile of mush in front of him. "Let me dress and I'll give you back your room."

He dropped my hand unceremoniously. "No need for that." He turned and strode out of the room, leaving me gaping at his sudden exit. Moments later, the sound of a door slamming echoed down the hall and through the house.

Whoa! His reactions were quite confusing. He seemed as though he wanted to grab me and pin me to the wall one minute, and the next, he dashed from the room as if it were on fire.

I grabbed my bag and quickly threw on my clean underwear and slipped between the sheets, my heart still pounding in my chest. I pulled the comforter to my chin, replaying what had just happened. A giggle suddenly burst from my mouth, overshadowing the embarrassment I felt at being caught naked. Another laugh erupted as I remembered the way he pretended disinterest when I caught him gawking.

Arrogant ass.

Well… if this were a sign of how my time here in Paris would be, I'd say I was off to a good start.

I snuggled deeper into the covers. But as sleep overtook me, so did my insecurities. And just as they had every night since my divorce, they jostled me awake.

What if I couldn't be as good at this job as I had once been? Could I flirt and be involved with a man without my heart becoming involved? It certainly wouldn't be with the owner of this gorgeous house, but perhaps I might find someone willing?

As I pressed a hand to the scar on my belly, I felt confidence and certainty rush back. I had lost a lot, but I wasn't going to let it rule me or my life. I was ready to move on.

Chapter Three

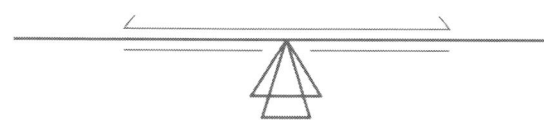

Remington

I leaned on the door, taking deep breaths to slow down my racing heart.

Bloody fucking hell!

I had just behaved like an uncivilized Neanderthal. What was it about Selene that made me behave like this? When I walked through the front door of my house, I knew Selene was already here, but what I hadn't expected was to find her in my room, naked.

Earlier this evening when I left her at the reception counter in the hotel, I had stopped to greet a few people and that's when I heard her talking to the receptionist about a room in the hotel. I had lingered long enough to learn she didn't have a place to stay for the night. What surprised me the most was when I heard her talk to my good friend Andrew. I couldn't believe my luck. What were the chances the same woman I had met and had spoken to was acquainted with a friend?

After she'd finished speaking with him, I had quickly dialed his mobile and asked him point-blank about Selene, then offered my house for the night. All he needed to do was come up with a reasonable excuse as to why he couldn't find a suitable hotel for Selene. He must have been very convincing because she was here now. I don't believe in beating around the bush, and if I want something, I go for it. Besides, I was being a good Samaritan, no?

After postponing my trip to Provence, I drove to the private hangar where my mother and my son had been waiting for me so we could travel together. Earlier this morning, she'd arrived from London and picked up Adrien from kindergarten. Adele had driven them to the hangar late in the afternoon to wait for me. I informed my mother I had some business to take care of in Paris tonight, and I would be seeing her the following day, then drove back to the townhouse with my son. After all, what kind of host would I be if I offered a guest a place to stay and not be there to keep her company?

Satisfied with my reasoning, I pushed away from the door and walked toward the bed while dragging my fingers through my hair.

Selene intrigued me. At first, when I laid my eyes on her at the hotel, all I saw was a confident woman, both beautiful and sensual. She was comfortable in her skin. Yes, she had completely knocked me on my arse the moment I saw those curves. But there, beneath all that, was something in Selene's eyes. Sadness, I think. It called to me. Fed on mine. I'm certain she didn't even know she had given off that reaction. I knew pain, hurt, and sadness, and that was what I sensed in her. Like attracts like, and that's probably the reason I was drawn to her so strongly.

And her breasts. *Mon Dieu*, she was perfect. I had come this close to pushing her against the wall and kissing her, touching her. I'd faked disinterest when she caught me staring at her breasts, but in truth, my cock had been unbelievably hard.

I forced my mind back to the issue at hand, knowing I'd need a very cold shower before the night was over. From the look on her face, both at the reception desk and in my room, I must have given her mixed signals. She'd caught me off guard and I was in a state of havoc, caught between lust and attraction for her, and my past. I shut my eyes, the image of Colette, Adrien's mother, flashing in my head. The anger that had burned inside me after her death had been replaced by acceptance. But it occasionally reared its head.

Other than Selene's physical attributes, was I intrigued because she bore some minute resemblance to Colette?

I pulled my phone from my pocket and scrolled through my phonebook to the letter G and then pressed dial.

"I need you to run a check on someone for me," I said, after a few words into our greeting.

I knew this was a bastard thing to do, but if I was going to pursue Selene, and I intended to, I wasn't going to walk into this without some background information. Right now, I had to cover all my bases. My friend Gilles owned a security firm. He was my go-to man; after knowing him for years, he was practically family. Two years ago, I'd started receiving unusual text messages on random days of the week, sent from an anonymous number. They were mostly flirty and sometimes disturbingly intimate but never threatening. Gilles had worked on tracing them, which proved to be difficult. He believed whoever sent them probably used disposable phones. Despite not being able to track down the sender, I trusted him implicitly.

After the call, I walked to the bed and lowered myself

onto it, rubbing my neck with one hand. Right now, I was a contradiction. I wasn't used to feeling like this, and I didn't like it at all.

I'd be leaving for Provence tomorrow. The distance should help me focus on more important things. The week-long Art Symposium had consumed all my time, and I'd hardly been able to catch up with other business. It seemed that *other business* was now going to include one sassy, beautiful American woman.

Chapter Four

Selene

Something prodded my cheek. My eyes popped open, clashing with the most adorable green eyes I'd ever seen on an even cuter face. A small hand appeared out of nowhere and swiped the black curls off his forehead. He blinked once.

Twice.

I pressed my hand on my chest, soothing the pain blooming there, and I tried to breathe. Quickly, I blinked back the sudden tears threatening to blind me.

Shit! I'm about to bawl all over the place and scare the child.

Would this feeling ever go away?

I inhaled deeply to ease the pain of loss that snuck up on me whenever I saw a child, especially one as sweet as this one in front of me.

I succeeded. Barely.

The boy leaned back, frowning down at me. Bet he was wondering what brand of crazy I was.

I cleared my throat and pasted a smile on my face. "Hey there," I said in a hoarse voice, hoping I didn't frighten him.

He continued to stare at me as if analyzing a very difficult math problem. Suddenly, a wide grin spread across his face, displaying a huge gap where his lower teeth were supposed to be.

"Are you Papa's girlfriend? You're wearing Papa's shirt. And you are…" He squinted hard as though he were searching for the right word. "Aha! *Belle*. Beautiful." He spun around on his heel and dashed out the room yelling, "Papa!"

Even before the sound of the boy's pattering feet on the tiles faded, I swung my legs from the bed and glanced down at the black, silk pajama top I'd put on after waking up cold in the middle of the night.

Then the word the boy had yelled slapped me in the face. Papa? As in Remington St. Germain? *Really?* He certainly didn't seem like the father type. Everything about him, the little I'd seen of his body, his face, his voice… I should stop thinking about him if I was going to make it downstairs and not die from embarrassment caused by the memory of being caught naked.

I scanned the room for a clock, narrowing in on the nightstand and groaned. I'd slept longer than I had intended, and now, I had a little over thirty minutes to get ready and meet Andrew at the Sara Arden offices.

I scrambled out of bed and headed for the shower. Moments later, I dashed out and dressed in a butter-yellow top with a plunging back and the blue jeans I'd worn yesterday before I quickly applied minimal makeup.

Shoving everything inside my carry-on bag, I straightened the bed, making sure to leave everything as it was the night before. After bounding down the stairs, I stopped at the entrance to a huge living room, which was part of an open-concept floor plan. Remington and the boy were huddled closely, with the younger version of him speaking non-stop, while Remington busied himself preparing what appeared to be a snack. I felt as if I was intruding on their morning routine, but I couldn't help myself.

I turned back to take in the view of the room since I hadn't gotten a chance to see it last night. The white walls were bare save for two paintings, both hanging on opposite walls in the living room. One was of a beautiful child about three years; the same boy who'd woken me up, I guess, with black, curly hair and adorable green eyes. The other was of a woman in her fifties with features similar to Remington. I wasn't much of an art connoisseur, but I could tell these paintings were extraordinarily good.

Three leather sofas were placed strategically in the room, pillows with warm-colored covers tossed haphazardly on the seats and a few on the floor. A box filled with toys stood in the right corner. Three photos in silver frames were placed strategically on the mantle above a stone fireplace. I shuffled closer, squinting to get a better look. All of them featured Remington, the boy, and the woman from the painting either standing in front of a Ferris wheel or sitting on a riverbank, fishing.

Where was his son's mother? Was he divorced? Was she dead?

I switched my gaze back to the kitchen counter. If seeing Remington yesterday had been overwhelming, watching him interacting with the boy this morning was simply beautiful. I hovered in the living room, taking in the scene before me. Remington was dressed in black, silk pajama pants slung low on his hips and a white T-shirt that emphasized his well-toned arms, which were dusted with dark, fine hair. The muscles beneath his T-shirt flexed as he prepared the snack. The boy said something, and Remington ruffled the boy's curly head, smiling.

Oh my God. That smile! It was as if the room felt lighter and brighter at the brief show of his teeth. He turned around, opened the fridge, grabbed something from inside, closed the fridge door, and carried on with whatever he was doing before. The boy shifted forward, pressing his forehead to Remington's, and kissed his father on the nose before squealing as Remington snatched him by the waist and tickled him. There was no doubt. This was his son. The way they angled their heads to the right as they talked and how they squinted while trying to think was freakishly fascinating.

His son shrieked, and this time Remington threw his head back and laughed. I gasped at the heavenly sound, deep and alluring. Two set of eyes whipped in my direction.

"Good morning." I smiled brightly as if I hadn't been watching them for the last few minutes.

His son jumped down from the stool and raced toward me, skidding to a stop while his father seemed frozen in place. The unreadable look was back on his face again.

What is he thinking?

Dropping my gaze from his, I sank to my knees to be at eye level and extended a hand to Remington's son. He was dressed in a pair of jeans and a cute blue sweater with a Spiderman picture on the front.

"I'm Selene. What's your name?"

He slapped a small hand on mine in greeting. "Adrien. You're pretty. Isn't she pretty, Papa?" He swung around to look at his father. "Is she your new friend?"

Remington's gaze was fixed on me, sending shivers of awareness all over my body. Eventually, he said, "She is beautiful and no, she's just here for the night. Come on. As I said last night, we will stay in Paris today. Adele will be here soon to take you to school, and you know she doesn't like tardiness." Even though the words were spoken gently, there was a firm note twined in his voice.

Not seeming in a hurry to do his father's bidding, Adrien turned to face me again, his eyes twinkling in joy. "Can't you stay with us? Please say yes. Please—"

"Adrien." This time, Remington's voice brooked no argument.

The poor boy snapped his mouth shut and shuffled back to the kitchen island, his shoulders stiff. He then perched himself on top of the stool he had been sitting on moments before. Silence reigned. My scalp prickled as tension filled the air.

Right. "Thank you for letting me stay, Mr. St. Germain. I need to get to the Louvre in fifteen minutes. May I use your phone to call for a cab?"

Remington's head came up fast, something like surprise registering in his eyes. Just then, the doorbell rang, followed by the sound of keys unlocking the door. Adele walked in a few seconds later. After exchanging pleasantries, she glanced over to the kitchen, her face softening as she took in the sight before her.

"Give Papa a kiss before you go," Remington was saying to Adrien.

I turned around in time to see Adrien wrap his short arms around his father's neck and peck him soundly on his cheek. After Remington handed a red lunch box to his son, Adrien shuffled toward me. Suddenly, he broke into a run and slammed his tiny body into mine, hugging my legs. I dropped my carry-on bag and embraced him.

God, he felt so right in my arms.

"*Au revoir,* Selene," he whispered in my ear before pressing a wet kiss on my cheek.

"Bye, darling," I said, pushing myself back to my feet as he walked away, smiling shyly.

As soon as the front door clicked shut, I turned around to find Remington staring at me. A scowl was on his face.

Why the hell was he pissed off? Had I done something wrong? Was he angry I slept in his room?

Crossing my hands under my breasts, I clenched my jaw. "I'm sorry to have used the wrong room last night. I was sleep-deprived and misheard Adele's instructions. Thank you for letting me stay the night though."

He continued to scrutinize my face. I wish I had a clue what he was searching for. "It was a pleasure."

I smiled politely and grabbed the pullout handle of my luggage, turning to leave.

"You could stay here if you want," he said. "I'm leaving for Provence for a few days."

I froze in my tracks. *Um, what? Stay here?* He had been reserved from the moment we met, sending mixed signals. Worse, I did not understand the reason he seemed cautious around me. "I'm truly flattered. Thank you for the kind offer; however, Andrew will sort out my accommodations today."

"It's no bother since the house will be empty."

I blinked at him. "We don't even know each other. Why would you want me to stay? I could be plotting to rob you as we speak."

He smirked. "You don't look like the thieving kind."

I rolled my eyes, fighting a smile. "Don't ever underestimate a pretty face. I could be the kind of person who whacks people on the head and steals stuff." His lips curled up in amusement, but he didn't say anything. "Thank you, but I can't."

As if he couldn't help himself, his gaze darkened as it narrowed in on my lips. There seemed to be a war of emotions going on inside him, but then as quickly as the lust-filled gaze had slipped onto his face, it vanished, and his expression shuttered.

"All right, I'll take you wherever you want to go. Allow me to do that, Selene."

A tremor traveled down my spine at the sound of my name on his lips. It was as if he'd inhaled the letters and exhaled my name in one swift, intoxicating breath. It had never sounded so good.

Ugh! This man was confusing. Finding a guy to flirt with in this city would be much easier than figuring out the mechanics of his thoughts and moods.

"I really appreciate it."

I leaned back against the door as I watched him stride up the stairs, his head held proudly and confidently, leaving me with a delightful view of his ass. I tore my gaze away, took deep breaths, and, for just a few minutes, thought of Adrien in my arms. It had felt unexpectedly good, considering I had always believed I'd feel the loss all over again if I ever held a child in my arms. I'd made a point of avoiding any contact with children in the past. But Adrien took me by surprise when he bolted toward me and hugged me.

I smiled, savoring that feeling all over again.

Remington

As soon as the door to my bedroom slammed shut, the scent, Selene's scent, still lingering in the room, slammed into me, and immediately, my anger vanished. I stumbled mid-step, pausing long enough to inhale deeply. Then I remembered what happened downstairs.

Being around Selene was intoxicating. I'm not sure what led me to open my mouth and offer her to stay in my house.

Ah, yes, I know. I was greedy and wanted her to myself. I was envious she'd be spending her nights in some hotel room.

Three sins down, but who's counting, eh?

I shook my head, remembering how Adrien had embraced Selene, the hopeful look on his face, and the way my body had reacted toward her. I wasn't the kind of person who slept with women just for the fun of it. Well, I had after Colette's death before I realized how wrong it felt and hated myself for it. After that, I'd steered clear of women and focused on raising my child. I had been in one long-term relationship since then, but it ended two years ago.

Which is why I wanted to punch something, preferably a wall. I wasn't used to contradicting myself with my own thoughts and feelings. Something about Selene was holding me back from pursuing her. An invisible flashing signal that said, "Tread with caution." Adrien's reaction to her had almost brought me to my knees.

I needed space to think, and Provence was the only place I could do that.

I stripped and stalked toward the wardrobe where I pulled out a T-shirt, jeans, and a pair of white boxer briefs from the second drawer.

When I was ready and felt more in command of my foolish feelings, I went downstairs, pausing long enough to admire her arse and full hips as she stood below the painting of Adrien. One of my best works yet.

"Ready?" I asked. She glanced over her shoulder, quickly scanning me from head to toe before bringing those hazel eyes back to my face.

She licked her lips. "Lead the way."

Chapter Five

Selene

It was official. Being in the same space as Remington was wreaking havoc on my system. Every single shift of his body, no matter how minimal, and each flick of his gaze toward me heightened the tension coiled tightly in my body. I was ready to snap.

As soon as the sleek, black Rolls Royce Phantom pulled in front of the Sara Arden offices, I grabbed for the door, ready to tumble out of the car. Remington's big, strong hand slid across the console and planted itself on my knee, freezing me in my seat. I flinched as the heat from his palm seeped through my jeans and into my skin. I wasn't made of stone. Not even his hot and cold moods could stop the shivers that had my stomach clenching with lust and my toes tingling with awareness.

I snapped my head around to face him and my brain screamed, *Jesus! Dude, warn a girl first, or you might end up with a case of hyperventilation on your hands.*

The touch was intimate, almost possessive, and the look

he gave me was a veiled command. My heart threatened to leap out of my chest and join the cars racing down the street.

He removed his hand, and before I knew what was happening, he'd rounded the car and opened the door for me.

No other touch had felt like his just had.

No other touch had ever left me so confused.

No other touch had ever left me wanting like his did.

Whoa, Selene. Back the hell up. His mercurial moods are too confusing for your sanity.

I climbed out of the car and stood there on the sidewalk, watching him as he effortlessly lifted my suitcases from the trunk and placed them on the ground. His body moved lithely, his movements precise. Purposeful. I could watch him all day and night, but then I'd be at risk of getting whiplash from his shifting moods.

"Come on." He rolled the suitcase inside the Sara Arden offices, giving me no other choice than to hike my carry-on over my shoulder and follow him inside.

Halting just inside the room, he propped his hands on his slim hips, studying the chic, black and hot pink interior in that inscrutable way he seemed to view the world around him. Then he finally brought those eyes back to me.

"*Au revoir*, Selene."

Caught off guard, I straightened beside him, my head hardly reaching his shoulder.

Did his voice have to be that… potent?

Suppressing a shiver, I crossed my arms over my chest and met his gaze. "Thank you for everything. I must say it was… interesting meeting you." I hitched my carry-on bag on my shoulder. "*Au revoir*, Remington."

I held out my hand to him. He took my hand in his

and pressed a kiss to the back of it before letting go. He strode through the doors, heading toward the car without a backward glance.

Man, that ass! I shook myself, grabbed my luggage, and headed toward the reception area.

Remington St. Germain was an enigma best forgotten. Fast.

Chapter Six

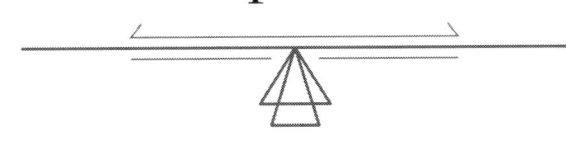

Selene

Five o'clock found me inside a black Peugeot 508 with Adele behind the wheel, compliments of Remington, according to the handwritten note I was holding. Andrew had arranged for a room at Hotel Catherine, a boutique hotel, a five-minute walk from the Seine River. He'd been delayed in Lyon, but he would drop by the hotel as soon as he returned to Paris. We still had a lot to discuss about the upcoming events.

I stared at the paper in my hand, the scribbled words bold and confident. This was a sign of someone in command of his life and surroundings.

"They must miss you over at Monsieur St. Germain's household," I said, trying to figure out Remington's motives for sending Adele. I could have easily taken a cab, but no. Mr. Tall, Dark, and Brooding was obviously in a very generous mood.

Adele's gaze flicked to the mirror and met mine before focusing on the traffic jam ahead again. "Monsieur St. Germain drives his own car most of the time."

I had many questions circling my brain, but I didn't want to pry too much and make her uncomfortable, so I leaned back and closed my eyes. I made a mental note to contact Remington to thank him for this kind gesture. After a day filled with dress rehearsals for an upcoming lingerie fashion show; a meeting with Grace, the owner of Curves Fashion House, to discuss the forthcoming lingerie photo shoot; and my program for the next few weeks, I was mentally exhausted, still jet-lagged, and famished. I'd hardly eaten anything after the two cups of *café au lait* and the chocolate croissant at breakfast.

After Adele dropped me at the hotel and handed me a card with a number to call whenever I needed to be driven around town, she left. With the help of two bellboys, I went inside Hotel Catherine to check in. The interior was breathtaking with polished counters, a huge glass and brass chandelier, cream marble floors, and baroque furniture interspersed throughout the room. How was the agency able to afford this? Seriously, this was like a two-hundred-and-fifty-euros-per-night kind of hotel. If I were staying here for the next three months, surely the agency would be bankrupt by the time I returned home.

Andrew was going to have to look for other accommodations. This was just too much.

"Welcome to Hotel Catherine, Madame Michaels," a thirty-something-looking woman said, startling me.

I smiled, trying not to feel too guilty about staying here.

After exchanging pleasantries, I left her to her devices. She flicked a curious gaze toward me every few seconds and quickly looked away when I caught her staring. James's inattention and disregard had affected me deeply. Whereas before I had been used to turning heads, both male and female on occasion, receiving looks of appreciation were now like healing balm for my damaged pride.

The check-in went fast. The clerk handed me a keycard and a white envelope sealed with a red wax stamp.

The initials on the stamp said it all.

RSG.

Remington St. Germain.

My hand trembled as I headed for the elevator.

The beginnings of a fluttering simmered in my stomach. He was like an ever-present shadow at my side, and he used wax to seal his letters.

Talk about style!

I reached my floor with the bellboy in tow and swiped my keycard to enter room 404. I forgot to breathe as I beheld the room. A fireplace and a crystal chandelier graced the chamber containing a canopy bed, draped in white and red. Heavy, red velvet curtains hung on either side of French doors leading to a balcony, which afforded an amazing view of the Eiffel Tower.

Snapping my gaping mouth shut, I dropped my bag on the bed and then distractedly opened the envelope while soaking in the view before me. My gaze veered across the room to the white, baroque vanity on which sat an intricately-faceted crystal vase with a bouquet of fragrant red and white roses.

I glanced down to the letter in my hand and came face-to-face with familiar, bold handwriting.

> *Selene,*
> *Welcome to Hotel Catherine. I hope your room is to your satisfaction. If not, please inform the front office manager and he will make the necessary adjustments.*
> *Au revoir,*
> *Remington St. Germain*

Had he arranged everything?

Shaking my head to clear my wayward thoughts, I grabbed one of my bags and opened it. I searched for my trainers, my jogging pants, and a tank top. It had been two days since I last did my usual morning run. I could already feel my thoughts clamoring inside my head. Jogging was my outlet. I didn't like staying inside my head for long because if I let my thoughts wander, they ended up muddled. I wanted to get outside to scatter my thoughts in a hundred different directions.

I grabbed my iPod and left the suite. After asking the receptionist where to find the safest and nearest place to run without interruptions, I took the small map she gave me and tucked it inside my pants pocket. I then shoved my earbuds into my ears, left the hotel behind, and soon was jogging on the sidewalk, savoring the sight of fallen leaves and the changing colors of the trees. My stomach growled as I dashed past a brasserie, reminding me I had barely eaten. Ignoring my growling tummy, I pushed my legs faster, knowing my reward would be a huge dinner when I finished.

When I returned to the hotel, I ordered room service and headed to the bathroom for a quick shower but halted at the door. Brilliant, beige marble tile covered the wall and floor. A wall-to-wall antique cherry vanity stood in the far corner, two sinks sitting on top with ample space in between. On one side was a shower big enough to fit four fully-grown men and next to it, a square bathtub so huge it could fit three people with room left over. Three shelves on the side of the tub were filled with books and magazines. A flat-screen TV was mounted to the wall. Installed into the ceiling was a window displaying the clear, starless sky above.

Forget the suite. I'd live in this room.

Of course, I intended to make use of the tub before I gave up this suite. But for now, showering was a priority, followed by dinner. Andrew would be arriving soon. I walked back into the suite ten minutes later dressed in a robe, and after checking the time difference between Paris and New York, I requested the receptionist connect me to my parents' home number.

The line crackled for a few seconds before it cleared. My younger sister, Marley, answered the phone. God, I missed her. She was my best friend and confidant. Mom and Dad were visiting some friends. I told her to tell them I had arrived safely and would try again later. After disconnecting the call, I quickly dressed just as room service delivered my dinner.

My family had been my cheerleaders through the times I needed therapy, and they had been there for me after my divorce. I hated how weak I had been at the time. However, I had later realized, in order to be strong, I had to be weak first and learn to fight my demons. It hadn't been easy, especially since I was dealing with self-esteem issues on top of everything else. When I was well enough to pick up the pieces of my life, I had visited my agent in New York. Even though it'd been almost six years since my last modeling gig, she'd been pleased to help me find some modeling jobs outside the country. When she told me Curves Fashion House had let go of their former "Face of Curves" and were still searching for someone who'd represent their brand, I had jumped at the chance. I needed space and distance to think about what I planned to do with my life once I returned back home. So, Marley had literally packed my luggage for me and sent me on my way.

Andrew arrived fifteen minutes into my meal. After pulling me to his huge body for a hug, he kissed my cheeks and shrugged out of his coat, tossing it onto one of the chairs. Then he sat across from me as I continued with my meal. He raised his eyebrows, his blue eyes twinkling with merriment. "What the hell did you do to St. Germain?"

The hand holding my chicken halted midway to my mouth. "Why? What did he tell you?"

He laughed. "I've known him for five years. I've seen him treat his women with respect, literally laying his money at their feet to make sure they were happy. However, allocating one of his precious, expensive suites for any of them in his hotel? I never thought I'd see the day."

Chapter Seven

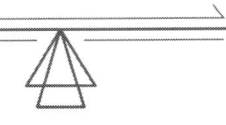

Selene

"He owns the hotel?"

Andrew nodded.

"Shit, no." My hand fell away from my mouth, my hunger dissipating. "What is he playing at?" I murmured, wiping my hand and mouth with the soft cotton napkin. Even the cloth felt classy.

Andrew's eyebrows shot up. "Apparently, he isn't the only one with their knickers twisted around their arse." He winked.

I rolled my eyes, took my tray to the table, and plopped back on the bed. "Is he always so… mercurial?"

He shrugged. "The Remington I've known for five years is laidback, almost to a fault. I can't wait to see how this plays out."

I grabbed the folder with my program for the coming weeks. "I can't stay here. This is just too much. Too expensive."

He lifted a hand, waving aside my concerns. "I'm sure St. Germain doesn't mind."

"Still, I shouldn't."

"What do you have against this?" He swept his arm across

the room, sounding as though I was making a big deal out of nothing.

It wasn't what I had against the room. How Remington affected me was what I was against. I wasn't ready for any kind of heart's entanglement, and in his case, Remington made my heart sprint the extra mile.

One thing I'd learned from my therapy sessions was that whatever had happened in my life up to that point didn't define the rest of my life or my future relationships. But also, I shouldn't go into a relationship blind, wearing my heart on my sleeve. So for now, I just wanted someone to flirt and go dancing with, have no-strings-attached sex, and then go back home and get on with my life. I had a feeling Remington was *not* Prince Charming, and he probably had no idea how to be that guy. He was the wolf. He took chasing prey to a whole new level.

I promised myself I wasn't going to dwell on my failed marriage. What good would it do me? It wasn't as if playing nice would give me James back. He'd already moved on. And to think I'd sacrificed my career for his cheating ass.

Taking a deep breath, I focused on the folder in Andrew's hands. I'd deal with Remington later. "Let's go through my schedule."

"Enough talking about St. Germain, I assume?" He grinned widely.

"Shut up!" I threw a pillow, hitting him in his face, but he kept laughing.

"You're allowed to move on with your life, Selene. Your ex was an arse."

I cocked one eyebrow at him. "I'm here in Paris, aren't I?"

"Touché, my lovely friend." He winked and then lowered his eyes to the file. "Ready for tomorrow's presentation at Lycée Saint Bernadette's?"

With a huge grin on my face, I nodded. If there was anything I was looking forward to more than the fashion show, it was talking to adolescents and teens while here in France. Being "The Face of Curves", I was asked to do presentations in schools, mixers, and other various events to promote the "Loving Your Curves is Sexy" campaign. I'd gladly accepted. The younger Selene who'd been bullied throughout most of her life was eager to come out and play.

Andrew and I went through the details on my schedule, and at some point, the phone rang. It was the concierge inquiring if I needed anything.

Remington must be keeping the staff on their toes. As much as his generosity overwhelmed me, it didn't stop my heart from dancing stupidly inside my chest from the knowledge someone was watching over me.

Andrew's serious expression turned smug as if he knew what I was thinking and feeling. I rolled my eyes, fighting a smile. Andrew was the closest thing I had to a best friend, other than my sister and Grace. I had lost contact with most of my other friends after leaving modeling years back. James's jealously knew no bounds, and he always said I'd leave him someday. Sometimes I wondered how can you hurt someone you say you love, someone who's been your best friend your entire life?

UGH. There I went again.

After ordering coffee and pastries from the hotel's patisserie, we picked up where we'd left off, with a short interruption from the wait staff delivering our coffee.

The next time we came up for air, it was 8 p.m. A cool autumn breeze swept through the room from an open window, ruffling the papers in the folder and nudging me awake. I was still jet-lagged and kept yawning every few minutes. Andrew tossed the folder on the table, stood up, and dug out a cell phone from his coat pocket.

"My number is in there."

Yawning again, I rose from the edge of the bed, took the phone from his hand, and then pressed a kiss on his cheek, following him to the door. "What time are we meeting downstairs tomorrow?"

"I'll meet you at Saint Bernadette's."

I frowned, and before I could say a word, he said, "St. Germain's driver will pick you up at 8 a.m."

"But I thought we—"

"He told me to tell you Adele will drive you. Besides, I have to run some errands before the presentation." Andrew's lips twitched in amusement. "He doesn't know how to react to you, which is a first. But he wants you. He just needs a few days to clear his head. Believe me, the determination I saw in his eyes… well let's just say, it's frightening."

I snorted. "Yes. He wants me like a hole in the head."

He leaned down to kiss my forehead, which was now heated by his words. I silently hoped my skin would scald his lips. "Goodnight, Leney." Yeah, he went for the kill with that one. He knew I'd soften up if he used my nickname.

Minutes later, a knock sounded on the door. The same waiter who'd brought coffee hours ago arrived pushing a trolley with a bottle of wine on it.

"Compliments of Monsieur St. Germain." He flashed a boyish grin as though he was holding onto a dirty little secret.

"Thank you"—I squinted to look at his badge—"Èric. When did Monsieur St. Germain order this?"

"A few minutes ago. He sends his warm regards." He shoved a white envelope in my hand, and just like the first one I received when I checked in, it was sealed with red wax, his initials on it.

As soon as Èric left, I ran a finger under the seal, shook my head, and then carefully pried the envelope open.

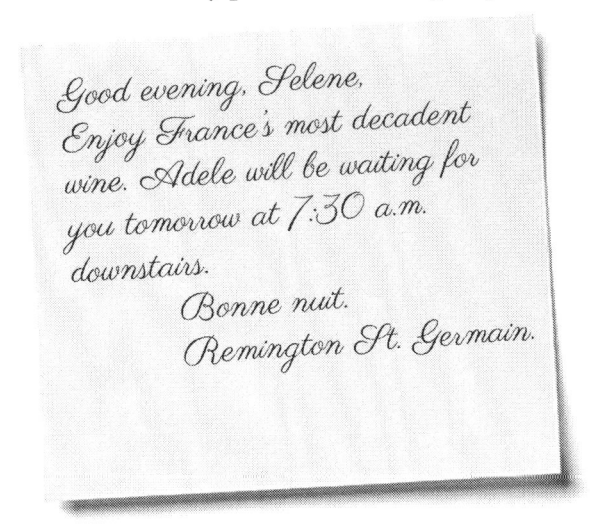

> *Good evening, Selene,*
> *Enjoy France's most decadent wine. Adele will be waiting for you tomorrow at 7:30 a.m. downstairs.*
> *Bonne nuit.*
> *Remington St. Germain.*

Dropping the letter on the table, I took the bottle of Rosé wine from the trolley to read the label.

Château Armand St. Germain, and below the wine name: *Only the best for the lady* with the letter *R* signed below the sentence.

Who the hell was Remington St. Germain? A dad, artist, hotelier, possibly a winemaker. What else was he? I seemed to be intriguing him, and I wasn't even sure how or why I'd captured his attention in the first place.

Color me fascinated. I made a note to ask Andrew tomorrow after the presentation.

Chapter Eight

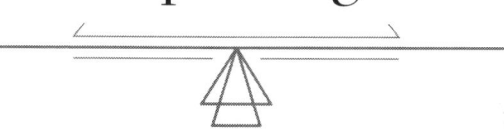

Selene

I woke up at 5 a.m., and after an intense workout session at the hotel's state-of-the-art gym, I showered and ordered room service. When I was done, I quickly slipped on a black pencil skirt, which hit slightly above my knees, and I tugged down the soft, stretchy fabric. Then I put on a plum, ruffle-neck blouse, tying the ribbon on my waist. I headed downstairs and outside to find Adele waiting for me in front of the hotel.

"Madame Michaels."

"*Bonjour,* Adele. And please call me Selene." I smiled and slid onto the backseat of the car, relieved to have Adele with me instead of driving with someone I didn't know. Digging inside my bag, I pulled out the letter I'd written last night. "Could you please give this to Monsieur St. Germain?"

She nodded, taking the note, and putting in carefully inside her black jacket pocket.

We arrived at Lycée Saint Bernadette in the *3rd arrondissement* with about five minutes to spare.

Andrew was hovering at the school doors, chatting with

Grace. After a quick look in our direction as the car arrived in front of the school, his frown was replaced by a huge smile.

"That was cutting it too close, Leney," he said, bounding down the stairs toward me as I opened my door.

"Traffic was a monster," I said, lifting up to kiss him on his smooth cheek.

"I thought you'd made up your mind not to take advantage of St. Germain's kindness anymore?" he asked, an eyebrow raised.

"Your friend is the persistent type, isn't he?"

"Only when he wants something badly," he said.

"Did someone mention St. Germain? As in Remington St. Germain?" Grace asked, brushing past Andrew, embracing me in a tight hug. "It's good to see you again, Selene."

"It's so nice to see you, too, Grace."

She smiled, her bright blue eyes filling with laughter as always. "You look well-rested. Did I mention yesterday how good it is to have you back with us again?" She linked my arm with hers, pulling Andrew with us toward the school.

I nodded, smiling. "Yes. But I don't mind hearing it again."

She bumped my shoulder with hers and laughed.

At five feet seven inches, Grace was a formidable presence in the fashion industry. Just like me, she'd had a hard time growing up. She'd started her company over ten years ago, spreading within Europe the first three years. Two years later, I was recruited through my agent in New York for a fashion show in Milan, where we met for the first time. Later the same year, I was honored with the title "The Face of Curves." Grace and I became good friends, until I left to make things work with James. When I told her I was getting back into modeling, she'd immediately offered me my former position. The outgoing girl had been let go after failing to maintain Curves' values. Respect others, respect your body, and above all, encourage others.

"So, St. Germain, huh? The handsome devil works fast, eh?" Grace said, pulling me away from my thoughts.

"You know him?" I asked, flicking a gaze toward Andrew as his phone buzzed in his hand. He excused himself when it started ringing and walked a short distance away.

She laughed. "Only that he's Andrew's friend and one newspaper called him 'one of France's sexiest, single fathers.' Doesn't hurt he's as close to Michelangelo as it gets when it comes to painting."

Wasn't there anything Remington did wrong? A guy so perfect and talented had to have some skeletons in his closet. "He was generous to give me a room at his hotel. And his driver."

"Oh, look at you, sweeping the Sexy Father off his feet." We laughed at that, heading for the doors, which led to the school hall.

As soon as I stepped on the raised podium, I was in my element. The real Selene, not the one who was always photoshopped in magazines to enhance or smooth her curves, but the one with a little tummy bump, which refused to go away no matter how much she exercised, and I loved it.

I was the girl. The girl who grew up in New York, who fought her way through childhood and teenage years, craving acceptance from society. The girl who, after bowing to her high school physical education teacher's pressure to lose weight, finally discovered the world of fashion. The girl who'd purchased a monthly *Vogue* magazine, wishing she'd magically transform to be like the tall, slender models gracing the glossy pages. And when she'd finally realized that wasn't in the cards for her, she'd accepted herself. Eating healthily and exercising took priority as she began to model part-time for plus-size clothing. She learned to embrace her body, her curves, and *she owned it. I owned it... because I was that girl.*

When I was finished speaking, I took a deep breath, my pulse beating wildly in my ears as it always did after peeling back those memories. Looks were exchanged, but the room remained silent. I was beginning to worry I might have said something wrong when a tall figure unfolded from a seat at the back of the room, clapping. Seconds later the room joined and, I swear, my heart's thudding overtook the clapping hands.

Remington St. Germain. A small smile curved the corner of his lips, his green eyes filled with approval, and damn it, I couldn't take my eyes off him. My stupid heart threatened to leave my chest and dash down from the podium to hop on his lap.

What was he doing here?

Andrew. I turned in his direction, but he just shrugged and raised his hands as if to say, "I didn't have a choice."

Taking a deep breath, I flicked a quick glance in Remington's direction, taking in how good he looked in a white V-neck T-shirt, hugging his toned chest, and a black coat.

Standing there, tall and hot, Remington was the picture of sophistication. If I hadn't seen him laughing with Adrien, I would have thought laughter was the rarest thing ever to grace his mouth.

I dragged my gaze from him. I had to in order to gather my thoughts, which were now splattered all over the place. I turned, walked out of the hall, and entered one of the classrooms designated for a question-and-answer session. A group of girls had already gathered inside, waiting. I needed to get my act together before facing Remington again.

Chapter Nine

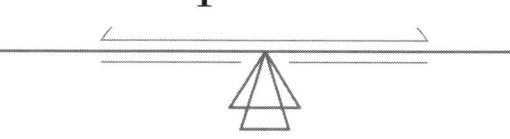

Selene

"If I didn't know better, I'd think you're avoiding me, Selene."

The poise I had maintained while talking to the girls shattered into tiny slivers at the sound of his voice.

I sucked in a breath, halted mid-step, and turned around to come face-to-face with Remington leaning on the wall behind me with his feet planted firmly on the floor. He was wearing black jeans, which hugged his strong thighs quite nicely. I glanced up to find him studying me. If he noticed me ogling him, he didn't show it.

"I wasn't avoiding you."

I totally was.

He chuckled, low, dark, and dirty. "Yet, here I am, waylaying you in the hall ten meters from the bathrooms. Lovely session by the way."

"Glad you approve." I smiled. "How long were you in there?"

"Long enough." He took a step forward. I didn't step back. For some reason, I was curious to see what he was going to do. He dipped a hand into his pocket and pulled out the letter I'd given to Adele. "I got your note from Adele. I did all that because I wanted to, and I want you to keep the suite for as long as you are in France."

"That's a bit too much—"

"Selene, please." He was in front of me in a second. "Let's not argue about this." His eyes were intense, the heat pouring off his body blasting mine. Such a simple word chipped at my resistance. I had a feeling him saying "please" was rare. Besides, I still had a date with the bathtub.

"Okay, I'll stay. Only because of the tub," I said playfully, surprised by how natural it was to tease him, especially when he was being this cordial. "Thank you."

He laughed. Whoa! He should do that more often. "It's such a beautiful thing, isn't it?" He lifted his hand toward my face but stopped inches from my cheek, staring at me as if he were waiting for my approval. I couldn't utter a single word as I waited to see what he wanted to do. His fingers first brushed my cheek and then slowly sank into my hair to untie the scarf I'd used to keep my hair off my face. He set my curls free and then flashed me an honest-to-God happy smile, one similar to the one I saw when he was chatting with his son.

"Have a coffee with me."

"W-what?" I stuttered, his request catching me off guard.

"You want to thank me. Have coffee with me."

There was just something in the way he was staring at me right now that if he asked me to sprint up Mt. Everest wearing a camisole, I probably would.

Oh, wow, Selene, back the hell up. These were very dangerous thoughts.

I finally broke away from his potent energy and took a step back. "How is that a thank you? It doesn't make sense."

"Unless you're scared of being alone with me." He smirked, eyebrow raised in challenge. Oh, he was in a playful mood. This side of him was new, and I liked it probably more than I should. "Besides, I want to show you I'm not this arse of a man you met two days ago. Call it a do-over."

"A do-over," I said. "You're convinced this will change my mind about you?"

He cocked his head to the side. "Yes." This man wore his confidence so effortlessly it was quite appealing. "Adrien and I are leaving for Provence later this evening. I'll feel much better knowing I didn't leave you with a bad impression of me. Unless you have other plans."

My plans included heading to town, doing some sightseeing, or visiting a museum or two. It took about one second to make up my mind. Remington had me curious.

"All right, I'll have coffee with you."

His eyes lit up, even though his smile was brief, and his shoulders visibly relaxed. "I'll meet you outside." He turned and strode away.

I headed for the bathroom and when I returned to the hall, Remington, Andrew, and a tall, burly man I had never seen before were speaking in low voices. Remington handed Andrew a piece of paper. Andrew frowned, and it only got worse as his eyes scrolled down the paper. He glanced up, said something to Remington before handing him the paper. As if he sensed me, he looked over his shoulder in my direction.

Three things happened. Andrew tucked his hands into his pants pockets and cleared his throat. The new guy shifted on his feet, mumbled something, and left. Remington's eyes narrowed as if gauging how much I'd heard of whatever they'd been talking about.

What the hell is that all about?

Pretending I wasn't bothered, I smoothed my skirt and stepped forward.

Remington's lips curled deliciously to one side. "Andrew, if you'll excuse me?" He folded the letter, slipping it inside the inner pocket of his coat, but not before a small piece of paper slipped and fluttered to the floor.

"Have fun, kids," Andrew said, winking at me as he shoved my handbag into my hands.

"You planned this, didn't you?" I murmured in his ear as I hugged him. He leaned back, placing a hand on his chest, wearing a wounded expression.

"Oh, drop the act already. Don't ever take up acting because you suck at it, Andrew." He laughed.

Taking a step back, I dropped my handbag right where the tiny snippet of paper was on the floor. "I'm such a klutz," I said, leaning down to pick up my bag along with the piece of paper, which I quickly slid into the side pocket of my bag.

"I'll drop Selene at the hotel," Remington said, his palm cupping my elbow to steady me.

Andrew's smile was smug as he turned to face Grace as she approached. She mouthed "call me" and waved.

As I walked down the stairs, Remington's hand pressed lightly on my arm, guiding me toward the Phantom parked a few feet away. He waited until I was safely seated and buckled before rounding the car and sliding into his seat.

My fingers itched to touch the dusting of hair on his arm. God, it was sexy. A majority of the men I'd seen shaved most of their body hair, so the fact Remington maintained his was devastatingly sexy. I turned my gaze to his fingers on the steering wheel, long and strong with clean, well-kept nails. And when I imagined them tugging my chin up for a kiss, I pressed my thighs together as the image flashed inside my head repeatedly.

I was attracted to Remington. I couldn't deny it. It wasn't only because of his looks. I was drawn to his elusive, mysterious nature. I wanted to know what made him tick. Maybe I didn't need a Prince Charming after all.

Chapter Ten

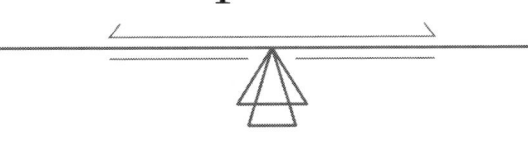

Selene

"Want to eat outside?"

"Sure." I glanced around, enjoying the warm fall weather. "I thought we were having coffee."

He flicked his wrist to look at the time. "We could have an early lunch." He jerked his chin, indicating to cross the street. He'd parked the Phantom close to the Hyatt, Hotel du Louvre, and we were walking toward Place du Carrousel.

My stomach chose that moment to announce how hungry I was. Heat crawled up my cheeks as I clutched my middle, my head snapping up at the dark chuckle from my right.

"Come on," Remington said, pointing me toward a brasserie to our left. He didn't seem as eager to touch me as he had when we left Saint Bernadette, but rather preferred to keep his hands clenched loosely at his sides.

Twenty minutes later, Remington was guiding me down a path flanked by trees in the Tuileries Gardens with our lunch in a bag. Red-orange leaves crunched under our feet as we strolled toward an empty bench close to a fountain. It was a beautiful day, and I was glad he'd suggested eating outside. I wasn't sure I was ready to be in close quarters with Remington just yet.

He handed me the lunch bag, strolled toward some chairs in front of the Octagon Basin, and dragged three of them toward me. Then he grabbed the bag and laid out our meal in one of the seats while I stood back, enjoying the view of him preparing our lunch.

"How am I doing so far?" Remington asked as soon as we sat down. He leaned forward with his elbows propped on his knees, hands hanging loosely between them.

"Hmm, let's see. I'm sitting in one of the most beautiful places in the world, and you're feeding me. So far so good. You're earning some very good points." I smiled, shoving a piece of rotisserie chicken in my mouth, following it with roasted vegetables. "As long as you feed me, we'll be friends."

He laughed, his eyes lingering a second too long on my mouth before he switched his focus to his food. "I'll definitely keep that in mind, Selene."

There it was again. The inflection in his voice on the last two letters on my name. His knee brushed mine, and even though we had clothing separating us, it didn't stop a shiver from scuttling down my stomach and settling between my legs. There was just something so intoxicating about him. Just a look from him, or a touch, made me feel lusty. I had been out of this flirting game for a very long time. James and I had dated since high school, so I had never dated anyone other than him. I obviously hadn't thought this through when I made the decision to jump back into the dating pool.

My stomach clenched, and I shifted on my chair. What if I said the wrong thing? But I was an adult, a single woman who hadn't had sex for ages, and was looking to have some fun.

We ate in silence, pausing to ask or answer questions. I told him I was having a good time in Paris so far, how long I'd been modeling. We talked about Adrien, conveniently skirting his mother. Adrien attended a preschool both in Paris and in Provence depending on where he was during the week. He spent at least a week every three weeks with his grandmother. I watched Remington, fascinated by how his face softened whenever he spoke about his son.

"Andrew told me you are an artist. Who's your inspiration?"

His eyes lit up further as he sipped wine from his plastic cup, then put it back on the chair between us.

"Caravaggio." I must have looked clueless because he pulled out his phone, and after tapping a few times on his screen, he handed it to me. He continued talking, his gaze never wavering from mine, making me feel like I was his only point of focus, and I completely forgot where I was.

God, this man was good and beautiful, especially with his face relaxed like that.

I returned his phone and dropped my gaze from his, suddenly feeling as though he could see what was going on inside me. How my resistance was slowly slipping away, how the thought of his sweet boy made my heart ache. Suddenly, the kind of loss I hadn't felt in a long time slammed into me. The months of therapy hadn't done anything to dull the pain. It had always been there, simmering beneath the surface, waiting for a trigger. And bam!

Blinking hard, I placed my plastic cutlery on the paper plate and snatched my cup of wine, drinking deeply, hoping to erase the ache right now wrenching my stomach.

"Selene?"

I couldn't look up. Dear God, I couldn't. If I did, I'd end up bursting into tears.

Gah! I hated when this happened. The sudden shifts in my moods were rare but there nonetheless.

Strong fingers cupped my chin and gently tugged it up to meet those vivid green eyes up close, darkened with worry. His ability to read me was quite frightening.

"I drank the wine fast," I said, laughing and gently wiping the tears from the corners of my eyes.

"Wine, huh?" He cocked his head to the side, and I just wanted to hide from his searching gaze.

Something vibrated nearby, and I leaped for my bag eager to distract myself, but Remington dropped his hand from my chin and pulled his phone from his pants pocket.

"Mother." His face softened marginally as he listened to the person on the other side of the phone. The conversation went on, shifting from French to English and back. Remington looked happy, occasionally laughing at something his mother said.

"I'm out for lunch. Can I call you back when I get home?" He leaned back on the chair, his eyes locked with mine. "Yes, Mother, a woman, and her name is Selene." Pause, then. "Yes… No, you can't talk to her… Yes, in time." He rolled his eyes, suddenly looking young and full of life.

A few minutes later, he hung up, sliding the phone in his pocket and ruffling his hair before resting his hand on the nape of his neck.

"Mommy giving you trouble?" I teased.

He chuckled. "She has been pushing me to find a woman for a while now. Whenever my mother hears I'm dining with a woman, her mind jumps ten feet ahead, and she wants me to put a ring on the woman's finger."

I laughed. This wasn't the Remington I first met, rather the one Andrew told me about.

"Don't you ever date?" *Where is Adrien's mother?* I bit back the question. We'd been having such a great time the past hour, and I didn't want to destroy the mood.

Something flashed on his face, and before I had time to decipher the expression, it was gone. "Occasionally. Ready to leave?" He changed the subject and stood up, collecting the plates, tossing them in the nearest bin, and corking the bottle of wine before holding his hand out to me. All I could do was stare until he raised one eyebrow in question or maybe a challenge.

I was going to touch him. Really touch him.

Pulse fluttering in my ears, I picked up my bag. When my hand touched his, I closed my eyes for a few seconds, enjoying the feel of his palm on mine. The strong way he held my hand made me feel safe. Stupid, I know, but true.

As soon as I was on my feet, he squeezed my hand before letting go. I wanted his hand back, holding mine, but I couldn't just grab it.

"Is Adrien's mother still around?" I finally asked.

"No." His voice dropped about twenty degrees, giving me a chill. "She passed away."

I froze mid-step, swiveling around to face him. "Oh my God, I am so sorry."

He studied me before shaking his head and laughing bitterly. "No apologies needed."

Shit. I didn't like that I was the one responsible for the dark look on his face.

Heading back to the car, we walked in silence while I

nibbled my bottom lip and Remington brooded silently at my side.

"I lost my points again, didn't I?" he asked.

I shook my head. "I think I lost mine. Thank you for lunch. And I'm truly sorry for asking you about her."

He waved a hand, brushing it off, and shoved his hands in his pockets.

There was a candy shop ahead of us, and I suddenly craved something sweet. I hoped I could find some kind of peace offering in there.

"Could you please wait for me? I need to buy something inside."

He nodded, and I left him standing under the shade of a tree.

After I placed my order for cotton candy, I stood back to wait and then remembered the piece of paper I picked up from the floor earlier. I dug it out, stared at the newspaper cutout of the letter C, and frowned.

What the hell is this? And what does the letter stand for?

I glanced over my shoulder at Remington before placing it back in my bag. He, Andrew, and the burly man had seemed worried, and when they realized I was hovering nearby, they seemed overly eager to discontinue their conversation.

"Got what you wanted?" Remington's sexy voice close to my ear snapped me out of my thoughts. His light scruff brushed lightly on my skin as he looked over my shoulder.

I nodded, pointing to the cotton candy being twirled into a huge ball.

"Cotton candy is the answer to every single problem." I took it from the man's hand, and once I paid for my purchase, I pinched a small piece and shoved it in my mouth.

Remington's eyes followed my fingers as the candy disappeared into my mouth.

He dragged his gaze away from my lips and laughed. "For world problems, too?"

"Especially world problems. If anyone ever took time to listen to me, the world would be a better place." I grinned, pinching a wad of candy and holding it out for him. "Want some?"

Before I could move my hand, his mouth, warm and wet, closed around my fingers. He twirled his tongue around them, his eyes dark and playful.

Oh. My. God. "Good?" I asked hoarsely when he finally freed my fingers from their delicious prison.

"Perfect." He licked his lips while staring at mine, his face much closer than before. I could see every single golden speckle in his eyes.

My head angled automatically as his did. Were we about to kiss? Wasn't it too soon for this? Oh my God. Why was I questioning everything? Right now, a hot guy looked like he wanted to devour me alive and I was *thinking*?

He pulled back slightly, studying me, and I kicked myself mentally. My eyes shifted to his jaw, trying to scoop up my thoughts now splattered at his feet. I'd been so absorbed by him, I hardly noticed what was hidden behind that sexy scruff.

"Is that... a dimple?" My finger was suddenly all over the small indentation. I found myself doing things without a second thought when I was around Remington. Before I could pull my hand back, he snatched it, bringing it to his mouth.

Again.

"If one little dimple drives you insane, wait until you see the second one." He turned his head.

God, I think I just came.

He swirled his tongue around my finger, nipping the tip gently. I groaned, struggling to pull my hand away before I embarrassed myself in front of the people littering the shop.

My heart was racing, and I was out of breath. All he did was show me his dimples and suck my finger.

Oh, shit, I am so in trouble.

"You're a dangerous man, Remington St. Germain."

He laughed, and everything seemed right in the world again. "Is that a bad thing?"

"No," I said, thinking how wonderful it'd be to live dangerously for once. Not care what anyone would think. "It's a very good thing."

As we walked toward his car, our bodies seemed to gravitate toward each other, our shoulders touching slightly with the occasional brushing of fingers.

At the hotel, he stopped in front of the elevator. "Have I earned my full stars yet?"

I shook my head, enjoying the twinkle in his eyes. "Almost. Can I ask you something? And you'll promise to tell me the truth?"

"Anything. I will always endeavor to tell you the truth."

"You seem shocked when you saw me the first time."

His expression shuttered closed. "Is that a question or a confirmation?"

"Both, I guess."

"Yes. You reminded me of someone from my past."

Someone from his past? Who? A girlfriend, a wife?

"And now?" I asked. "What changed?"

"I realized you were as different as day and night. You're

so full of light and kindness. Any other girl would be shoving something up my arse for how I treated you. But you, you amaze me."

"And you, sir, are good for my ego." I laughed, but he maintained the serious look on his face.

"I'm truly sorry for behaving like I did, Selene. Forgive me?"

I nodded, wondering what really happened to Adrien's mom to make him go from hot to cold in one second flat when I asked a few minutes ago.

And as if it was as natural for him as breathing, his fingers circled the nape of my neck, pulling me close. My mouth parted, ready. Waiting, but he only pressed a kiss on each of my cheeks.

"*Bonne nuit*, Selene," he whispered against my skin, turning and walking away from me.

"Goodnight, Remington," I murmured, rubbing my fingers on the place his lips had been.

Chapter Eleven

Selene

Not much happened the next few days. I hadn't seen or heard from Remington since our lunch in the park. However, he had made his presence known by making sure I was well-fed. Just yesterday, he had one of his staff deliver a huge bag of cotton candy with his usual red-wax sealed letter. I kind of missed him even though it didn't make sense to miss someone I had known for a few days.

My next assignment was a lingerie photo shoot, and until then, I was free. My agent in New York had spread my assignments out so I could have some free time. As much as I missed my mom, dad, and sister, I wasn't ready to go back home. I needed some time away to clear my mind. Live before I moved into the next phase of my life. I'd already accumulated enough money to start my own business designing plus-size lingerie.

Andrew was busy planning upcoming events, and Grace had travelled to Germany for work. So I spent my early mornings either in the gym, going for walks and jogging, or letting myself be pampered in the hotel's spa. I hadn't felt this relaxed and spoiled in a very long time.

One evening, I was readying myself to go out to Arena 31, a recommendation from Èric, the waiting staff who was becoming a regular at my doorstep at the hotel. There was no way I was going to spend the night indoors when Paris sparkled with life outside my four walls. When Andrew called to check on me, we made plans to meet in the club.

When choosing my ensemble, I was going for elegant, yet flirty. I chose a sleeveless, black skater dress with gold filigree on the front bodice, jammed my stocking-clad feet into a pair of gold heels, and put on a knee-length trench coat to keep the night chill away. Then, I was out the door with a gold clutch tucked under my arm. Adele was still at my disposal, but today, I wanted something different so I ended up taking a taxi. Twenty minutes later, I was standing outside Arena 31, in front of a suited-up, tall man with familiar blue eyes.

"Èric?"

A slow grin appeared on his lips. "Madame Michaels." He opened his arms as if he wanted to hug me, then seemed to remember himself and held out his hand in greeting. He was a hyper one, this guy.

I wrinkled my nose. "You've seen me in my, um… pajamas and dry drool around my mouth. Selene will do," I said. His face turned red, obviously remembering two days ago when he delivered dinner at ten o'clock, courtesy of my Sexy Knight in Brooding Armor who seemed to keep an avid eye on me. I'd fallen asleep at six in the evening, promising to wake myself up to order room service, but was startled awake and raced to the door without really checking how I looked. I realized too late that one side of my camisole had hiked up, revealing a breast. We had carefully circumvented that little episode ever since.

"So you moonlight as a bouncer?" I asked, scanning the entrance and beyond, frowning. A woman dressed in a short leather dress, that barely covered her ass, and thigh-high boots sashayed past me, followed by a group of men and women wearing clothing that showed a varying degree of skin. Was I overdressed?

He nodded, then seemed to sense my confusion because his grin widened. "It's Fantasy Friday. Everyone dresses in what they have been fantasizing about, something they cannot do in public."

"Oh." Apparently, the clubbers seemed to fantasize about showing a lot of skin.

My phone pinged. It was Andrew asking me where I was. After waving to Èric, I ambled inside, careful not to touch any exposed skin, and a lot of it was hanging out. By the time I shouldered my way to where Andrew and his wife, Marie, sat, I had been bumped, grinded, and my hands had touched places they had no business touching.

"So you didn't get the memo either, huh?" I asked after hugging Andrew and Marie. He was attired in dress slacks and a white shirt, and Marie wore a cute short, white, lace dress.

"It's my first time here. We know what to do next time, don't we, gorgeous?" He pulled Marie close and quickly took her lips in a deep kiss. Even after having three kids and being married for almost eight years, they behaved as they did when I first met them.

"Jeez, it's fantasy night where people play dress-up. I don't think it was a voyeur invitation to a kiss-her-like-you-want-to-fuck-her night," I said, laughing.

They pulled apart. "Don't give him ideas, Selene," Marie said with a giggle, tucking herself into her husband.

My chest tightened as I watched how easy they were with each other. How in love they were. Don't get me wrong, if anyone deserved to be happy, Andrew did. He'd had a lot of crap growing up. He'd moved from home to home, unable to find a couple who'd take him in. His parents had died in a car crash, and because they'd been estranged from their own parents, no one was willing to care for him. Eventually, a couple took him in, giving him the love he deserved and the medical attention he needed.

I couldn't help the sliver of jealousy snaking through my gut though. We ordered wine for Marie and me and beer for Andrew, then sat back and chatted while watching the semi-naked crowd on the floor. The music kept changing from one fast beat to another. I wasn't good with all the hopping everyone was doing on the dance floor, so I just kept swaying my body in a slower beat until I saw Èric making his way toward us, grinning. He was cute—the dark blond, ice-blue eyes kind of hotness.

"Any chance of requesting something that doesn't involve breaking an ankle?" I shouted above the music so he could hear me. He nodded and winked at me before striding away toward the DJ's cubicle.

"The boy likes you," Andrew said, his bottle pressed to his lips, studying me under his lashes.

I rolled my eyes. "I'm like his mother."

Did Èric like me? I had seen his eyes linger too long on my chest, but yeah, that could have been because he'd seen more than he should have.

Oh God, I'd almost blinded the kid.

"He does, Selene," Marie piped in. "Lock the boy down before some girl snatches him away. You have like six years age difference between you two. It's not so bad."

"You two are crazy." I laughed, standing and swaying as the music changed to a slower, seductive beat. "Come on." I grabbed both their hands, dragging them to the floor.

Marie and I danced around Andrew until the song ended.

As another song started, Andrew snatched Marie; at the same time, he shoved a passing Èric into my arms. And boy, Èric was a good dancer, light on his feet.

"Aren't you going to be fired?"

"It'd be worth it," he whispered in my neck, a smile on his lips.

Am I actually going to do this?

"Just this song and then you go back to work. I don't want you getting in trouble." He stared at me, giving me a look resembling one from a dog that'd been kicked in the ribs. *Oh, shucks!* "So, you're a bouncer," I said, trying to come up with something to talk about while our bodies got used to each other's movements.

"*Oui.* The benefits are amazing."

Oh, man, he's tall and really cute, especially when he grins at me like that. He's going to make some woman very happy someday.

"Benefits, really?" I raised a brow at him. "Did you always want to work in a hotel? It seems like music is more your thing."

"I like to interact with people, and working in Hotel Catherine gives me the opportunity. I trained for combat in the army but unfortunately had to leave due to an injury. I went back to school to study hotel management, and the rest is history. Now, I work nights in clubs and get to meet beautiful women." He gave me a crooked smile, waggling his eyebrows.

I laughed just as he twirled me around. His hands moved around my waist, framing my body, then slid down my legs. I gasped, swiveling around to face him, missing a couple of steps, and when I righted myself, I was in Remington's arms. "*Bonsoir*, Selene."

"Remington?" My heart was beating fast, and I blinked several times to make sure the god holding me was real.

I had missed him. Sort of. And I wondered again if it was logical to miss someone you've known for only a few days.

"What are you doing here? Where's Èric?"

He pulled me flush to his body, pressing his cheek on mine. His arms were like bands of steel around me as if he had no intention of letting go. "Was he your date?"

God, his voice did me in.

"No, he referred me to this place. How did you know I'd be here?"

Not that I was objecting.

He suddenly swung me around, his hold secure. Sure. Confident. And when he brought me back to his body, my breasts pressed against his hard, *hard* chest, his hands automatically going to my hips as if they belonged there. "Andrew, but you already know that. I want to have your number so I don't have to threaten to throttle him for your whereabouts every time. Did you miss me?"

I smiled, laying my face on his shoulder. "Did you?"

He sighed. "Yes, I did. I couldn't stay away for long." He pulled me tighter into him and moved one hand from my hip, sliding up my arm until he found my hand and linked our fingers together. The other hand skimmed my hip and came to rest on my lower back, pushing me to him right *there*, where I could feel the huge bulge in his pants. I shivered and snuggled closer, enjoying the feel of his arms on my body more than I probably should. The music continued to pound all around us. I inched closer, subtly inhaling his cologne that smelled minty with a slight woodsy edge in it.

Not knowing what to do with my free hand, I let it drift upward to his neck, twirling my fingers around the silky, soft hair on the nape. The longer we danced, the tighter he held me until I was certain not even air could pass between our bodies.

I felt the hand on my lower back flex several times before it framed me harder.

"*Mon Dieu*, your arse. I want to play dirty. Bite. Lick. And bite again."

I giggled, swaying, feeling happy and free and intoxicated by being around him. "What happened to the Brooding Remington?"

"Brooding?" he asked, pulling back to peer down at me, his lips twitching slightly. "I do not brood. How much did you drink?"

"One or two glasses of wine. Oh, yes, you've mastered the art of brooding," I said, shimmying my shoulders. I didn't make a habit of drinking too much, especially in social gatherings with crowded places. I was too paranoid someone might slip one of those infamous date rape drugs into my drink. Or I might not be in control of what happened around me. He pulled me closer. I could feel his erection pressing harder on my belly, and I felt delirious that I had this effect on him. Did he just grow bigger in his pants? "Tell me what else you'd do to this ass of mine."

He cocked his head to the side and stared at me through narrowed eyes. "I would rather show you than tell you." His eyes remained on mine the entire time, watching me. Devouring me. Sending every single breath in me scattering. I was lost in his touch. Lost in his gaze and in the middle of a thousand gyrating bodies, it was him and only him. His heart was beating fast and hard where our chests met, or maybe it was mine. But holy shit! Remington St. Germain was very intense, sexy, and enthralling. I could feel him in my veins like a drug.

"Have dinner with me," he murmured in my ear.

I didn't answer him immediately. I couldn't. My mind was still trying to catch up and regroup. I let my eyes wander aimlessly around the space full of clubbers. Remington seemed to sense my reluctance; he didn't pressure me. Just held me close, swayed with me, let me be.

"Yes, I'll have dinner with you." I finally breathed out the words as my gaze fleetingly fell on a man a few feet away. His fierce gaze flicked around the room, before returning to where Remington and I were standing. He put on a pair of dark sunglasses and then turned and left. He looked very familiar. "Remington, who's that man over there?"

His arms tensed around me. "What man?"

"He's gone," I muttered. "I swear I've seen that face before in the past few days."

"Probably one of the bouncers from the club."

I snorted. I felt how his body tensed at what I said. In addition, there was the mysterious letter and the tiny piece of paper I'd snatched from the floor. I needed a clear mind to think about all of these things.

When the song ended, I leaned into Remington's ear and told him I needed a break. My heels were killing me, and I needed to rest my feet. As soon as I slid back into our seats, Remington followed, keeping a respectful distance despite the way we danced. Then he pulled my feet onto his lap and removed my heels.

God, his touch was as beautiful and exhilarating as the man himself.

He beckoned a passing waiter while massaging my feet; this time, I asked for water and he ordered a beer. Remington was here, and given the way I was reacting to him, I wanted to think clearly. I had been brave and shockingly flirtatious on the dance floor, but now, I was scared of what I might do if I were fully intoxicated.

We spent the next two hours talking and laughing with Andrew and Marie, hopping on the floor at intervals and switching partners. The more I watched him, especially when he was dancing with Marie or seemed deep in thought, the more fascinated I became. Every time he took her hand and pulled her to the floor, I wanted to pull him back to me. Of course, they were just friends and I knew he wasn't really mine. What right did I have to feel jealous?

It didn't stop me though.

After we said our good-byes to Andrew and Marie, Remington drove me back to the hotel, and just like the last time, walked me to the elevator and stopped.

"I'll pick you up at seven tomorrow. Wear something to show off those curves and leave your hair like this. I like it." He leaned forward, brushing a thumb across my lips and bringing his mouth to my ear. A shiver raced down my spine. "I like it so damn much."

Gah! This man was going to destroy me with his words and his dark, seductive voice. He was as devastatingly charming as he was frighteningly broody.

"Well then." I found my mouth leading the way, letting my brain catch-up. "It seems as though pleasing you might be in my best interest, too, kind sir."

The amusement in his face vanished, and for a second, I thought I'd said something wrong until I noticed his eyes darkening and his long, spiked lashes lowering. His gaze dropped to my mouth for several moments as he just stared.

He inhaled deeply, seeming to need all his energy to drag air into his lungs.

"Until tomorrow, Selene." He brushed his knuckles along my jaw to my mouth, lightly touching my lips with the tips of his fingers, leaving a trail of heat on my skin. All I could do was just stand there, looking into his eyes, hypnotized and savoring the slight tremble in his fingers. "I have this overwhelming need to find out how it feels to kiss you." And before I could say, "Shut up and kiss me," he stepped back and squeezed his eyes shut for a few seconds. And when he opened them, hunger still shone bright in his eyes. He shook his head as if to clear it and then walked away, leaving me with a perfect view of his tight butt framed in those black pants. I realized I had a thing for his butt. How could I resist when it all but screamed, *Bite me, spank me?*

And I have this overwhelming need to do all sorts of things—some of them probably banned in several countries—with your mouth and your butt, Remington St. Germain.

I shook my head, smiling as an idea began to form in my head, and as I walked into my room, it bloomed into something so frighteningly exciting.

Tomorrow couldn't come fast enough.

Chapter Twelve

Selene

If anyone would have told me a few days ago that I'd be heading out for a date with Remington St. Germain, I'd have thought them insane. Nevertheless, here I was, planning what to wear.

I stepped out of the shower, rubbed a towel on my hair to dry it, and headed for the bed where everything was perfectly laid out. After slipping on white, seamless, silk underwear with lace trimming around the waist and a bra and garter stockings to match, I sat on the vanity close to the window to do my make-up.

Remington stood at the door at exactly seven o'clock. If Remington in jeans, cable knit sweater, and a blazer looked hot, Remington in a tuxedo looked simply stunning. My gaze moved upward, halting every single dirty thought beginning to pour through my head.

Something was wrong. His chest rose and fell rapidly as though he were struggling to breathe. Tiny beads of sweat popped up on his forehead. His face was flushed, and his fingers were trembling at his side. He looked… frightened.

"Hey," I said, moving aside to let him in.

My hand automatically pressed on his forehead without thinking. He leaned his head into my palm, his eyes falling shut.

No fever. I dropped my hand, and his eyes snapped open, giving me a clear view of the turmoil thrashing within. What had him so shaken? God, this was worrisome. And for just a second, I wondered if he had different personalities. Did Andrew forget to warn me about this?

"Come in and sit down for a bit." I took his hand when he showed no sign of following me inside.

He lowered himself onto the chair, and as I turned to grab a bottle of water for him, he buried his face in his hands, his elbows propped on his knees.

As soon as he had the water in his hands, he downed three-quarters of it before lowering the bottle. Then he sat back as color returned to his face.

Not sure what to say or do, I sank into the seat beside him, waiting. Was the dinner still on? Or maybe cancelling the whole thing was the better option?

"I've never had anyone so enthusiastic about taking me to dinner before." I tossed him a look.

He lifted those stunning, green eyes, now clear of torment, and scrutinized me for what felt like minutes, his expression unreadable.

Then he chuckled, and soon it turned into full-blown laughter. Such a beautiful sound from a delicious mouth.

"I arrive at your door, looking like some mad man, and all you do is make a joke of it?"

I shrugged, smiling. "I have a black belt in karate. I could kick your ass before you had a chance to touch me."

He blinked. "You do?"

I laughed. "Not really. I always wondered how it would feel to say that so casually though."

"And how does it feel?"

"Like I could actually kick someone's ass."

"God, you're a precious little thing, aren't you?" he said when his laughter cooled down a notch.

"I'm not sure 'little' would be a word to describe me. Precious, yes." I grinned at him, enjoying how his eyes twinkled with amusement.

"Brave and breathtaking." He took my hands in his, rubbing his thumbs on my wrists. "Small, enclosed spaces scare the shit out of me."

Wow. This man had so many facets. I had a feeling I was just starting to discover them.

He said it as if it didn't matter. The small tremor in his body said otherwise.

I squeezed his hand to comfort him.

He rose from the chair, pulling me with him, finally realizing I was all dressed up. His gaze slid down my body, taking in every single inch of my five-feet-ten-inch, size-twelve body. When he brought those eyes to my face, he swallowed. Hard.

"We still have a dinner to attend, *ma belle*." He released my hands.

My eyebrows shot up. *"My Beautiful?"* This man was full of surprises.

"You're mine for tonight, and you're beautiful." He glanced around the room, searching for something. "Are you wearing those?" He pointed at the red-soled Louboutin stilettos under the vanity.

I nodded and turned to go get my shoes, but his hand shot out, grasping my wrist.

"Sit." The command was soft, yet stern.

I settled in my chair, enjoying the view of how the black pants framed his thighs as he strode across the room. He returned, holding the shoes, and then dropped to his knees in front of me.

I waited, my breath a tornado in my chest, wanting to break free. My skin tingled with awareness as he bowed his head.

God, he smelled *so* good!

As soon as his long, strong fingers wrapped around my ankle, air rushed from my lips, my eyes squeezing shut. His touch was heat and ice, his breath a soft caress on my skin, his skin wet against—

My eyes snapped open in time to see him lean back, licking his bottom lip, and smiling wickedly.

Did he just kiss my calf?

He straightened and took a step back as if everything was right in his world, while mine was on a constant repeat of that single, hot kiss.

"We need to leave before they cancel our reservation."

He did have pretty lips. Kissable. Devourable. I shook off lusty thoughts and stood up, tugging down my deep purple dress as I smoothed my hands around my backside. Then I walked to the bed to get my black clutch, earrings and necklace.

He sucked in a deep breath, his hot gaze a brand on the skin exposed from the slight dip in the back of my dress. I grinned widely, knowing he couldn't see my face.

Works like a charm. Every. Single. Time.

Chapter Thirteen

Selene

As we reached the elevators, Remington's step faltered, his eyes darting to the door on our right leading to the stairs. He tucked his hands inside his pants pockets, and looked at me, before turning to stare as the red numbers scrolled upward on the tiny display above the elevator.

What had traumatized him so much that the thought of getting inside the elevator terrified him?

"We could take the stairs." His face was growing pale at an alarming rate.

"No." His gaze fell on my shoes. I rolled my eyes, leaned down, and pulled off my shoes, dangling them in my hands.

He snatched them from my hands and crouched to put them back on, then stood up, his face set into a stubborn scowl. A young couple emerged from a suite down the hall, giggling and kissing, ignoring us, at the same time the elevator dinged.

"Take the next one," Remington said in a voice that brooked no argument, grabbing my arm and pulling me inside the velvety interior.

He dropped my hand, turning his back to me, and pressed

his forehead on the wall. His breathing grew erratic with every passing second.

The man was going to hyperventilate and probably faint right there in front of me.

"Why do you have to be so stubborn?" I muttered, dropping my clutch on the floor and wedging myself between Remington and the elevator wall.

He lifted his head and slowly peeled his eyes open, meeting my gaze in confusion.

"Put your arms around me."

He did without hesitation, and I pulled him to me. I began to rub a hand down his back, occasionally threading my fingers through his silky, soft hair. God, it was *soft*. And smelled like heaven. He was hard *everywhere* my hands touched. I wasn't sure what I was doing, but it seemed to be working. He dropped his head to my shoulder, tucking his face in my neck. His hard breathing eased up slowly, and the grip around my waist loosened.

Moments later, the elevator dinged. He pulled back, staring at me as if he were seeing me for the first time.

"Thank you." He dropped his arms and picked up my clutch from the floor before stepping out.

"Anytime," I said quietly, following him out.

He flashed a smile. "I might take you up on that offer. How did you know what to do?"

"I didn't. Frankly, I just wanted to make everything go away."

He broke eye contact as someone called his name.

"Be back in a second." He strode toward the reception desk, clutching my bag under his arm possessively as though it might grow legs and dash away.

Two minutes later, he returned, placing a hand on my

lower back as he led me out Hotel Catherine's doors and toward the Phantom parked five feet away.

The evening had progressed from fascinating to enchanting with every single word that passed from the man sitting across from me. Or maybe it was all the wine I'd been sipping while letting myself be charmed by Remington St. Germain and his accent. Dear God! It seemed to hover between very British and very French. It was the sexiest thing that'd ever teased my ears. He kept a constant flow of questions about my family and my job. I found myself answering without hesitation. He was so easy to chat with. I couldn't explain why I felt this pull toward him.

"So you intend to open your own lingerie design line?" Remington asked, tracing a finger along the rim of his glass.

I nodded. "I graduated with a Bachelor of Fine Arts. I didn't have start-up capital, so when I saw an advertisement looking for plus-size models, I jumped at the chance. I intend to model for the next year or so and then open my own line."

"Sounds like a very good plan." His eyes shone with what I thought was admiration. "Have you drawn up some designs yet?"

I nodded. "I usually have a notebook with me in case inspiration strikes. What about you? I noticed the wine bottle had your surname on it. Is there a story behind that?"

"Yes."

He leaned back and stared at me.

"What? What's the story?"

"Hmm, if I tell you, then I will no longer be mysterious to you."

I laughed. "That's very narcissistic."

He raised an eyebrow. "I'm still not telling."

I shook my head, smiling. "Fine. So when did you know you wanted to be an artist?"

"For as long as I can remember, my mother fed my need by buying canvas after canvas and brushes." We held each other's gaze until I dropped mine, shying away from the sea of questions shining in his.

The silence between us stretched, punctuated by the cutlery and conversations from the other patrons. Finally, he leaned forward, bracing his arms on the table between us and took my hands in his and stared at my fingernails. "You have beautiful hands," he said, ignoring the fact the nails were now chipped around the corners. I had worried them to death whenever he'd asked a question that hit too close to home. I needed a manicure after today. "Tell me about your ex-husband."

I blew out a breath and tried to pull my hand away, but his grip was strong. His eyes were filled with so much compassion. I caved. If I was going to get over the aversion, the pain of my past, I would eventually have to deal with everything. "His name is James. I've known him literally my entire life. We attended the same school, and he was my first boyfriend. He proposed when we were seventeen. Logically, I married him." I smiled, remembering how eager James had been while sitting in front of my father, trying to impress him by being a gentleman and properly asking for my hand in marriage. My father had been impressed.

"I loved him. I have been divorced for almost two years

now." I waited for the pain that accompanied those words, but nothing happened.

Nothing happened! Did this mean I was finally free?

I grinned to myself.

"You should smile often," Remington said, and for umpteenth time since he picked me up from the hotel, his intense gaze lingered on my lips.

Kiss me, darn it!

We fell silent again, and this time it felt comfortable. I couldn't recall a time when this level of comfort had been felt between James and me, no matter how many years we had been together. This was the kind of comfort where two people said everything with just a single look and understood without uttering a word all while sitting across from each other. At least that is how I felt.

"I don't want to sound like a bad cliché or a dreamer, but do you believe things happen for a reason? Like people meet for a reason?" I asked, stumbling over my words. We were attracted to each other, but that wasn't a reason to say things that could end up being construed as desperate and send him running.

He studied me thoughtfully before bringing my hand to his lips. He pressed a kiss to my palm, and I felt dizzy and breathless at the contact. "I believe people come into your life for a reason. We could have met five years ago or two years ago, but we met when we did. Maybe it was a sign for us to acknowledge the bad, so we can appreciate the good when it comes along. I don't know, Selene." He covered my hand with both of his. "I don't believe in fairy tales. But I feel like I have known you forever."

I swallowed, watching him watching me.

"Wow."

He smiled, laid my hand on the table, and leaned back.

"I have a talent of shocking people to silence." He grinned. "So, your name. I was wondering about it. Isn't Selene a French name?" he asked, a slight frown on his face.

"My mother is French and my father Jamaican. They met in a culinary art school here in Paris, fell in love, and moved to the United States thirty-five years ago. So yeah…" I shrugged.

"The name suits you."

I grinned again like an idiot. I'd been doing that the entire night. This man was very good for my ego.

I leaned forward, enjoying how his eyes kept slipping down my dress. The front was designed in a way so the neckline drooped slightly, giving a hint of skin, but not overly so. "I hear you're France's sexiest single father."

He seemed to be having a hard time dragging his eyes from my chest. "I'm actually interested in what *you* think."

My eyebrows shot up. "You are? Why?"

His expression grew sober, and the playful look in his eyes vanished. "I don't know. It matters, I guess."

Hmm. Another quality indicating Remington wasn't all that perfect. It was quite endearing.

"I think you are a great dad. As for the sexy part, I'm holding my verdict for now."

He laughed. "Haven't I proven my sexiness yet?"

Oh, he had done that and more.

"You might have to work harder." We laughed, then I sat back, devouring him with my eyes, planning my move. God, I was feeling brave and sexy. I wanted to live on the edge. "You know, we've been chatting for a while now, but I still don't know how old you are."

"Does it matter? As long as we enjoy each other's company, it should not, no?"

I shrugged, not eager to destroy the mood, but unable to resist teasing him. "I just want to make sure I'm not breaking any laws or something."

He laughed. "I'm thirty-three. And you're twenty-six." I rolled my eyes, smiling. I guess Andrew couldn't resist filling him in with details about me.

I sipped my wine, studying him from across the table. "What happened in the elevator?"

Crap! That's not what I wanted to say.

He stiffened, and his lips flattened with obvious displeasure.

"When I was eleven, I got stuck in a lift while visiting my father in his office in London. It took almost an hour before someone got me out of there. Apparently, my father had seen fit to punish me by ordering his staff to stay put until he said otherwise." His lips curled in what I thought might be hate. "He was teaching me a lesson for disobeying him. I never visited him again after that."

God, such cruelty. No wonder the man was a mess in that elevator.

The mood had changed, and it was my fault. I shouldn't have asked him. I needed the carefree Remington back.

"I have a proposal for you." I pounced on the first thing in my head. "Call it an arrangement."

His eyebrows shot up, and he sank deeper in his chair. Curiosity sparkled in his eyes.

"An arrangement," he said, tracing his bottom lip with the tip of his finger. Gah! "Let's hear it."

I licked my lips, attempting to regroup the words in my

head, which was proving difficult with the way he was staring at me.

Where's the lusty devil when I needed her? And as though summoned, she hopped on my shoulder, and I felt braver.

"When I left New York, I promised myself I wasn't going to hold back if I wanted something. And for the three months I'd be here, I wanted adventure and—" He continued to study me, his intense gaze never leaving mine. "What I'm trying to say is—"

"You're trying to get over your ex-husband by getting involved with another man?" he asked. There was no judgment or rebuke, or even curiosity.

I shook my head. "That's not why I'm doing this."

The restaurant manager, who'd been checking on us every so often, appeared at our table, his hands folded in front of him. His glanced at me, a small smile on his lips before turning his attention to Remington to ask if we needed dessert. The rest of the words got lost in translation as they chatted in French. The manager left moments later, a satisfied look on his face.

"Then why are you, Selene? Why are you doing this?" He fixed me with such an unreadable look I couldn't tell if he was furious because of what I'd said or if he was just gauging how serious I was.

The past few hours talking to Remington had been so much fun, it'd cemented my decision to ask him. As much as the thought of him being my Paris fling had sent me running the other way before, he wasn't as bad as I'd originally thought.

"Because I want to do this for myself. I'm tired of being

the girl who gives without posing questions. I want to be the girl who takes what she wants and gives in return."

There. I said it.

Remington leaned forward, staring at me under his lashes, then bit that bottom lip. "What if I don't want to settle for just flirting?"

My heart rate doubled in my chest, but I mirrored his move, leaning forward. His eyes widened slightly, and his lips twitched at the corners, apparently amused by my bold move. For once in my life, it felt good being in charge for something this delicious. Slutty, but very, very good.

"What do *you* want?"

"Sex. Hot, dirty, vigorous sex." One eyebrow raised in question. A challenge.

Chapter Fourteen

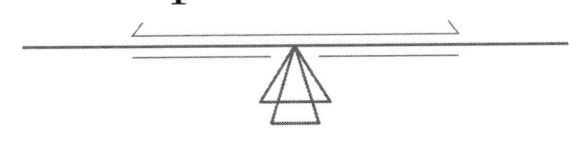

Selene

Heat filled my cheeks as what felt like a flock of sparrows took flight in my belly. "Anything else?" I asked him. *Sweet, mother! I was on a roll.*

"I get to touch you, whenever and wherever." His fingers flexed on the table as though he was fighting the urge to do just that.

"Done."

Wow and yay to the new me.

One side of his mouth tilted up. "Selene, I keep thinking I've figured you out until you throw another curve ball."

"Is that a yes, then?" I raised an eyebrow. This was so much fun, challenging him.

He threw his head back, laughing, then brought those strong painter's hands to my temples, pushing the hair off my face. "Yes."

"Good," I studied his face, halting on his scruffy chin.

A waiter stopped by our table, placing two plates of éclairs and coffee in front of us, but Remington's gaze never left mine.

I was beginning to realize he was very intense when he set his mind on something.

Needing a short reprieve from his gaze, I grabbed the fork and knife on the table and devoured my dessert.

"God, I love how you eat with such dedication." He sipped his coffee, watching me above the rim of his cup. Then he placed it back on the saucer and started on his éclair. Watching a guy lick chocolate cream off a spoon has never been so arousing.

"I don't shy away from food."

I polished off my dessert under his appreciative gaze. When he was done, he pushed his plate aside, then stood up and effortlessly lifted his chair and placed it next to me. He sat down, making sure his knees touched mine.

Cool is the word, Selene.

I swallowed and watched as he bent slightly forward. He traced a finger down my neck, halting where my pearl necklace lay against my skin, then wound it around his finger and tugged it slightly. He leaned forward, his eyes taking in every feature on my face, before bringing them back to mine. He cocked his head to the side. "I have a proposal of my own."

"Why am I not surprised?"

His eyes lifted to mine. "I want to draw you."

I jerked back, but his grip on the necklace wouldn't let me. "*Draw* me? Why would you want to do that?"

He moved forward an inch, warm breath brushing my lips. "Because you're sensual and beautiful. You wear your curves with pride. It's sexy and utterly breathtaking."

Oh, God, he was serious about this.

I snagged my bottom lip between my teeth, feeling nervous yet curious. I was used to being the focus of a photographer, but somehow this felt more intimate. How would it feel, being the center of his attention? I'd seen how focused he was throughout dinner, but I had a feeling he was intense when it came to painting.

I nodded, unable to keep my distance any longer, and did what I've been dying to do since we sat across from each other. I brushed my lips across his, and the hand on my necklace loosened as he pressed the calloused pad of his thumb across my top lip, resting his palm on my jaw.

"Is that a yes?" he asked, the deep timbre in his voice sending heat to pool between my thighs.

Is it?

Life doesn't always hand out second chances. We always tell ourselves we need a break; we need to take things slowly. Fuck slow. I was done with it. I wanted crazy flirting, insane hot, dirty, vigorous sex, crazy everything. I wanted both the brooding and the laidback Remington St. Germain.

I nodded, breathless at the thought of this beautiful man with his strong hands, using them to immortalize me on canvas. And touching my neck, breasts, and thighs.

Jesus!

I clenched my thighs and let out a shaky breath as that image teased me.

He wanted me. Me, Selene. The slightly overweight girl who'd suffered through childhood, The Face of Curves, taking the world one tiny storm at time, and at that minute, the object of Remington's attention.

Remington exhaled a controlled breath. He turned around, his eyes scanning the restaurant. When he found what he was searching for, he nodded once. The same waiter who had served us before materialized beside him. They spoke in French in low tones. I could hardly hear what they were talking about. Then the waiter left without sparing me a glance. Remington switched his focus to me, his hot gaze straying to the gentle dip of my gown.

What was he up to? Well, other than looking like he's about to devour me, just like he had his dessert.

The waiter returned minutes later, handed Remington a set of keys, and then left again.

The muscles under his white shirt flexed as he stood. He bent forward until his mouth met my ear, and then he flicked his tongue to trace my earlobe before nipping it. My body was coiled so tightly, I almost jumped out of my seat at the contact. "On your feet, *ma belle*."

"Where are we going?"

"The lounge rooms."

"Wait, wait. Why?" I whispered, my pulse beating in my ears and heat racing all over my body. The look on his face—lust, mischievousness and a challenging glint in his eyes—was destroying whatever brain cells I had left after our titillating dinner.

"For you, three months of debauchery and indulging in several acts of hedonistic pleasure. Me, I get to draw you and touch you. Whenever. Wherever." His eyebrows rose slowly in that challenging way I was getting used to. "Sounds like a deal worth sealing in private, no?"

"We could do that in here." I waved a hand around the restaurant. I didn't trust myself to be alone with him. My body had been fighting some serious gravity to slam myself into him the entire evening. I hadn't had sex in a while, and I was afraid I'd rip his tuxedo from his body and do dirty things to him. Given the way he'd been looking at me the entire evening since we sat around this table, I was sure he wouldn't mind.

"I prefer to do it in private. You aren't afraid of a little kiss, are you?"

My back straightened. My previous thoughts of not trusting myself around him vanished.

Afraid? "Where are the rooms?"

He smiled, and for a second, I wondered what I was really getting myself into. "Third floor. *Chambre trois*. Take the lift down the hallway." He pointed the direction with his stubbled chin.

"I'll meet you there in two minutes," I said. *Afraid my ass!*

"Don't keep me waiting, Selene." He grinned wickedly, turned, and strode away with his usual gait. Measured, confident steps full of purpose.

It dawned on me that Remington had a way of making me do things I wouldn't have done before. It was as though he could read my mind, see the things I was afraid to do but wanted them badly. He knew when to challenge me, how to challenge me.

The old me would be fiddling with my clutch bag, contemplating how safe meeting Remington in a secluded room was. The new me savored the recklessness of the situation, the idea of making out with him in public as foreign and intriguing as the man himself. Moreover, that grin hit the right spots, sending me shooting from my chair and following him, anticipation and lust fueling my legs.

Chapter Fifteen

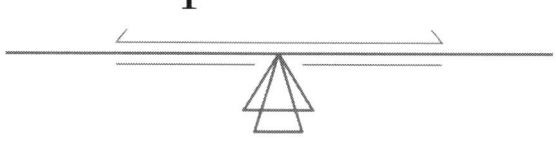

Selene

I stood in a red-carpeted hallway, staring at the gold plate with the number 3 on it and trying to bring my fast breaths under control. My body contradicted my mind; I wanted this, but I was afraid of what awaited me on the other side of the dark hardwood door.

It's just Remington. Yeah. A man whose moods changed like the wind, and for some reason, I wanted to know what made him tick. Or what made my body tick whenever I was within his vicinity.

Don't keep me waiting, Selene.

With those words in mind, I glanced quickly over my shoulder before twisting the doorknob and pushing the door slightly inward.

"Remington?" I called out breathlessly.

"Come in, Selene."

I stepped into the room and glanced around the space lit by three pendant lights hanging strategically on the ceiling. An oval table with six chairs around it stood close to the floor-to-ceiling windows. The curtains were open, giving a view of a sky full of stars and the street below. A pool table stood in the middle of the room, and in the far corner was a cabinet, which I assumed held beverages. There was only one painting decorating the white walls. This was just a normal room that restaurant patrons—probably an all-male room—retired to if they wanted to extend their stay.

Finally, I turned to face Remington and swallowed hard. He stood at the far end of the room, tall, strong, broad-shouldered, his chin thrust up and his hands behind his back. The flirty and fun Remington was gone. In his stead was a man radiating sexual power, control, seeming to take up space in the large room. For just a second, my step faltered and my grip on the doorknob tightened. We stared at each other from opposite sides of the room.

What was he thinking?

He dropped his arms to his sides and ambled toward me in long, measured steps, his eyes now dark and hooded, fixed on mine. I wet my lips and swallowed the ball of nervous anticipation in my throat. I waited, unable to move, stealing little breaths of air and failing miserably.

God, I was already panting shamelessly, and he hadn't even touched me.

He stopped in front of me and leaned forward, his cheek brushing against mine. He covered my hand with his around the doorknob and pushed it shut, twisting the key. The click of the lock echoed around the silent room, causing me to jump. He pried the clutch from my hands and tossed it on a small table on my right. He then ran his hand up the exposed skin of my back, his fingers digging into my hair, grabbing it, and tugging gently.

He dragged the tip of his nose along my jaw, inhaling deeply.

"Are you afraid of me?" His deep voice was hoarse.

Oh, dear God. "You're quite intense."

"You don't like intense?" He pulled back to look at me.

"I've never had intense," I said, breathless and panting. Surely, this was torture.

"Get used to it. Because this is the only way I know how to be. I want you to be comfortable around me."

Then he pressed his lips to the side of my neck. I stopped breathing completely, waiting. He lifted his hand from mine and slid his fingers to my hip, around the curve of my butt, squeezing gently. He groaned, his chest vibrating with it. I exhaled and closed my eyes, giddy, knowing I had this effect on this man.

"I've wanted to do this since I saw you naked in my room," he murmured, and I could feel his smile imprinting itself on my skin.

My eyes snapped open. "You have?" He nodded into my neck, his hand inching underneath my dress and drawing circles on my stocking-clad thigh with his thumb. "You didn't seem impressed that night."

"Oh, I was very impressed. For once in a long time, my cock, mind, and body were in synchrony. If I hadn't left, I'd have thrown you on that bed and fucked you. Hard. I took two cold showers to cool myself down, and that was after my failed attempt to satisfy myself with my hands twice."

"I wasn't very impressed with the way you treated me when you saw me. I'd have maimed you if you had tried to touch me."

"I want to apologize for that."

Before I could prepare for it, one of his arms hooked under my knees, lifted me up, and headed for the oval table. I gasped, shocked by his immense strength as my arms flew around his shoulders and clung to him.

Color me impressed. This is a man who could lift and carry

me without me having to worry I'd do some damage. I couldn't remember anyone ever lifting me so effortlessly, as if I weighed nothing. Remington had my full attention.

He lowered me on the smooth surface and spread my legs, moving his body between them, before grabbing my hips and pulling me forward, right where his arousal pressed against my core. I squeezed my thighs around his hips, causing him to groan again.

"I have to touch you, Selene," he murmured, his hand moving under my dress and up my thigh, stopping at the edge of my garters. He pulled back, his eyes focused on where his fingers were tracing the lace. He looked up and swallowed hard.

"I thought we were here just to kiss. Not that I'm objecting." My fingers slid to the nape of his neck, twirling the curls there.

"Never trust a man when he says he just wants to kiss you." Those strong fingers inched up and between my legs, brushing the lace of my panties. He paused, a question clear in his eyes while flirting, when I wanted those thick, long fingers inside me.

"Including you?"

"Especially me," he said hoarsely, pressing his lips to mine. He sucked my top lip between his lips. "If I kiss you, I fuck you. Whether it's with my cock, my fingers, or my mouth, I go all the way. When I finally have you naked and spread before me, every little part of your body will be mine to worship. My mouth will lick and suck, my hands will caress you, and I bite, *ma belle*, hard and light. But I do bite. And when I finally slide deep inside you, stroking in and out, you'll think of nothing else but me and my cock and my mouth." His teeth grazed my lower lip, lightly. The tip of his tongue swept along the seam of my parted lips, and mine darted out to touch his.

My body was on fire, fuelled by his words. Remington was the first man ever to say something so sinfully dirty and, holy shit, it was the most arousing thing. He was pushing all the right buttons with just his words and hands. My thighs trembled and my breathing was ragged, mirroring his. Somehow, I found the strength to wrap my legs around his hips, pulling him closer. Wanting more. Needing more. I slid my hands up his chest, savoring the hardness beneath them. Then I did something I'd never done before, startling myself and apparently Remington, given the way his eyes widened and darkened even further. I wrapped his tie around my fist and tugged him forward, brushed my lips on his jaw, inching toward his strong neck, and sucked.

He groaned, and his fingers left my hips and dug into my hair, fisted it, and jerked back, bringing his lips to my ear. "Selene, Selene, Selene. You're so damn beautiful." My name fell from his lips, like a prayer from a desperate man.

Then his mouth was on mine. There was nothing gentlemanly about the kiss. It was aggressive, possessive, utterly and deeply claiming. His tongue tangled with mine, tasting, exploring, teasing. He pulled away and my tongue followed his, tracing his bottom lip. I nipped him like I'd wanted to do for a while now. A growl escaped his mouth, making my whole body vibrate. I pushed my hips forward. I rubbed against him. I couldn't get enough as he gyrated his pelvis. "You've bewitched me with your body, your mouth, *this*."

He released my hair and cupped my breast through my bra while the other hand continued its trail down my body to pleasure me through the soft material between my legs. His thumb brushed against my nipple, so sensitive and hard. He bowed his head, taking one nipple between his lips, and sucked through the material, tugging gently.

"Remington. God, Remington." A breathless moan poured

between my lips. I felt reckless, a need unlike any other coiled inside me.

"*Mon Dieu,* I can smell your arousal. So good. You're so wet. Tell me what you want. What's your pleasure, my beautiful?"

I felt him everywhere. My body was bombarded by all these feelings, things I hadn't felt in a long time, things I had never felt in my entire life. Remington didn't just kiss me and touch me. He breathed life into my skin. He consumed me. He'd reached inside me with just a breath, took my uncertainties and insecurities, hurt and chaos, and turned them into wild passion. I couldn't find the words to tell him what I wanted. I didn't even know what I wanted.

I pulled away to catch my breath, but he pulled me right back and kissed me as if to let me know I wasn't going anywhere.

Of course, I had no intention of leaving his arms. I wanted what he was offering me. I wanted it bad.

He buried his face into the crook of my neck. "What do you want?" I tilted my head to the side, giving him access to my throat. There. Right there, he licked my skin, tasting it, and then traced his nose along my jaw. When I didn't respond, the hand between my legs halted their sweet, delicious torture. "Say it. Tell me what you need."

How would his lips feel on parts of my body other than my neck and lips and breasts? Would it be better, more explosive?

Suddenly, he moved away from my body, leaving me cold. He grabbed my hand and dragged me past the pool table and straight to the windows. Dropping my hand, he pressed me against the cool glass and then stood back, scrutinizing me with dark, hungry eyes. I held my breath, waiting, my hot body shivering at the contact with the cool glass

"Hands on the glass and leave them there."

I did as I was told.

He stepped closer and placed his hands on my shoulders. "Keep your eyes on me."

I nodded quickly and licked my lips in anticipation. As soon as his hands wandered down the sides of my breasts, I released a breath and closed my eyes. He squeezed gently, a warning. My eyes flew open to see him following the path his fingers were trailing down my body, leaving me trembling.

"God, your touch, Remington; I love how your hands feel on my body."

He looked up at me, a small smile on his lips. "And I love how your body feels in my hands. Utterly breathtaking." He fingered the edge of my skirt and then lifted it, caressing my inner thigh. He pushed my panties aside with one hand and teased my clit, watching me intently, and slipped the other around my back to cup my butt, pushing me into him.

I darted a look over my shoulder to the dark street below. "Remington, I don't think…"

"Don't think, just feel. Spread your legs wider. I want to taste you."

My thighs squeezed together instead. "What?"

His eyes widened slightly, and I knew he had figured it out. He removed his finger from inside me and brought both hands to my waist. "Have you never done this before?"

I shook my head as heat spread across my face. James hadn't been the oral sex kind of guy. He rarely ever touched me down there with anything other than his dick. But, Remington seemed to revel in the idea.

His eyes darkened even further at this revelation, and the hand now on my hip trembled, tightening. "I'm your first?"

I nodded, unable to read his expression. I felt his hands loosen around my waist.

This was it. Maybe he wasn't interested in going beyond kissing me. I braced myself for the rejection I knew was coming. Without warning, he dropped to his knees and pushed the skirt up around my hips. He buried his face between my thighs and pressed little kisses there. His scruff rubbed against my skin, and I lost the ability to breath for a second or ten.

Holy fuck! I was getting my first tongue-fuck ever from this complicated, hot man.

His hands left my dress and went for my panties. He hooked his fingers around the band and slid them down to my ankles. Then he brought those strong hands back to my thighs and opened them wider. With one last look at me, he brought his face back between my legs. As soon as his tongue touched my folds, I forgot that we might be giving a free show to the pedestrians below. I lost myself to the most pleasurable feeling I'd ever experienced while I watched his dark head bob as he continued to give me what I've been missing my whole life.

Every thought melted away, and my body coiled tightly in anticipation as his warm breath caressed my skin. His kissed me unhurriedly as if he had the entire night at his disposal. Then his fingers were there, spreading and stroking me in and out, alternating between gentle and hard licks. He knew what to do to make me moan.

My hands left the window, desperately in need of holding onto something, and gripped his soft hair, pulling tightly. He moaned, and the sounds vibrated all over my body, causing my knees to weaken.

"Your hands, Selene."

"But I want to touch you."

"No," he growled, and I shivered at his response. God, he was bossy and I loved it.

I returned them to their original place, afraid he might stop if I didn't follow his orders.

His lips moved to my inner thigh and nipped my skin. I screamed and trembled, my body torn between pleasure and pain, and my knees gave out. His hands gripped me harder, pinning me on the glass to support my weight. He did something with his tongue, hitting a particularly sensitive bundle of nerves. My back arched as I moaned. He groaned in obvious satisfaction and wrapped his mouth around my clit, sucking. Alternating between gentle and fast. He slid a finger inside me and continued working me with his tongue. I couldn't take it anymore.

"I… I'm coming!"

"That's it, Selene, come all over my tongue." His hands cupped my butt, holding me to his mouth as he continued his assault. He grunted in approval, the sound vibrating thorough my clit. "You taste so good. I could do this all day and still want to spend the night doing it some more."

Those words were my undoing. I sobbed, screamed, thrashing my head from side to side as I crashed into my climax head-on. Unable to keep my eyes open, I shut them and stars exploded behind them. My hands dropped from the window and I fell forward, but my body didn't hit the ground. Instead, I felt strong arms catch me and hold me tight, my back against a warm, hard chest. I let myself drown in Remington's scent and strength until my breathing returned to normal.

When I finally resurfaced from my orgasm, he was kissing my shoulder, nuzzling my neck, and murmuring words of endearment in French. His fingers caressed my jaw softly. "Are you okay?"

I opened my eyes to find him staring down at me with a gentle expression. "I'm… perfect. Thank you for catching me."

"I would catch you anytime." He fisted my hair in one hand while the other slid around my neck to cup my chin. He tugged my head back and crushed his mouth into mine. I moaned, tasting myself on his tongue, and I deepened the kiss. It ended as abruptly as it had begun. He loosened his grip on my hair, pushed it off my shoulder, and kissed the spot between my neck and shoulder.

"Turn around and look at me, Selene," Remington said roughly. I did, and we stared at each other. For some reason I felt embarrassed, which was weird because I really enjoyed what his mouth did to me.

"You're so responsive," he said, finger combing my hair.

If only he knew!

The last time anyone touched me sexually was my husband. Even then, he'd just groped my breast, stuck his dick inside me, and when he was done, he pulled out and walked out the bedroom door without looking back.

Now, in the hands of another man, I fell apart like it was my first time having sex. Which only made me feel a bit awkward. What was the etiquette for facing the man who just gave you your first epic oral in your life?

What do I do?

"Hey, are you okay?" He tugged my chin up to stare into my eyes, and I could feel heat spreading over my cheeks. He narrowed his eyes. "You have the most expressive eyes. For a minute there, I thought I lost you. Where did you go, Selene?"

"I'm here," I said, as he helped me to my feet. "I just… Did you come?"

He kissed my hair and chuckled softly. "I wanted to fuck you so badly. When we snuck in here, that was what I had in mind. I've never held back before, but I did." He shook his head as if he couldn't understand why. "I want to be inside you when I do that. Is that what has you troubled?"

I opened my mouth but closed it again and shook my head. My mind was still tangled up in so many thoughts, I was afraid I would say something I'd regret later. "We need to go."

I turned to leave, but he caught my elbow, turning me around. "Believe me, Selene, I need to be inside you like I need my next breath. But"—he waved his hand around the room—"not here."

I nodded, unable to talk. I wasn't sure what bothered me more. The fact that I liked him more than I thought I would or the shock of how fast I was getting used to *him*.

We left the room, my eyes focused forward as we passed a group of men, heading toward one of the lounge rooms. Heat filled my cheeks as a few eyes wandered to the sexy beast beside me. Did I look as ravished as I felt? Remington's hand on my waist was gentle, yet claiming, as he tugged me into him. Secure.

After paying for our dinner, he laced our fingers together and led me outside. We hopped in the car as soon as the valet brought it around. As much as my feelings were all over the place, I didn't want the night to end.

He slid a hand on my knee, squeezing it a little. "What are you thinking about, Selene?"

"I had a lot of fun tonight. Thank you."

"It's not over yet." He grinned at me, looking very carefree and young. I realized he'd been like this the entire evening, other than when he arrived on my doorstep. He turned his focus back to the road. "You wanted adventure. I'm the man to give you that."

We left the restaurant and fifteen minutes later, parked in front of what looked like a warehouse. He left his side of the car and came to mine. Holding out his hand to me, he led me toward the building. Giving me a playful look, he turned and removed something from his pocket and angled it in front of us. Immediately, the pull-down metal doors on the building slid slowly up, revealing a sleek, black sports car. It reminded me of a panther.

"What are we doing, Remington?" I asked as excitement and fear ratcheted up a notch.

"Have you never ridden in a sports car before?"

I shook my head, my eyes still on the car.

"Consider this your first." He grabbed my hips, pulling me into him. "It looks like we have a lot of firsts ahead of us."

Then he kissed me hard, snapping me out of my daze. I could live in this man's mouth forever.

"Ready?" he asked as soon as we were inside the car, safely buckled.

Feeling the high from being inside this car and the smell of leather surrounding us, I nodded, grinning widely and gripping my seat.

The thing roared to life, sending heat rushing through my veins and arousal between my legs.

Holy wow!

Remington pressed on the gas and the car sped off, throwing my body against the seat. I screamed and laughed as he raced through the streets around the outskirts of Paris. At one point, I wasn't even sure where we were, but in that moment, I trusted him to keep us safe.

By the time he drove me back to the hotel in the Phantom, I was breathless with exhilaration from the ride. We stopped at the elevators, and he warily glanced at the steel doors. But when he leveled a hungry gaze on my mouth, my excitement morphed into lust. He tilted his head, licked his lips, and he leaned toward me. He pressed his hands to my cheeks and I felt them tremble, whether from the adrenaline of racing or from desire, I couldn't tell. His eyes fell shut as his mouth met mine, softly kissing me as if learning the map of my lips with his own. Gently, he pulled my upper lip into his mouth, sucking lightly. He never went past my lips, yet it was the softest and most erotic kiss I had ever experienced. I wanted to see him as he kissed me, so I didn't close my eyes. I was rewarded with the most blissful look I've ever seen on anyone's face.

"*Bonne nuit*, Selene," he whispered against my lips, his eyes now open and watching me, watching him.

"*Bonne nuit*, Remington."

He leaned back and strode away, leaving me clutching the wall by the elevators.

Remington St. Germain's kiss had just spoiled me for all other men.

Chapter Sixteen

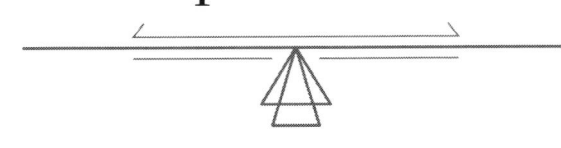

Selene

Yesterday was one of the most enjoyable evenings I'd had in a long time. Admittedly, my ex and I had dined out while dating. After getting married, everything went well until things started to dwindle and finally stop. Most nights, I found myself eating alone or heading over to my parents' for dinner. So the past few days were stuck in my Hall of Great Memories. Maybe it had to do with me finally not letting anything hold me back. Or maybe it was Remington. I could see myself becoming addicted to him. I wasn't sure how I felt about that. I had to tread carefully—have fun, but keep my heart out of it.

My phone, on a towel beside me, vibrated before playing a classical music tone. I frowned and shifted on the bench where I was sitting inside Hotel Catherine's swanky indoor swimming pool. When I picked it up, heat crept up my cheeks as I saw the name on the display. I didn't remember having that tone. Remington probably added it yesterday when he put his number in my phone.

"Don't tell me you're one of those classical-music-obsessed guys who can't function without it."

Remington's chuckle was slow, and as usual, seductive. How did he manage to do that so effortlessly? I bet he had no idea how sensual that sound was.

"I *am* one of those classical-music-obsessed guys. Would you like to come over?"

Smiling, I sat up on the bench, pulling my legs to my chest and resting my chin on my knees. "Hmm. What's my incentive?"

"Adrien is having some friends over, and I need company."

His son was enough to make me grin like a fool. He was so cute and—

I stilled, freezing my train of thought. I could not think like that. This was someone else's child, and I was already forming a mental bond with him, yet I would be leaving in three months.

I wonder what my therapist would say to that.

"Selene?"

Remington's voice snapped me back to the conversation.

"Sorry, um… I drifted off for a bit."

He was quiet for a few moments. "Are you all right?" His voice was low and worried.

"Yes. It is a bad habit of mine. Just ignore me." I laughed nervously. "What were you saying?"

"The incentive, I'll feed you. Not only am I one of 'France's sexiest fathers,' I'm an excellent cook."

"Careful there, St. Germain. Your head might not fit through the doorway if you aren't careful."

He laughed. "So what do you say?"

"I suppose I'm in the mood to be fed and spoiled."

"You have no idea how much I want to spoil you, Selene." His voice was low and intimate, sending a thousand tiny shivers all over my body.

I closed my eyes tight, biting my lip. "You're good with words, Remington."

"I'm good with other things as well."

I blew out a breath, opened my eyes, and looked around. A few hotel guests were scattered around the pool area, all appearing to be distracted in one way or another.

"I'll send someone to pick you up in twenty minutes."

I was dressed and waiting in the lobby ten minutes later. I was wearing fitted jeans with a chiffon blouse and a light sweater. It was an afternoon with kids playing around the house, so my makeup was minimal. And anyway, I might end up having food and who knows what else tossed on my face.

Even that thought didn't take away the excitement of seeing Remington and Adrien. In fact, I was looking forward to it.

A man who looked like he could lift a small hill with his bare hands entered the lobby and slid off his sunglasses. I knew him. He was the same guy who'd been talking to Andrew and Remington at Saint Bernadette. His eyes zeroed in on me as he strode, or rather prowled, toward me. My back straightened as he halted in front of me.

"Madame Michaels?"

"Yes."

"Monsieur St. Germain sent me. This way, please."

"Where's Adele?" I blurted out. This guy was very scary. The impassive look in his eyes didn't make him appear any friendlier.

He just stared at me before jerking his head toward the

entrance and then turned around. I quickly pulled out my phone.

Who's the Vin Diesel guy you just sent?

I stood up and adjusted the strap of my handbag on my shoulder. Gripping my phone, I hurried after him and then stopped as my phone pinged in my hand.

Adele is off today. Sorry I forgot to tell you Gilles was picking you up. He is a good friend of mine. You're safe with him.

My step faltered.

Safe with him? I pressed send, and the answer popped up immediately.

I meant he is a good driver. Almost as good as me. ;)

I laughed, followed Gilles to his car, and made a mental note to knock his ego down a few notches when I finally saw him.

Ten minutes into the drive to Remington's townhouse at Montmartre, I noticed Gilles's head quickly darting to the mirrors every few minutes. His eyes were safely hidden behind his sunglasses again. Turning in my seat, I craned my neck back to check what had him so jittery. I didn't see anything unusual. Traffic was light this time of day.

I leaned back in my seat, the same uneasiness I'd felt the past week coiling in my stomach. I was so lost in thought that when Gilles suddenly swerved the car and dashed into a side road, I shrieked, shaking in my seat. Horns blared and car wheels screeched on the tarmac outside the window.

"What happened?" I asked, my hand on my chest, darting a glance out the window and back to Gilles.

"Just avoiding some crazy drivers on the road." His voice suited him. Rough, deep, and rumbly.

I glanced out the window again. Gilles was driving on

a narrow street, frequently checking the mirrors. As the Peugeot slowed at some traffic lights, the car suddenly shook hard. I screamed, throwing my hands around my head and shoving it between my knees.

Oh, God, OH, MY FREAKING GOD!

Silence descended. The only sound was the pulse beating violently in my ears and my labored breathing.

"Gilles?" I called, lifting my head slightly and looking around.

"Everything's all right, Madame Michaels." His voice sounded strained. I pulled my hands down cautiously, peeking around his seat. "Everything is fine," he said while dialing his phone. Seconds later, he was talking in a low voice. My French wasn't the best—even though my mother had insisted on speaking to my sister and me in her mother language and I regretted not making the effort—but *danger* and *car* were tossed around a lot. Then his voice dropped further, and I leaned forward. It was nosy and probably rude, but if this was about me, I *had* to know.

"I didn't see the face," Gilles was saying. *"The idiot drove away before I could catch the plate number."* Then, *"She is okay. She asked, but I didn't tell her."*

Suddenly, rage flared inside me. I fisted my hands on my lap, and my body shook with pent-up fear. That unsettling feeling I'd had for a while now spread through my chest, and by the time we arrived at Remington's place, I was ready to explode.

What if… what if…

I shook my head as all kinds of possibilities rushed through my thoughts.

If this person, whoever it was, was after me… but no, I

wasn't *that* famous. I'd heard of models being stalked, but I was just a small person in a sea of fashion.

I had to talk to Remington before I drove myself insane.

Glancing up from my hands, I realized Gilles was standing there, watching me, waiting. I couldn't tell what he was thinking behind those sunglasses. Slinging my handbag strap around my shoulder, I placed my hand in his and allowed him to help me from the car, and somehow, my nerves settled a bit.

Chapter Seventeen

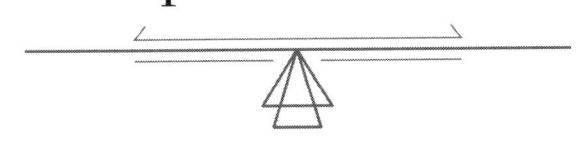

Selene

Remington wasn't in the living room or the kitchen when I walked into the house, but I could hear voices drifting from somewhere inside.

I dashed upstairs in search of the bathroom. I splashed water on my face, grabbed some tissues, and flipped the toilet seat to sit down, waiting for my nerves to settle a bit more. After quickly reapplying my eyeliner and lip-gloss, I tossed everything back into my bag and left the bathroom.

Remington was leaning on the wall outside the bathroom door, his arms folded across his chest. The white T-shirt hugged his chest and upper arms, and a pair of blue jeans framed his muscular thighs.

Voices drifted from downstairs, a child squealed followed by laughter so infectious I wanted to head down to join them.

But Remington was back to being Mister Intense.

"Are you okay?"

I walked around him to lean on the wall next to him, leaning my head back. "Am I okay? Hmm. No. Not really." I rolled my head to the side to face him, pretending I was calm, but deep down my stomach still twisted at the memory of what happened on our way to his home. "What's going on, Remington?"

He dropped his arms to his sides and stepped in front of me, placing one arm on the wall beside my head. He leaned forward, running his nose along my jaw. "Nothing you need to worry about."

I inhaled deeply and held my breath, fighting the shiver travelling down my spine. "Does this have anything to do with me?"

He placed the other arm on the other side of my face, caging me in, and pressed his lips to the side of my neck.

I groaned, moving my head to the side. "Oh God, Remington." My fingers twined in his hair. "You're distracting me, St. Germain." I brought my lips to his, kissing him deeply before pulling apart. "I want to know."

He buried his face into the crook of my neck, his warm breath on my skin. "Let's talk about this later, yes?"

"No."

He pulled back to look at me. "Not right now. Not with the children here."

I huffed out a breath, breaking his gaze to stare in the direction of the stairs. "Fine. No distractions?"

He grabbed my chin, forcing my attention back to him. "No distractions."

As we descended the stairs, Adrien saw his father and me and came hurtling toward us, skidding to a stop at the bottom of the stairs.

"Selene!" he shouted, flashing the cute grin I'd fallen in love with the moment I saw those green eyes staring down at me.

Dropping Remington's hand, I hurried down the stairs and scooped him in my arms. I squeezed him gently, savoring the feel of his little, squirming body.

"How are you, tiger?"

He pulled back, slapping a hand over his mouth, giggling. "Good. Papa? Can we swim outside?"

"It's cold out—"

Adrien interrupted, pleading his case in a torrent of French words. Laughing, I put him back on the floor, tossed my bag on a side table, and headed to the kitchen to see what I could do to help.

"Did you do all this?" I asked, glancing at the tray of food in front of me.

"I told you I was a good cook." He winked, and I laughed. He looked so carefree and beautiful, and I loved how self-confident he was in his masculinity. It was such a huge turn-on.

"You managed to handle those kids out there on your own?"

He nodded and smiled briefly. "I have been doing this, having Adrien's friends come over to play, for years. When you are the father and mother of a less than one-year-old child, you learn to take things in stride. Sometimes Adele helps and at times, when I have a lot of work to do in my office, I hire help. But mostly, I do it myself. I would do anything for him."

Oh my. How did this man manage to leave me breathless with just his words and actions?

I walked to where he stood, slid my hand to the back of his neck, pulled him down to me, and kissed him hard on the lips. I leaned back, watching hunger play in his eyes.

"What was that for, *ma belle?*"

"Because you are so…" He cocked his head to the side as I dug around inside my head for the right word. Then I remembered I was on a mission to teach his ego a lesson. "Cute," I finally said, dropping my hand and heading back toward the kitchen island. I could feel the heat of his gaze on my back. I tossed him a sassy smile over my shoulder, and my step faltered.

His eyes widened in obvious disbelief at my choice of words before narrowing. "Cats are cute. Dogs are cute. Adrien and the rest of the rug rats out there are *cute*."

He started toward me, the look on his face as dangerous as the prowl in his walk. I bolted around the island, heart pounding in my chest, giggling. I kicked the ballet flats from my feet and adjusted my stance. "Cute."

"Take that back before I make you, and I won't be gentle about it."

I shook my head, dashing to the other side as his long legs covered the distance between us. "Nope. We need to cool you down a little. Your ego is getting out of control."

"My ego," he growled, feigning a left. I darted to the right but too late; he pounced on me, tackling me flush into his body, my back to his front. "Is exactly the right proportion. Cute, you said, huh? I will have you know the word doesn't describe me. Not even close."

I wiggled my butt against the bulge in his jeans, highly aware of the blast of heat from his body, along with the shouts and fits of laughter from the children's playroom down the hall. "All right. Give me a word that would describe you without inflating your already large ego."

He ran the tip of his nose along my cheek, dipping his head to nip the underside of my jaw. His hand snuck under my blouse, his rough palm caressing my skin in circles. I sucked in a breath at the contact as unrestrained need settled between my legs.

"I am Remington *fucking* St. Germain. No amount of words can sum me up."

I turned my head to look him in the eye, laughter fighting for release in my throat. Then I saw the amusement and hunger fighting for dominance in his eyes, and I burst out laughing.

"So, you find that funny?"

Before I could respond, his mouth was on mine, stealing my breath and my laughter. He kissed me as though this were the first time our lips had met. He kissed me as if he had been waiting his entire life for this chance. He kissed me with a passion so deep that when he finally dragged his mouth from mine, we were panting and smiling.

"I could spend my life listening to your laughter, Selene."

"And I could kiss you an entire lifetime and never be sated. You are an excellent kisser, St. Germain."

"It's because of this mouth of yours. So bewitching and perfect."

My chest warmed all over the place at his words.

Spending the afternoon with Remington and the six boys was something I was going to remember for a long time. He played the part of a horse, neighing and galloping. I was a cross between a queen and a witch. Remington let the kids poke him with plastic swords as he pretended to be a dragon and then turned around and tickled them in turns.

Right after dinner, the parents stopped by to retrieve their children. Adrien yawned, rubbing his eyes.

"Papa, can she read me a story tonight?" Adrien asked, pointing a finger at me.

"Her name, Adrien," Remington told him, a soft reprimand in his voice, as we finished rinsing and putting the dirty dishes into the dishwasher.

"Selene!" Adrien shrieked as I dropped the dishcloth, rounded the corner, and dashed after him. He giggled as I caught up with him.

Laughter died in my throat when I turned to face Remington. He was leaning on the kitchen island, staring at us. His hands flexed at his sides, and different emotions flashed across his face as if he was fighting himself over something. Finally, he seemed to come to a decision. He nodded at us.

"Are you sure?" I asked him. I didn't want to barge into their lives and disrupt their system.

He mouthed "yes" at me, as Adrien yawned again.

Right after brushing his teeth and changing into his pajamas, Adrien dove under the covers and settled himself before looking at me expectantly.

"Which book would you like me to read for you, tiger?"

He pulled out a picture book on top of the nightstand drawer.

This... this feels wonderful. I inhaled deeply and began to read. Getting back into reading in French was difficult at first, but after a few passages into the story, it became easier.

Twenty minutes later, I left Adrien's room, smiling.

When I walked back into the living room, Remington was sprawled on the couch, shirtless, with a glass of wine in his hand. I paused long enough to admire this beautiful man, so lost in thought he hardly heard me enter the room. My eyes moved back to study his physique. Ripped stomach, muscled arms but not overly so. Dark hair dusted his chest and merged into a narrow line trailing down his stomach to disappear under his jeans where the top button was popped open.

Holy shit.

As if he could read my thoughts, he titled his head around. His mouth widened into a crooked smile, his eyes moved down to my legs and right back up to rest on my chest. My nipples hardened at the memory of what happened in *chambre trois*.

How hard I came under his ministrations.

"Ready?" That single word filled the room, increasing the tension between us.

I cleared my throat and crossed my hands over my chest

before heading in to stand in front of him. He stood up from the chair, bringing the glass of wine to my lips and tipped it slightly. I drank deeply, heat curling between my legs.

What was I supposed to be ready for? Sex? Or talk? Since our dinner, my mind had been on a loop, imagining how he'd feel naked and on top of me. Filling me. And the fear I'd felt when the car rammed into ours on the way to Remington's house.

"I want to draw you."

Chapter Eighteen

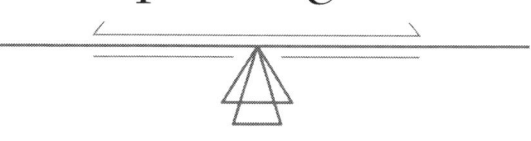

Selene

"And I want to talk."

He tensed and rubbed a hand down his face, before placing the glass on the table and starting to pace. "Let's forget this for now. Let me paint you."

I scowled at him. "Why?"

He halted mid-step, turned, and stalked to where I stood. "Because I don't want this person coming between us. This afternoon went so well. I want to enjoy this feeling a little longer. Gilles is handling this problem. Come with me, please. We can talk after this, I promise you." I could feel the urgency in his voice. He held out his hand to me, his palm facing up. "Let's enjoy each other's company a little longer."

"You know I'm holding you to that promise, right?"

He nodded. I placed my hand on his, and his shoulders relaxed visibly. We had the entire night to talk anyway.

Remington led me past the kitchen and down a hallway with white walls. Paintings decorated both sides of the wall.

"What kind of art do you do?" I asked, darting a glance

over my shoulder to Remington behind me and caught him staring at my ass. "You have a thing about my ass, don't you?"

"Hmm. I have a thing about every little part of your body." His hand was suddenly trailing down my back. He spread his fingers and squeezed my butt gently. "My art is realistic."

"Well, you have the license to own my ass tonight for the painting."

I was flipped around without warning and pressed against a wall. He caught my wrists in both his hands and leaned in. "Just for tonight?"

"Yes. And by the way, you're distracting me. We were supposed to talk about what happened earlier today, St. Germain."

"I know." He pressed his forehead to mine and shut his eyes. "I just wanted to end this night on a lighter note. We can do that, right? Talk about the other stuff later?"

"Just answer me this first. Does it have anything to do with me?"

His eyes opened slowly, and he pulled his bottom lip between his teeth, staring at me through those long, spiky lashes. "I promised always to tell you the truth, so I will. Yes. And no."

I exhaled, my body slumping forward. "What the hell does that mean? Do you know who this person is?"

He shook his head.

"I'm hardly anyone important or famous. What would they want from me?" I paused, remembering something. "The letter. You and Andrew were reading a letter at Saint Bernadette. Was that... mine?"

He blew out a breath. "No." I stared into his eyes for a few moments. He was telling me the truth. *What was in that letter?*

"Let's not think about this right now, all right? We had a great day; let's not spoil it." He slipped his hand down my arm and linked our fingers. "Come with me, *ma belle.*"

That endearment spread warmth through my body as he tugged me toward a room, flipping the lights on before we walked in. He dropped my hand and strode to some cupboards on the right. I turned, taking in my surroundings. This room was completely different from any other room I'd seen in this house. Terracotta walls with one side splattered in a range of colors: blue, green, red. A stool was positioned near a chaise lounge at the far end of the room. An easel stood on the opposite side of the room with a large collection of brushes, paint, and something looking like charcoal on the table behind the easel.

"You're wearing too much for our first session, Selene."

He appeared in front of me and lifted a hand to rest on the top button of my blouse. He looked up at me, a question in his eyes. When I nodded, he unbuttoned each slowly, letting the blouse fall to my feet. His hand drifted lower to rest at the band of my jeans and this time, didn't hesitate.

Seconds later, I was naked save for my white lace bra and panties. His eyes moved slowly down my body, lingering on my breasts. He swallowed hard, flicking a gaze up to my face. His eyes were dilated and dark, a look of hunger I'd never witnessed before on any man's face but his. I glanced down the soft trail of hair on his stomach, and this time, I was the one fighting for air as I saw the thick bulge in his jeans.

Wow, just wow!

When I looked up again, his gaze was stuck on my stomach, staring at the tattoo peeking from behind my panties. I shifted on my feet, feeling extremely naked and vulnerable. A devastating grin lifted the corners of his eyes, and suddenly, I felt bold.

"Another thing we have in common. We love art," he said, looking very smug.

If only he knew! My tattoo wasn't for love of the art, but a way to hide a painful memory.

"We do?" I said to cover the pain twisting in my chest. "What other things do we have in common?"

"We make each other laugh, and our sexual chemistry is off the charts."

He was right about that.

Feeling more confident, I slid my hands to the bra clasp on my back and stopped. He nodded, clearly reading my hesitation. He wanted me completely naked. I tossed it on the floor and then hooked my fingers on the lace band around my hips. He placed one hand on mine, stopping me.

"Let me." And with that, he dropped to his knees, taking the soft material with him down my legs, placing tiny kisses on my hip and toes as he reached my feet. He returned his focus to the tattoo, now fully exposed to his eyes.

He pressed his lips on my navel, tracing his tongue along the edges of the tattoo, then the middle. Panting, I reached down and tangled my fingers in his hair, tugging gently. As soon as his tongue touched the scar, I shivered and shut my eyes tightly. I didn't want him to see how that single touch affected me.

His mouth was pain and pleasure, my death and resurrection. I was a goner.

Pulling away from me, he straightened to his feet; he took my hand and led me to the vintage velvet, red chaise lounge. I sat down and then looked up at him with uncertainty.

"Lie down." The carefree Remington had disappeared. Before me, stood the Remington who had driven me wild during our dinner. Controlled and in his element.

"How flexible are you at pushing your boundaries, Selene?"

I frowned. "Boundaries?"

He brushed his knuckles down the side of my face, a gentle expression in his eyes. "Have you ever done anything unconventional?"

I didn't have any idea what he was talking about; if he was talking about sex, well, James and I never strayed out of the ordinary. Missionary position or him taking me from behind.

"If I do something you don't like, let me know, all right?"

I nodded and watched him stride toward a set of built-in cupboards to the right, anticipation and lust warring inside me. Also fear. My mind kept drifting back to today's incident and the conversation with Remington before we came in here. Dropping my head back on the soft surface, I stared at the square tiles on the ceiling, those thoughts running rampant inside my head.

"Selene?"

I jerked my head to the side to face Remington holding a long, red, silky piece of material in his hands.

"Where did you go?"

I shook my head, releasing my lip from between my teeth.

"You think too much, and right now, I don't want you getting lost inside your head. I want you here with me. Experience this with me, all right?"

I blew out a breath. "I'm not sure today is a good day to draw me. I'm too distracted."

"Well, I'll just have to take care of that right now."

The muscles on his shoulders tensed as he once again dropped to his knees and gripped my hips.

"Spread your legs, Selene."

"What?"

One eyebrow shot up in challenge. "I want to make sure the only things on your mind right now are you, me, and this room."

His eyes darkened even further, his chest rising and falling in quick breaths. He placed his hands on my hips, running his palm along my inner thighs and on my stomach. I loved the fact my full thighs and not-so-flat stomach aroused such lust in him.

"Jesus, you are so very beautiful, spread here before me. I'm dying to fuck you right now, Selene. I'm certain if I take you, I might not stop until we are exhausted. Even then, I would want to live inside you. So for now, I'll settle for tongue-fucking you and make damn sure you'll never forget it. Spread your legs, *ma belle*."

As if hypnotized by the dark eyes full of desire so profound they had me shivering, I let my legs fall open. His eyes moved between my legs, and a groan rumbled in his chest.

"*Vous etês belle*," he murmured, lowering his headful of dark, wavy hair between my legs and pressing his lips on my inner thighs. Even though I was expecting his lips on my skin, I started at their softness, the pure intimacy of that single act alone.

Every thought melted away, and my body coiled tightly in expectation as his warm breath caressed my skin. His lips pressed on my pussy before languidly kissing and licking until I was squirming on the chaise. My back arched as I moaned. He grunted in obvious satisfaction and wrapped his mouth around my clit, sucking, alternating between gentle and fast. He slid a finger inside me and continued working me with his tongue. I couldn't take it anymore.

"Remington, I… I'm coming!"

"Fuck, Selene, I love how you taste." His hands cupped my butt, lifting me to his mouth as he continued his assault. He grunted in approval, the sound vibrating through my clit.

"Oh God!" The release hit me so hard I couldn't catch my breath. I felt like I was riding a never-ending wave of pleasure.

When I came to my senses, Remington lay at my side with his elbow propped on the chaise and his head in his hand. He leaned in and kissed me. Tasting myself on his tongue, I groaned.

"Now, this is the look I was going for." He caressed my jaw

with his knuckles. "Next time, you will be coming around my cock, *ma belle*."

He kissed me on the lips before sliding from the chaise lounge, and seconds later, repositioned me the way he wanted. My fingers itched to touch him, and I wiggled on the lounge, feeling as if I were on fire. When I couldn't take it anymore, I pulled my hand from above my head. My fingers snagged the belt loops of his jeans, yanking him forward. I was hungry for him. I wanted his hard body on mine, his hot skin branding mine.

Caught off-guard, he stumbled forward. His hands shot out, bracing on either side of my head.

"Let me take care of you." I slid my hand down to the huge bulge in his jeans. He sucked in a breath and closed his eyes as if in pain. "Come on, Remington, just a few minutes."

"Bloody hell, Selene. If you keep doing that, I might not stop myself from fucking you until we pass out." He pressed his mouth to mine, sucked my bottom lip, and nipped it gently. Then he dropped his lower body to mine and rolled his hips, sending heat into my core. I'd just had an orgasm, but I could feel another building.

"That's the point."

He groaned. "Jesus." He kissed me hard, before pulling back, adjusting his crotch, and brushing a finger along my inner thigh. "First, let me draw you, and then I will show you how to touch me. Rough, soft, everything." The way he said "everything," it sounded like it should be right up there with the seven deadly sins. And darn it, I was in the mood to commit some sin.

"It's all your fault," I said, pouting.

One dark eyebrow shot up, amusement dancing in his eyes. "My fault?"

"Yes. You're irresistible, and you make me want you and I haven't stopped thinking about the kiss and how it will be when we finally… fuck."

"I love it when you say that word. Fuck."

He grabbed the silky material he'd been holding before, tied one end around my ankles, and slipped it between my thighs so it was covering the area between my legs. He brought the sash around my waist once, draped it around my breast, and finished by tying it around my wrists. I was stretched out, the material wrapped in a way that displayed teasing glimpses of my skin.

He stood back to examine his handiwork, grunted in contentment, kissed my forehead, and strode away.

I'd walked down the runaway nearly naked, posed in front of a camera with a wrap around my body and nothing underneath. I'd done so many things that made me feel completely exposed.

But never like this. I felt stripped bare. Was I comfortable lying there, watching Remington study me with a look so indescribable I wanted to hide? Hell, I wasn't sure about that. I knew I was beautiful. I'd worked hard to get back to where I was before I married James. However, somehow, Remington made me feel more sensual, especially when his eyes seemed to stare where the rose tattoo peeked out.

"Stop squirming, Selene."

That voice. Christ. A quiet, simmering fire laced the warning and I stopped moving. I shifted my gaze from his bare feet to his muscled, denim-clad thighs and up to his face. He narrowed his eyes in concentration, all business, very stern.

Moments later, he strolled away from me. Within seconds, dramatic classical music poured into the open space from hidden speakers on the ceiling. I craned my head back in search of Remington. He was already lifting the easel with ease, walking toward me.

"Classical music?"

He nodded. "Sergei Prokofiev. Do you like it?" He waved one hand toward the ceiling to indicate the song.

With the music filling the room, we fell into a tension-filled silence. The combination of Remington's heated gaze and the cadence of the music had my stomach in knots. This was the most erotic thing I'd ever done, and I was lucky this talented man, who seemed to do everything perfectly, was doing this with me.

Chapter Nineteen

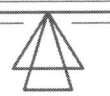

Remington

I took deep breaths, wrestling the control that was merely seconds from snapping.

Wrong move.

I could still taste her on my tongue. Her scent was still embedded in my senses, and my body was coiled so tight it was physical pain to even think beyond the woman lying on the lounge, naked and breathtakingly beautiful. Up until now, I had successfully managed to leash my lust, the urge to rip her clothes off, bury my cock deep inside her and fuck her until she screamed my name. Until nothing dominated her mind. Just me and how I made her feel.

My grip on the paintbrush tightened as visions of her sweet body writhing beneath me as I pumped into her as our bodies moved together taunted my mind. My breath came out in pants. My cock pressed hard on my jeans and my sight blurred, overwhelmed by my desire for her. The brush in my hand snapped, jolting me from the reverie. I glanced at the useless pieces of wood, my jaw clenched.

Mon dieu!

I needed to get my starving body in control until this session was over. If I went to her like this, I might scare her. What I was feeling was unusually alarming, even to me. I couldn't remember ever feeling this way. I wanted her on so many levels. I wanted to protect her from the world so no one ever hurt her again. I wanted to fuck her, hold her, cuff her to my bed so she never had to leave.

Just a few more minutes and I would have her. There was no way I would let her leave me, leave this house, until I had satiated my hunger over and over. Until I had her body bowing in my hands. Until I'd made her come several times over.

I let that thought wash over me, calming me.

When I turned to look over my shoulder to where she lay looking like my personal wet dream, I noticed her eyes were unfocused. She was once again lost in her own thoughts. Looked like I had some work cut out for me.

I turned back to my easel, readjusted my cock in my jeans, groaning inwardly before picking another brush, and smiled.

I was up for the challenge. I would make sure I was the only thing in her mind and fuck if I won't have her thinking about me every time she touched herself.

She was mine for tonight and every fucking day for the next three months.

Chapter Twenty

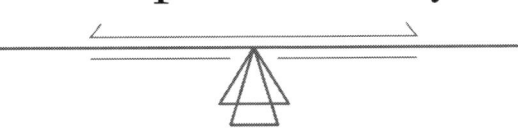

Selene

When the session was over, Remington untied the sash, draped a soft blanket over my naked body, and went to the bathroom around the corner to clean up. He returned ten minutes later, rubbing his hair dry with a towel. He was barefoot and bare-chested, dressed in another pair of hip-hugging jeans, as he padded toward me.

He tossed the towel on a side table before crawling up on the chaise lounge. He slipped under the blanket and climbed on top of me, covering my mouth with his in a soul-stealing kiss. He pulled back to stare into my eyes as he slid his palm to my stomach, brushing feather-light strokes around my navel.

"How was it?"

I wiggled closer, eager to feel his skin on mine. "Amazing. Have you ever drawn anyone other than me? Nude, I mean."

His eyes clouded and he averted his gaze, his jaw tightening. "Adrien's mother."

A stab of envy shot through my chest at the thought of him doing this with someone else. I shook my head, cringing inwardly.

Jeez, Selene, he had a life before he met you.

He brought those potent eyes back to me, tugging my chin up. "But never like this. You're the only one I've done this with."

"Can I see it when you're done?"

He flashed me a grin. "Of course."

We fell into a comfortable silence as I tried to bring my mind around to asking about what happened earlier today. I was curious about other things concerning the man wrapped around me like a warm, unbreakable shield.

"You are really good with Adrien, and he likes you. I thank you for that."

I smiled, snuggling closer. "He is a wonderful kid and easy to love. Besides, he has good taste."

He sighed deeply, warm breath ruffling the hair on the nape of my neck. "Why would anyone not stay in love with you?" he mused, probably not aware he said those words aloud.

I shrugged. "Sometimes love isn't enough. Sometimes people realize after years of being together, they didn't receive what they needed from the other person. I don't know." I took my bottom lip between my teeth. Why was it easy talking to Remington? Was it because of the way he held me in his arms? Or the way he focused on me with undivided attention? Or maybe his voice? I didn't know. All I knew was it felt easy to tell him things.

"James and I met in elementary school, so we literally grew up together. I was overweight and always made fun of by the other kids. One day, James appeared, like a knight on a white horse, and rescued me from being bullied. From then on, he was Team Selene." I laughed, remembering how James's eyes flashed in anger and challenge at the other children. "He and my best friend, Gena, made going to school, and life in general, almost bearable.

"We married two years after I started modeling. I was twenty-one. It's strange how you wake up to realize the one person you've known and loved all your life has suddenly turned into this person you don't even know anymore."

He pulled me tighter and kissed my hair.

"James is a good man. He just wanted something different from what I could give him."

"Something *different*?" He sounded confused.

"We had known each other for years. I probably had nothing to offer. I don't know. Love fades, I guess." I wasn't going to tell him James had found love in another woman's arms. It was too embarrassing just to think about it.

He flipped me on my back, cupping my face in his hands. "Love is a theory. I believe that… Love doesn't fade. And you have a lot to offer. I feel fortunate to be discovering every little piece of you, each step of the way."

He kissed me, his tongue sweeping inside my mouth. Kissing the sense into me. I could feel his dick pressing against my hip as he rolled his. His leg nudged my thighs apart as he wedged himself between them. He kissed my neck, sucking and nibbling. A deep growl rumbled in his chest, setting off a thousand shivers inside my body.

"I love what you did with your tongue and your hands before. Shouldn't that be forbidden in every country in the world? It was out of this world."

"Not in France. This is the land of love and apparently fucking. In addition, I hold the patent for it. Aren't you glad you're in France, *oui*?" he teased.

I laughed, and when I met his gaze, the teasing was gone. He stared at me as if he was seeing me for the first time. I realized he did that quite often. Unnerved by the look, I brought one hand to his neck and pulled him down to trail kisses on his jaw while the other slid down his abs between our bodies. I'd never tire of touching him. I felt his hand cover mine and lead me down to the huge bulge in his jeans. I started moving them up and down, alternating the pressure. He stopped, tossed the blanket aside, and lifted himself on his elbows so no part of his body was touching mine.

"Open my jeans and take me out."

I did as commanded and Oh. My. God! He was huge and hard. Tentatively, I ran my palm along his length, savoring the silken feel of his skin.

"You feel amazing," I whispered and then looked up at his face. His eyes were focused on my hands as they stroked his cock. His breath was ragged, and veins popped along his neck.

Hmm. Let's see how far his control will take him.

I slid my hand lower to the base of his cock and squeezed lightly.

He cursed repeatedly in French, but his body didn't lower to mine.

"Get the condom inside the back pocket of my jeans," he growled the words.

Quickly, I did as he asked, and not waiting to be told, I tore the wrapper and rolled it over his straining erection and then pushed the jeans down from his hips. He kicked them from his legs, fast.

"Spread your legs for me, Selene."

My legs fell apart. As soon as he wedged between them, he grabbed my legs and brought them to either side of his hips. He brought his eyes to mine while angling his cock to my entrance, and my pulse doubled its beating in my ears. My breathing came out in pants, and my butt lifted off the chaise, eager to feel him.

He held my gaze as he slid inside me, inch by inch. Sweat beaded his forehead, a sign of how much effort he took to control the urge to bury himself inside me. He groaned and slammed into me. I screamed as tiny pinpricks of pain scattered from my pussy. He *was* huge! My fingers searching wildly for something to hold on to and managed to find the curved arm on the chaise lounge, which I grabbed with all my strength.

Oh, God, I'm going to explode. So many feelings… I squirmed and moaned, raising my hips farther up to feel him deeper.

His grip tightened in warning against my skin. "Do *not* move," he said gruffly, his jaw tense and his eyes closed as if he was in pain.

Seconds ticked by, the only sounds that filled the room were our pants and the loud beating of my heart. Suddenly, I tensed, remembering there was a child in the house.

"Adrien," I whispered, not wanting my voice to carry across the room.

Remington's eyes slowly opened, blazing with desire. "He will not wake up until the morning." He shifted his hold on my thighs and began to move languidly at first. "You feel amazing, Selene. Your body is my weakness, *ma belle*. I've had an insatiable hunger for you for a while now. To fill you with my cock. Look, Selene. Just look how perfectly we fit together." His voice was rough, untamed. Awed. I was wonderstruck myself. Having Remington inside me, thrilling me, doing things that made my body bow in worship, had surpassed my wildest imagination. He shifted his focus on the place where we connected between our bodies. A smile full of pure male satisfaction burst across his face as he ground himself into me. I shivered in response to that look. I had done it. Brought that expression of unbridled passion. His hips moved hypnotically, his thrusts vicious. Purposeful.

When he looked back up at me again, his expression changed and I knew he wouldn't last long. I wanted to please him, make him feel as good as I'd felt on the two occasions he'd devoured me and made me come hard.

He shoved hard inside me. "Get out of your head, Selene," he gritted out the words. "I want you here with me. Do that for me, and I will make it worth your while, *d'accord*?"

I nodded.

He pulled out of me and grabbed his cock, stroking himself. *Fuck, that's hot.*

Remington sat on the edge of the chaise, grabbed my ankle, and dragged me forward to him, pulling me on his lap, with my back facing his chest. He gripped my hips in his big, strong hands, and I lifted on my toes as he guided me down onto his erection. We simultaneously groaned as he filled me to the hilt. God, this felt so good. One strong arm slid across my waist, holding me flush to his chest, and the other slid to my breast, kneading then tugging the nipple. Sharp, sweet pain shot from that area and settled a delicious ache where his cock filled me. He moved to the other breast and did the same, and I shuddered, groaning. I felt his lips on my spine as he kissed me before he started moving, slowly at first. He thrust more forcefully, and I bore down on him to meet his furious plunges. His teeth nipped my skin, and his mouth soothed the marks, kissing me better. This was pleasurable pain. The only kind that comes when mixed with pleasure. If only this moment could go on forever. But sooner or later, this feeling, this moment, would come to an end. A beautiful pain, and holy crap, I loved it. This was wild, uninhibited fucking.

He did something with his hips, causing me to groan and sob. My back arched, leaving his chest, but he quickly shoved me back into him, grounding his pelvis into my butt. "You feel so good, Remington. So big. More. I want more. Give me more," I said desperately.

"Do you like being fucked hard, *ma belle*? Tell me, Selene. I want to hear you say it."

I nodded quickly, unable to put in words what I really wanted. This was new ground for me, and I felt embarrassed just saying the words.

He continued to swirl those hips torturously slow, his breath hot as he brushed his lips on the shell of my ear and nipped my earlobe hard. "Say. It," he growled.

"I like it." The words flew from my lips. "Yes, I want you to fuck me hard."

He grunted his approval. His hand left my waist, caressing my body roughly with his fingers as if marking his territory, learning the curves and soft swells of each part of me. His fingers veered downward and parted me gently, while his other hand left my breast and grabbed my jaw, tilting my face to the side. His mouth came crushing against mine, taking and giving. I took greedily, needing more.

"Dammit, you have bewitched me, Selene. I can't wait to take you over and over, because one time is not enough for me."

His hand left my face and he brought both arms around my waist, yanking me back to him.

The jerkier his movements, the dirtier the words fell from his lips and the wetter I got until I thought I couldn't take it anymore. I could feel myself begin to climax. I closed my eyes and lost myself in the feeling, the scent of sex surrounding us, Remington's hard body and the groans and words spilling from his mouth. He was quite expressive, this man.

He pounded into me frantically before thrusting once. Twice. His body tensed, and his shout was muffled as he slammed his mouth on my back. I felt it vibrate in my body as it sank into my skin. We clung to each other as our bodies shook in the aftermath of our fucking. I smiled, delirious. Now that was some good sex. It gave a whole new meaning to the phrase "rocked my world."

He held me like this as we both came back from our climaxes and then rolled us onto the chaise. He pulled the blanket from where it had been abandoned and covered me again before sliding out from inside me. After removing the condom, he left for the bathroom to dispose of it and returned moments later, slipping under the blanket. He pulled me back and spooned me, tucking his head in the crook of my neck, and sighed.

God, that sound. If there were a way to describe it, I would say it was a thousand unspoken words, wrapped in one small, breathy sigh.

The sound of the doorbell ringing jerked us out of our little bubble. Remington frowned, flicked his wrist to look at his watch, and slowly untangled himself from my body. He grabbed his jeans from the floor and slid them on. I shivered, missing his warmth, and I pulled the blanket tighter around me.

"It's almost ten o'clock. Who'd be visiting at this hour?" he muttered as he left the room to answer the door.

I dropped my head back on the soft velvet, remembering the last two hours, and smiled like an idiot. God, being with Remington was an entirely new level of fun. My heart squeezed at the thought of him. Such a great dad and lover, yet from what I'd learned so far, a tortured man.

I stretched, turning to stare at the door, willing him to come back to me. After waiting a little longer, I wrapped the blanket around me and left to go in search of Remington. He stood in the hallway with his back to me. His head was bent, and the muscles around his shoulders were taut. His breathing was labored, and one hand was clenched into a tight fist at his side.

My heart plunged to my toes as I stepped closer, catching a glimpse of white paper in his hand.

"Remington?"

He spun around, his eyes wide and his jaw clenched. Anger flared in his eyes. My gaze dropped to his hand and nausea rose in my throat. He pulled back his arm when I stepped forward to read what was in that letter.

"Remington?" I called his name again. "I need to see what's in that letter."

He continued to stare at me, indecision, anger, and determination in his eyes. Well, I wasn't budging, either. I clutched the blanket and stared back at him.

Eventually, he exhaled deeply, running his fingers through his hair and held it out for me. I fought a grin as I took the letter from his hands. Then I froze.

I was going to throw up. Or faint.

But neither happened.

I breathed deeply, staring at the words—the letters cut from newspaper—and re-read the words written in French.

Do you think you can get your wife back by having a woman who resembles her?

Think again, Remington. Get rid of her, or you will regret it.

I blinked. I lifted my head as I tried not to let the pain and fear writhing in my chest choke me.

"Is this true?" I whispered. "Are you interested in me because I resemble *her*?"

He shook his head vigorously, his arms stretched toward me in a desperate plea.

"Selene, listen. It's not like that." He paused and took a deep breath. "Remember the first time I saw you in the hotel? I was so confused, hurt, and angry. But you're not that woman. You are not *her*." The last sentence was uttered in a whisper.

My mind was working overtime, trying to connect the

dots. "The incident this afternoon, is this connected to what happened today?"

"Gilles seems to think so."

I shook my head. "Whoever this person is, he or she will not give up. If I stay, God, Remington, if something happened to you and Adrien, I could never forgive myself."

What if the person who sent the letter was keeping an eye on the house, waiting? My fight or flight response kicked in with dizzying clarity. If this made me selfish, then so be it, but they would be *safe*.

"I have to leave." I dropped the letter in his palm, spun around, and walked back into his studio, my stomach clenching with pain from what I'd discovered and fear for what might happen to him or Adrien if I stayed.

After getting dressed, I hurried back to the living room in search of my handbag.

"It's in my room," Remington said in a quiet voice. "Please listen to me, Selene. This is not the first time, whoever this person is, has sent me letters. This is most likely something they do to scare me."

That got my attention. I swept a hand over my tear-streaked face, wondering why it hurt so much. Remington and I hadn't known each other for that long, but *shit*, it hurt. He covered the distance between us in two long strides and took my face in his large hands, his tortured gaze meeting mine.

"What do you mean it's not the first time?"

He pressed his lips to my cheeks, kissing the tears away.

"Every time I start a relationship with a woman, the letters start arriving. It used to be text messages, and now, letters."

"Did these women, you know… resemble your wife?"

He stared at me longer than necessary, dropped his hands from my cheeks, and shook his head.

My shoulders relaxed a bit. "What happened to them?"

He seemed to hesitate, and his hands clenched loosely at his sides. "I ended things as soon as the threats became serious."

I straightened, wiping a hand at my damp face. "I can't stay here, Remington. Whoever this person is… I can't put you and Adrien in danger. I have to leave now." I started for the door, but he appeared suddenly in front of me, blocking my way.

"No."

"No? This is my decision, Remington. I'm leaving." I stopped to contemplate my transport options and then looked up at him. "Can I call for a cab, please?"

"You… are… not… leaving, Selene!" He grasped my forearms crushing me to his chest. "You can't leave."

"Don't do this, Remington. You have a son to think about, to keep safe. You don't know me well enough for you to risk that. "

"I know you well enough to protect you any way I can."

I stilled, stunned by the declaration. "You ended things with the other women. I want you to do the same. Please, please, Remington." I took his face in my hands, pressing my forehead to his. A face that hid scars I suspected ran deeper than the blood in his veins.

"You're not the other women. And I'm not ending anything."

I rose on my toes and pressed my lips to his, but he quickly deepened the kiss, his hands wrapped tightly around me.

"I will not risk you two." I pulled away and headed for the door. "Could you please tell Adrien good-bye for me?"

"Wait!"

I stopped and looked over my shoulder, my heart breaking at the defeated look in his eyes.

"I'll call Gilles to take you to the hotel." He grabbed his phone from the table and dialed, while climbing upstairs. He came back a few moments later with my handbag. "Could you please do me a favor? Give me a call when you get to your room?"

I nodded, reaching for my bag from his hands.

Gilles arrived a few minutes later. I climbed into the car without looking back. As the car started to pull out of the driveway, I finally looked out the window and saw Remington, his shoulders slumped forward, standing on the path leading to his house. I waved. He waved back, his shoulders lifted, and a look of determination crossed his features.

I turned away, my vision blurred, my body feeling like lead. Things had been going so well, until a crazy person with an insane agenda stormed into my life. And that damn letter.

Stupid me and my crazy heart.

My emotions were in a state of havoc, but I'd get them under control again. I hadn't known Remington long. I'd get over it. I had to. I'd get on with my life. *Been there before.*

Then why did I feel as though I had left my soul inside the glass and brick house?

Part Two

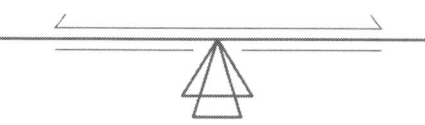

We all have our demons,
and every once in a while,
we have to dance with them,
embrace them.

Remington St. Germain

> "One of the deep secrets of life is that all that is really worth doing is what we do for others."
> —Lewis Carroll

Chapter Twenty-One

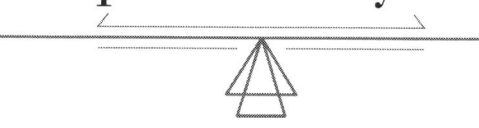

Remington

I knew the moment I gave in to the need to pursue Selene that trouble would follow me.

It always had.

I should have resisted harder.

Easier said than done. Selene had caught my attention, and I couldn't shake her off. However, I was beginning to realize that when it came to Selene, my heart overruled my mind, eliminating any rational thoughts. Those memories of the first time I saw her at the hotel—the speech she'd given at Saint Bernadette's that made me want to stand and applaud all over again, the way she made me laugh, every single minute with her—were treasured.

Within a short time, she had become an irresistible and unforgettable force, and my mind was in chaos because of her.

She was the first woman who didn't look at me as if I were made of gold. I craved her with a need so ravenous it throbbed painfully in my chest, something I had been missing for a long time. Was I about to lose her before I'd even had a chance to know her? She was only here in France for three months, but I'd be damned if I wasn't going to spend those days with her. Every single fucking one of them. I wanted Selene as I'd never wanted any other woman in my life. Call it lust or love at first sight; I couldn't care less about all those fancy definitions. All I knew was my sights were set on her and there was nothing I could do about it; we had amazing chemistry. In the time I'd spent with her, she'd been a bright light in my life.

And apparently, my cock agreed with me. I rearranged myself, groaning at the thought of her curvy body. How these emotions were possible in my current state of mind, this cocktail of lust, frustration, anger, and determination, was still a mystery to me. The night she left, she asked me if what the letter said was true, and I had denied the truth. Selene bore some fleeting physical resemblance to Colette, the woman to whom I'd once given my heart, before she turned around and ripped it out of my chest. While Colette had been an olive-skinned brunette, Selene was a rich honey-brown with curly hair that seemed reluctant to be tamed. The only things they had in common were the high cheekbones and the uncanny way their noses upturned at the tip. I couldn't tell Selene the truth because I was afraid she would think I wanted her to replace Colette, which was the farthest thing on my mind. Fear like none I had ever known had filled me, forcing the lie from my mouth. Yesterday, I went to Hotel Catherine for my monthly staff meeting. As much as I had wanted to walk up to her hotel room and see her, I had to respect her wish to stay away.

For now.

Later, I met with Èric to discuss him being part of Selene's security team. I knew he'd been in the army and could easily neutralize a threat. I was also aware he had feelings for her. I had seen it in his eyes the night I arrived from Provence and tracked Selene to the club where Èric also worked. There was no way he would let anything happen to her.

I glanced at the letter that had arrived earlier this morning and then to the red irises next to it on the table. I growled under my breath and swiped the letter, crushing it in my hands, and hurled it across the room before picking up my pacing on the carpeted floor of my living room.

Shit. Bloody fucking hell!

I pulled my phone from the pocket of my trousers and punched in Gilles's number. It rang twice before he answered the call.

"Any news yet?" I barked into the phone, any trace of civility or patience long gone.

"No. I sent the letters to a friend of mine, a police officer. There were no fingerprints. It seems the sender is very keen on not being found, so we are looking into other ways."

I clenched my jaw, forcing myself to stay calm. "When? When will you get the results?"

He sighed. "I can't promise you anything at the moment, Remington. He has to employ other methods to find out who the sender is. He will forward the letters to a document examiner to work on this. I have done some favours for him, and he knows how important this is."

I rubbed my neck, fighting the urge to hurl the mobile against the wall and said, "Keep me posted."

I disconnected the call and shoved it back inside my pocket. I lowered myself on the chair next to me and dropped my head in my hands. I was desperate, and I had no idea how to deal with what I was feeling. I couldn't remember the last time I'd felt this way. I closed my eyes and all I could see were Selene's, reflecting her terror for my son, Adrien, and me. But there was something else in there, too.

Concern.

Maybe I should let this be. Let her go.

She would be safe. Adrien and I as well.

I rose from the seat, and after confirming the alarm was on, I climbed the stairs and walked past my room and into Adrien's. I sat down on a chair and stared into the dark, my thoughts in total chaos over the hazel-eyed woman I'd watched drive away with Gilles.

I had two choices: Give her time to think about it, to remember how good it felt for us to be together, or forget about her and move on with my life.

Given my intense feelings and Adrien's ardent love for her, the latter was not an option. Especially now that I realized how much he had been missing. Being with Selene had proven to be an eye-opener. I had gotten a glimpse of how my life could be with her in it. It didn't matter that she was here for a short time. I wanted her any way I could have her.

Chapter Twenty-Two

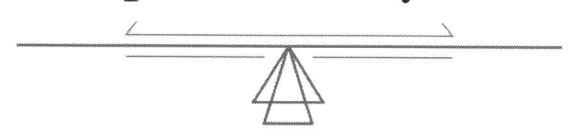

Selene

Remington was a creature of habit and apparently, persistence. I came to realize this after I walked out of the townhouse's front door and rode away with Gilles while Remington stood outside his house, watching. I hadn't heard from him since and I kept hoping he wouldn't call, for his safety and Adrien's. But he still kept his vigilance, making sure that dinner—minus the wax-stamped letters—was delivered at my doorstep whenever I was within the hotel. Èric shadowed me everywhere I went, and I caught glimpses of his tall stature, no matter how stealthy he was about it. Maybe he intended for me to see him to feel safe. I didn't mind at all. I was still shaken by that last letter Remington received, and I appreciated his need to keep me safe.

I fought hard not to remember his voice, his face, his laugh, but it proved to be exceedingly difficult considering he was the first man, other than James, I had ever felt anything more than mere 'like'. The memories of his hands, his scent, were stubbornly imprinted in my brain, my bones.

Last evening, as I was coming in from a run, I saw him

standing at the reception area, talking to one of his employees. I knew the moment he saw me. How could I not? His eyes were like a hot flame as they followed me all the way to the elevators. As soon as I stepped inside and turned around, our gazes locked. I saw torture, pain, hunger, and finally determination before his expression shuttered and the doors slid closed. From the little I knew about Remington, he wasn't the kind of man who sat back and let everything take its own course. *He* was his own course, and he'd be back. It was only a matter of time.

Every time I scrolled through my phone and saw his number, my fingers hovered above it, itching to call or text him. Then I'd remember the words on the letter, threatening the man and his son I had begun to care about. Never in my life had my mind and heart had mixed feelings.

I had let my feelings run away with me, charmed by his passion, adventurous personality, and the way he cared for his son, even though his own father had been an obnoxious ass. This was supposed to be a short affair, but something about Remington pulled me to him. Perhaps the glimpses of sadness, which at times broke through his confident façade, were what drew me—add Adrien to the mix and I was a goner. Maybe I was using the boy to replace my loss. I wasn't sure anymore.

I needed to stay the hell away from those two.

Fall seven times, stand up eight. I repeated this over and over, a Japanese proverb that my mother kept repeating to me when I was recovering. These six words were a pledge to myself.

Taking a deep breath, I focused on finishing the final details of the strapless corset I drew after I left Remington's house. I could already envision this in sheer, black lace. I planned to use my body measurements when I finally sewed them before moving to other sizes.

Satisfied with the finished design, I smiled and dropped

the pencil and notepad on the bed before heading for the bathroom. I grabbed the remote control and scrolled through the channels on the TV mounted high on the wall, directly across from the tub. I selected a romantic comedy, set the language to English before placing the remote back on the miniature vanity, and turned off the water. I had left the tap running so I could fill the huge tub while I finished up my design. After adding a few drops of my lavender essential oils, I shrugged the silk robe from my body and stepped into the hot water. I settled back with the autumn twilight sky showing through the glass ceiling above me and felt the tension and anxiety melt from my bones into the scented water. I pushed away any lingering thoughts of Remington and Adrien, shut my eyes, and focused my hearing on the movie.

I jerked awake at the feel of my shoulders being shaken so hard my teeth rattled. My eyes snapped open and I blinked rapidly, trying to focus on the face above mine.

What the hell is going on?

My sight finally cleared, although my body felt as though all my bones were disjointed. I stared back into vivid green eyes, filled with absolute terror.

Remington?

Had I fallen asleep in the tub and dreamed about him, or had I missed him so much my thoughts conjured him to life?

I blinked several times to make sure *he* was here.

His scent slammed into me, reawakening the feral desire and need for him that I barely succeeded to tame. He stood above me, larger than life. His entire body was shaking, and a wild look dominated his eyes. His mouth opened and closed, but I couldn't hear what he was saying. Every nerve in my body was focused on his large hands on my shoulders, strong, warm, and comforting.

Without warning, he yanked me to him, crushing my wet body to his chest, and buried his face in the crevice of my neck. He murmured, "*Dieu merci, que tu ailles bien*" alternating the words with, "Thank God, you are okay."

My arms remained trapped at my sides until I felt him loosen his grip around me. He raised his head and stared at me as if he couldn't believe I was real. He exhaled deeply and brought his hands to my face, pushing the heavy, wet curls from my forehead. Sweat beaded his temples, and his face was flushed in obvious agitation.

"What's wrong?" I asked, smoothing the frown between his brows with my fingers. His eyes fell shut as he leaned his cheek into my palm when I traced his jaw. "Remington, you're scaring me. Please say something."

He opened his eyes, his gaze searching mine. The fear in them had waned off, replaced by relief. "I was worried about you. I tried to call you on your mobile phone, but the call went to voice mail. I couldn't reach you on the hotel telephone either."

"I…wait, you called me? Why? Did something happen? Is Adrien okay? I was in the tub and fell asleep." *Oh, God, please let everything be okay.*

"No, no. He is safe. Adele would protect him with her life if it came to that." He smiled briefly, dragging one hand through his hair.

I heard feet shuffling in the next room before the bathroom door swung open. "Is she in here Monsieur St.—Oh, pardon!" Remington growled and Èric jerked his head in the other direction, backtracking while I scrambled to cover myself by bending over to my waist with one hand placed between my legs and the other arm covering my boobs. A useless effort. I snapped my head up and scanned the room, searching for something to cover my naked body.

"What is Èric doing in here?" I asked, my voice unnaturally high, like a bad imitation of Lisa Simpson.

As soon as the door shut behind Èric, Remington, who had quickly stepped in front of me to shield my body, shifted around to face me.

"I got worried—" He smiled sheepishly. "I guess I got carried away." Muffled sounds slipped into the bathroom from the bedroom.

How many people are out there? "And you brought an army?"

His lips twitched, fighting a smile. Still shaking from the abrupt interruption, I watched him turn and head for the vanity without answering my question. He grabbed a towel, strode back to the tub, and began to wrap it around me.

"Who else is out there?"

"The hotel security. Stand up. Lift your arms."

I did, shivering as his fingers came in contact with my skin when he tucked the edges of the towel into the top. Then he scooped me up as if I weighed nothing. Water splashed on the expensively tiled floors, but he didn't seem to mind everything getting wet. His jaw was set, his eyes held a determined look, and I knew nothing would stop him as he strode out of the bathroom.

"Leave us," he ordered the men in the room. Èric flicked a gaze toward us before he hurried through the door with three burly security guards in tow.

One of these days, Èric's blood pressure will hit the roof. Seriously, I'd flashed him so many times, not only a part of my body but, in today's case, my entire body.

Remington laid me down on the bed before standing back to stare at me. I squirmed under his intense gaze as it raked every inch of my body. Even with the towel around me, I felt the heat from his eyes burn through the terrycloth.

I sat up at the same time he crouched in front of me and placed his hands on each of my knees, squeezing gently.

I closed my eyes, savouring the feel of him, even though I knew I probably shouldn't. My body was betraying me, yet my mind knew this wasn't a good idea.

God, I've missed this. I missed him.

I opened my eyes and caught him staring at me while chewing his bottom lip. "You need to start talking, St. Germain, or I might sit on you and torture the information out of you."

He chuckled, but there was no humour in the sound. "When you didn't answer my calls, I panicked." He stood up suddenly and began pacing, before stopping as fast as he'd shot to his feet. He faced me. "I'm not the kind of person who panics easily. I don't remember the last time I was ever messed up this bad, but you, Selene, my heart is so twisted over you. The thought of you being in danger almost gave me a bloody heart attack."

He put a hand to the nape of his neck, squeezing as if it would ease some of his frustration. Even though I had a thousand different questions flashing through my mind, I waited for him to speak. I had a feeling he wasn't done talking.

"I received another letter, a warning to remind me I should stay away from you. I realized something after reading it. Whoever is sending these letters will never stop. They will keep torturing me, threatening me, and so, I made a decision." He sank to his knees in front of me, took my hands in his, and kissed my knuckles. "I have this chance, a second chance. I care for you very much, and because of this, I will not let anyone take you away from me. I'm—"

I pressed my hand over his mouth, cutting off whatever he

wanted to say. "Remington, no. No. You can't do this. I leave in three months. Surely, you don't want to risk yours and Adrien's lives for something like this."

He nipped the soft skin on my palm and I squealed, dropping my hand away. He grabbed it and placed it on his thigh, covering it with his bigger one.

"Selene." His voice had taken that no-room-for-argument kind of tone. I felt the fine hairs on the nape of my neck rise, ready to fight him.

"This is my decision, too, Remington. Don't try to pull that shit on me."

He blinked, obviously surprised by my tone. The last thing I needed right now was to be controlled and told what to do. I left that crap behind the minute I signed the divorce papers back home.

He took a deep breath, a muscle twitching at his temple. I could see how difficult it was for him, but I wasn't going to back down on this. I had learned a lesson a long time ago. You give someone a slice of your control, your trust. Instead, they turn around and rip it out of your hands. I wasn't about to repeat that mistake.

"I am sorry, *ma belle*. My intention wasn't to order you around. *Mon Dieu*, I have no clue how to restrain myself when it comes to you."

I lifted his palm and pressed it to my cheek. "A clever man once said that 'Change is inevitable. Change is constant'. This is something we have to accept."

He cocked his head to the side, his eyes narrowed at me. "Are you ready to accept that? Because if you are, I just might prove you wrong. You want this as much as I do. Look me in the eye and tell me I am wrong."

"That's not the real issue here and you know it."

He grunted impatiently. "I know that, damn it. I promised to keep you safe. Gilles is looking into the matter. We will find out who this lunatic is, all right?"

I dropped my gaze to my lap, afraid he would see how his words gave me hope. Vivid memories of spending time with him and Adrien flashed in my head. Then I remembered I had promised myself to stay away from them. I shook my head while raising my eyes to meet his hopeful gaze, and I felt my resolution slowly crumble.

He nudged my chin up with his thumb, forcing my eyes to stay on his. "Well, I know of this brilliant man who said, 'Life is a series of natural and spontaneous changes. Don't resist them; that only creates sorrow. Let reality be reality. Let things flow naturally forward in whatever way they like.' I really prefer to follow Lao Tzu on this one."

I rolled my eyes, fighting a smile. Looks like quoting was another thing we had in common. "Let me think about it."

His grip on my chin tightened. When I flinched, he loosened his hold. He was coiled so tightly, he probably hadn't realized his own strength. "I know your stay in France is temporary, but I would rather have those few weeks with you than none at all. I'm not trying to control you or tell you what to do. I am sorry if I gave you that impression. But know one thing; I will do everything in my power to protect what is mine."

Didn't he realize he had controlled some aspect of our relationship since we first met? He had ordered Adele to drive me places and gave me a room to stay in for the three months. Not that I was complaining. I enjoyed being spoiled as much as the next woman. I sensed he did this because he cared and not to undermine my independence. I pushed those thoughts aside and focused on what he had said before.

Chapter Twenty-Three

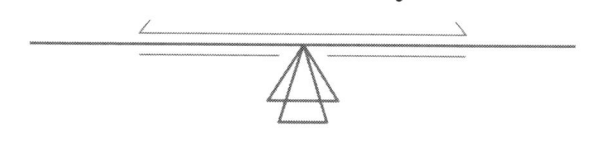

Selene

I *was his?*

Warmth curled inside my chest, even though I probably shouldn't have allowed myself to bask in those words.

"You don't even know who this person is. How will you protect me or Adrien or yourself for that matter?"

"You underestimate me, *ma belle*. If I say I will do something, I tend to do it without fail. All I need is your answer. Just say yes, and you will have the most unforgettable three months of your life. Let my actions prove I can take care of you."

Uncertainty and fear warred in my head. I shouldn't want him like I did. If there were a way to command my heart not to miss him so much, I would do it in a heartbeat. It wasn't just because of the sex, although that was a huge plus. No. It was him. *Remington*. He had a way of making me feel special, something I craved with a hunger so wild it shook my very foundation. I was a different woman with him, carefree and with no worries. Remington let me be *me*, explore a side of me I thought was non-existent. He had given me a part of him, his past, when he told me about his fear of being in an elevator. Most men wouldn't be caught confessing something that would make them appear weak, especially a man as self-assured and in control of his surroundings and life as Remington. I'd already met Gilles, that mountain of a man, so I was confident Remington was capable of taking care of us.

His fingers grasped mine, pulling my hand from my mouth before clasping it between both of his, warm and calloused. My gaze fell on my fingers, and I realized my thoughts had once again swept me away. My nails, like always, were suffering the consequences of my turbulent mind. I brought my eyes to his, and my breath caught in my chest. The look in them was gentle, filled with need. Every single emotion was in there, conveying a thousand unspoken words.

Remington was quite impressive when he was stubborn and determined. There was a recklessness about him, but the safe kind, the controlled kind, which was quite appealing.

"Where did you go?" he asked, his eyebrows scrunched up in a worried frown.

"I'm here," I said. "Sorry. Old habits die hard."

He ducked his head, meeting my gaze. "Stay with me, all right?"

I nodded.

He squeezed my fingers. "I am just a man on his knees before you, asking for a chance to spend time with you."

My defences melted further and I felt giddy, breathless. *This must be how it feels to swoon for a guy.* Where were the smelling salts when I needed them? I had a feeling I might need some before the night was over. "God, Remington, what am I going to do with you?"

One side of his mouth pulled up into a smile. "Anything you want. Take whatever you need from me, *ma belle.*"

I lunged forward, tackling him into a hug and a deep kiss, catching him off guard. Nevertheless, he caught me, sank his fingers into my hair, and held me in place as he kissed me back. He tasted like coffee and chocolate, and dear God, he smelled so good, a heady combination. I traced kisses along his jaw, enjoying how his bristly beard tickled my cheek. I pressed my lips on his throat and flicked my tongue on his hot skin, tasting him.

"Is that a yes, Selene?" he asked, shivering as I nipped his chin.

I sat back on the bed, nodding and grinning so hard my cheeks hurt.

He flashed his devastating smile that always made me melt. Ah, there went those dimples, hidden behind that sexy, sexy scruff.

Dropping his gaze to his fingers, now flirting with the edge of the towel near my crotch, he leaned down to brush the tip of his nose along the inside of my thigh.

"Are you sure about this, Remington?" I asked.

He looked up and nodded. "What's stopping us from seeking the most unimaginable pleasure from each other?" His hand moved and cupped the back of my neck, rubbing it. I shivered at the contact and the huskiness of his voice. "What's stopping *you*?"

God, he was irresistible, especially with his piercing eyes on me like that. My body was already coming alive from his overwhelming force. I knew there was no way in hell I could be close to this man and not feel as though I were burning. The good kind. I needed him as much as he needed me. I wasn't sure how healthy it was for us to need each other like this. It was more than physical attraction. There was some intangible reason I couldn't describe, and believe me, I tried to evaluate this in the past few days we had been apart. Would we be able to survive after three months of this intensity?

He pulled me to him and rested his forehead against mine. Everything faded away, and it was just him and me.

"You're gonna fall for me," I teased him, laughing.

He murmured, "My sweet Selene. It will be the sweetest fall."

Before I could take my next breath, his mouth was on mine, molding and shaping my lips to fit his. I gasped, caught off guard as his tongue swept inside my mouth, tasting and claiming me. He shifted and somehow he was above me without breaking the kiss, his fingers gripping my hair.

"Beautiful mouth," he murmured against my lips. "Scoot over."

I crawled backward, watching him as he came at me on all fours. God, his eyes were consuming me completely.

As soon as I settled back on the large pillows, Remington pounced on me in a hurricane of eager hands and lips, a hard body, and a huge erection in his pants. The soft material of his V-neck T-shirt and the coarse fabric of the jeans rubbed against the already sensitive skin on my chest and thighs, heightening my senses. I squirmed and moaned, wanting him closer. I moved my hands to the edge of his T-shirt, but he grabbed them, sliding them above my head and shackled my wrists with one of his hands. He buried his nose into the crook of my neck, his breath hot, and his kisses hotter.

"I missed you so much, Selene," he murmured against my skin, tracing the vein there. "You have no idea how much not touching you and kissing you almost drove me to near madness. One more day without seeing you would have been my ultimate death."

I rolled my eyes, giggling at his melodramatic words, while tilting my head to the side to give him access to that piece of heaven between my ear and neck. We both knew this thing between us was temporary. As for the looming threat, I felt I could trust him to keep me—us—safe. I'm not even sure why, but I did.

"I missed you, too, Remington," I said, pressing my body into his. "I missed you a lot."

He stilled, his body tightly coiled as if he were about to snap. Then he let out a sigh, bringing his mouth back to mine. This time the kiss wasn't gentle. It was a clash of teeth and duelling tongues, both punishing and forgiving, passionate and desperate, as though his lips on mine was what he needed to survive. He rolled his hips, pushing his pelvis into mine. I spread my legs wide, hooked them around his waist, and locked my ankles on his back just as he dipped his tongue into my mouth, reclaiming me in his usual wild passion.

Why again did I stay away from him? I wanted him so damn much.

He pulled back, and without losing a beat, gripped the edge of his T-shirt and removed it, tossing it over his shoulder. He slid out of bed and wrestled with his jeans, followed by his black boxer briefs.

His cock sprang free, and I moaned deep in my throat, squirming on the bed. He was just as I remembered, when I first saw him fully naked after the drawing session.

I peered at him under my lashes. "God, you're hot. I want to lick every part of your hard body."

He grabbed his jeans from the floor, pulled a condom

from his wallet, and tossed it on the nightstand. "I've missed you so much, so forgive me if patience is not one of my strongest virtues. I want inside you now."

I shivered as his words stoked the fire inside me. "I'm not feeling very patient right now either. Stop talking and come here."

His eyes widened in surprise, and he chuckled in appreciation. I felt as if I were about to burst into flames with need. I watched him as he tore the foil with his teeth and slid the condom over his hard cock, pumping his hand, up then down. I couldn't take my eyes off him.

That is the sexiest thing I've ever seen.

"As much as I want to take time making love to you, Selene, I can't. Right now, I want to fuck you hard and fast, surround myself with you."

"Take me any way you want, Remington. I want you, too, any way I can get you."

He grunted, obviously pleased with my words. Then he smiled.

God, he is so hot.

I clutched the sheets to stop from throwing myself at him. The bed dipped as he crawled forward and stopped only when he was on top of me. Parting my thighs, he moved between them. He slid a hand between our bodies, took his cock in his hand, and stroked my entrance, and without warning, he slammed inside me and my body arched.

"Remington!"

His arms gave way, and his body dropped on top of mine. He buried his face in his favourite place on my neck, breathing hard. "Did I hurt you?" His voice sounded strained.

"No! No. I was just caught off guard, that's all," I replied, trying to catch my breath. I thought my heart might give out from beating so hard. "God, I love how you fill me. So good. Now start moving or you'll lose points, St. Germain."

He chuckled, a hoarse laugh that sounded dirty and heavenly at the same time. "As you wish, *ma belle*."

He pushed himself up with his arms, and as though I had released a demon with my words, he started pounding inside me. In, out. In, out. He groaned. I moaned. He grunted. I screamed. Then his mouth was on mine, inhaling my breaths and breathing his into me. His tongue demanded and soothed, claiming, giving. I served him right back, letting myself go. I felt free and incredibly desirable. He pulled his mouth from mine, slowing his thrusts as he brought one of his hands to my breast, kneading then rolling one nipple between his fingers. He moved to the next one, doing the same thing before lowering his wicked mouth to take my breast in his mouth.

This was Intense Remington times ten, and I loved it, loved the passion tangled with desperation.

Pressure built inside my belly, sending shivers of pleasure down my spine and to my toes. Remington seemed to sense it. His mouth lifted from my breast, and he braced himself with his hands beside my head. He picked up his pace, his smooth thrusts becoming uncoordinated, and I knew he wasn't going to hold back anymore.

The thought of him coming apart, and knowing that I did this to him, hit me hard. I climaxed, screaming Remington's name repeatedly as he continued pounding into me. Still riding the wave, he rammed into me once, twice, and shouted my name as he came, grinding himself inside me. He leaned forward, taking my mouth in a gentle kiss while shoving his hand into my hair and giving it a quick, sharp tug as we came back down.

Remington rolled over, removed the condom, and strode to the bathroom to dispose of it. He returned seconds later and crawled back between the sheets, spooning me. He slid his arm around my waist, pulled me to him with my back to his chest. He squeezed my hip, sighed before sliding his palm across my belly, and settled it on my scar.

I smiled, content. "That was amazing."

"Phenomenal." He kissed my shoulder as his thumb traced tiny circles on my skin.

I closed my eyes, lulled by his caresses and the warmth from our bodies. I knew he was curious, given the way his palm flattened over the scar beneath the tattoo. I cleared my throat, snuggling deeper into the comfort of his strong arms, and braced myself for what I was about to say. The only people I'd talked to about this were my therapist and my family. Yes, and Grace. I had told her what happened after I made up my mind to get back into modeling.

I opened my mouth to speak, closed it. My throat felt dry.

God, please give me strength. "Um—about three years ago, I …lost my baby." The words came out in a rush, and I tucked myself farther into him. The hand stroking my belly stilled. I covered his hand with mine and stole a bit of his strength into my body, allowing my mind to wander back to the day that altered my life in the most unimaginable way. I'd never felt so lonely in my life, and I wondered if something had happened in Remington and Adrien's lives to alter it as mine had.

"I was seven months pregnant when it happened. I had been feeling sick for a while, and the doctor ordered me to take full bed rest in my sixth month. James used to work long hours back then. Anyway, to cut the long story short, I was hungry and restless so I decided to go downstairs to make a snack. Halfway to the kitchen, I had these sudden pains in my stomach and before I knew it, I'd tumbled down the stairs. When I woke up, I was in a hospital bed with no baby bump." I swallowed hard to get rid of the lump in my throat, shivering at the memory of how I woke up and how my hand traced where my bump was supposed to be, only to find it gone.

Sadness threatened to rip me wide open, so I breathed in deeply. I was strong. I had learned to cope with this over the years. I could do *this*.

Remington's arm tightened around my waist as he pulled me tighter and tangled his legs with mine. "Where was he?" he asked in a voice that sounded like it was being forced from his chest. "Your—this James?"

"At work. He had been stressed for a while because he was closing in on this partnership at the law firm he'd been working in."

A string of curses fell from Remington's lips. "He left you alone and worked long hours while you were unwell? What kind of bastard would do that?"

The sort of bastard who cheated on me with my best friend from almost day one of our marriage, that's who. I stared at the wall across from me, willing myself not to cry. I'd done that every single time I'd talked about what happened. But now—

"*Je suis désolé*," he murmured, turning me around to face him. "I'm very sorry, Selene." He brushed his fingers on my cheeks, and I realized I was crying. I'd shed enough tears in the past three years; I thought I had nothing left in me.

He pulled me into his chest and I tucked my head under his chin, basking in his strength and warmth.

"I'll bet you didn't get the memo that tonight was confession night, did you?"

He rubbed his hand in circles on my back. "I was curious about the scar, but I knew you would tell me when you were ready."

We stayed like this, two souls locked in a bubble of intimacy. It was as though the demons that roamed our minds recognized each other, and instead of stoking the fire that caused them to burn, they stroked them, silencing them, *calming* them. For once in a long time, I felt peace settle over me. I could really get used to this.

Chapter Twenty-Four

Remington

I slid out of bed and immediately felt the loss of Selene's warm body against mine. God, she was a true beauty both inside and out. But I couldn't linger in her bed any longer. I promised Adrien last night that I would drive him to kindergarten today. I went to the shower and walked out twenty minutes later, my thoughts dominated by the woman sleeping in front of me.

 I picked up my clothes from the floor, before turning to face Selene, and dressed while devouring her with my eyes. I thought I might never have the pleasure of watching someone sleep, other than Adrien. But there she was, her lips curved in a serene smile. She lay on her stomach with her hands crossed above her head. The white sheets covered her beautiful arse. My gaze followed her shapely thighs, down to where her legs were crossed at the ankles, and my cock hardened with the thought of burying myself deeply inside her again.

 "Hey, you," Selene's voice was breathy and hoarse and sexy. How would that mouth of hers feel around my cock, sucking me?

It took effort to drag my eyes from her body to her face. Her smile was sexy and her hazel eyes dark with sleep.

Mon Dieu, this woman was going to be the death of me. Or my awakening. I couldn't wait to paint her looking like this, as soon as the first portrait was done.

I closed the distance between us, crawled on the bed, and kissed her. She moaned deep in her throat and shifted to her back, then slid her hands around my neck and pulled me down to her. I could kiss her mouth the entire day and never want to leave.

By the time I pulled away, I was fighting for breath and my cock pressed hard against the zipper of my jeans. "You make me crazy. I need to leave before I rip my clothes off and fuck you senseless, Selene."

"As if I'd object to that," she said, her fingers playing idly with the hair on the nape of my neck. I loved it when she did that. It was amazing that Selene knew how and where to touch me. "Come back to bed and let's play dirty."

"You know I can't resist when you seduce me with words like that." I kissed her elegant neck as she moved her head to the side, giving me better access. "I promised Adrien I would drive him to school today. And I'm sure Adele is eager to start her day," I murmured against her skin. Would it be too much to drag her from this room and take her with me so I could have her any time? She would probably think I was an oversexed Neanderthal.

Her forehead creased slightly but cleared fast when she caught me staring at her. She cleared her throat, avoiding eye contact.

"What is it, Selene?"

"Um…it's nothing really." She tried to wiggle out of my arms. I pulled her back, trapping her legs with one of mine and just stared at her, hoping to will her into submission with a look.

"Could you stop looking at me like that? It's so unnerving."

I laughed. "Like what?"

"Like you're waiting for me to confess every dirty thought," she mumbled.

I had to admit that sometimes I wondered where she went when she had the unfocused look in her eyes.

I sighed. "How will I fulfil them if I don't know what they are, hmm?"

She laughed. It was still one of the sweetest sounds I've ever heard.

She cleared her throat, her expression turning serious. "Do you think Adele has some feelings toward you? I mean, beyond the 'you are my employer' kind?"

This statement jolted me from my thoughts. I pulled back and stared down at her. "What?"

She bit her bottom lip between her teeth. "There's just something in the way she looks at you. Maybe I'm wrong."

Really? And why hadn't I noticed that? "Adele has been with us for four years. Not once has she displayed anything other than fondness for Adrien and me. Especially Adrien."

"Is she married? Boyfriend?"

"Not as far as I know. Come to think of it, the only thing I know about her is that she is twenty-three years old, speaks English perfectly with no trace of a French accent, yet she has a French name." I frowned, not liking what I just said.

Adele had never seemed a threat to us, and her employment papers seemed legit to me. I had never bothered to think beyond that, and she had never shown any instability in her manner. If anyone asked me to describe her, I would have said she was a constant calm.

Another thought hit me hard. Was the friendliness I saw in Adele a ruse? Could she be the person who sent the letters and the flowers?

Merde! Had I been blinded by a beautiful, kind face? I made a note to ask Gilles to dig deeper into her past.

"Jealous?" I asked Selene playfully, trying to hide the fact that I was worried about what she pointed out about Adele.

"Yes. A little bit."

I was surprised by her honesty. Most women I knew wouldn't admit to that emotion.

"Don't be. My eyes and every other part of me are set on you and only you." I kissed her neck, breathing in her scent, and I felt content. "What are your plans for today?" I asked as my hands found their way to her breasts. She moaned and her body arched, pressing her bare chest into mine.

"I have a modeling shoot at Curves. Lingerie."

My sight blurred as visions of Selene in lingerie taunted me. "Can I watch?"

"Yes." She lifted her hips, rolling them and rubbing her pussy against my cock. "You'll have a chance to undress me, if you're a good boy."

I laughed, enjoying her flirtatiousness. "What do I need to do?"

"Bring me cotton candy, and I'll be your slave for the night." She put her hand on my crotch, massaged me, and licked her lips.

Fuck.

I had to be inside her. Now.

I pulled back and unbuckled my belt, my hands shaking with anticipation. God help me! I felt like a young boy about to lose his virginity. What was it about her that had me wanting her with a desperation I'd never experienced? Or the fact that I was always eager to please her? This was uncharted territory for me, given that in the past, the women had always strived to please *me*.

Before I could lower my body to hers, she grabbed the loop of my jeans and pulled me to her with determination that rocked me to the core. Her fingers worked the zipper, and soon my cock was in her palms. One hand slid down to take my balls.

"Selene." I groaned, sinking my fingers into that wild mane of hair and jerking my hips forward. She stared at me from under her lashes, a slow smile forming on her lips as she brought her mouth to my cock. I watched her, hypnotised, waiting, my balls tight and aching. Then she seemed hesitant as her mouth hovered above my length. She swallowed and smiled nervously. I traced a finger on her lips.

"You don't have to do this."

She cleared her throat, her smile turning shy. "Um—I've never done this before."

I loosened my hand around her hair. "You haven't? Even with … him?" Just uttering that bastard's name made me want to fly to New York and punch him. Hard.

She shook her head.

She wanted me to be her first? I fought the urge to beat my chest but managed a grunt of satisfaction, which was still a caveman trait. It was quite easy to revert to our predecessors' tendencies when she made me feel like I was the only man for her.

I placed my hands on hers, tugged them off me, and stretched on my back. "Come here."

Confidence flooded back to her face as she moved closer and threw one leg over my thighs, realising my intent as my hands gripped her hips. I pulled her higher toward my mouth.

"No. I want you inside me, Remington."

As if I needed a second invitation. I rolled her over,

reluctantly left the bed, and picked up the jeans where they lay on the floor. I dug the last condom from my wallet, sheathed my cock, returned to Selene, turned around and sank inside her.

"Fuck, you feel incredible. Put your legs around me. Yes, like that. I love it when you do that." She dug her heels into my arse, and my cock hardened even further. "I missed this, feeling your pussy wrap tightly around my dick. *Mon Dieu,* you drive me insane, woman." I slowly slid in and out, wanting this to last longer. She sucked in a breath, a groan passing through her lips, and my lust rocketed. "Did you think about me, fucking you like this, Selene? Did you miss me filling you with my cock?" She nodded quickly, her bottom lip caught between her teeth. "*Très bien.* I'm going to fuck you so hard that you won't leave me next time."

"I will have to leave eventually, Remington."

I tried to hold back the irritation those words caused but ended up scowling down at her. She stared back at me, defiance and arousal shining on her face. I loved it.

"Now you're just turning me on with that scowl. Were you angry when I left?" she asked, sliding her hands between us to cup my balls. I spread my legs wider. She tugged while holding me captive with those bewitching eyes of hers.

"I was livid. Now, I just want to show you what you missed and make certain I am the only damn thing in your mind long after I've finished claiming back what's mine."

Her fingers moved up, and as soon as the tip tentatively brushed my anus and my balls, my cock tightened harder. "Christ! Do that again," I growled.

This time, her touch was bolder as she brought her finger between our bodies, lubricated it before sliding it back, caressed, and then gently prodded.

I panted, my body a fucking bomb with only seconds to

explode. I forgot I was angry, forgot where I was. I was certain I couldn't remember my name then, and if I were standing, I would be a bloody mess on the floor. No one had touched me like that before.

"So, you forgive me?" she asked.

I tried to focus on this woman who was annihilating any restraint left in me. "You've destroyed me, Selene." I panted the words. "I can't go back to being who I was, because you've done …this …to …me."

Unable to control myself, I grabbed her hands and shackled her wrists with one of mine and pounded into her, fast. Unlocking her legs from my hips, I pushed them to her chest and lifted them over my shoulders, leaning forward to kiss her while sliding in and out.

"That's, oh, my God, Remington, you feel so good inside me. So huge. Harder, please. Harder." She panted out the words.

God, she was as greedy as I was. "Hands on the headboard." She did as I ordered. I readjusted my position between her thighs. "I'm going to fuck you hard, Selene; you will remember this the whole day."

I didn't give her a chance to respond. I pounded, hard and fast into her, and her back arched off the bed to meet my thrusts. Her moans became louder, and then she was screaming my name as she sobbed and shook under me. Those erotic sounds were my undoing. I slammed into her twice, grinding myself into her, before a shudder tore through me, threatening to split me in two. Right then, I wanted to crawl inside her so I could have her with me always. I slumped forward, making sure to keep half of my weight off her and buried my face into the crevice of her neck—my favourite place—panting. She wrapped her legs and arms around me and sighed, her soft, generous curves pressed on my hard planes.

"That felt … that was even better than the sex before," she said breathlessly.

"It was. What am I going to do with you, Selene?" I murmured, echoing the same words she had said to me a while ago. I pulled out of her, took my cock in my hand to remove the condom, and froze.

Shit! The fucking thing broke.

"What's wrong?" she asked, staring at me, then down to my crotch. Her eyes widened. "No wonder it felt different this time around. Different good." She added the last part quickly.

I nodded, cursing in my head, and stalked to the bathroom to get rid of it and returned to the room. I had been so carried away by my need for her I hadn't stopped to think. All I knew was that having my cock buried deep inside her was like a cure for me. What if she got pregnant? Was she on birth control pills?

She seemed to read my mind. "I'm clean and on birth control. I take them because they help me with my periods and …" She trailed off, burying her face in her hands, embarrassed.

This woman was quite the contradiction. One minute she was brave, funny, and shy, and the next second, sweet. I pushed her hands back and caressed her heated cheeks with my knuckles. I leaned forward and kissed her forehead, appreciating her selflessness about this situation.

"I'm clean, too. I haven't slept with a woman for a long time." Her eyes widened at my revelation. "I haven't had time. In between taking care of a demanding five-year-old, painting, helping my mother with the vineyard whenever I could, and managing the hotel, I've been distracted."

"But what about your needs, you know … er …" The blush on her face deepened, and her eyes dipped to my crotch.

I laughed. She was innocent in so many ways. "I had other means. I have very talented hands, *ma belle*." I winked at her, and she laughed. I pulled her into my arms, letting my eyes wander to the tattooed skin on her stomach, and traced my fingers around the scar. She shivered, snuggling closer to me, and sighed.

The world felt perfect.

I wasn't about to let this woman slip through my fingers. Ever it seemed.

Chapter Twenty-Five

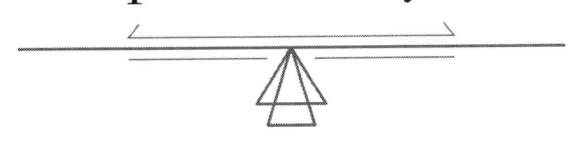

Selene

Wow. *Just freaking, wow!* Sex with Remington had been a completely new level of adventure. After shaving my legs and armpits silky-smooth, I made sure my bikini line was clean. I didn't need any strays making an appearance. Then I slipped on my dark blue jeans.

After putting on a pair of black flats, I grabbed my handbag from the vanity. I left the room feeling lighter and happier than I'd been in a long time.

Remington was leaning on the reception counter, speaking into his phone when I arrived downstairs. He glanced up, straightened to his full height, and raptly watched me as I walked toward him with a little extra sway in my hips.

Seconds later, he shoved the phone inside the pocket of his jeans and strode toward me with his eyes trained on my mouth. He grabbed my hips and walked me backward until my back hit a wall. He pressed his hard body against mine. I lifted my legs, wrapped them around his hips at the same time he growled low in his throat, crushing his lips on mine. He kissed me deeply, as though he hadn't spent the better part of the night and morning devouring me. He pulled back and framed my face in his hands, caressing my lips with a thumb.

Dear God, I was such a slut when it came to Remington. Besides, locked between two hard places had never felt so good.

"You truly are beautiful, Selene," he murmured. "What are you wearing under these jeans?"

"Nothing."

His lips parted and air rushed out. "*Nothing?*"

I nodded. "Want to know why?"

"I'm sure your reason will probably kill me, but yes, please. Tell me," he said indulgently.

"I love the feel of the jeans rubbing me *there*."

He groaned, rubbing his strong fingers between my legs while his lips sucked and licked my neck.

Someone cleared a throat nearby. I froze, pushing away from Remington with my hands, but he was like a mountain. Immovable, hard, and stubborn. I peeked over his shoulder to find Èric, trying very hard to look everywhere but in our direction.

"Monsieur St. Germain, Adrien is looking for you," Èric announced, his ears and cheeks pink and his head turned the other way as if looking at us would burn him alive. It probably might, given the heat coming off Remington and the lust setting my veins on fire. Poor guy! Not only was he scarred from seeing my boobs a while back and what happened last night in the bathroom, but now he was forced to watch us behave like some horny teenagers.

"Control yourself, St. Germain," I whispered in his ear, while Èric spun around and left us in our little alcove.

"My body doesn't know the meaning of the word when I'm around you." He slid me down his hard body at the same time Adrien rounded the corner, dashing in our direction, and hurled himself into me.

He looked up, grinning wide. "I've missed you, Selene."

"Me, too, tiger." I ruffled his curly hair and looked up at Remington, who was staring at me as though he was about to pounce on me.

I winked at him, adjusted the handbag strap on my shoulder, and headed out of the hotel with Adrien at my side.

When he didn't follow us out, we went back inside to check on what was keeping him, and I froze mid-step. He stood next to the reception counter, his back to us, and his shoulders stiff. My heartbeat sped up as my gaze fell to his hands.

"Èric, could you please keep an eye on Adrien?" I said when I caught his eye. He nodded, smiled, and took the boy into the back office.

I inched closer to Remington, coming to stand next to him. "Remington? What's that?" I stared at the bouquet of red irises, tied with a yellow ribbon around the stalks.

He breathed out, lifting his troubled gaze to meet mine.

"Do you think they were sent by the … person?"

He nodded, pursing his lips, showing me the paper similar to the one he received the night I walked away from him.

"Do you have any idea who sent them? Do they have a meaning? Say something, Remington," I whispered, glancing around the lobby and back at him.

"There are about four women I suspect who might have sent them. Women I had relations with during the first two years after Colette."

Okay. At least we are getting somewhere. I tried not to let the huge lump in my throat choke me and reminded myself he hadn't led a solitary life before we met.

I shook off the feeling and focused on Remington. "Maybe one of the women wasn't happy about ending things with you."

"I treated each and every one of them with respect. I made certain we had a mutual agreement." He dragged a hand through his hair. "I don't understand. Why would someone do this?"

I stared at him and shook my head. Seriously? This man had no idea of his appeal to women.

Suddenly, with his jaw clenched, he straightened, spun around, and thrust his hand toward the male receptionist behind the counter. "Get rid of these. Where is Adrien?"

As if summoned, the boy came running from the back office, holding a Lego figure in his hand.

We started for the hotel's exit, but I halted when I felt the hair on the nape of my neck curl in awareness of someone watching me. I spun around, scanning my surroundings. Everyone seemed busy, caught up in whatever they were doing. I turned to look at the entrance and caught a glimpse of a woman on my right, farther ahead of us. She had on dark sunglasses and had stared in our direction a heartbeat too long, then turned and hurried from the hotel. At least it looked like a woman, but I couldn't tell the shape of the body underneath the long black trench coat with a hood pulled over the person's head.

"Remington, look at that—" I stopped and frowned at the doors. No one was there. Had I imagined everything?

"What? What is it, Selene?" he asked, his gaze darting from my face to the hotel's entrance, then back to me.

"Nothing."

A deep V formed between his eyebrows as he stared at me with obvious disbelief. "Are you sure?"

"Yes. No. I thought I saw someone staring in our direction just over there." I gestured to the place I saw the person only moments before.

The frown disappeared, replaced by a neutral expression. Unreadable. "Wait here."

He strode out of the hotel and returned after a few minutes, his jaw clenched. He scooped Adrien in his arms before turning to face me. "Whoever it was is gone. Are you all right? You don't look so well." He brushed his fingers along my cheek.

"I'm fine, just a little shaken." I smiled, hoping to reassure him.

Fifteen minutes later, Remington dropped me in front of the Curves offices and waited until I was inside the building before driving away. I took deep breaths to clear my head and forced myself to relax. Grace was waiting for me inside her elegant office. We hugged and she turned around, pulling me inside the studio—a large room painted in white and black with lights propped strategically around the space.

"We haven't had time to really catch up, Selene. Forgive me for abandoning you for so long. I'm in Paris for a little longer now. Maybe we can catch up, yes?"

"I wasn't lonely for long." I smiled slyly at her. When she cocked one eyebrow at me, I murmured, "Remington."

"And ...?" she prompted, her eyes wide with excitement.

He's addictive, adventurous, and since the recent developments, dangerous to be around. "What you see is what you get. He is that kind of guy. And by the way, he will be dropping by later."

"Oh my! Looks like your plan to experience pleasure is going very well," she said, her brown eyes filled with amusement as we halted in front of the dressing room. "I really have missed you, Selene. You are taking care of yourself, yes? Because that idiot ex-husband of yours did not know what he had."

I shook my head. "Water under the bridge, honey. Look at me. I'm here in Paris, back to my job and," I swept a hand down my body, "healthy." I had told her about the baby because I knew the chances of her figuring it out were high, considering I had a tattoo on my lower belly. Frankly, I didn't want to start our work relationship based on lies. Thank goodness she didn't pity me. I loved her for that.

She nodded, hugging me one more time before shoving me into the room with a smack on my butt. "Go ahead and look pretty for the camera. The lingerie is numbered so you know which one you will wear and when. Have fun, lovely."

I laughed, closing the door behind me. It felt wonderful to be treated with such love and appreciation. Time in therapy, wholehearted love from my family, Grace and Andrew's fervent encouragement, and now Remington's determined effort to be in my life? All those things combined were destroying the negativity that had built within from being married to James.

Chapter Twenty-Six

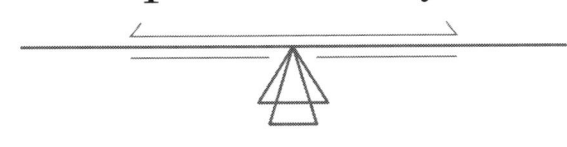

Selene

Sultry, seductive French music played in the background while I posed in different positions on the wide, four-poster, canopy bed. Sheer, white curtains were draped on the black frame with large white pillows tossed haphazardly on the bed.

We had been shooting for the past thirty minutes when the photographer, a tall, spindly guy with a ponytail, announced we were taking a break. He glanced at me, a frustrated look on his face. I heaved a breath, tossed aside the large pillow I'd been holding against my chest, and slid off the bed. This session had been a bust. From the moment Remington dropped me at Curves, my mind had been in total chaos, and kept wandering back to the flowers and the person in a trench coat. Even the Chardonnay I'd been sipping to loosen me up hadn't worked.

I fluffed my hair before grabbing a ribbon from a table and tying it back as I walked toward one of the women who was assisting with the shoot.

"Thank you," I said, smiling, and took a white silk robe from her hand and slipped it on.

I caught sight of Remington, standing beside Grace, talking in low tones. His eyes were focused on me as I padded barefoot toward them.

"Hey, baby," I greeted him, pressing my lips to his cheek, but he moved his face so our mouths collided. One of his hands slid around my waist and pulled me to him. One thing I enjoyed about Remington was he wasn't shy about showing his affection in public. No one seemed to mind anyway.

By the time I pulled back, my body felt alive with this man's attention and kisses. I glanced at Grace to find her smiling hugely, giving me a thumbs-up, and fanning herself.

"Are you enjoying yourself?" Remington asked, his deep voice teasing the lust in me as his hand traced circles on my lower back, sending tingles down my spine.

"Um … yeah. Sure, I am."

He narrowed his eyes.

"This girl needs to relax. Let herself go," Grace said, waving her hand. "I have never seen you this nervous, Selene."

Remington's hand halted its soothing motions. "I just need a few minutes. I didn't think I would be this nervous, getting back into modeling."

"Please excuse us, Madame Dresner," Remington said, flashing Grace a smile.

Grace patted her flushed cheeks, and I rolled my eyes at Remington's blatant use of charm. "Certainly, and please, call me Grace."

"You're incorrigible, St. Germain," I said as he led me into the hallway, his arm a steel band of heat around my waist.

He grinned at me, hitting me with a smile more potent than he had given Grace. "The room," he murmured. I frowned up at him, wondering what he was talking about. "Your dressing room."

"Oh, yes. I need to freshen up a bit …"

"Not what I have in mind." He squeezed my butt to make his point.

"Oh!" My face heated at the suggestion. "So what do you have in mind?" I tossed a flirtatious smile over my shoulder as I opened the door, letting us in. He kicked it shut with his foot as soon as we were inside and swung around, pushing me against the door, and pressing his body against mine. He gripped my hips, pulling me to him.

"This."

His mouth came crushing down on mine, while his hand slid under the white lingerie. His fingers traced the curve of my hip, edging around to cover my butt. Caught off guard, I gasped and his tongue swept inside my mouth. I closed my eyes, and even then, he was all I could see, feel, and smell. I eagerly returned his kiss with helpless abandon.

My body needed this man, and my soul desperately demanded his presence. It was impossible to imagine how my life had been before him. At that moment, he was my sweetest distraction and I was a slave for his attention, for his touch. He told me I had cast a spell on him, but he was wrong. He had bewitched me with his green eyes, his addictive touch, and sinful mouth. When that mouth pulled away from mine, I opened my eyes and laughed. His lips were covered in red lipstick.

Ignoring my amusement, he leaned to my ear, gently nipping my earlobe, and asked, "What are you thinking about?"

I shivered at the sensation. "Those mysterious flowers and …" I stopped, suddenly feeling stupid for what I was about to say. The thought had not occurred to me until now, and I wasn't sure how I felt about it. I closed my eyes, breathed out, and shook my head to chase away those ugly thoughts.

He pulled back, running his knuckles against my cheek. "And what? Open your eyes, Selene."

My eyes met his, filled with concern and warmth. "It has been eight years since I did this." I waved a hand down my body.

"You mean look like my own personal wet dream?" he asked, one eyebrow raised.

My heart did this hummingbird-wings flutter like it always did when he said things like this. I grinned, his words feeding my ego and boosting my confidence.

He squeezed my hip in warning. "Truth, *ma belle,* we always tell each other the truth."

"I thought I'd gotten over some body issues, but apparently, I haven't."

He frowned at me, looking confused, but the look in his eyes when he took me in was appreciative. There was so much hunger infused in that single look.

"The last years before James and I got divorced, he used to say some pretty mean things. Eventually, I believed him. He shredded every wall of defence and confidence I had built since he had come into my life. I shouldn't have believed him, but I did. Every ounce of negativity I'd gotten rid of while growing up came rushing back twofold. It only takes someone to tell you something a few times for it to ingrain itself in your head."

"Oh, Selene," he murmured, pulling me into his arms.

"Please, don't pity me. Instead, give me a good kick in the butt and kiss me hard. Then send me out there to finish this photo shoot. I shouldn't let myself think like that."

He leaned back, cupping my face in his hands, his eyes intense, before kissing my forehead. "I want you to go out there and be the alluring, seductive temptress I know you to be. Do you hear me, Selene? Your ex-husband was an asshole. But let me tell you one thing. I love your body. Every little curve of it and I cannot get enough."

Then he kissed every single insecurity out of my bones and fed my soul with pieces of his, stealing another bit of my heart.

My mind was still hazy from the kiss. My body shaking from it, I startled when a sharp pain on my right butt cheek swept through my body. I squealed and glanced up at Remington. Before I could open my mouth to sass him, he dropped to his knees. Grabbing my hip, he ran his hand over my skin, soothed the stinging with a caress as he kissed and licked it better.

Remington St. Germain was becoming a welcome distraction and my addiction.

I grabbed some make-up removal tissues and cleaned the lipstick off his mouth, his eyes never leaving my face.

The make-up artist dropped by a few moments later to retouch my make-up. The rest of the shoot went well, and I was on fire. Remington was a few feet away, his hungry gaze never leaving me as the photographer continued excitedly snapping pictures. The photographer didn't need to tell me what to do, because my body was doing everything on its own. At one point, I caught Remington discreetly adjusting the front of his pants. I met his gaze and winked at him before coyly running a finger down the front of my purple, lace bra.

During another short break, he strolled forward and whispered, "I hope you don't mind being tied to a bed because that's what I'm thinking about right now. Tie you up, devour your pussy, and fuck you hard. Later tonight."

Heat curled low in my belly, but I couldn't let him have the last word. My gaze darted around the room. No one was paying us any attention, so I did something I would never have done before in public. I palmed him through his jeans and I was rewarded by a growl, dark and sexy. "This, in my mouth, will be heaven."

His hand slid to the nape of my neck. "Fuck, woman. You're driving me insane."

He dropped his hand when the photographer returned and resumed his position on the wall on the far end, hands crossed on his chest and feet planted on the floor. Watching. Every movement on the bed seemed to bring my senses to life as I imagined his hard body on top of mine. Heated cheeks, tingling limbs, sultry eyes.

"*Magnifique!*" The photographer repeated with every click of his camera, grinning. "*Très belle.*"

My body felt alive, and I was back in my element. At this moment, seeing Remington's reaction to my poses on the bed and knowing I was the reason for that possessive look on his face, seduction was my super power.

Chapter Twenty-Seven

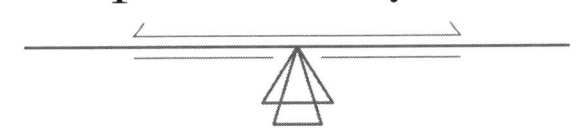

Selene

Right after the photo shoot, we said good-bye to Grace. She hugged and kissed us on both cheeks in turn before retreating into her office where she had a meeting with one of her designers. Remington grabbed a black leather jacket from the hook on the wall next to the door and put it on before holding out my trench coat for me. Once I slipped it on, he took my hand and led me outside toward the parking lot and into the cloudy morning. We stopped in front of a sleek, black motorcycle. I glanced up at him, then at the gray skies above, and back at Remington.

"You okay with this?" he asked, smoothing the frown between my eyebrows with his thumb.

I bit my lip. What if it rained? The roads would be slick and we could end up slipping …

"I will not let anything happen to you. I promise."

I licked my lips, nodding. This was part of enjoying the little pleasures I'd promised myself when I left home. Besides, as much as he radiated recklessness, he was very cautious. It was in every movement of his hard body.

I smiled. "I know."

He nodded, seeming pleased with my words. Maybe it was the way he looked deeply into my eyes as he made the vow or the pure confidence in his voice; whatever it was, I trusted him.

After pulling out another jacket from the storage compartment under the seat, I removed my trench coat and folded it, shoving it inside the compartment and shrugged on the bike jacket. Then he picked a helmet, slid it over my head, and worked the chinstrap, his eyes never leaving mine.

"You have beautiful eyes."

He grinned. "Thank you. And you, my lady, look absolutely breathtaking." He tugged the wild curls behind my back before picking the second helmet and working it onto his head.

"Flattery won't get you anywhere."

"And here I thought it would turn you on enough to let me do dirty things to you on this motorcycle." He sighed dramatically as he lifted one strong thigh, straddled the bike, and then held his hand out for me.

Sweet mother of all that is holy, that is hot!

I placed my hand in his as I settled myself behind him, my pulse thumping hard in my ears at the thought of us doing it on the bike. I squirmed, pressing my thighs around his, and gripping his taut waist. "Where are we going?"

"I want to show you something." He sounded calm and collected, but I felt him tremble as he pressed his hand where mine linked on his tight abs.

I smiled and buried my face into his back. Remington wasn't as controlled as he wanted everyone to believe. At least not with me.

Remington in control of the bike was such a turn-on. The muscles beneath his jacket shifted and his thighs tensed as we swerved and raced down the street. Some curls escaped the knot, slapping my face. I peeked around his back, and my gaze was drawn to his hands. His strong fingers wrapped around the handlebars, looking capable of anything. He swerved around corners, raced down streets, and slowed down when traffic got too heavy. Riding with him was addictive.

Remington parked the bike on Rue Rouget de Lisle and lifted me off before unbuckling the chinstrap. He removed the helmet and his as well. He stored them inside the bike's storage compartment.

"You lift me as if I weigh nothing. I love it."

He shrugged. "You don't weigh much."

I rolled my eyes, at the same time flattered by his words.

He reached out for my hand, guided me down the street and toward the Tuileries Garden. Surprisingly, it felt natural, as though I'd done this for years. I glanced up at him, wondering if he remembered our first lunch date, and met his knowing gaze. His lips curled up, faintly flashing his dimples as he lifted my hand to his lips, and I knew he was thinking about the same thing.

I was so lost in him and taking in our surroundings and breathing in the scent of wet leaves that when I looked up I realized we were walking toward the L'Orangerie Museum.

We headed toward the checkpoint and Remington presented two museum passes, then linked our fingers as he led the way to the top floor.

"When did you buy the passes?"

"I bought yours after dropping Adrien at school."

Before I could thank him, he was already tugging my hand and grinning playfully over his shoulder. I grinned back; I couldn't help it. When he looked like this, he resembled Adrien. We stepped into a large oval room with pristine white floors. The walls were covered in water lily paintings as far as the eye could see. Everything around me faded—the crowd of tourists, the low murmurs—just the feel of Remington's hand in mine and Monet's Nympheaus' remained.

I sucked in a breath, pressed a hand on my chest, and studied the painting, the way light played across the greens, blues, and whites.

"Wow," I whispered, breathless at the beauty surrounding me. In all the times I'd visited Paris, I'd never had a chance to visit this museum. I'd seen images in magazines and the Internet but never this close. Never like this. Why didn't I ever take time to visit this place?

I turned to Remington to ask him about the paintings but stopped to take in the look on his face. A look I could only describe as peaceful. The first time I saw this expression was when I walked into the kitchen and saw him interact with Adrien when I stayed over in his house, and while we danced in the club, and then again, after we had sex following our painting session. And yes, again today, while holding me in his arms on my bed.

He moved to stand behind me, pulled me into his chest, and slid his arms around my waist, holding me flush to him. "Welcome to my Fortress of Solitude," he whispered in my ear. I leaned my head back into his shoulder, and I couldn't restrain the giggle bursting from my lips.

"Fortress of Solitude? Like Superman?"

He nodded. "When I was a child, whenever my mother brought me to Paris, she would bring me here. The first time, I sat on the bench over there and never wanted to leave. I loved how peaceful this place was. Pure, as if nothing could permeate its walls and destroy me. After a while, it became a ritual for us. She would drop me here and go ahead with her business, and later, pick me up in time for lunch or dinner before flying back to Provence. When things were bad with my father, I came here. I would sit here and stare at this painting, imagining my life was different. After Colette passed away, I spent most of my time here wondering how I was supposed to continue. I wondered how I could raise a nine-month-old on my own, even though I had practically done that for the previous four months."

His voice was cold when he said her name. I wanted to ask him what happened to his wife, but I didn't want him to stop talking. I'd wanted to know more about her for a while now. The fact he was opening up to me was a huge step. So I brought my hands to his, squeezing them gently to let him know he had my attention.

"I met Colette for the first time in a club I was visiting with my friends here in Paris. She and I got along very well from the beginning. She was twenty-one and had just lost her parents in a car crash six months prior to our meeting. They were traveling together to Paris after spending their summer holidays in Marseilles. She was a mess. Vulnerable. My need to protect her, be there for her, overwhelmed me. She did not have anyone else other than her estranged aunt and me. She never visited her grandparents. She refused to tell me the reason, so I stopped asking about them. One year later, we were married.

"Colette was an archaeologist, and she used to travel a lot before she became pregnant with Adrien. She picked up where she had left off after our son's birth, as if he didn't exist. I suppose she was bored and in a hurry to resume her work." He sighed deeply. "Nothing could hold her down. Not our child and definitely not me. She travelled but always came back to us. One day, she came home in an exuberant mood and told me her company had discovered a site in Chile. She had been chosen as part of the excavation team."

Remington fell quiet as though he was gathering his thoughts.

"She left you and a nine-month-old baby." It was question, but also a statement. I was still trying to wrap my mind around the fact that a mother could leave her child, a baby, and go for days without a care in the world.

"Yes. This time she did not return. Her aeroplane to Paris crashed during takeoff, killing everyone aboard. I remember burying her bones, whatever pieces of her they found. I was so lost after that. I had no idea where my pain began and loss ended. I was a complete mess. I dated women who resembled her or had something that reminded me of her to cope with my loss. Whether it was a smile, their hair, or even the eyes, anything to bring her back to me in one way or another. My mother took care of Adrien and me for a while." He inhaled deeply, as if to steel himself for the next words, and shook his head. "One day, I woke up and it finally hit me, the depths I had gone to to deal with all that. I didn't like the kind of person I had become, and my boy needed me. I cleaned up my act and tried to be the best father and son I could be."

"Oh, my God, I'm so sorry, Remington." I turned around and quickly hugged him, not caring that the room was full of strangers. I could only see him, feel his pain. "How did you do it?" I asked. "How did you finally pick up the pieces of a shattered life and go on?"

"Adrien," he answered simply, took my hand and walked around with me as two groups left the room. "And I had already promised myself before my son was born that I wasn't going to be the kind of father mine had been."

I wondered how a love could be so deep, so potent, that it crippled a man seemingly as strong as Remington. She must have been one special woman to occupy his heart and soul. I tightened my hold around his hand, hiding the slash of envy tearing my heart, and closed my eyes, wishing that horrible feeling away.

Jesus, Selene. The man is probably still hurting.

There must be a reason he seemed angry and hurt when I asked him about his wife on our first dinner date. Then I remembered the letter, referring to the fact I looked like his wife. Would it be tactless if I asked him about that?

"One afternoon, a woman approached me outside the townhouse and introduced herself as Madame Girard. Her husband had worked with Colette and had been on the same team that had been sent to Chile. The name sounded familiar, and then I remembered Colette had mentioned him quite often."

For some reason, a sick feeling coiled in the pit of my stomach. I couldn't breathe as I waited for his next words.

"His wife told me Colette had been having an affair with Monsieur Girard for over two years. She had hired a detective to confirm her suspicions."

"Oh, Remington."

"After that, I knew there was a possibility that Adrien might not be my biological son. But I didn't care. He was *my* son." He thumped the left side of his chest passionately with a fist. "I decided not to have any tests done. I just knew. My blood runs in that boy's veins."

Of course it did. Adrien's and Remington's facial features were so similar, one would be blind not to see they were blood relatives.

We continued to stroll around the room, my mind in turmoil from what I'd just learned. Now I understood his anger and hurt when we first met, which begged the question …

"What did she look like?" I asked. I still couldn't get that darn letter out of my mind.

He froze mid-step, forcing me to stop as well. He studied me, before exhaling hard. "She was a brunette with brown eyes. The only thing that was similar was your nose. You know, the slightly upturned tip and your cheekbones. Other than that, you two are different as night and day. You," he said, tightening his hold on me, "you are the calm to my storm."

Anger simmered low in my veins. "I asked you if I resembled her before I left your house, but you did not tell me the truth."

He grimaced. "I was afraid if I told you the truth, you would leave. It didn't matter because you left anyway." There was no judgment in his voice.

And just like that, I was torn between letting my anger free or leashing it. What did one do when a man served you truth in your face? *God, I love this man's honesty.* I felt it required the same amount of truthfulness. Something that had been missing in both of our marriages. "You understand why I left, right?"

He nodded, leaned down, and kissed my forehead. "I do."

I huffed out a breath and laughed. Today was taking some very insane, unexpected turns. "You realize we are two somewhat messed-up people?"

"We might be that, but you make me stronger. It sounds insane, doesn't it?"

"No," I whispered, pondering his words. "It makes perfect sense. Strange, yet perfect."

Because it did.

Chapter Twenty-Eight

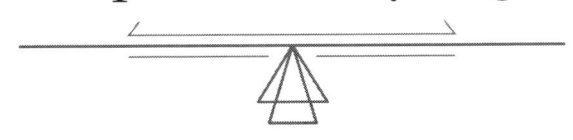

Selene

By the time we made it to the exit, the clouds were hanging low in the sky, and it was drizzling as if to underscore the tragedy of what Remington had told me inside the oval room. My heart still felt heavy for him. There had to be a slice of happiness in his life.

"Do you have any siblings?" I asked Remington.

"Two step-brothers. I hope you will have a chance to meet Luc and Dom."

I glanced up quickly at this new information and fought a smile. "*Luc* and *Dom*?"

"Lucien and Dominique. My mother married when I was fifteen to Luc and Dom's father, Bernard. He was my father in all ways but one."

"Was?"

"He passed away two years ago." I heard the wistfulness in his voice. He must have had a good relationship with his step-father.

I slid my hand into his, twined our fingers together and squeezed them, offering him consolation.

"Then there's Caleb, my half-brother. We attended a boarding school in Hertfordshire together."

He fell silent, and his mouth tugged down into a little frown. I fought the urge to ask him what he was thinking. Anything to explain his relationship with Caleb. Seriously, this man had gone through so much at such a young age, and as much as I wanted to know more about his past, this wasn't the place.

I made a mental note to ask him later. Much later. Today's confessions were enough to drain even the strongest of men.

I stood on my toes, grabbed the collar of his jacket, and pulled him down to catch his attention. He turned to look at me with a million questions swirling in his beautiful eyes. I slid my hand to the nape of his neck, feeling bold, and kissed him, capturing his startled gasp with my lips. When he caught on to what I was doing, his hands cupped my face, returning my kiss.

"What was that for?" he asked when we broke the kiss.

I swept his tousled hair back from his forehead with my fingers and said, "Even Superman should be kissed senseless every once in a while."

The frown on his face vanished, replaced by a smile, and I swear the clouds parted and the sun shone. On the other hand, maybe it was just me basking in that sexy grin.

"Fancy a walk in the rain?" he asked me, his eyes darting to my hair, then back to my face. "That is, if you don't mind getting wet. Even though I have to say, I love you wet." He whispered those last words in my ear, and I almost combusted on the spot.

I nodded, excitement rushing through my veins like a drug. I couldn't remember the last time I walked in the rain.

He took my handbag and slung the strap over his body. I grabbed his hand and tugged him forward and into the drizzle, laughing. I wanted to run with his hand in mine and feel my heart thumping in my chest while the cool rain fell around us. His legs were long, but he slowed down enough to accommodate my strides.

We stopped next to the Octagon Basin, out of breath, laughing. When the drizzle turned into a downpour, I grabbed him by the neck and crushed my mouth to his. This time he was ready.

We finally made it to the motorcycle, just as the rain eased off a bit. He carefully weaved in and out of traffic as we drove to his townhouse. My front was plastered to his back, and his warmth seeped into me.

"I'm so wet for you right now," I whispered in his ear. His back vibrated from his growl. "Remember that illegal move you did in your art room? The one that ought to be forbidden in every country? I want that, Remington."

"You're killing me, Selene. You know what this means, don't you?" he asked, pulling to a stop as the lights turned red.

I kissed his back, before whispering, "Tell me."

He darted a look at the lights and then over his shoulder at me. "When we get home, I will rip your clothes off and then kiss, suck, bite, and lick every part of your body. I can't wait to taste you. *Mon Dieu*, the thought of burying my cock inside you is driving me insane; I can't get enough of you." He grabbed one of my hands from his waist and dragged it down to his crotch. "Do you feel this? This is for you, *ma belle*. Are you ready for it, Selene?"

"Yes!" I almost screamed as my heart raced and my breathing became harsh, matching his.

"*Très bien, ma chérie.*" His accent deepened with lust. He released my hand and squeezed my knee. I just about jumped off the bike at the contact. He laughed low and dirty as we sped off when the lights changed.

He rolled the bike up the drive, haphazardly parking it before jumping off and lifting me from my seat. After quickly divesting our jackets and helmets, he scooped me in his arms and headed for the door.

"God, I love your arms. So strong," I said, snuggling deeper into his chest. No one had ever tried to carry me like this, so I was going to enjoy being spoiled while it lasted.

He laughed, pressing a kiss on my forehead and stopping at the door. "Keys in my trousers. Right side pocket."

I repositioned myself and did as instructed. Jesus, the man had strong thighs. And oh, my God! Was that his—?

"Found something you like in there?" He grinned at me.

"Yes, I did." I flung the door open, and as soon as we stumbled through, he kicked it shut, slid me down his body and pushed me up against the door.

"Well, then." He jerked his pelvis forward, hitting me right where I wanted him. "So I have the license to do very dirty things to you."

Before I could speak, his mouth was on mine, kissing me passionately and desperately as if he couldn't get enough of me, as if the thought of not having his lips on mine was driving him to the point of insanity. And I loved it. I fisted his hair, tugging it hard. A groan rumbled in his chest as his tongue swept and plunged into my mouth in the same rhythm as his hips. He pulled back, breathing hard as his shaking fingers fumbled with my zipper, and for a moment, I thought he'd rip my jeans off as he had promised. He growled in satisfaction when he finally got through, and I lifted my shaky legs. He tossed the jeans behind him, and his eyes shone with lust as he realized I had told him the truth. I was commando. He hooked his hands inside my lilac lace bra and ripped it off my body.

"Holy shit! That's so hot, even though that was my favourite bra. God, Remington," I screamed his name as he tore the blouse from my body, his lips kissing, sucking, biting, and then kissing me better, just like he'd promised.

Then I remembered he had a son, and he might be stumbling around in the house. "Oh, God, Remington. Where's Adrien?"

"He won't be home for another hour." He dropped to his knees, grabbed one of my legs, and hooked it over his shoulders. He shoved his head between my thighs and brought his mouth to my pussy, the sexy sounds he made in his throat vibrating through my body, making me wetter. He pulled back and slid his hands to my breasts.

"I love how your breasts fit in my hands. Hmm, just right." He rolled my nipples between his fingers, and then, slid his hands down my body to my hips. "Touch your breasts, *ma belle*."

I stared at him, feeling very turned on and awkward. I had never done this before. Would I look silly? Who touches themselves?

"Do it," he commanded softly, his heavy-lidded gaze sweeping down to my chest. He licked his lips, and his Adam's apple bobbed as he swallowed. He glided his strong hands down the sides of my body in encouraging, worshipful strokes, and I felt like a goddess. "I want to see you touch yourself."

I did as he asked, basking in his fervent gaze, boosting my confidence. I squirmed at the contact.

Oh, holy wow! That was ...interesting. I peeked at him through my lashes and smiled seductively. Or I hoped it was a minx-like smile. He looked like he was about to pounce on me any second and complete the task himself.

"Yes, that's it. Don't stop." He brought his mouth to my pussy and used his fingers to bare me to his tongue. His scruff rubbed against the inside of my thigh, arousing me more.

I screamed as he flattened his tongue on me, stroking my

clit, then sucking gently. He rumbled deep in his throat, the sound humming its way up my body, and I shattered. My orgasm shook me to my very foundation. Without warning, he shot to his feet and crushed his mouth with mine, passionately, possessively, and claimed me. Jesus, I could taste myself on his tongue.

He wrapped his arms around me, holding me as I rode my orgasm.

"Are you all right?" he asked, hoarsely. I nodded into his chest, unable to raise my head. He scooped me in his arms and closed the distance to the sofa, tossed me on it, any signs of gentleness gone and straightened.

"Don't move. I'll be right back."

As if I would. "Where are you going?" I asked, following his delicious butt up the stairs with my eyes and then grabbed a pillow, plunked it on my face, and giggled.

I am in heaven.

Moments later, the pillow was yanked out of my hands. Remington stood above me, his eyes dark and hungry.

"Give me your hands."

Holy shit! He was in Intense Remington mode.

"Why?"

He stared at me, his jaw set and one eyebrow raised. Apparently, he'd decided to wield his 'stare her into submission' look.

I sighed dramatically and shoved my arms toward him, but inside my body, anticipation bubbled furiously.

One hand went to the back of his jeans as he spun me around with the other, and seconds later, my wrists were shackled in handcuffs.

I wiggled my wrists and quickly looked up at him. He must

have read my confusion because he grabbed my chin and said, "I want you to give me all of you."

"Haven't I done that already?"

He shook his head. "You've been holding yourself back. Give me your fears. I don't want you to surrender your control to me, but I would like you to trust me enough to know that I would never hurt you."

I shifted on the couch, more aroused than before. He watched me closely, as though waiting for a reaction from me. After our earlier conversation, he knew how I felt about giving up control. Holy shit, the thought of being at the mercy of his strength and passion at this moment was driving me insane with need. But allowing him a glimpse of my fears? It felt too intimate. On the other hand, the thought of freeing myself from that weight, if only for one night, sounded quite appealing.

"Trust goes both ways, you know," I said, scrutinizing his face for a reaction to my words. "Would you do that? Trust me with your fears?"

He narrowed his eyes on me, sensing the challenge behind those words. Finally, he nodded.

"I will hold you to that."

His expression shuttered. He probably hadn't expected me to say that. But darn it. If there was a way to wipe his slate clean for another chance at life, I would do it in a heartbeat. But then, he probably wouldn't be this strong, exceptional man standing in front of me. After what he told me today, I had a feeling it would take a huge effort to get him to let go of his reservations.

He had promised me three months of debauchery and hedonistic pleasure. I wanted that and everything else he had to offer.

This is it. I took a deep breath and nodded, surrendering a slice of my control and fears to him.

His shoulders relaxed a notch. "Thank you for trusting me, *ma belle*."

He stood back to survey his handiwork as uninhibited hunger flooded his face again. He quickly stripped off his jeans, his movements uncoordinated. He seemed to be losing control, fast.

Then he sat on the couch next to me and gripped my hips, pulling me to him.

"Spread your legs and sit on my lap."

He guided me forward to place me right above his shaft. He looked up at me with raised eyebrows as if to ask me if he could enter me naked. I love how he paused long enough to check if I was okay with what he was doing. Strangely, there was no hesitation on my part. Plus he'd already been inside me, bare, earlier on today when the condom broke. I shivered at the thought of having sex with him skin on skin. I wanted him completely. I smiled at him, answering his question.

Seeming satisfied, he squeezed my hips, and I lifted myself to my knees.

I loved this version of Remington. He didn't need to say a word for my body to bow to his touch and command. I looked down at his thick, hard cock and did as instructed. He lowered my body, his gaze never leaving mine. I held my breath as I took him in.

Oh, holy fuck! Surely, I was going to die. My legs shook, and my body clenched with eagerness. I wasn't going to last long. How was it even possible for a person to orgasm twice in the span of thirty minutes?

My legs gave way, and I sank onto his lap.

"Oh, fuck, Selene!" he shouted, before burying his face in the crevice of my neck. "I think I've died and gone to heaven. You feel incredible."

I grinned smugly into his chest, loving how his hands

adored my body. After a few moments, he pulled back and began to lift me up and down his length. Since my hands were cuffed behind me, I hardly had much control other than lifting myself up and down on my knees. But darn it if I was going to let him have all the fun. I mirrored his undulating movements, leaned forward, and kissed his throat. His scruff rubbed on my face and chin as I made my way to his ear. I nipped and sucked his earlobe. He groaned, grunted, and cursed. I bit my lip, moaned and whimpered.

"Don't hold back, Selene. I want it all. I will not be able to hold on too long," Remington said as his thighs tensed beneath me and he seemed to harden even more inside me. His hands and mouth worshipped my body, sucking, caressing, kneading, nipping, gripping, squeezing, and licking, and there was nothing I could do about it other than squirm on his lap, scream, and savour it.

I leaned forward, pressing my lips to his throat and gently sucked the skin there. "I don't want you to. Come with me, Remington," I whispered hoarsely.

There was nothing tender or sensual about it but an act of fulfilling a raw need. Pure hunger of two bodies, two souls that needed each other to make them whole. It was explosive, almost desperate, intense. He took what he needed from me, and I did the same. This wasn't sex, but something between sex and fucking.

And he came at the same time I did, shouting my name. His arms shot around me, my breasts flattened on his hard chest, and he hugged me tightly to him as our heartbeats thumped against each other's chests.

I inhaled, taking in the scent of sex and Remington's cologne and exhaling all the frustrations and fear, which had held me captive the entire day. I quite liked being handcuffed, especially by Remington. The only downside was that I couldn't touch him like I'd wanted to. But knowing that he was doing things to me with his hands and mouth and I wasn't expected to return the favour, but enjoy what was being done to me, gave me a high unlike any I'd ever experienced before.

"You ruined me," he said. "I can hardly stand on my feet."

"I guess we will just have to crawl upstairs," I announced with a lack of conviction. Remington's shoulders shook, but no sound came from his mouth.

"As long as I go first; I'm incapable of staring at your ass without thinking of fucking you."

I laughed, and the next second, Remington leaned forward, grabbed his jeans, and pulled out a small key from the pocket. After unlocking the handcuffs, he tossed them on the floor and then cradled me in his arms as he marched upstairs and into his bathroom. His hold around me was strong, giving me the feeling that, with him, I would always be safe.

Chapter Twenty-Nine

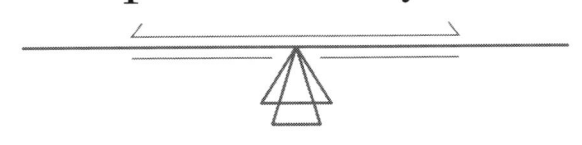

Remington

I sat back on the seat and quickly read the report Gilles had handed me a few minutes ago, but my mind was still on my reunion with Selene yesterday, how I had fulfilled my promise after Adrien was in bed—tied her to my bed and fucked her until we both couldn't see straight.

I blinked to focus on the papers. I had already read them three times, and nothing seemed to stick inside my brain. Apparently, my mind had other plans.

Gilles shifted on his chair, staring at me with his eyebrows raised. I knew he noticed how distracted I was. It wasn't in my nature to be this inattentive.

I was not about to give him the opportunity to interrogate me.

Heaving a deep sigh, I forced my mind back to the matters at hand and reread the document for the fourth time. "Is this all?" I asked, tossing the papers on the table and focusing on Gilles. "Gilles, you and your team had enough time to look into this. Is that all you could find out? My son and the woman—" I stopped short, realizing what I had been about to say.

The woman I love.

Shit.

I rubbed my jaw, thinking back on the words she had spoken jokingly. She warned me I would fall for her. But had I really? Or was I hanging on to the fact that Selene made me feel self-confident and the ache in my heart bearable? It did not hurt that Adrien obviously adored her. The boy had practically mourned her absence after she left.

At that moment, I could hear their laughter from outside the library's closed door. My lips quirked as I turned my attention back to Gilles. As a former member of GIGN—*Groupe d'Intervention de la Gendarmerie Nationale*—he had an extensive knowledge of undercover surveillance, among other qualities. He was a mean son of a bitch when he put his mind on something.

"Did you check the whereabouts of the women on the list I gave you?"

He nodded. "The first two women on the list have been out of the country for the past two months."

"But that does not disqualify them from being suspects, does it?" I impatiently tapped my finger on the smooth, dark surface of the oak table.

"No, it does not."

I rose from the chair, massaging the nape of my neck, and turned to face the black Paris night out the window. "I need to make arrangements for us to travel to Provence for a few days. I think it might be easier to keep everyone safe there. I need you or a member of your team and Èric to accompany us. Are you up for it?"

The thought of Èric anywhere near Selene still made my hackles rise. I wasn't fond of the way he looked at her, but his easy smile and cheerful eyes masked a lethal man. He was the kind of man I wanted at my side when shit hit the fan. Gilles knew this about Èric, and he'd been thinking of recruiting him to join his security firm.

"Us? Does she know of this arrangement?" he asked.

I looked over my shoulder. "Not yet." But I wasn't going to leave her unprotected.

"Did you say something?" Gilles asked, amusement thick in his voice.

I rolled my eyes. "Just make the arrangements and I will handle the rest."

He chuckled, shaking his head. "I know you asked me to stop any background checks on Selene. Are you sure?"

"Yes," I said in a steely voice. "I told you I wasn't interested, Gilles." How could I explain to him that, somehow, I trusted Selene? She had willingly walked out of my house in order to keep my son and me safe. From what I knew about her, she wasn't the kind of person to hurt people out of maliciousness. She had a pure soul. Even after everything that happened to her, she had the strength to carry on.

What was I going to do when the three months were over? And what about Adrien?

I rubbed a hand down my face, my mind flooding with different options. I could ask her to stay. Was it too early for that? All I knew was I couldn't see myself letting her go without a fight. I just hoped she felt something akin to more than like for me. She obviously adored Adrien.

Gilles studied me for several seconds before he nodded once and rose from his seat. "I haven't gotten anything on Adele yet as you requested yesterday. Do you think she could be this person sending the letters?"

"I just want to be certain she's not."

He nodded. "I'll keep you updated."

We left my office and returned to the living room. After Gilles muttered good night to Selene and Adrien, he nodded curtly before heading out the door.

I wasn't going back on my decision about checking up on Selene. I'd made up my mind; I was going to enjoy being with her. Besides, as I'd gotten to know her, I trusted my instincts. But I still wondered about some of the things I did when I was around her. Was I in way over my head here? Yesterday had been perfect. I hadn't planned to tell her about my father or Colette. But there was just something about her—the way she stared at me with her large, hazel eyes full of softness—that snapped my control and made me bare my soul to her. I didn't regret telling her, though. I'd been holding so much inside me; it felt liberating to finally talk to someone who did not judge me. Or pity me.

I strode into the living room and stopped, taking in the scene before me: Adrien and Selene sitting next to each other in the dining room, thumb fighting. Selene's face was screwed up as she pretended to be losing, and then she dropped to the floor, causing my son to scream joyously. Then he turned and saw me.

"Papa, I won, I won!" Adrien shrieked, waving at me with his fork, then pointing at Selene. "She made macaroni with cheese."

"Her name please, Adrien." I ruffled his hair, my heart swelling and, unable to stop myself, I leaned forward and kissed Selene's forehead and then helped her up. She smiled up at me and I blinked at her, spellbound.

"Selene." Adrien smiled shyly, scraping his plate clean of the lingering specks of macaroni and cheese Selene had made for dinner.

"Hey." She walked toward the kitchen, and I followed her like a smitten, young schoolboy. "Hungry?"

"I am really trying not to answer that right now."

She smiled, biting her lip, and I knew she remembered our reunion.

"Yes, I am starving." My gaze tracked her every move around the kitchen as she prepared hot chocolate, adding two marshmallows, and took it to Adrien. It was rather pathetic how much I craved her. "How is your schedule for the next few days?" I finally asked when she returned to the kitchen.

"I'm free until Grace finalizes a contract with a design house in Berlin. Why do you ask?"

"I was wondering if you'd like to join Adrien and me in Provence for a few days."

She bit her lip, turning away to serve an enormous heap of food on a plate. "I don't think that's a good idea."

"Why not?"

"That's taking things a bit too far, don't you think?" she asked, looking at me over her shoulder, and I frowned. "Your mother?"

"What about her?"

She exhaled as if exasperated that I wasn't getting the point. In truth, I wasn't.

"Don't you think she'll think something is going on between us? Something more?"

Oh, that. "Well, my mother is in London meeting with some wine sellers at the moment and will not be returning until the beginning of October."

Her shoulders loosened at little, and she smiled. "All right. I would love to. I'm not sure about meeting your mother just yet."

I wasn't ready for them to meet yet, either. My mother had been pushing me to marry again, saying Adrien needed a mother. Yes, my son needed a mother figure in his life. I hadn't given up on love even after what happened with Colette, but that didn't mean I would get involved with any woman to make sure that happened. Everything had its time and place.

She tilted her head to the side and narrowed her eyes at me in scrutiny. "Something else is going on. Want to talk about it?"

I had opened myself up too much to her, and her eyes saw through me, more than felt comfortable. "I want to keep you safe while we try to find out who is behind the threats. The château is much safer."

"You own a château?"

I grinned, relieved she was distracted from what was truly bothering me. "Actually, my mother owns it. It has been in our family for a long time."

"Are you guys some kind of monarchy or something?" she asked in a joking voice.

"My great, great grandfather was a marquis," I said, remembering how my mother had made sure I had my family history straight.

"Well then …" she said, seemingly at a loss for words.

"Does that change things between us?"

"You are still the same man you were one minute ago, so no. It doesn't change a thing."

Just then, Adrien hopped down from his seat and took his plate and mug to the sink, yawning. Selene had given him a bath earlier on while I was in the office with Gilles.

"Time for you to go to bed."

After he kissed Selene good night, Adrien skipped ahead of me, dashing up the stairs. I glanced over my shoulder and caught Selene's hot gaze trailing my arse.

"Insatiable minx," I mouthed the words to her.

Not that I could blame her. I felt just as insatiable.

Chapter Thirty

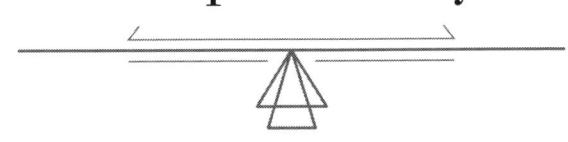

Selene

The following day we drove toward a privately-owned hangar near Charles De Gaulle Airport. Remington filled me in on his two brothers. Lucien was the mad race car driver, as he put it, and Dominique was into horseracing. They sounded like a crazy bunch, and I couldn't wait to meet them. Adele was traveling with us as well. Earlier today, Remington informed me that Gilles was doing some checks on her to make sure she wasn't a threat. So if she pulled a stunt, Gilles and Èric would catch her in the act. Personally, I didn't feel as though she was dangerous. I felt responsible for this. I probably shouldn't have made Remington doubt himself over Adele. After watching her since Remington and I got back together again, I came to realize what Adele felt for Remington was respect coupled with simple affection and nothing more. The way her eyes lit up when he or his son walked into the room made me feel happy for Remington that he had one more person who loved him. He was so easy to love.

I stopped breathing.

Shit! Love? Did I say love? I meant, easy to grow fond of.

I gave up grappling with my feelings and took in my surroundings.

There were several small planes scattered around. We boarded a white one with blue lines along the sides. Apparently, Remington believed in traveling in luxury. Impressive.

"Are you comfortable?" he asked as soon as he had settled Adrien across from us.

I nodded. "You're quite the Prince Charming. I feel spoiled, Remington."

He snorted. "Prince Charming? I told you I'm not that man. I'm sure even my tamest thoughts would scare the shit out of him. And I enjoy spoiling you, princess." He flashed me a heated look.

"Can't you think of anything other than dirty thoughts when you look at me?"

He sighed dramatically. "I've tried really hard but failed miserably. It's as though, when I look at you or have even the slightest thought of you, it knocks all sensible notions out of my head." He shrugged. "You are the muse to my thoughts."

"Wow, don't hold back, St. Germain."

"I promised you the truth. Always." He grinned as he buckled his seatbelt.

A few minutes later, we were on the way to Provence.

As soon as our plane reached our destination, the tension coiled in my bones melted away. As we disembarked, I glanced around while Adrien bolted toward a tall man with dark, curly hair standing a few feet from us.

Remington's palm was on my lower back as we left the plane behind. I loved the way his hand felt on my body, possessive and attentive.

We stopped in front of the tall man. *Those eyes and a strong jaw!* The air here in Provence must do wonders for the male population.

He was very good-looking with about a day or two's worth of scruff, a straight nose, and full lips, which were pursed as if he were deep in thought. His eyebrows were scrunched up in a small frown resembling confusion as his brown eyes studied me. Remington nudged him in the ribs, breaking the man's scrutiny.

Man, this is awkward.

They hugged each other before turning to face me.

"Lucien, this is Selene," Remington announced. He sounded proud and almost adoring. I loved it.

Oh, the mad race car driver. Sweet.

I saw a thousand questions flitting in his eyes. He darted a loaded look at Remington and then back at me.

I shifted on my feet nervously, knowing he was seeing what Remington saw the first time we met.

Lucien's face cleared, a slow smile spread across his features, and he quickly pulled me into a hug, kissing both my cheeks, then once more on my left cheek. "Well, Selene. No wonder Sunshine over here was twisted over you when he was here a few days ago. You're utterly breathtaking. And by the way, call me Luc." I could sense an accent in some words, but otherwise his English was perfect. Too perfect.

Sunshine? I snorted.

"Enough buttering her up, Lucien." Remington turned to me. "This idiot of a brother has a sarcastic way of showing his love."

Lucien didn't change his focus on me, and Remington's lips flattened as irritation flashed in his eyes.

"How is Charlotte doing? You know, your girlfriend?" Remington asked, interrupting Luc as he guided me toward a Jeep parked a few feet away, while Adrien skipped, then scrambled inside the back seat of the car. Adele, Gilles, and Èric were driving in a different vehicle, so they headed toward a Peugeot parked a few feet away.

Luc laughed, slapping Remington on his back. "She's fine, actually."

"Keep that in mind."

Luc rolled his eyes at Remington's tone as he slid into the driver's seat. I laughed. It was so refreshing to see this side of Remington. It was as if the moment the plane landed, he was a new person who was lighter and carefree, albeit very possessive, something I'd noticed since we got back together.

Lucien drove like a maniac. A very confident maniac. I spent half the trip gripping the leather seats, my stomach in knots. Thank God the traffic was almost non-existent. Adrien squealed and laughed, clapping his hands, while mine searched for purchase to stop from banging into the seat in front of me. Even the motorcycle ride with Remington didn't make me this scared.

"My child and Selene are in this car, Lucien. This is not the right time to show off your skills."

"*Mon Dieu*, but you are such a party pooper, Remington."

"It's called responsibility, idiot."

I chuckled under my breath at their banter.

We drove about ten minutes in silence at a moderately slower speed while I took in our surroundings. Adrien had finally dozed off and snuggled into me, snoring softly. The feel of his tiny, warm body next to mine was like a balm to my heart, temporarily chasing away the pain lurking in the corners and crevices, just waiting to rear its ugly head.

"Grape Harvest tours in Luberon," I read on a billboard as the car drove by. "Is it the season?"

"*Oui*. Would you like to do that sometime?" Luc asked,

and Remington cursed under his breath. Luc laughed. "Come on, Remington. Relax. There is no need for you to scowl at me. It was just an offer."

I couldn't see Remington's face, but from Luc's playful expression, I knew he was baiting Remington and it was probably something Luc did often, teasing his brother to get a reaction.

"Remington and I haven't talked about our plans yet." I leaned forward, slid my hand on Remington's shoulder and rubbed his strong jaw with my fingers. He flashed a dimpled smile at me, and dear God, heat pooled between my thighs.

After we stopped at an intersection, Luc turned left onto a road flanked on both sides by vineyards. I breathlessly admired the scenery, the rolling hillsides and hilltop villages in the distance, a smile tugging at my lips. A hand on my knee pulled me away from the window. Remington had twisted his body around in the front seat and met my gaze before glancing down at his son and back up at me. His regard was warm, and for a second, I thought I saw something more. Something that made my pulse flutter like tiny butterfly wings. Then he turned to face the front, taking that look with him, and my stomach clenched delightfully. I couldn't stop myself from reacting to him. My heart still pined for him, even sitting so close to me. Maybe I needed to teach my heart to hold back, to look before leaping because this jump might lead me to a place I could never climb out of. But a heart is stubborn, greedy, selfish, and it wants what it wants, thrives on being fed its favourite food, so I let mine feed as I took in Remington's side profile.

Ten minutes later, a huge house, well, not a house, a château came into view, growing larger as we drove up a hill. We pulled up a cobblestone driveway minutes later, and my eyes couldn't absorb the view fast enough.

Holy freaking WOW!

"Welcome to Château St. Germain, Selene." Remington sounded content as he said those words. "Your mouth, *ma belle*," Remington whispered, as soon as Luc climbed out of the car. "Or I might just crawl back there and do something about it."

I gave him a dirty look and snapped my mouth closed. He chuckled as he slid from his seat and rounded the car to scoop Adrien in his arms. The boy's eyes blinked open. After scanning our surroundings, he squealed and wiggled out of his father's arms and dashed toward the front entrance. I smiled, enjoying the little ball of energy that was Adrien.

Stepping out of the car, I was immediately wrapped in the faint scent of lavender. Teasing me. Seducing me. The weather was still warm around here. I stared at the enormous Renaissance stone building, painted in a very pale yellow colour. Several rooms spanned both the east and west sides. Rows and rows of grape vines, now blazing in gold, brown and bronze colours of autumn, striped one side of the château's hillside and bushes of lavender covered the other side.

It was simply beautiful.

"How old is it?"

"The west wing, which is the oldest part dates back to the thirteenth century, while the east wing, around the eighteenth."

By the time I was done taking in the view, Remington's arms were wrapped around my waist and his chin rested on my shoulder. Everyone had already gone inside the house, and our luggage had magically disappeared.

"Gilles and Èric took the luggage inside," Remington said when he saw the frown on my face.

I nodded. "How do you keep this place so well-maintained?"

He twined his fingers with mine, leading me toward the entrance. "We have staff who drop by at least three times a week. This place would fall apart if we didn't have people to help take care of it. My mother travels a lot, although she knows more about wine making than I do, and Lucien is mostly on racetracks or practicing. As for Dominique, he's either traveling or racing his horse. They are hardly ever in Provence. We have someone who's in charge of all the workers in the vineyards and keeps an eye on things."

The inside was as breathtaking as the exterior. The walls were a light shade of terracotta with a few colourful portraits decorating the open space. A fireplace stood at one side of the big living room. Pillows in soft hues of blue, yellow, and red were scattered on the black leather sofas, the only thing taking away the historic feel of this place. However, they suited the room just fine. On one of the walls stood a realistic painting of Adrien as a baby, cradled in a woman's arms—Remington's mother, if I had to guess. Their resemblance was uncanny.

"This place is beautiful."

He smiled, seemingly pleased with my words. "I'm glad that you like it. Our rooms are on the west side. Adele, Èric, and Gilles are on the east," he said, guiding me up a flight of stairs that curved smoothly, leading to the next floor. About ten rooms lined the hallway. "This is ours." He pointed to a door to our left. "And Adrien is right next to us."

Ours. He had used that word twice. My heart skipped a beat as the words caused little flutters of bliss inside my stomach. I loved the intimacy that word elicited.

As we entered the room, someone shrieked, followed by a child's laughter. I made a beeline for the window, and once again, my lungs couldn't absorb air fast enough. Two small brick houses—I supposed one was a shed—stood to the right, then a flight of steps leading directly to open, green lawns with trees placed strategically to offer shade from the sultry summer days, their autumn gold and orange colouring adding to the already landscape-like scenery. A fountain bubbled gently a few feet away, close to the patio, the sound hypnotizing, relaxing. I moved my gaze to the swimming pool I had bypassed while taking in the view and smiled. Èric and Adrien were in the pool, splashing water at each other. Adele had changed into a conservative black swimsuit and sat with her back to me, her legs submerged in the water. Had Remington and I stayed that long outside? Or had Èric, Adrien, and Adele been too eager to get in the water? Clearly, despite Adrien growing up without a mother figure in his life, he was surrounded by a lot of love.

Adrien was one of the happiest children I'd ever come across. I couldn't remember a time I'd seen him sad.

"I love this place," I said, turning around to find Remington standing near the bed, his intense gaze on me.

"And I love looking at you. You're quite the vision, standing there." He held out his arms to me, and I walked into them happily and willingly.

"Thank you for inviting me."

"You're very welcome," he said. "I'm glad you said yes."

Chapter Thirty-One

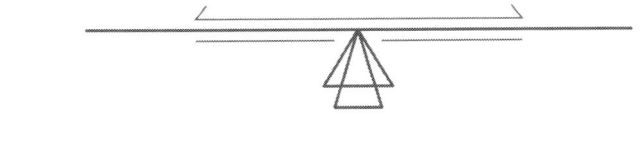

Remington

After unpacking our luggage, I left Selene inside our room and went in search of Luc. I had seen the way he'd stared at her when he picked us up from the hangar. He must have noticed the same thing I did when I first saw her at Hotel L'Arc. The infinitesimal resemblance that caught someone off guard until they really looked at her and realized she and Colette didn't really look alike.

I found Luc sprawled in a chair in the living room, reading one of his race car magazines. He lifted his gaze and sat up as soon as I lowered myself onto one of the seats.

After updating each other on what was going on in our lives, I leaned back in the chair and stretched out my legs. I knew we were dancing around the topic, and it was making me jittery and impatient. I wanted to get it out in the open.

"So what do you think of Selene?" I asked him, watching him carefully.

"Very beautiful. And curvy. Man, she has some curves on her."

"Shut up, arsehole," I growled at him. He grinned, and

I knew he'd been baiting me. He always did, even when we were children.

His face took on a serious expression. "She reminded me of Colette in a very small way. But when I looked at her more closely, she didn't. I can't really explain it."

I exhaled, relieved. "She does." I shrugged. "I wondered about her as well. However, there is a theory that we all have someone we resemble somewhere in this world. This must be it in her case."

He studied me through narrowed eyes. "Is that the reason you're dating her?"

I rubbed my neck, feeling tension start to curl at the base of it. "No. She is more than that. She understands me without pitying me. I don't know how to explain this without sounding like a completely smitten fool."

He cocked his head to the side. "Try."

"I feel a connection toward her I haven't felt with any woman in years."

"Connection. Is it the sex?"

"Part of it, yes. But the other part …" I shrugged, letting the words trail off.

"You, my dear brother, are either starved for sex or attention," he declared, and I wanted to wipe that smug smile off his face.

"It's nothing like that, smartarse."

He chuckled. "What about Adrien? You made certain he didn't meet the women you dated before."

I dragged a hand through my hair. His question echoed my thoughts. I had no clue how to answer that, just like everything else that involved Selene. "He loves her. For once in my life, I don't know what to do."

"You will. You always find a way. That's one of the things I admire about you."

"You admire me?" I asked, raising a brow.

He leaned forward and took the glass of wine from the table, tipped it toward me, and said, "Don't let it go to your head."

I laughed, feeling the tension ease from my body. This was one of those things I missed in my life, spending time with my brothers like we used to do when we were children. Life had thrown us into a frenzy of busy schedules.

Selene came downstairs half an hour later dressed in a strapless, yellow dress that hugged her body in all the right places, yet not giving much away. It was a sneak peek to a body I had learned every curve of with my hands and mouth. My fingers itched to touch her, yet my body had me rooted on the seat, wanting to savour the sight of her. I remembered Luc's words, turned, and saw how his eyes unashamedly took in her body. I glared at him.

"What's that noise?" he asked, his eyes widening in what I assumed was surprise. "Did you growl at me?"

I did? I couldn't remember making that sound. It showed how deeply Selene affected me, to the point that I did things unknowingly.

Luc lifted his hands as if to placate me. "Take it easy, Tarzan. Jane is all yours."

I narrowed my eyes at him, and he had the grace to drop his gaze back to his magazine.

I shot to my feet and strode to where Selene stood, smiling at me.

"Breathtaking," I murmured and kissed her forehead, breathing in her scent from one of her body lotions I'd watched her rub all over her body just this morning. Citrus and uniquely Selene.

Slipping my arm around her waist, I led Selene to the patio and down the steps leading to the rest of the open grounds. Just seeing the joy and awe on her face as she took in her surroundings or watched as Adrien played with Èric in the swimming pool, while Adele's laughter rang through the quiet gardens, made me happy and proud of my decision to bring her here.

We later dressed for dinner, while I fought the urge to pin her on the bed and have my way with her.

In my opinion, dinner was perfection. We dined on the patio together: Lucien, Gilles, Adrien, Selene, Èric, Dominique, who arrived an hour ago, and Adele. Music played softly from speakers hidden around the grounds. I glanced around the table, wishing my mother were here. These were the people in my life, and to say I wouldn't do anything for them, *anything*, would be a lie. I turned my gaze to Selene. I loved having her here with me, the place where I grew up. I couldn't wait to show her around. My eyes automatically honed in on her chest, the way the dress hugged her full breasts, and my cock stirred to life. My hand, resting on her knee, inched up under the short, yellow dress she wore and squeezed her thigh.

I leaned into her ear. "Did I tell you how much I love this dress? So accessible."

"Can I tell you a secret?" I nodded eagerly, loving the wicked look in her eyes. She brought her lips to my ear. "I'm not wearing underwear."

Fucking hell! I should have fucked her earlier. I slid my hand up her inner thigh, tightened my grip, and her breath hitched.

Good. At least we were both hot and bothered.

I returned my hand to her knee and focused on Dominique.

"So how is the horse racing business?" I asked Dom while taking a sip of my rosé, made from grapes grown in our vineyards. Delicious.

"Just neighing all the way, I guess." He laughed at his own joke.

I made a note to tell him to come up with some fresh jokes. He had been using that one for the last five years or so.

"How are you enjoying your stay in France, Selene?" Dominique asked.

"So far, it's great. I've visited a few places. I've been to Paris before, but I didn't realize how much I missed it until I was actually there again. I have never been to Provence though. It's amazing. I'm glad I got a chance to visit." She sent me an affectionate look.

I loved how she said that with confidence and warmth. I grinned like a fool.

"Anything special you want to see while here in Provence?" Dom asked again, smiling lazily. He was obviously thinking about showing her his horses. I chuckled quietly, and he sent me a scathing look before turning to focus on Selene.

Lucien perked up like a hunting dog that had suddenly caught an intriguing scent. "Actually, I was thinking of showing her around Monte Carlo." I scowled at him, and he rolled his eyes.

I knew he didn't mean anything other than show her his 'play toys' as he liked to call his cars. He had a warehouse similar to the one in Paris, where he kept sports cars for whenever he was in the cities he visited often. He had given me a spare key so I could drive whenever I felt like it. It had been exhilarating, watching Selene's face as we raced down the streets after our first dinner date in Paris.

But damn it, Luc was bringing out the worst in me. My hackles rose every time any man looked at her for longer than a few seconds, let alone talked to her. My selfishness to share her with the world rivalled the possessiveness I felt, and I wanted her to play with *my* toys and no other man's, even though the context was different here. I was never good at sharing before, and neither was I now. But I needed to control myself before I ended up handcuffing her to my wrist to keep her by my side.

Luc was reckless at best, and letting him take Selene with him would be insanity. I loved my brother, but sometimes he drove me to madness. I can't even count how many times I'd sat in a hospital room, praying he survived one of his near-fatal accidents. He always bounced back, more energetic than ever.

I shook my head without uttering a word and turned to Adrien. "Come on. Time for bed, Adrien. Say good night to everyone."

After he fell asleep, I went back downstairs and pulled Selene on my lap, enjoying the feel of her body flush to mine. She was wearing a pair of heels, similar to the ones she wore on our date at the restaurant, the day she made a proposal that left my world spinning. She kissed my jaw and then rested her head on my shoulder.

"Have Gilles and his men found out who sent those letters?" she asked quietly. "And just so you know, I don't think it is Adele."

At the back of my mind, I knew it wasn't her. But it didn't stop me from being cautious about the situation. "No. It looks like the person who sent them knows how to hide their trail very well."

Her hands tightened around my arms. "Don't you think it would be easier to involve the police?"

"I would rather solve this without involving them, not that I have anything against the police. The only thing the person has managed to do is send letters and the flowers. Gilles is more than qualified to handle this case. I've known him for a long time, and I trust him completely."

Once again, I searched my mind, wondering which of the women could have been callous enough to send the messages. I glanced at Adele, chatting with Èric, before sparing Gilles a look. He shook his head, and I breathed out in relief at the confirmation. Nothing strange had happened so far. I liked Adele very much. She had been there for me and Adrien. How would I handle the situation if she turned out to be the mysterious stalker? How would I explain that to Adrien?

"Let's go upstairs," Selene whispered, sounding tired and effectively pulling me out of my thoughts.

We said good night to everyone and climbed the stairs. By the time we undressed, Selene had yawned three times in a row as she slipped between the sheets and held out her arms to me. As soon as I settled next to her and wrapped her in my arms, she snuggled into me, tucking her face into my chest and sighed contentedly.

I stayed awake long after she had fallen asleep, thinking about our conversation during dinner. If Gilles didn't find out who this person was by the end of next week, I was going to hand this case over to the police. We hadn't received any new flowers or messages. I was getting nervous and didn't like it.

I pressed a kiss to Selene's hair. As much as my body desired her, she needed her rest. Moreover, holding her completed me and opened doors to things I hadn't allowed myself to think or feel in a long time. And as always, my need to confirm that she was real overcame me, and I slid one hand up to rest where her heart beat steadily in her chest. My arm tightened around her, enjoying the feel of her curvy body, soft and warm nestled in to me, and I closed my eyes as sleep overtook me.

Chapter Thirty-Two

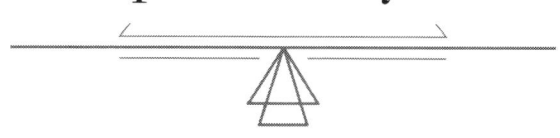

Selene

Right before Dom and Luc left the next day, Luc caught up with me as I was descending the stairs.

"Can I talk to you, Selene?" he asked, the playfulness from yesterday long gone, replaced by a resolute look.

I nodded, following him as he led the way out the back door that led to the patio and gardens. Dom sat in one of the lounge chairs, leaning his head back on the arm of the chair as if absorbing the sun's rays. He opened his brown eyes, so similar to Luc's, and smiled warmly as we joined him.

What is going on?

"We wanted to talk to you." Luc shifted in his seat on my right, leaned forward and braced his elbows on his thighs.

"Is this the 'what's your intention toward our brother' talk?" I grinned, trying to hide how nervous I felt, being the centre of their serious expressions.

They exchanged a look before turning to look at me.

This is not the time to make jokes, Selene.

"Yes, it is," Dom said, putting me out of my misery, and my body loosened a bit. I could handle this. "Remington seems quite taken with you. We have never seen him interested in any woman before. Not like he is with you. Other than Adrien's mother."

I nodded, the urge to grin wide overwhelming. I was beginning to realize how special, how freeing it was to be the centre of Remington's attention as his lover. "I like him a lot, too."

They exchanged another look, and this time I felt as if my stomach had dropped to my toes. "What's wrong?" Was that the wrong thing to say?

Luc cleared his throat. "Remington doesn't know how to 'like.' He shoots straight from casual interest to love. When he loves, he gives himself completely. And when he does that, he doesn't let go easily. He hasn't shown any woman anything other than interest."

I nodded again, letting those words sink in.

"And you think… you think he loves *me*?"

"*Oui*," Luc said. I glanced quickly at Dom. He wasn't much of a talker. I had a feeling he preferred to sit back and study people silently. I returned my focus to Luc. "Remington would kill us if he knew we told you this. But we had to talk to you before we left. Colette almost destroyed him, and we don't want to see that happen again. He's crazy about you." Luc paused as though to allow me some time to let those words sink in. "He is restless when you're not around. I've seen murder in his eyes when he thinks any man is trying to capture your attention for too long. He might not act on his feelings soon. But we wanted you to know. Please just…" Luc looked at me square in the eye, various emotions flashing through his face. He inhaled deeply and said, "I hope you let him down gently when you leave."

I sat back on the chair, pressing a hand on my chest. I could hear Remington's laugh as he and Adrien worked on Adrien's tree house. He had promised him yesterday that they would do that today.

He loves me?

I tried not to let those three little words do crazy things to me. Wasn't it too early in our three-month-agreement relationship to feel that?

"But we've only known each other for a few weeks."

Dom shifted in his chair. "Remington is just—" He paused as if searching for words but ended up saying, "Remington. Whether it's a few weeks or a few days, it doesn't matter."

They were right about that. Remington was just that. Remington. He lived by his own rules and no one else's, which was quite scary if I allowed myself to think about it too much. Scary, because as much as I enjoyed being the centre of his attention and wanted to play by his rules, I had allowed the 'what ifs' to linger in my thoughts far too often. Was I ready to take a step in that direction? I shook my head, shoving those thoughts to the back of my mind.

"Thank you for this," I said, forcing myself to focus on the two men. I could see loyalty and love for their brother as clear as though they had just shouted the words aloud.

After saying their good-byes to everyone, Luc and Dom left. I went upstairs and pretended I was working on my designs. I knew Remington would notice something different about me. I wasn't good at hiding how I felt. I needed some time alone to evaluate the revelation and my own feelings.

The next few days, I mastered the art of being calm. Remington divided his time between working in his office and building a tree house with Adrien. Not to mention our day tours around Provence. Yesterday, we went on a hot air balloon ride at six thirty in the morning. The sunrise was astounding and the landscape, painted in the gold and oranges of autumn, was simply breathtaking.

We cuddled up on the patio at night after everyone had gone to bed, and then later, we slipped between the sheets. Sometimes he'd take his time pleasuring me, and when he finally slipped inside me, he'd make love to me as if he had all the time in the world. Other times he was so impatient and almost desperate that he'd slam his cock into me, pounding me like he couldn't get enough. Remington could be as demanding as he was giving, and I loved that about him.

Today was a lazy day, spent around the swimming pool. I had drawn some lingerie designs and a few marketing strategies. I was excited about how everything was turning out.

Right after dinner, we settled down on the patio, sipping wine. Adrien, as usual, was a whirlwind of energy, running along well-lit pathways and finally dropping on either my lap or his father's.

Earlier today I'd called my parents to let them know I was doing well. The only person I told about Remington was Marley. I didn't tell my parents because there was nothing to tell, really. This was temporary, and I knew they'd worry about me. They had already done enough of that to last them a lifetime. I forced any thoughts of leaving France out of my mind and simply enjoyed the moment.

Adrien hopped on my lap and pulled up his knees before fully focusing on me. Jesus, the boy's eyes, so much like his father's, disarmed me.

I combed the locks off his forehead with one hand, smiling at him. "What is it, honey?"

He pursed his lips, shifted on my lap, and said, "Can I call you Mama?"

I almost choked on my wine. My throat closed, and I

clutched the glass tightly in my hand. From the corner of my eye, I saw Remington go still. I couldn't face him because I didn't want him to see the devastation tearing at my heart.

Adrien blinked up at me, his huge eyes full of unguarded hope.

"Could you please bring the wine opener from the kitchen, Adrien?" Remington's voice interrupted the panic storming inside me.

Adrien hopped down from my lap and shuffled his way into the kitchen.

"Selene. I am so sorry for that. I've been foolish to assume something like this would never happen," Remington said, colour rising on his ears. "He loves you, but I never expected him to say something like that. I'll talk to him when he comes back."

I swallowed and shook my head. "No need to apologize. He has good taste," I said, trying to ease the tension swirling around us. Before I could say something else, Adrien returned with the wine opener, gave it to his father, and turned to look at me. God, the look in his eyes completely wiped out any reservations in me. Adrien and Remington were both my strength and my weakness. Adrien had a way of filling the hole in my chest because he loved wholeheartedly. Remington gave me back something I'd been missing all those years. He made me realize my sexuality, and every single look from him made me feel like I mattered. He also loved freely and strongly when he finally dropped the hot-and-cold mood swings. However, my stay in France was short. Forming any attachments would end up destroying us. Me. After James, I had promised myself I would never let myself be vulnerable again. Yet here I was. However, this time, someone else needed me. Remington depended on me for more than just sex. We had both gone through so much in our lives. We understood each other.

It hit me then. Flirting wasn't something I could do without getting my heart involved. I had unwittingly become deeply involved in this relationship and if something would ever happen to Adrien and Remington ...I shut my eyes tight, not wanting to think about it, and when I opened them again, Adrien's big, green eyes were on me, waiting. Why wasn't Remington saying anything?

I flicked a gaze at him, catching his guarded expression.

"Come here, Adrien." Remington held out his hand to his son, the look on his face heartbreakingly gentle. Adrien flicked a gaze at his father before turning to me. I bit back a smile as I watched the father-son interaction. Remington had just been served the I'm-busy-right-now look. Exasperation filled Remington's face, and his lips tightened in irritation. He moved to stand up.

"Don't you want to call me Selene anymore?" I asked quickly before Remington could haul the boy away. From the corner of my eyes, I saw him shift on the edge of his seat.

He shook his head. "I don't have a mama, and all the children in my class have mothers." He squinted and cocked his head to the side, as if mulling over something in his head. "Well, what do you think, Papa?"

Finally, Remington stood up, pulled his son toward him and onto his lap. "Selene is with us for a short time. She has to go back home eventually, you know." His expression said differently. Why did he have to be so confusing?

"I know, Papa. Why can't she stay here with us forever? You love her and she loves you, no? I've seen you kiss her, and only people who love each other kiss."

Remington stared at me with a look I was becoming used to. A look that dried my throat and mouth, and one that spoke of so many things without uttering a single word.

His gaze left mine, and he took a deep breath. He seemed conflicted, unlike the man I'd come to know.

"Excuse me, I'll be right back." I stood up and left for the bathroom, shaking my head slightly when I saw Remington shift in his chair as if he wanted to follow me.

Inside the bathroom, I locked the door and braced my back on it. I took deep breaths, trying to calm my speeding heart.

Shit. What was I going to tell Adrien? The boy held my heart in his tiny hands. Was there a way this could work when I returned to the US?

I had to talk to Remington before confirming anything to Adrien.

After splashing cold water on my face, I patted it dry with a towel and went back to the patio. Remington and Adrien were thumb wrestling, and it looked like the boy was winning—his father was letting him. My chest warmed all over again. *Damn stupid heart.*

Adrien yelled my name from his father's lap and told me he had won. I chuckled at the comical pretend-defeated look on his father's face.

If Remington had intended the game to be a distraction, it didn't work because the next minute, Adrien fixed those adorable eyes on me and asked, "Can I, Selene? Can I call you Mama?" The wall of resistance crumbled completely.

"Yes, honey. You can call me Mama." The words poured from my lips before I could stop them, negating the decision I had made in the bathroom.

Crap, crap, crap! I opened my mouth to rectify the situation, but Adrien was already scrambling off his father's lap and hurtling toward me. I caught him in a hug.

Remington stared at me, caught between anger, shock,

and disbelief, and what I thought was the slightest touch of hope.

"Time for bed, Adrien." His voice was firm as he stood from his chair.

What have I done?

Adrien gave me a wet kiss on my cheek. *"Je t'aime, Selene,"* he whispered, pulling back and holding my face in his small hands.

My eyes burned, and I swear my heart did this crazy dance inside my chest. I never expected to ever hear those words from him. Somewhere in the back of my mind, I knew this was a point of no return for me. For him. *"Moi aussi, je t'aime, Adrien,"* I said, smiling. He planted another kiss on my cheek and sprinted upstairs. I quickly brushed my eyes with my fingers just as Remington turned around to face me, rifling his fingers through his hair and tugging it back.

"You had no right to tell him that, Selene. Why didn't you wait to talk about this with me first?" He started pacing, his hands propped on his hips. "I've been trying to protect him from situations like this, but I met you. And somehow, I couldn't stop myself from seeing you." He seemed angrier with himself than with me.

"I'm sorry," I whispered, feeling my eyes burn. I blinked back the tears. I wasn't going to do that now. "I know I shouldn't have told him to call me that, but …" I let the words trail off, unable to finish them.

He dragged his fingers through his hair again, stared at me for a few seconds, looking as if he wanted to say something. His eyes filled with regret and confusion before he turned and stalked out of the room. This situation was getting complicated too fast.

Shit! Had I messed this up? The thought that Adrien

might one day ask something like this never occurred to me. It should have, but I was busy soaking up each moment with them. His question had thrown me into a tailspin. All I could think about was the hopeful look of longing on his face and the constant craving that feasted on my memories of what could have been. I should have been prepared, but I was blinded by my stupid feelings. My vision blurred. I swiped a hand on my cheeks to wipe the tears.

God, give me strength to handle this.

I went inside the château to wait for Remington in the living room.

He came down the stairs half an hour later and stalked into the kitchen, his stride a combination of fury and elegance, and I was still turned on. What was wrong with me?

I straightened, watched him as he poured wine into two glasses even though we had unfinished wine on the patio, and then strode into the living room and slid one toward me. He placed his on the table, took the seat opposite me, and continued to brood in silence while he stared at me the entire time. The look on his face was one I imagined a cat would wear while watching a mouse run around in circles before finally pouncing on it. I lost my patience, and the hopelessness I had felt moments ago melted away.

I am stronger than the woman who was married to James. Remington and I needed to be honest and talk about things.

"Do you want to talk about this or what?"

He steepled his fingers, pressing them against his lips.

Anger flared inside my chest, setting my blood on fire. I hadn't allowed myself to feel anger in a long time, so it felt refreshing for that dam to burst. "You pursued me, Remington. I was gone, but you followed me to that hotel and pulled me back. What did you think was supposed to happen? Please understand I'm not heaping any blame on you, but damn it, Remington. You pursued me." *And brought me back to life.*

He continued to watch me silently, his eyes narrowed and his hair tousled from dragging his fingers through it. I'd forgotten how sexy Brooding Remington could be.

I shot from the seat and stomped across the room with no particular direction in mind. I was annoyed with myself, with Remington, and the stupid threat looming over our heads. Then the floodgates of my soul burst open. The old hurts, fears, and rage I'd locked away nearly two years ago flared to life, and I jerked to a stop and whirled around.

"Aren't you going to say anything?"

He sat back, stretched out his legs, and watched my little tirade, his expression unreadable. The urge to get a reaction out of him was overwhelming. I glanced at the glass of wine, then down at my feet. Probably throwing a shoe at him would be safer than the glass.

"Oh my God, Remington. You are so frustrating!" No reaction. "Oh, fuck off!" I shouted at him, spinning around and heading upstairs. I hadn't spoken that word out loud in a long time, and it felt very liberating. "Fuck you very much," I muttered under my breath, but loud enough for the words to travel across the quiet room and slap him in the face. The effect was ruined when I brushed my face and felt the tears burning a trail down my cheeks.

I reached the landing, made a beeline for his room, and froze, glancing at the rest of the rooms down the hall. If he wasn't at least going to talk to me, I wasn't sleeping in his bed. I hoped he'd be cooled off by morning. I hurried inside his room, grabbed my toothbrush, camisole, and sleeping shorts and left.

"Where do you think you are going?"

I stopped and turned around. "So you want to talk now? Leave me alone. I'm tired."

His gaze fell on the stuff in my hands. He closed the distance between us in two long strides and tugged the items from my grasp. At the same time, his free hand went around my waist, pulling me close, and his lips were on mine in no time.

"Leaving you alone is not something I can do, Selene. Don't you know that by now?" he murmured against my lips.

I pushed his chest with my hands, but he didn't budge. Instead, he pushed his lips to mine, nipping my bottom lip and forcing my mouth open while his hand gripped my hip in slow, tantalizing squeezes that sent shivers up and down my spine. His tongue plunged into my mouth in deliberate strokes. I could taste the sweet flavour from the wine. My cami and shorts dropped to the floor, and his fingers circled the nape of my neck, holding me in place. The kiss shifted; he kissed me furiously as if punishing me for something I had done. The anger that had been roaming my body minutes ago morphed into lust, and my hands sank into his hair, tugging and holding him in place.

"I was an idiot," he said hoarsely, pressing his forehead against mine.

"Y—yes, you were," I breathed out the words. "You hurt me."

"I'm sorry."

"You should be. Why didn't you let me go when I left your house? If you didn't want Adrien getting close to me, you shouldn't have let me in your lives."

"I'm very sorry," he said remorsefully. "I have never been in a situation like this before. I handled this badly, Selene. I promised myself I'd never hurt you, but I did that tonight. Tell me what I can do to make it up to you." He was quiet for a few seconds. "You told me to fuck off." He sounded amused.

"And I meant it."

"Hearing that word from your mouth was very sexy."

I rolled my eyes, moving away from his arms. "You were angry with me for what I told Adrien." It wasn't a question, just a statement.

"At first I was. Then I realized I was angrier with myself than I was at you."

I remembered what he said before, and anger stirred back to life in my blood. "So you regret letting me into your lives?"

"No. Never." He bit his bottom lip between his teeth and peered at me under his lashes. "Are you going to tell me to fuck off?" The side of his mouth quirked up and he reached out, grabbing my upper arm and dragging me back into his embrace.

"I'm going to bed." I finally wrenched free and grabbed my stuff from the floor, heading toward one of the guest rooms.

"Don't walk away from me, Selene." His voice sounded so close. When I looked over my shoulder, his face was all I could see as he trailed nearby. He grabbed my arm, spun me around, and before I could gasp, I was in his arms again, and he was stalking toward his room.

"Do you know what it feels like to watch you walk away from me, Selene?" His breath was warm against my cheek.

"Pain. It feels as though my chest has been cut open, and my heart ripped from it. I don't like it."

My heart broke a little at his words. This confident, proud man had been hurt so deeply, yet he was strong enough to utter such honest feelings. James did a lot of damage to my self-esteem. Remington seemed to be intent on building it back up again, and comments like these did so much to my heart. However, in some ways, I was still angry with myself and also the way we'd handled the situation. Yes, it was selfish of us, and perhaps as we had continued this dance, we had neglected to consider the impact on Adrien's young heart. Remington thought I had the ability to rip his heart from him, but he and his son held mine. I was completely at their mercy. I remembered the conversation I had with Luc and Dom a few days ago. I opened my mouth and answered him honestly. "I'll never walk away from you."

He nodded, and the demons in his eyes receded. "And no, I don't regret meeting you. Never."

Chapter Thirty-Three

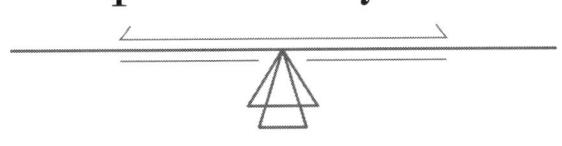

Remington

I'll never walk away from you.

Selene's words rang through my mind as I placed her on the bed and immediately missed the feel of her body in my arms. I was trying hard to restrain myself from tearing our clothes off and burying myself inside her. Taking deep breaths, I helped her out of her clothes before stripping mine with shaking hands. I desperately needed to feel her naked body around mine. It calmed me.

I had been so angry after what she told Adrien, and when I went back downstairs later, I knew I wasn't angry with her. I was angry with myself. I had no control over time, which was slipping through my fingers, fast. In a little over two months she would leave France, leave Adrien and me. My affection for her had roots, and they kept digging deeper with every passing second.

I had nearly broken the promise I made when I decided to pursue her after she left my townhouse: to enjoy the little time I had with Selene and not to waste it on trivial matters. Although now I saw I had been missing out. Seeing Selene angry had been a turn-on. I had stared at her like a bloody fool, speechless. Her eyes had lit up with unconcealed fury, and her chest heaved with laboured breaths. She had been quite a sight. Maybe I'll just break my rule and make her angry more often.

She glanced up at me, stubbornness glinting in her eyes.

"Let's take one day at a time. We will deal with everything when the time comes. Are you okay with Adrien calling you that?"

She bit the corner of her bottom lip, her eyes searching mine. Her face had always been quite easy to read, but right now, it was impossible to do so. "Are you? He's your son, Remington. You need to decide this."

We locked gazes, communicating without words. She looked so certain, and I suspected she needed this. I had seen how her demeanour changed whenever she was with Adrien. It was like everything around her faded. I had done my son an injustice. He needed this, a woman who loved him fiercely and vice versa, someone he could call "mother." Every child needed someone like Selene, loveable and freely giving of her love, but that didn't mean I could let her shoulder this responsibility. I scrutinized her face longer, searching for a sign that told me she wasn't sure about this decision, but all I saw was a fierceness born from the decision she'd already made.

Finally, I nodded and pulled her into my arms, curling my body behind her. I simply held her. Then something occurred to me. As much as my need to be inside her at this moment was as ferocious as it was the first time I saw her, having her in my arms released another kind of calm within me. I couldn't explain it, though.

I didn't want to define it.

Chapter Thirty-Four

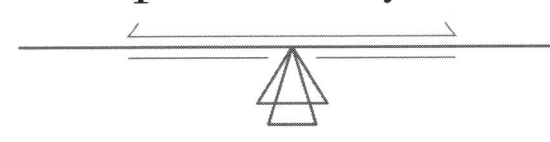

Selene

I woke up feeling anxious, hopeless, and empty. I couldn't breathe, and the room felt as if it were closing in on me. My chest hurt, and I felt as though my heart had bled dry during the night, even though I had spent most of it curled in Remington's arms.

My body trembled as sweat poured from my temples and body, soaking my cami.

Oh, God, not now. I couldn't be having one of my panic attacks here with Remington lying next to me. The last time I had one was over six months ago, which had freaked the crap out of my family. I'd been living at home with my parents and sister, and without warning, I had begun hyperventilating.

I glanced over my shoulder at Remington, illuminated by the moon spilling from the window, sleeping with his lips slightly parted. I slowly pulled his hands from my waist. They tightened slightly but relaxed again. I stumbled to the bathroom as nausea rose into my throat. I braced my hands on the sink and heaved. Nothing came out. I tried again, my eyes stinging with tears. Finally, my knees gave way, and I sank to the floor.

God, I was dying. I had to leave the château. I needed air, and my heart was beating wildly in my chest. Then huge sobs escaped my lips. I didn't even know why I was crying, but the tears kept falling. I remember on the night I had the attack months ago, my mother had held me in her arms and rocked me. She'd told me that crying was a way of cleansing the heart of heartache and pain. However, this felt worse than that night, and I wasn't sure my heart could take it anymore.

I trembled, my body going from hot to cold, and I whimpered. I drew my legs to my chest and tried to take deep breaths like those that I had practiced with my therapist.

In. Out. In. Out.

My breathing slowed, but I was still shivering and cold. I craved warmth, but there was no way I could reach the shower.

Will Remington think I am weak if I wake him?

Somehow, I didn't care. He had already seen me at one of my weakest and most vulnerable times when I told him about losing my baby. Not only that, but he knew what it was like to be terrified, paralyzed by fear.

"R-Remington," I called out, my teeth chattering. I called his name again, but my voice wasn't loud enough. Nausea hit me again, and I leaned to the side and heaved, unable to hoist myself to my feet.

"Selene? *Mon Dieu*, what's wrong?"

"I'm s—so cold," I whimpered. "So sorry to wake you up—"

"Shh." He dropped at my side, snatching me up and wrapping me in his arms and hot body. "Take deep breaths."

"I did."

"Do it again. Slowly."

I did as ordered, filling my lungs and letting it all out. He rubbed his hand on my back and along my arms, and my body started to warm up against his, my muscles relaxing with every breath.

"Wait here. I'll go and start the shower."

I nodded, missing his warmth as soon as he left my side. He returned moments later and reached out for my hands. I stood up, and he quickly scooped me in his arms and stepped into the shower. He put me down on my feet, sat down, and pulled me into his lap.

"Better?"

"Yes, thank you." After a few minutes with hot water beating on our backs, I whispered, "Sorry for this."

"You should never apologize for something you can't control. What happened?"

I told him what happened and then wiped my eyes and gave him a wobbly smile. "This is the kind of madness you'll have on your hands if you stick with me. I'm a mess, Remington. Sometimes I am such a mess that I don't know my right from my left."

He ducked his head to meet my gaze. "I don't see any madness. What I see is a strong woman. Life has knocked you down several times, and you're still standing."

I chuckled, a sound between a sob and a laugh. "I keep asking myself why I didn't know you before."

"Because, like everything in life, this is how it was meant to be. Life doesn't give us reasons. It just gives and takes. It's a bastard."

He held me longer, urging me to take deep breaths while murmuring endearments, encouraging me, distracting me.

We stepped out of the shower and dried ourselves. After wrapping our bodies with towels, Remington settled me in the bed, then went to the kitchen and returned holding a mug filled with some liquid, steam rising from it.

"Drink this slowly."

I took the mug, lifted it to my lips and blew to cool it before taking a sip. Chamomile tea. He nodded in encouragement for me to take another sip. When I was done, he took the mug and placed it on the nightstand. He headed for the closet and returned with two T-shirts and two pairs of boxer shorts.

I dressed and then looked up at him. "How did you know about the tea?"

He shrugged. "My mother used to make this for me when I was young. She'd say it cured anxiety." He smiled fondly. I nodded, smiling back at him as I slipped between the sheets. "Never, ever think you are weak, Selene. And, please know you can wake me up anytime, all right?" he whispered in my ear as he settled behind me, moving his front flush to my back.

I nodded, snuggled into him and absorbed his warmth into my body. Remington charmed, spoiled, challenged, comforted, and made love to me in equal measures. Shit, there went the waterworks. It was quite overwhelming when I thought about it too much, so I refused to dwell on it. "Thank you for everything," I whispered in the dark. He swept the hair off my shoulder and kissed my cool skin, his arm tightening on my waist.

I lay there in his embrace, breathing and re-evaluating my breakdown. My therapist had warned me even though the attacks had lessened through the years, they might be triggered by something as small as seeing a child smile or seeing a pregnant woman. Adrien's question must have prompted it.

I needed to get ahold of myself to avoid incidents like this from happening again. I closed my eyes, allowing Remington's hard, warm body to guide me into my dreams of him.

Chapter Thirty-Five

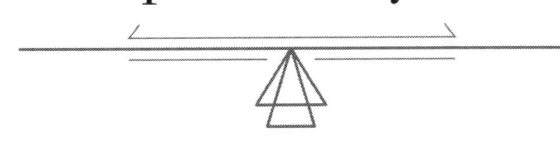

Selene

I woke up to the feel of Remington's lips on my body, his strong, eager hands kneading my breasts, and his fingers teasing my nipples.

"Good morning, *ma belle*."

I moaned and stretched as he took one breast in his mouth. "This …I love waking up to this."

"Stay," he whispered, his voice hoarse and full of need. "Stay with me and I can spoil you like this forever."

My eyes snapped open, and I felt his hands freeze. My head swam, prompted with all kinds of possibilities provoked by his words, feeding that part of my heart that longed for this. A man like Remington.

He buried his face into the crook of my neck, his warm breath fanning my skin. "I am sorry. I shouldn't have said that."

Disappointment shot through my blood, settling low in my stomach.

I shook my head. "It's fine."

He pulled back and fixed his gaze on me, his bottom lip caught between his teeth. "Truth time." I shook my head, not in the mood to play any kind of games, but he held my face in his hands. "What would you do if I asked you to stay a little bit longer?"

"I would tell you that I couldn't."

"You couldn't? Or are you afraid?"

"We've known each other for a very short time, and my family is back in New York." He continued to stare at me. "Remington, you don't know me. You don't know the girl inside this body. Remember what happened last night?"

"I do."

"And?"

"And what?"

I pushed him off me and sat up, watching him as he sprawled on the bed, naked and, oh, Jesus, so beautiful. "Remington, weren't you scared? I'm sorry that you had to see me like that. And I can't tell when something like that might happen again.

He stared at me calmly, one hand thrown behind his head. "Are you done?" He squinted his gorgeous, all-knowing eyes at me, and I could feel them focus on my fears. Don't get me wrong; I was confident about myself, and I had worked very hard to be where I was today. But times like these snuck up on me, reminding me that beneath my facade was a woman still trying to find her footing. Remington's easy acceptance of me, especially after he witnessed one of my worst fears, had thrown me off guard.

I slid out of bed, headed into the bathroom, stripped off my clothing and hopped in the shower, wanting some distance to gather my thoughts away from his distracting gaze.

Why wasn't I happy about this? Remington cared, and he didn't seem shocked after what he saw last night. Then the truth hit me hard. I sucked in a breath and leaned my forehead on the opposite wall to absorb the impact of what I was feeling. I *was* happy, but at the same time, I was terrified of taking that step and opening myself completely to this man.

I heard the shower door open and then slide shut behind me. Cool air swirled around me before a hard body pressed against my back. Remington's arm circled my waist as he swept my hair to one side, kissed my shoulder and then nipped my skin, and I felt the fire ignite low in my belly.

"We all have our demons, and every once in a while, we have to dance with them, embrace them. Having bad memories doesn't make you broken," he murmured against my skin, punctuating his words with a kiss. "It doesn't change a thing about who you are. Even if you were broken, I would take a chance and glue all the pieces together, to make you whole. Because you're worth it. Life is a gigantic ball full of heartaches, breakups, both good and bad memories, making up, and falling in love. It's messy, but it's also fun. "

God, what is he doing to me? He says all the right things at the right time. He disarms me.

He splayed his fingers on my stomach, pulling me into his body. "If you think for a second that I'm bothered by what happened last night, I'm not. I admire your strength and will to go on, even after everything that has happened to you. "

I couldn't take it anymore. I turned in his arms and kissed him hungrily. He pushed me against the shower wall, returning my kiss with fervour, and murmuring endearments under his breath. I soaked up the words, soaked up the kiss, and soaked up every single breath he poured into me.

"Your legs." He said the words against my lips. "Put them around me."

I did, at the same time he slipped his hand between our bodies, stroking me before guiding his cock to my pussy. He leaned forward so the hot water ran down his back. I couldn't take my eyes from his even if I wanted to.

He kissed me firmly, then slammed into me hard, and I groaned. A stream of French words poured from his mouth as he thumped the wall with a fist. "God, you feel fucking incredible. What's your pleasure, Selene?"

I squirmed and moaned in desperate need of friction. I cupped his neck and yanked him down, nipping his throat, and he trembled, groaned again, pulled back before thrusting back in. "Yes. Just like that. Remington!" I screamed into his shoulder as he continued to leave me both speechless and thoughtless.

"You're not perfect, Selene. I wouldn't be this crazy about you if you were perfect. You hear me?" He rammed his cock into me to make his point.

"Yes! Oh, my God, Remington, yes!" I threw my head back, and his mouth found my neck, kissing and nipping hungrily. "Please, fuck me harder! God, I love it when you do that."

He slowed his thrusts, grabbing my thighs and squeezing them.

I moaned, ragged breaths filling the room. "Why did you stop? I need you so damn bad, Remington."

"Did you hear what I said?" He rolled his hips torturously slow, grinding himself into me.

I blinked at him, wiggling my butt, my lust-filled brain unable to comprehend what he wanted from me.

He groaned deeply, slid out of me and then reached around me to turn off the water. Then he pushed the shower door open, cupped my ass in his large hands to stop me from sliding down his body and carefully negotiated his way on the stone floor as he headed for the marble counter. He put me down, and as soon as my feet touched the floor, he growled, "Turn around."

I did, my skin humming at the closeness of his tightly coiled body against my back. God, he looked sexy and untouchable. "Tell me what you want to do to me." I peeked at him over my shoulder and met his dark, hooded gaze.

"First, I need to make something clear, even if it means fucking you senseless to get the point through."

"What point?"

"You're not perfect."

"Damn it, Remington, can't we have this conversation later?" He wielded his 'stare into submission' look. When I didn't reply quickly, he pressed a hand on my shoulder, bending over, and then pressed my lower back, grabbed my hips and slammed into me. I screamed his name, panting.

"You're not perfect," he repeated again. "And everything about you drives me insane." He pulled back and thrust deep inside me. "*Est-ce clair?*

"Clear as a bell," I gritted out the words. I was close to orgasm, but I couldn't reach it if he kept torturing me like this. "I want to come, Remington. I can't take it anymore."

He pressed his lips to my ear while his hands squeezed my butt, before slipping a finger to stroke my clit. "I love how wet you are for me, Selene. You better hold on tight and get ready to scream my name because I'm going to fuck your sweet pussy. I'm going to own it, *ma belle. This.*" He cupped me with one hand. My body trembled as his words slid down my body, sending heat straight between my legs. "Hands on the counter."

I did as I was told, eager for him to own every part of me. He already did anyway. His hand skimmed over my lower back and then pressed gently. He brought his free hand to my chin and tugged it up.

"Look how beautiful you are, Selene." My gaze met his in the mirror. "Keep your eyes on the mirror."

He pulled his hand back, slid out of me and back in again,

his eyes never leaving mine. His jaw was clenched tightly as if he were in pain; however, his eyes said differently. They held so much emotion I was terrified of acknowledging it, so I focused on how he made me feel. This was exquisite torture. I pressed back, but he gripped my hips, a warning flashing in his eyes.

"Hold on tight, Selene."

I gripped the counter tightly as he began pounding into me furiously. His lips were parted in pleasure, the sounds coming from his mouth spurring me on. Just seeing the look on his face—a mix of wild hunger and tenderness—weakened my knees. He quickly caught me around the waist and continued to pump into me. My climax hit me hard.

"Don't even think about closing those beautiful eyes." He growled out the words that proved to be my undoing. My body shivered as I rode my orgasm, and Remington followed me not long after. Unable to hold myself up, I slumped forward and he leaned on me, kissing me on my temple, down my neck and spine.

Oh. My. God. That was intense. Remington had a way of making every session an all-consuming experience.

Is this how it would always be if I stayed? Could I have this in my forever?

Chapter Thirty-Six

Remington

Like every morning, my day started out with running alongside Selene at five thirty. She rarely slept in, and I wasn't very fond of letting her run alone.

The last few days, I watched her closely, checking for any signs of a panic attack. I still shuddered every time I remembered walking into the bathroom and finding her curled on the floor, how terrified I was at first before I realized what was really happening. Every time Adrien called her Mama, my eyes would automatically hone in on her, waiting. She would smile and as soon as he turned away, her eyes would glaze over, her thoughts sweeping her to a place only she knew. I'd walk up to her and pull her in my arms, and she would hold me as if she depended on my strength to keep her afloat. She'd say, "He is a cutie," with awe in her voice, and my reply as always was, "Yes. With an extra dose of mischief," and then she would laugh.

We returned to the château an hour later after our run, showered together, and took breakfast on the terrace. Today, Selene, Adele, Adrien, and Èric were going out for a morning excursion. I opted to stay behind and finish some paperwork for an upcoming art auction scheduled to take place at the end of October. I also planned to call Gilles. He'd left for Paris four days ago. He called me yesterday and informed me that his office had been broken into. He was yet to confirm the extent of the damage. Whoever the burglar was had made sure to ask him to stop his investigations by leaving a letter similar to the one I'd received a while back. I couldn't imagine anyone who was resourceful enough to infiltrate a security company's office, and not just any company, but Gilles's.

At ten o'clock, after meeting with Monsieur Laurent, the estate's winemaker, I took a break to see Selene and the gang off.

"We are leaving for Saint Didier. Adrien wanted to visit the Jardin trains again," Selene said, coming down the stairs. At the same time, Adrien came rushing into the living room and toward me. I scooped him up and hugged him.

"Sele—Mama is taking me to see the trains. Come with us, please, Papa?"

"I have a bit of work to do. How about you and I play in the swimming pool when you come back?"

He nodded and wrapped his arms around my neck. „Je t'aime, Papa!"

„Moi aussi, je t'aime, Adrien."

He squirmed from my arms and ran toward Adele.

"Hey, Adele, are you enjoying yourself?" I asked her, watching her hover near the door.

"Yes." She gave me her usual calm smile and waved, walking out the door. I scrutinized her face. If her feelings extended further than employee to employer, then she had a talent of hiding it well.

"Adrien adores her," Selene said, wrapping a hand around my waist as I walked her out to the car. "And I believe her attentions are now claimed by another."

I laughed. "So does that mean she doesn't give me the lover's eyes anymore?" I asked teasingly. She swatted my chest, smiling.

"You get the lover's eyes from me and no one else." She lifted her chin up, the look on her face pure stubbornness.

I cocked an eyebrow, surprised. I had sensed irritation from her when women looked at me. She had made a point of claiming my hand with hers or a quick kiss on my lips. But she had never said a word. I felt pleased to hear those words now.

"That goes both ways," I murmured, eyeing Èric. He seemed less bothered by whatever was going on. "Did you call your family at home?"

She nodded. "My mother went back to the hospital and will be starting the insulin therapy in a few days. How about you? Have you spoken to your mom?"

"She signed a contract with a wine distributor in London and will be back home in a couple of days." She frowned at the information. I made a note to talk about that later, and I kissed her as I fought the urge to haul her over my shoulder and carry her upstairs. It seemed like my mind always wandered in that direction these days.

We stopped next to the car and I stood back, watching as everyone settled inside, then stepped back and waved as the car sped off. I glanced up at the darkening skies. We had talked about Selene's trip to Berlin. Grace had called two days earlier to let her know that the deal had gone through and she would need to be in Berlin by Thursday the following week. At least we had six more days before her trip. As much as I wanted to keep her close to me, I couldn't. Èric would travel with her for this trip. And yes, his interest for her had diminished. I had made sure to lay my claim on her with a touch or a kiss without resorting to thumping my chest and growling whenever he stared at her longer than necessary. I still needed the man on my side, and I didn't see any reason to make things awkward. I smiled at the thought as I turned and went back to my office.

Chapter Thirty-Seven

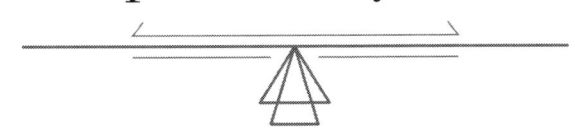

Selene

Thirty minutes into our drive, it began to rain, the heavy drops beating relentlessly on the roof of the car. Adrien was cuddled into me, sleeping and unaware of his surroundings. Adele and Èric kept sneaking heated glances at each other. I had noticed this tension-filled exchange during the last couple of days. I hadn't been certain, but the way they were acting in the car confirmed to me that they were, in fact, attracted to each other.

Good for them.

The sound of a phone ringing interrupted Adele and Èric's constant glances in the mirror.

Oh, thank goodness!

Their staring contest had reached the point I wanted to yell at them to just stop somewhere on the country road and fuck each other's brains out. She wasn't much of a talker, but still, it was painful and uncomfortable to watch them.

Adele dropped her gaze as she dug out her phone from her pants pockets, and a little frown formed on her smooth forehead, her eyes on the screen. She answered, speaking in a low voice, and her eyes levelled on her lap the entire conversation. By the time she was done talking, her face was pale and her body was shaking.

Èric shot me a questioning look, any signs of flirting long gone. I shook my head and focused on Adele.

"Adele?" She raised her face, her blue eyes swimming in tears. "What's wrong? What happened?"

She shook her head and pressed her fingers to her lips. "I must speak with Remington. Please … God … Èric?"

The sound of Èric's name spoken in a broken whisper was enough to have him making a U-turn on the empty country road and racing back the way we had come.

As soon as the car pulled to a stop outside the château, Adele jumped out of the car and bolted for the door. I balanced Adrien in my arms and followed Adele inside with Èric in tow, holding an umbrella over our heads. After setting Adrien on a nearby sofa in the living room, I headed for Remington's office. Adele was pacing inside the room, wringing her hands, while Remington sat back in his swivel chair, his forehead scrunched up in an expression of confusion.

"What's going on?" he asked, his gaze moving between Adele, Èric, and me before settling back on Adele.

When Adele didn't answer, Remington stood and walked toward a built-in cabinet and poured some sort of alcohol from a decanter. He strolled back and shoved the glass into her hands.

"Drink," he ordered softly.

She did and then blinked rapidly, her eyes watering even more. Shit, that must have been some strong stuff. It seemed to have given her the boost she needed. Her back straightened, but just as she was about to speak, the house phone rattled mercilessly on Remington's desk.

I touched her arm to draw her attention. "Come, sit over

here." I pulled a chair for her next to the desk while Remington tended to his call.

"What the hell do you want?" Remington literally snarled into the phone.

Immediately, I pitied whoever was on the other end of the line.

His back was to us, so I couldn't see his face. He dragged his tense fingers through his hair and rested them on the nape of his neck.

"Caleb?" He sounded shocked. "What happened?"

Adele shifted on the chair. A few tendrils escaped from her neatly-coiffed hair, and her fingers started fiddling with the edge of her blouse.

When Remington was done with his call, he replaced the handset but didn't turn around. I moved around to stand in front on him.

"Baby, what's wrong?" I asked, ducking my head and meeting his stricken eyes.

"I have to leave for London."

London? Is his mother okay? Or his brother? He'd mentioned his half-brother's name at the museum a while ago.

"When?"

"Caleb was taken to the hospital this afternoon. The doctors are still doing some tests, but they think his kidneys aren't working as they should."

"You'll travel to London to see him?" Adele asked, infusing so much hope in that single sentence.

He cast a look at Adele and nodded.

"Thank God," she whispered under her breath. "He needs you."

He needs you? How does she know? And why is she so concerned about this situation?

Because Remington was distracted by his thoughts, I guessed he hadn't absorbed what she'd said. But seconds later, he frowned and then turned to face her, a million and one questions flashing in his eyes.

"You know him? You know Caleb?"

Adele nodded, wiping her cheeks with the back of her hand. "Caleb … he's my brother."

Chapter Thirty-Eight

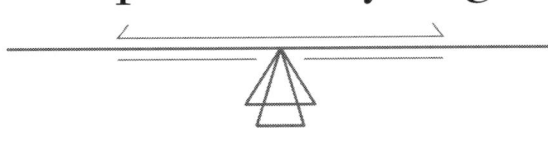

Remington

My pulse thudded hard in my ears, and my vision blurred.

"What did you just say?" Had the shock of hearing my father's voice on the telephone damaged my hearing? Sure, this had been the first time in over twenty years that he had thought of calling me. The worse thing about it was that it hadn't been his idea. Caleb asked him to do it. Probably forced him to do it.

I reined in the rage that thoughts of my father provoked in me and focused on the issue at hand.

"Could you please excuse us, Èric?"

He nodded, then flicked a worried look at Adele before turning and leaving.

"Caleb is my brother," she said in a quiet voice.

I pulled away from Selene's arms and stalked toward Adele.

She stared at me with red-rimmed eyes as if begging me to understand. "I'm your half-sister, Remington."

The impact of those words hit me squarely in the chest.

Is this some kind of joke?

"Your mother named you after our father. Remington."

"The only thing I inherited from him," I spat. "I don't remember Caleb mentioning you. He is an only child as far as I know."

She shook her head. "He's my older brother. He's ten years older than I am. He told me you two attended the same boarding school in Hertfordshire."

I continued to watch her, my mind wandering back to the best two years of my life before my mother moved back to France from London. All I had needed was my best friend who was my brother, Caleb, and my mother.

"Caleb also told me how my father behaved toward you. Those two years in that school were the best of his life, and he regrets the way things went after you and your mother left for France."

I started to pace the length of my office, confusion and hurt raging a war inside me. "Why didn't you tell me the truth? Is your name even Adele? You have been living under my roof. You befriended my son and me while pretending to be someone you were not. You know how I feel about being lied to, but you have done exactly that for four years. Fucking hell, Adele. Why did you do it?"

"I was afraid of how you would react if you knew who I was. I knew you hated our father, and the only person you had a connection with was our brother. You see, after Caleb told me everything, I wanted to get to know you. So I decided to take matters into my own hands. After secondary school, I procured papers to show that I'd previously worked as a nanny. I got references from some parents I had babysat for in my teens. My name is Adele, but I changed my surname, Newport to Dufort." She stood up and blocked my path, a very bold move. I stopped pacing and glared at her. "Remington, I'm very sorry for lying to you, but I did it out of necessity. I know this isn't a good reason; however, I hope that you'll understand why I did this."

My hands itched to punch something; at the same time, I wanted to take her in my arms and comfort her. Then Selene was right there beside me, covering my twitching hand with her smaller, softer one. Some of the tension left my body, but most of it churned inside my stomach.

I have a sister, and she has been living in my house.

"How old are you?"

"Twenty-three."

I couldn't stay in this room any longer. I had to leave to sort through all this new information before I said something that I'd regret later. I turned away from her. "We will talk about this later."

I turned to leave, my feet eager to pound some ground to purge everything I was feeling.

"I'm leaving tonight."

Merde!

I breathed in deeply, closing my eyes and letting Selene's touch on my back calm me. I felt betrayed, lost, and manipulated. I could throw Adele out the front door, but wouldn't that make me worse than my father? I had spent the entirety of my teenage years and adulthood trying not to let my childhood shape who I was. I had succeeded.

"Èric will drive you to the airport." I started to walk out of the room with Selene's fingers twined with mine, but I stopped at the door. "I will see you in London, Adele."

She smiled, tears streaming down her face and hurried toward me. "Thank you, Remington. You are a good man. I love you, big brother." She lifted on her toes and without warning, kissed my cheeks, then ran out and up the flight of stairs to her room.

Selene stepped in front of me, her eyes searching mine.

"I need to go."

"Where?" she asked, her eyes wide and worried.

"I don't know. I can't stay here right now. I need some air."

She gripped my shoulders and embraced me tightly until I felt as if she were trying to prevent my body from splintering into pieces. Then, she pulled back, her eyes bright with tears. But I couldn't stay. I didn't want her to see me like this, and Adrien would be worried.

"Where is Adrien?" I asked, looking around.

"He's sleeping on the couch in the living room."

"Good. Take care of him. I don't want him to worry. I just want to clear my head, all right?"

She stared at me, stood on her tiptoes, and kissed my cheek. "Take all the time you need, Remington. We will be here when you come back."

With that, I crushed my lips to hers and kissed her hard. They were the words I needed to hear, but I still had to get out of there. I turned and left the room.

Chapter Thirty-Nine

Selene

By two o'clock in the afternoon, Remington hadn't returned from his run. He'd changed into shorts and a T-shirt and taken off. I didn't offer to run with him because I felt he needed some time alone to process everything that had happened today.

Adrien kept asking where his father was, and I was getting tired of lying that he went to town, and I was worried, wondering if he was okay. Èric returned from dropping Adele at the airport over an hour ago and took Adrien out to the fields to watch the grapes being harvested. Gilles was in Paris, sorting out the issues in his security firm.

I was about to ask Èric to go for a drive to search for Remington—I wasn't a good driver—when I saw Remington jogging tiredly up the pavement. My feet refused to leave their place on the steps, so I watched and waited. He trudged up to me, took my face, and kissed me hard on the mouth, then shuffled past, leaving me reeling in the aftermath of the furious kiss. He didn't stop until he reached the back of the house and made a beeline for the shed, stalked in and back out seconds later, holding an axe and headed for the firewood arranged in piles, waiting to be chopped. After positioning the logs, he swung his arms and brought them down, splitting chunk after chunk of wood until a mountain of it formed on the side. Watching him do all that muscle work was so darn sexy. Then I remembered he was hurting, and I slapped away my lusty thoughts.

When he was done, he returned the axe and came back out. He stood with his back to the château, his gaze on the vineyards in concentration as if memorizing them for his next painting. Barely-contained anger rippled down his arms and back as he flexed his hands at his sides.

Isn't he tired after running and cutting wood?

"I ran for two hours non-stop. But I still feel this anger screaming inside me. How is that even possible?"

I inched closer and wrapped my arms around him from behind. "It was a lot to take in all at once."

He inhaled deeply and shook his head as if to clear his head. "When I was a child, my mother left her life here and moved to London. My father hardly acknowledged me, us, while we lived here in Provence. I think she hoped that if I were close to him, things would get better. What she kept forgetting was my father had a wife and a life in England, which was very different from ours. My mother and father met here in Provence. He seduced her and lied to her, telling her he wasn't married. He had been on a business trip to the law firm where she worked part-time as a paralegal, while learning how to run the vineyard from her father. While in London, she enrolled me in the same school as Caleb because she wanted me to have the same opportunities my father gave his other son. She was relentless.

"The only place my father and I used to meet was either at the school, some restaurant, or in his office. My mother, in all her goodness, would arrange for a father's day out. What she didn't know was this man, the man who fathered me, called me a bastard every chance he could get." He inhaled deeply. "I'm not certain when his wife left him. He blamed my mother and me for destroying his marriage. He would use his whip to mark me in places no one could see. I couldn't tell my mother. She was already working too hard; there was no way I could break her heart. Plus, there was Caleb, my best friend, who accepted me without judgment. I was glad when I had to go back to school because it meant that I wouldn't see my father for a while. One day he took things a little too far; he whipped me and the belt cut into my forearm. My mother saw it when she walked into my room as I was changing into my pajamas.

"I had never seen her as angry as she was that day. We left London the following week and away from the only friend I'd ever known. I wrote Caleb letters, but I never received any reply from him. I finally gave up."

He turned around to face me. "Today was a little too much, and I couldn't handle what I had just learned."

My eyes burned, and my chest hurt with this story. I squeezed my eyes shut to stop the tears because he would think that he had upset me. In truth, I wanted to cry for him. I kissed his chest, pressing my face onto his drenched shirt.

A bastard. Now I understood his unwavering devotion to his son. *God, his father is such a dickhead.*

I cleared my throat to get rid of the lump stuck in there. "Just because he called you a bastard doesn't make you one, Remington. It doesn't define who you are. You chose your path and made a life of your own. I'm so proud of you."

He pulled me into him and hugged me tightly. I sank into his arms, smiled, and breathed in his sweaty body, glad he was safe.

I leaned back and took his face in my hands. His haunted

gaze searched mine, but behind it, I could see the strong man I'd come to know. "You are human, Remington. No one expects you to handle everything," I said. His jaw was set into an angry, stubborn line. I wasn't sure what I said got through to him; he was such a proud man.

After making sure Adrien was distracted, I led Remington upstairs to our bedroom, locked the door and guided him to the bed. I placed my hands on his hips, looked up and found his gaze focused on my face. I pushed his running shorts down his thighs, my eyes never leaving his, and felt him shiver as my fingers connected with his hot, sweaty skin.

"What are you doing, *ma belle*?" he asked in a hoarse voice.

"I want to make something clear," I echoed the words he'd spoken to me not long ago. When he was naked, I stripped off my clothing, tossing them on the floor and turned around. His cock, already hard, stood proud and ready. I placed a hand on his chest, pushing him backward. He landed on his ass on the bed. I crawled on his lap and straddled him. I bit back a smile. *Yay to this new Seductress Selene.* "Put your hands on my hips." He licked his lips before doing as I ordered and lifted his gaze, now dark and hungry with desire.

"You are human. You are allowed to hurt. To cry even. Your father is a selfish son of a bitch, but you, baby, you turned out to be this exceptional man who hides a big heart inside this tough exterior. You are human, Remington." I lifted myself on my knees, guided his dick to my entrance, and then stared into his eyes. I watched him as I slowly lowered myself, taking him inside me. "Give me your fears, Remington. Trust me enough to let me in. I'm here, baby. I'm here to catch you."

With that, I moved up and down, his strong hands lifting and lowering me with exquisite care. Our gazes locked on each other. I felt the minute he let himself go because his hands left my hips, and he slid his arms around mine to hold on to my shoulders. I wrapped mine around his waist. He pulled me to him, burying his face into my hair. His thrusts became urgent and his groans deep.

We climaxed at the same time and it was explosive but quiet, which was a first for us. I held him as we came down but realized he was shaking as if his body was about to break into pieces. I hugged him tighter, rubbing a hand on his back. His sobs were muffled by my shoulder, and it felt as though his heart were being ripped out of his chest. Had he ever shared how he felt with anyone? When did he last cry, really cry?

As painful as the sounds soaking into my bones were, I was glad he had opened up to me and let me see this side of him. I admired him a lot for that.

Chapter Forty

Selene

Remington had been gone for two days, and even though he called any chance he got, we really missed him. Caleb wasn't doing well. His kidneys weren't responding to the medication, and the doctors were looking for a different solution. So far, Adele and Remington had taken a donor crossmatch test, and Remington was a match.

The rooms in the château still echoed with memories of him, walking in and out. Adrien missed his father, too, but was easily distracted by Èric. The fact that Remington had trusted me enough to leave his child behind floored me. My thoughts kept drifting to Remington as a child, stuck in an elevator, and then images of his father beating him. He'd gone through so much in his thirty-three years that it put my own experience to shame. Remington was such an easy man to love, and being with him made me realize how exhausting it had been, trying to make James love me back, especially during the last year before the divorce.

Curling up on a lounge chair on the patio, I opened my notebook and closed my eyes, pushing those thoughts away and conjuring up a photo shoot. Something sexy, like a boudoir session. What made them so sensual? My mind's eye flipped through my memories and when I opened my eyes, I started drawing, filling page after page with drafts of different designs, including as many details as I could. I would go back to the designs and fill them in later. Some of them were hideous, and some I could imagine would be breathtaking. Because I had been caught up in my task, I didn't catch the additional scent in the air …like burning trees.

My head snapped up from the book and I looked around, and I felt blood drain from my face. Smoke rose from the fields beyond the lush garden. I jumped from the seat, scanning around. Most of the workers who tended the fields had gone home.

Where the hell is Adrien?

My heart pounded in my chest as I dashed down the paths, calling his name. Seconds later I heard someone call *my* name. I spun around and saw Èric sprinting toward me.

"I saw it from my room," he said, his eyes scanning the compound quickly and efficiently. "When did you last see him?"

I pointed at the muddy patch close to where I'd been sitting. "He was there." *How could I have let him out of my sight?* "Let's split up and search for him." He nodded and we parted, heading in different directions.

Suddenly, classical music blared around the garden, loud and frightening. I spun on my heel, searching for the source, but I couldn't see anything. My heart thumped with every single beat, and sweat trickled down my temples and spine.

I know this song! It was Tchaikovsky's 'Dance of the Sugar Plum Fairy'. Among all the operas, *The Nutcracker* was my favourite. I'd always loved this piece, but now, it sounded creepy. The smoke, swirling in the air, didn't make things better.

Adrien. I snapped out of my trance and bolted toward the tree house, climbing up the wooden steps on trembling legs, but he wasn't there. Desperation and nausea swirled inside my stomach as I ran down the path leading to the wall where the fire was feeding on whatever vine or grass was in its way.

"God, please. Keep him safe," I murmured repeatedly. I squinted as tears ran down my face brought on by the smoke and dread. He had to be safe. Determination fuelled my feet forward, and I ducked as the fire roared, sending tiny sparks of flame in the air.

As I rounded the corner, heading toward a little pond on the east side of the garden, I heard a small cry. I peered through the smoke, pulling my shirt over my nose. Adrien scooted farther into what looked like a cave or an alcove.

"Thank God," I muttered under my breath, ran toward him, and ducked low to avoid bumping my head on the stone. He was curled into a ball with his legs pulled into his chest. His eyes were wide with fear. Soot covered his face, his cheeks were streaked with tears, and his body trembled in fear. I crouched low, my arm gripped his little body to mine, and we crawled out of there.

I took him in my arms, held him tightly, and suppressed a sob. I pressed a kiss on his hair. "Everything is all right now, darling," I said soothingly. "Are you okay?"

He nodded, his bottom lip trembling. The music stopped as suddenly as it had started.

Holy crap! What in the hell is that music all about?

By the time I made it back to the house with Adrien in my arms, the men from the fire department and the police were just arriving. They spoke in rapid French, and seconds later, they rushed out through the gardens. Èric must have called them from his cell.

A few seconds later, Èric raced inside the house, panting. As soon as he saw the boy, relief washed over his face, replacing the worry and panic that had been there.

"Is he all right?" he asked, his eyes roaming over Adrien's face and body. Adrien whimpered, turning to hide his face into my chest as he sobbed softly.

"He looks okay, but he needs a doctor to check if everything's all right." I turned to leave to search for the doctor.

"Selene." Èric touched my shoulder. I stopped and turn around. "Wait here."

He scanned our surroundings before jogging out the door and heading out toward the poolside lounge chairs. He squatted down and picked a bouquet of flowers from the floor.

A bouquet of red irises.

My heart sped up as panic flooded my veins.

What if the sender was watching us, getting off on the fact that we were scrambling around in the mayhem he or she had created? Were they working alone? Maybe one of the château's workers was involved in this. In all the time I'd been here, I had only seen one person inside the château, Monsieur Laurent, the winemaker. But according to Remington, Laurent's family had worked in this estate for years. Why would he risk his family's good name to destroy their reputation?

Adrien whimpered, pulling me from my thoughts.

"I have to get him checked by the doctor," I told Èric as he strode back toward us. He nodded, changing direction and heading toward two policemen standing next to the kitchen counter.

As soon as the doctor was done and reassured me that Adrien was okay and hadn't inhaled too much smoke, I carried him upstairs to give him a bath.

"Please don't leave me," he said in French, his eyes huge and panic-filled when I walked the short distance to get a towel.

"I won't leave you, honey. I'm here. I just wanted to get this." I gestured to the towel. This was the first time he'd spoken since I found him huddled in the alcove.

"I want my papa," he whispered as I wrapped him in the towel and carried him out of the room. Just then Èric walked into the room with a plate of sandwiches, a glass of milk, and orange juice and placed it on the desk by the window. He informed me he couldn't get ahold of Remington on the phone. A complete disaster. The boy cried. The only thing I could do was hold him. He was inconsolable. Eventually, he fell asleep in my arms.

God, I've never been so exhausted in my life. I felt helpless, scared, and tired.

After tucking Adrien in bed, I left Èric watching him and grabbed a pair of shorts and T-shirt from our room before hopping in the shower in Adrien's room. I was out within five minutes. As soon as Èric left to deal with the policemen, I slipped in beside Adrien, too worried and nervous to eat anything.

How were we ever going to sleep peacefully inside this house, knowing someone might be inside here or still hanging around nearby?

After the police left, Èric locked up and returned upstairs about an hour later to let me know he hadn't reached

Remington, but he would keep trying. Also, Èric had informed Gilles about what happened and was scheduled for an early-morning flight to Provence the next day. I requested that Èric let me know if Remington called back. I placed my phone next to the pillow where I could hear any incoming call. This time Èric looked confident, albeit grim, as he went back downstairs to keep watch. He didn't own a weapon, but according to Remington, he was an expert in hand-to-hand combat. With that thought in mind, I tried Remington's number again, but the call went to voicemail. After several tries, exhaustion finally pulled me under.

Chapter Forty-One

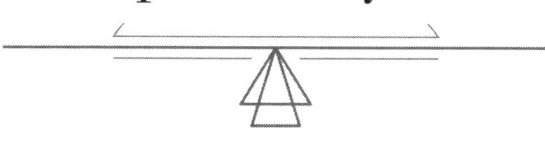

Remington

I ran a hand down my face, my thoughts wandering back to Provence. I hadn't spoken to Selene or Èric in the past few hours. The mobile phone reception inside this hospital was complete shit.

I missed her and Adrien. I couldn't wait to talk to them later when I left the hospital. I'd arrived earlier for an appointment with the doctor in charge of Caleb's case to discuss his condition, options, and the probability of surgery, and because I wanted to spend some time with Caleb.

Unfortunately, so had Remington Newport, my father. Adele wasn't around to act as a buffer as she had done the last few visits.

I flicked my wrist to check the time and then turned to stare at the man sitting across from me. He was nothing to me but a father in biological terms only, a stranger. His face had acquired more wrinkles between the last time I saw his photo in a newspaper, almost one year ago at a charity ball in London, smiling for the cameras, and now. His black hair was filled with grey. The eyes that always sparkled with power and confidence were dulled in defeat whenever he regarded his son, lying on the bed between us. When he flicked a gaze in my direction, a slight glint of what I thought was hope would lighten them.

Currently, I was Caleb's only hope, and my father knew that. The doctors had tested Adele for compatibility. Unfortunately, her blood wasn't a match. This was one of the areas where my father's power couldn't cure his own son or control the inevitable. Yes, he could shop around for someone to donate a kidney, but time was of the essence. Caleb's kidneys were shutting down fast, and he needed dialysis to aid them.

I should have been smug because he couldn't wield control and power in this instance, as was his style. Instead, I felt sorry for him. I wanted to hate him so much for destroying my childhood when I needed him most, but I couldn't. I'd been surrounded by love while growing up. My grandmother, who passed away when I was twenty years old, my cousins, my uncles, and my mother had made sure to love me twice as hard to make up for my bastard of a father. Surrounded by so much love cancelled the hate for my father, and what remained was indifference.

The beeping from the machine connected to Caleb to monitor his vitals filled the room. That and the whoosh sound coming from the bed whenever he exhaled. I hadn't had a chance to speak to Caleb again. The only time I did was when I arrived two days ago, but he'd been too weak to talk, just lifted a hand, and patted my head like he used to when we were in school. When I saw him, my heart broke. He didn't resemble the healthy boy with a head full of dark-blond hair, the boy whose laughter was as infectious as his friendship. My brother.

"We need to talk about this, son," my father said, interrupting my thoughts. I felt awkward calling him Remington. I didn't want to associate my name with the likes of him, which was difficult, given that I was named after him.

My jaw clenched and my fingers curled around the armchair as anger arose inside me. He was referring to the conversation we had when he found out I was his son's only hope. Whenever he could sneak a chance to confront me, he always started the same conversation. I wasn't in the mood to be bribed with money, promises of a place in his company or on the board of directors, or whatever else he kept babbling about. I thought my father was a complete arsehole, but his announcement that he would pay me to donate a kidney to his son—my own flesh and blood—had been the absolute height of arrogance and callousness.

I stared at him coldly. I flicked a gaze to Caleb before turning to face him. "Can I talk to you outside?" I stood and strode from the room, not bothering to check if he was following me. It was time to set the wanker straight once and for all. As soon as he stepped into the hall, I rounded on him. "Looks like you haven't changed, *Father*. Everything is all about money for you. Well, listen very carefully because this is the last time I'm going to say this. Fuck you and your money. I'm doing this because that's my brother in there. I'm not your son. I've never been your son and never will be. Get that through your head. As far as I'm concerned, you only exist in my distant memories." Rage shot through me, and I realised that I hadn't forgiven him. Not really. I had suppressed my emotions regarding him. My hands shook, and my breathing was ragged as I fought for the control not to punch his arrogant arse. "Stay away from me if you know what's good for you."

Someone cleared his throat. "Mr. St. Germain?"

I took deep breaths, schooling my expression as best as I

could, and turned around. The doctor cleared his throat before his fingers started to fiddle with the brown file in his hands.

"I'm sorry for keeping you waiting. We could step into my office if you're ready …" The doctor trailed off, his gaze moving over my shoulder to my father before returning to me.

I nodded and started to follow him but halted when I heard the sound of feet shuffling on the laminated floor as if to follow us. I threw my father a don't-you-dare-come-near-me look over my shoulder, freezing him on the spot, before I continued on my way to the doctor's office. Caleb was Remington's son, but I didn't care at that moment. It was my kidney after all. Besides, I was certain if my father happened to stand in a ten-metre radius of where I was, he would end up taking up residence in this hospital.

The doctor was clever enough to pretend he hadn't seen anything unusual in the hallway.

Wise man.

By the time I left the hospital, it was seven p.m. and Caleb was still sleeping. I had gotten a chance to chat with him for all of five minutes before exhaustion finally won the battle.

As soon as I stepped out of the hospital, I pulled up the collar of my coat to ward off the cool October weather. Then I turned on my phone, frowning at all the missed calls from Èric and Selene. The timestamp on them was a little over two hours ago. What could have happened? Different scenarios flashed through my head, each worse than the one before, causing blood to pound loud in my ears. I dialled Selene's number first, but it rang several times before diverting to voicemail. Fear closed in on me as I called Èric's number. He answered on the first ring and told me what had happened, confirming my worst fear. The notorious stalker had struck again while I was away, and this time, he or she seemed to be out for blood. *Shit, why hadn't I brought Adrien and Selene to London with me?* What if something had really happened to them? There was no way I could have survived it. I climbed inside the waiting taxi and sank into the seat, feeling as though I was losing grip of everything I held dear in my life: Caleb, Adrien, Selene, the château.

Forty-five minutes later, I was at the hangar where the St. Germain family jet was waiting to fly me back to Provence, my heart pounding hard in my chest. The thought of Adrien and Selene in danger made me nauseous. I hadn't prayed in a while, but now I did. The words poured from my lips repeatedly, like a mantra.

God, please keep them safe.

After the plane touched down, I rushed to my car that had been parked on the other side of the hangar when I left for London. I climbed inside and took deep breaths. My hands gripped the steering wheel so tightly that the veins were prominent under the skin. I had to calm down for the short drive home. Easier said than done. I drove to the château like a man possessed. Unable to wait long enough to park in my usual spot, I left the car in the middle of the drive, jumped out, and dashed inside. Èric was pacing in the living room, dragging his fingers through his blond hair in agitation.

Èric›s head shot up and saw me. The frown left his face. His shoulders drooped immediately, but at the same time, I saw wariness enter his face.

"Where are they?" I asked him when he halted in front of me.

"Adrien's room."

I dropped my traveling bag on the floor and dashed upstairs.

Selene lay on her side with Adrien tucked safely in her arms. My heart swelled at the sight of such tenderness, and a feeling that had now become familiar whenever I saw these two together unfurled in my chest.

"Dieu merci!" I whispered under my breath. I closed the distance to the bed and sat on the edge of the mattress. I leaned down to press a kiss on Adrien's forehead, and then I turned to brush my lips against Selene's. She stirred, and her eyes flew open. She blinked several times as her vision adjusted to her surroundings. She stiffened, and her arm tightened around my son as she pulled him into her body. When it finally dawned on her who I was, she gasped and the fear in her eyes receded, replaced by relief.

"Oh, my God, Remington," she said hoarsely. She flicked a glance at Adrien and slowly unwrapped her arm to keep from disturbing him in his sleep. Then she pulled the covers to Adrien's chin and twisted around to face me, her eyes filled with tears, which overflowed and rolled down her cheeks. She fell into my arms, and I held her as she buried her face into my neck. "It's so good to see you. When did you arrive?" Her voice trembled and her body shook.

"A few minutes ago."

She nodded but didn't lift her head. I hadn't noticed any traces of tears on her face when I came into the room before. She must have been holding them back until now.

I continued to hold her, my arms tightening even more with her every sob. My eyes locked on Adrien, sleeping peacefully on the bed. I wanted to touch him so badly, but I didn't want to wake him. He needed the rest after such a horrific ordeal.

We didn't talk, and I was grateful for that. My throat felt swollen, and I was sure no words could pass through my lips just then.

Finally, Selene pulled back and smiled, even as tears lingered in her eyes. Then, she wiped her nose with the back of her hand and sniffed. "I can't tell you how good it is to have you back, Remington. I've never been so frightened in my life."

"If I had known what was happening, I would have gotten here faster. I'm so sorry for taking this long, *ma belle*."

She shook her head vehemently. "Caleb needed you. Besides, no one knew this was going to happen."

I stared at her. Even crying, she was beautiful. She wasn't throwing a fit and blaming me for not being here on time. She thought about Caleb instead.

This woman was amazing. "Do you want to talk about it? Tell me what happened?"

She took a deep breath and poured out the whole story. She got to the part where the music blasted through the compound. And when she mentioned the song had been 'Dance of the Sugar Plum Fairy', I felt the hair rise on the nape of my neck. When she was done, I excused myself and went back downstairs to speak to Èric. He gave me a short version of what happened and then told me Gilles would be arriving the next day with two of his security personnel.

I had one more thing to check before heading up to join Adrien and Selene. I went to the cabinet located between the fireplace and the television. I opened it and did a quick inventory of the CDs inside. The case with the soundtrack for one of my favourite ballets, *The Nutcracker*, was missing.

Whoever this person was clearly knew their way around the château. They also knew how that song affected me and how much I treasured it. When I was thirteen, my mother took me to my first ballet in Paris. It was at that time she met Bernard, the man who had completely changed our lives for the better. He had given me the CD as a gift on my fourteenth birthday.

It held my most treasured memories. Once again, I tried to recall if I had shown anything other than casual interest to the women I dated before, but none came to mind. But how would they know their way around this place? The thought of someone I probably knew working with this person niggled at me in the back of my mind.

I closed the cabinet doors and returned to the living room. After activating the alarm system, I said good night to Èric, who still wore a troubled look even after I assured him the incident wasn't his fault. Finally, I went back upstairs, my thoughts clamouring in my head.

Selene had slipped back into bed, but she was still awake. I lifted Adrien in my arms and gestured for her to follow us. Inside my room, I lay my son on my bed, changed into a pair of pajama bottoms and a T-shirt, and joined them in bed. There was no way I would sleep without, at least, stretching a hand and feeling the two of them nearby.

Chapter Forty-Two

Remington

The last couple of days, the château had been a very busy place. The police stopped by regularly to investigate the site. They confirmed it as arson, but I already knew that. Everything was getting so bloody fucked up, and I felt as though control was slipping out of my grasp. Caleb's situation was getting worse, and the doctors were considering operating soon.

Most of the vineyards had been destroyed in the fire. The garden and east side of the château had also been grazed by the blaze and needed repairs. I spoke to my mother and told her what happened. She would be arriving tomorrow in one of the family aeroplanes. Then we would travel to Paris until the building was repaired, although I knew that getting my mother to leave this place was going to be impossible. I hadn't told her exactly who or what caused the fire. I wanted to speak to her face-to-face. I knew she'd have questions as soon as she met Selene, and I was prepared for that.

Today, we went into town to get away from the château, which ended up being a good thing. Adrien seemed more cheerful and lively, much more than he had been since the fire.

Right after dinner, I went outside to speak to the two men from Gilles's security firm. Gilles had returned to Paris to follow up on a trail he was positive was the person causing all the havoc in our lives. One of the hidden surveillance cameras in his office had recorded what had happened in his office, confirming it had been a woman by the shape of her body and how she carried herself. Other than that, her face had been covered in a fitting mask. The only thing that gave her away had been the label peeking on the back of her trousers that appeared to be custom made. After further investigation, Gilles found a boutique located in the 10 arrondissement.

Feeling relieved that we were finally getting somewhere with this madness, I led Adrien to his room. After brushing his teeth, he climbed in bed, pulled the bed covers up to his chin and took the book he had chosen for tonight's reading from the nightstand.

"Can I ask you something, Papa?"

"Always." I settled in the rocking chair next to the bed. I never could bring myself to remove it from the room. It held too many memories of me rocking little Adrien to sleep.

His eyebrows tugged into a frown. "Why does Selene have to leave? We could keep her here with us, and she could be my real mama."

I placed the book on the bedside table and reached out to smooth the frown away. I had known this question would come up eventually.

I studied my little boy, renewing my vow to convince Selene to stay with us longer. "We can't *keep* her, Adrien. She has a family back home. I'm sure they miss her a lot."

"Doesn't she want to be with us? You two love each other, no?" He cocked his head to the side, his eyes intent on mine.

I rubbed a hand across my jaw, thinking of the best way

to answer his question. This was new ground for me. Adrien never got a chance to meet the women I had dated before because I never felt any real connection with any of them, but Selene made me want a second chance in life.

Adrien shifted on the bed impatiently as he stared at me with a fierce, hopeful look in his eyes. It made me want to give him anything he wanted right there.

"She is a very special woman," I answered him, fighting the urge to blurt out my real feelings. If I were going to tell anyone how I felt, Selene would be the first person on my list. I wanted to look into her eyes when I finally bared my soul to her. She might have the same feelings as I, or maybe not.

My son stopped fidgeting, and a smile replaced the frown on his face. "I love her and I want her to be my mama."

"Me, too," I whispered and then leaned forward and pressed a kiss to his hair.

Mon Dieu, I loved this boy so much. The thought of something ever happening to him almost brought me to my knees, and sweat broke out on my forehead. The fact that Selene had lost a child and survived made me admire her all over again.

"Time to get some sleep. Are you happy to see *mamie* tomorrow?" I asked him, reminding him my mother was arriving the next day. Selene was still nervous about meeting her. I, on the other hand, was anxious for my mother to meet the woman who'd succeeded where other women had failed in the past four years. The woman who had managed to erase the pain and hurt of betrayal and claimed my heart.

"*Oui, Papa!*" he squealed happily and snuggled deeper into his covers.

I retrieved the book, opened it to the bookmarked page, and started to read. Five minutes later, Adrien was still restless, turning and kicking the covers all over the bed.

I sighed and stopped reading.

Tonight, I had been looking forward to spending more time with Selene. Even though we'd had sex after we arrived home just over two hours ago, I still wanted more. We hadn't had quality time since the incident. My need for her knew no bounds, and I was a glutton for her. Blood pumped loud in my ears as the thought of her sinful, naked body pinned beneath mine flashed in my head.

I groaned inwardly. I had to stop this. I was in my son's room and having naughty thoughts about the minx sitting downstairs.

I shifted on the chair, biting back a groan as my cock throbbed painfully inside my jeans, and tried to focus on my son.

"What's wrong, Adrien?" My voice sounded hoarse. Adrien gave me a funny look, and I cleared my throat.

"I saw her again today."

It took a moment for my lust-addled brain to catch up. "Saw who?"

"Her. The woman who visited me in school in Paris."

Those words cooled me off, and my heart rate sped up. He had never mentioned any woman visiting him in school. "What woman?"

He shrugged. "She told me soon she would be my new mama. I don't like her."

Sweat formed and slithered down my spine, even though the room was reasonably cool. "When did you see this woman?"

"After dinner."

I opened my mouth to ask him what the woman looked like, but I was interrupted as my mobile vibrated inside my jeans pocket. I dug it out impatiently and swiped the screen without looking who it was.

"St. Germain," I announced myself, leaning back in the chair.

"Gilles here. Listen, I know you told me to call off the background check on Selene."

"Yes, I did," I snapped impatiently. "Any news about this woman? Did you visit the boutique?"

"Yes. The owner will fax me the receipts and any other details about this special customer. He was reluctant at first, but when I told him what would happen if he didn't cooperate, he gave in." A pause then. "But that is not why I'm calling you. Some information about Selene arrived in my email earlier today."

I stood and walked toward the window, my heart thumping hard in my chest. "What the bloody hell? I told you I wasn't interested in investigating her behind her back, Gilles."

"Calm down, Remington," he said in a cool, gravelly voice. "The man I hired stumbled on something he thought you might want to know. Would you like me to destroy the information or would you like to know?"

I dug my fingers through my hair and shut my eyes. I'd asked Gilles to hire a private investigator in the heat of the moment, but finally, when I realized it didn't matter who she was, I asked him to call it off.

I blew out a breath. "Sure."

"Right. So—" He inhaled deeply. "According to this report, Selene Michaels is twenty-six years and her address—"

"Cut to the chase, Gilles," I growled on the phone, eager to return to my conversation with Adrien.

I heard the click of what sounded like a computer mouse, followed by a few keyboard taps. "So, Selene was born twenty-six years ago in—*merde*! Where did you say she was born?"

My stomach clenched at his hesitation. I glanced over my shoulder at Adrien. He was busy, playing with two Lego men.

I turned back to stare out the window at the moonless night. "New York."

Gilles was quiet for a few minutes. "According to this report, she was born in Paris to Monsieur Anthony Michaels and Madame Inés Dubois in the Armand Trousseau Maternity Hospital."

My pulse thudded in my ears, and my breathing was ragged. "What did you say?"

He repeated the words.

I shook my head, wanting to shake off Gilles's words. Had Selene lied to me about where she was born? Why would she do that? She had mentioned her mother was French, but I hadn't thought to dig deeper. I couldn't do this with Adrien in the room. I cleared my throat to relieve the emotion choking me. "Give me a second, Gilles."

I strode to Adrien's bed and dropped a kiss on his hair. "I have some things to take care of, okay? I will ask Selene to come up and finish reading the story for you."

Adrien nodded as he made some funny aeroplane noises, swooping his hand up and down. I turned to leave but stopped when he called out, "Papa?"

I turned to face him. "Yes, Adrien."

"The woman downstairs. She told me to tell you,"—he squinted as if thinking really hard and I squirmed impatiently—"one, two …bang."

One. Two. Bang? My fingers shook, and bile rose in my throat. "Adrien, do you remember what she looked like? Where exactly did you see her?"

"In the kitchen when I went to get ice cream. She had brown hair, and she was tall."

Bloody fucking hell! How had she made it past the two security men? Unless she had someone working with her. One of the people who work in the château. The thought chilled me further. I gripped the phone tighter in my hand, then remembered Gilles was still on the line and jammed it back to my ear.

"I will call you back." I disconnected the call before he could answer and turned to Adrien. "Stay in here and lock the door. Do not open it unless you hear my voice or Èric's, all right? No one else."

I didn't want to mention Selene. The woman had somehow managed to get inside the château, so I was worried she could impersonate another woman's voice.

As soon as Adrien nodded, I rushed out of the room, making sure he locked the door before dashing downstairs.

My foot hit the last step, and I frantically scanned the room. Selene wasn't where I left her. I shoved my fingers into my hair and pulled, the pain keeping my sanity at bay. I had promised her I would protect her, yet the château had been infiltrated under the noses of Èric and two security men.

I rounded the dining room and stopped cold. Selene lay on the floor, unconscious. Her skin was pale, and blood gushed from a cut on her temple. Her beautiful red lips were caked with what looked like vomit.

"Oh, Christ, Selene." I dashed to her side and dropped to my knees. I placed two fingers on her wrist to check for her pulse, but my hands were trembling and I missed the count several times. "I need help over here!" I shouted to the two men standing just outside the front door.

I needed to control myself; otherwise, I wouldn't be able to help her. I took deep breaths, and even as my eyes burned with tears, I checked her vitals. Her pulse was weak and her breathing shallow.

Blocking the background noise of shuffling feet, the sudden blaring of voices from the security men's walkie-talkies, and panicked voices, I concentrated on remembering my first-aid basics. I couldn't think properly. Someone touched my shoulder, and I turned around to face Èric. He said something, but all I saw were his lips moving. He pushed me aside and dropped to his knees beside Selene while I stood up and watched him without really seeing.

I thought I knew the true meaning of the word pain. The feeling of having my heart torn from my chest repeatedly until I felt as if I was in purgatory and hell at the same time. Turns out I didn't. Watching Selene lying on the floor, helpless and unconscious, made me feel powerless.

Different thoughts flashed in my head:

I should have let her go when she left my house weeks ago.

I should have forgotten about her.

But I had done none of those things because I needed her, craved her. My physical and emotional hunger for her knew no bounds, and I was a selfish bastard. I had been selfish to my son as well. His heart would break when he saw Selene. The thought renewed my determination. I had protected him his whole life, and I would keep doing that for as long as he lived.

I called the ambulance, and after telling them what happened, I disconnected the call, returning to Selene's side.

Both road and air ambulances arrived, and I stood back reluctantly as I watched two men check her vitals, this time with their equipment. Everything was a flurry of activity after that, so I turned around to face Èric. He looked shaken and pale.

"I failed. I failed twice, Monsieur St. Germain."

I clenched my jaw as anger and fear poured through me. "Yes. You and Gilles's men. How could one woman slip under your noses undetected?"

He opened his mouth to speak, but I cut him off with a furious look. "Keep an eye on her," I told him, pointing at Selene as I bolted upstairs toward Adrien's room. I knocked lightly on his door. "Adrien, it's me, Papa," I said, trying not to smash the thing down. "Adrien?"

The room was quiet on the other side of the door. I gripped the doorknob, twisting it. "Adrien!" I shouted, feeling panic, worse than finding Selene downstairs, twist in my chest.

"Papa?" a tiny voice called from inside, followed by feet shuffling, then the sound of the door being unlocked. The door cracked open and two large, green eyes filled with fear peeked through the doorway.

"Dieu merci!" I snatched him up from the floor and held him close, panting in relief. "Thank God you're okay." I had to prepare him for what happened. How would I do this without breaking his little heart? "Something happened to Selene. I need you to be brave for me, all right?"

His eyes grew ever larger than before, and his lips trembled. I could see panic and tears shining bright in his eyes. "Where is she?"

"The ambulance is taking her to the hospital," I said, leaving the room and hurrying downstairs. I felt his hands tighten around me, but he didn't say a word after that.

By the time we arrived in the living room, Selene had already been transferred to a stretcher with an oxygen mask fixed around her nose. She looked even paler than before.

"How is she?" I asked, walking alongside the stretcher as they pulled it out the door and headed toward the helicopter. Adrien whimpered in my arms, tightening his hold. I gripped him even harder.

One of the medical men flicked his eyes to me before turning away, and in that second, I saw the uncertainty in his eyes. "She seems to have received quite a blow on her head and lost a lot of blood." He pointed to the lump on her forehead covered with a bandage. "Her blood pressure is unusually high, and she is unresponsive to the tests we did." He flung the ambulance doors wide. "We will know more as soon as the hospital performs more tests. We will fly your wife to Marseilles. You and your son can sit with her inside the helicopter."

I nodded but didn't attempt to correct their assumption that Selene was my wife. After the stretcher was loaded inside the helicopter, Adrien and I settled on the seat next to Selene.

"Papa? Selene … is Selene going to die?"

As a parent, you are expected to do anything to protect your child no matter what. But was lying to him really protecting him? What if something really happened to her? "I don't know, son."

We arrived at the hospital in Marseilles, and soon Selene was being rushed through the hospital doors.

Chapter Forty-Three

Remington

"Monsieur?"

I shifted Adrien in my arms and turned to face a tall man with a stethoscope and a chart in his hand. "How is she?"

"Are you Madame Michael's relative?"

"I'm her husband," I replied, hating that I had to lie, but it was necessary, otherwise he wouldn't disclose any information to me about her condition. "How is she? Can I see her?"

"I'm the doctor in charge of her case. My name is Jean Blanchett." He stuck his hand out, and I shook it.

"Remington St. Germain."

His eyes widened slightly, and I knew he had an idea of who I was. The St. Germains were a large family, spread throughout the Provence region.

The doctor scanned his chart and cleared his throat. Of course, he wasn't stupid. He knew Selene wasn't my wife. Most people in the area knew I hadn't remarried since Collette's death. But I was willing to do anything to get the information. Even wield the St. Germain name, if it came to that. I was desperate, and the guilt of not protecting Selene was like a hand around my neck, choking me.

"She has no other relatives here in France. I'm the only person she knows, and she was with me when this happened," I said.

He nodded and raised his head. "She is in a private room as per your request, in our ICU ward. She suffered quite a blow to her head and is unconscious and sedated. After performing some tests, we will need to keep her here at least a few nights to monitor her closely. Right now, we need to know what happened. We also need her medical background information for our files. We found traces of some sort of poison in her blood. Do you know what she ate or drank during the past hour or so?"

Poison? Had the psychotic woman also poisoned her?

I provided the doctor with as much information as I could on what happened tonight and that the police were aware of this case. I also told him about her miscarriage and her condition after that loss. Then I stood there, trying not to look like a fool, while he shot question after question.

"I put my son to bed right after dinner, so if she was poisoned, it must have happened while I was away from her."

"We suspect at least some of it was removed from her system when she vomited. We are looking into that before we start a therapy to detoxify whatever she ingested."

A public address system cackled loudly, paging him. He excused himself and hurried away, promising to let me know more as soon as he could.

I had to call her family immediately to get the information the doctor needed. I was relieved when he didn't call me out on the lie. What kind of husband doesn't know if his wife is allergic to certain medications?

After calling Èric and asking him to check Selene's mobile for her family's telephone numbers, I disconnected the call and sat in one of the plastic chairs in the waiting room while Adrien slept in my arms. He had cried himself to sleep, and my heart broke with his every sob. It felt like hours, just sitting there powerless to do anything. Eventually, feeling as if I would go insane, I tracked down the doctor.

"Can we see her?" I asked.

He cleared his throat. "What about your son? He's quite young and it might be unwise, for now, to see his mother in her current state. Perhaps we should wait for …"

He trailed off when I narrowed my eyes. "Are you telling me that my son is not allowed to see her?" There was no way I was going to let Adrien out of my sight, especially after what happened to Selene. "The last thing he saw was my wife on a stretcher disappearing through the ER doors. He kept asking after her, and now he thinks she is dead. I spent the past four hours trying to calm him and assuring him that she is alive. I will not deny him the chance to see for himself that the woman he loves is still breathing." I took deep breaths to calm myself. "Do you have children, doctor?" His face softened, and he shifted on his feet before nodding. "Then as a father, you know that I'd do anything for my son."

He studied me for a few seconds, his eyes lingering on Adrien. Then, he nodded again. "Come with me. I will prepare him as much as I can for what he will see when he walks into your wife's room."

I exhaled, relieved. "Thank you."

With Adrien snoring softly in my arms, I followed the doctor down the hallway and inside what looked like a conference room. I nudged my son awake. It took several minutes before he was fully conscious. The doctor used a television screen mounted on the wall to explain to him what he will see inside Selene's room: the ventilators, IV tubes, the different sounds from the machine connected to her body. He continued to speak to Adrien in a gentle voice, checking to see my son's reactions or if Adrien had any questions.

When the doctor finished the presentation, we left the room and he requested us to wait for him. He'd come back and accompany us to Selene's room, as a precautionary measure. He wanted to monitor Adrien during the short visit.

About forty-five minutes later, Dr. Blanchett returned and led us to Selene's room. Two armed policemen were positioned outside her door. After nodding to them in greeting, I entered the room. The doctor warned me that she was still too weak, and we could only stay a few minutes.

Selene lay on a bed, covered in a white sheet. Her face was still pale, and her head was covered in a white bandage. Her chest rose and fell in a steady rhythm. A monitor was attached to a machine that stood beside her bed, displaying her vitals and beeping every few seconds. Several wires stuck out from under her hospital gown, linking her body directly to the machine. An IV-drip stand stood beside the bed. A nasal tube was placed at her nostrils, providing oxygen. I glanced at the doctor, frowning.

"We did not detect any damage to her brain, but her oxygen levels are quite low. The nasal cannula will help provide the amount her body needs," Dr. Blanchett explained.

Adrien had fallen asleep after the doctor's lesson. He stirred awake in my arms and blinked, looking around before finally realising where we were. His eyes grew wide as they settled on Selene lying on the bed, with a white bandage covering half of her head.

"She's sleeping," he said.

"Yes."

"Will she die, Papa?" he asked again, but this time his voice was almost a whisper.

"She has a good doctor taking care of her. And I know that angels are watching over her, too."

Adrien shifted in my arms, burying his head on my shoulder and exhaling a shuddering breath. "She is alive," he said with wonder in his voice

I nodded, savouring the small giggle of relief escaping his mouth. The doctor glanced at me and nodded in affirmation. Seeing Selene had been a good thing for Adrien.

We left the room ten minutes later. After thanking the doctor, I called Èric back to get the numbers. Making the call to her family was the hardest thing I'd ever done. I was responsible for her, yet she was lying in a hospital bed.

Marley answered the phone. Selene had spoken so highly of her sister, I felt as if I knew her. My mind was still trying to accept the fact that Selene might have lied to me about other things as well. Was she hiding something? I couldn't dispute the fact that she had gone through a lot in her life, had lost so much. But, who was Selene, really?

Shoving the myriad of questions aside, I introduced myself to Marley, and she laughed and told me she had heard of me. Then her tone turned serious and asked why I was calling. I gave her a short version of what happened without including the details about the threats or the woman who was trying to hurt both my family and Selene.

"The doctor in charge of her case needs her medical background information. Could you please fax it to my home number or scan and email it to me tonight?"

She hesitated at first, bombarding me with questions, trying to make sure I wasn't a malicious person trying to find out more about her sister to hurt her.

Good girl.

"Do you or your family have time to fly to France?" I asked her as soon as I told her where to send the information we needed. "I think it would be great if she wakes up with her family here."

We made arrangements for Marley to get on the next available flight. I told her I would make provisions for the ticket and would call her with the details as soon as everything was ready.

In the background, the PA blared to life, followed by an announcement paging Dr. Blanchett to room 201.

Selene's room.

I quickly wrapped up the conversation and then rearranged Adrien in my arms as I strode in the direction of her room.

Beeping noises filled the air, and four medical staff stood around the bed. One of them was punching buttons on the monitor while a different male nurse was pulling the sheets off her body and yet another held up defibrillator paddles.

Everything was happening so fast, and soon someone was pushing us out of the door. My last glimpse of Selene was her body arching up as a nurse slammed the paddles on her chest.

"What the hell is happening?" I shouted, as I fought the person who was busy taking us away from her.

"That's what we are trying to find out. Look, we suspect there might be some swelling inside her head. We were ready for something like this."

"Fuck no! No, no, no!" I whirled around to face him and grabbed the front of his coat with one had. "Don't let anything happen to her. Promise me!"

"We will do everything we can."

My eyes burned with tears, and my throat felt raw with pain. I finally loosened my hand from the lapel of his coat and watched him as he disappeared back inside her room, feeling helpless. I stared at the white door, my mind blank and my chest aching, then I wiped my cheeks with the back of my hand. I had to pull myself together for the sake of Adrien, sobbing into my chest.

Had my past interfered with my present, obliterating any chance of happiness in my life? Or with Selene?

I couldn't remember when I fell in love with Selene. I was fascinated at first, pulled by that curvy body of hers, and curious about certain features that resembled Colette's. It was as though I'd closed my eyes for a few seconds, and when I opened them, she was there, right in front of me. Her presence larger than life. Her heart pure, unsoiled by the events life had thrown at her.

I knew with all my heart that I loved her, even after the blow Gilles delivered while I was in my son's bedroom. There was no doubt. She had seen me at my lowest point in my life, yet she hadn't run. She knew more about me than any other woman ever did, even my own mother. Selene understood me, and she wasn't afraid to tell me off. She came into my life, stole every reservation I had in me, replacing it with pieces of her warmth and loving nature. Sometimes there is no pride in love; you fall hard and fast with no chance of reverting to the person you were. When Adrien asked me earlier, I had hesitated to answer him, but I wanted Selene to be the first to know. She was in there, fighting for her life, and I could do nothing to help her.

She had to be all right. She just had to. My life couldn't survive losing her. Everything made sense when she was around me.

I pulled my mobile from my pocket and dialled Gilles's number. It rang once before he answered the call. After giving him the short version of what happened in the house and the possibility that the woman who had broken into his office might be the same person who'd gained access to the château under his personnel's watchful eye, I paused long enough to let rage replace the hopelessness consuming me.

"Find who did this to her, Gilles." My voice was cold, exactly the way I felt inside. "I want you to use every resource you have and turn over every fucking rock, search every damn crack and hole until you find who hurt Selene. I don't care how much it costs. Find this woman."

I was filled with unquenchable wrath, and I was out for blood. I didn't give a damn who had hurt Selene. Justice would be mine.

Part Three

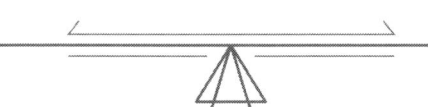

> The woods are lovely, dark, and deep,
> but I have promises to keep,
> and miles to go before I sleep,
> and miles to go before I sleep.
> —Robert Frost

Chapter Forty-Four

Remington

I was living and breathing my worst nightmare.

Three hours.

Three hours since the doctors wheeled Selene into the operating room. I hadn't heard from anyone. She was in there, fighting for her life.

Selene. The woman I had vowed to protect; yet there was nothing I could do to save her. Heal her. Take away whatever pain she was going through.

I pulled out the letter from my shirt's front pocket. I had written to her a few days ago when I woke up before dawn, unable to sleep. I hadn't had the nerve to give it to her at that time, and I'd been planning on surprising her before she left for the assignment in Berlin.

Taking a deep breath, I reread the words, the honesty in them leaving me breathless.

Merde! Everything was completely fucked-up. But I was going to make it right.

Folding the letter neatly, I slipped it back inside the pocket and turned to face Adrien, sleeping on the couch. I pulled the cotton sheet provided by one of the nurses up to his chin and then ran my hand down his hair, pushing the dark curls off his face. The last forty-eight hours had been a tremendous trial on him. Having him near me gave me a sense of control. He had spent the last hours sobbing into my shoulder, and for the first time in my life, I felt vulnerable. Not even when my father had threatened me, taken a belt to my back, had I felt this powerless. I had stood tall and taken whatever he'd thrown at me. But now, shit. Everything was a bloody fucking mess.

I leaned back on the chair, thinking back on the past few weeks. The first time I saw Selene in the hotel, our first lunch in the Tuilleries Gardens, dancing in the club and how her eyes had lit up when she'd realized she was dancing with me. I still couldn't believe how fast I had dropped my guard when I was around her, even though I'd known her for only a few days.

Rage boiled through my veins as scene after scene of what happened to Selene played in my head. The instant I had taken Adrien to bed a few hours ago, the damn PA had gone off, announcing Dr. Blanchett was needed in Selene's room. There had been a flurry of activity from the medical team surrounding her bed as they tried to help her. I should have protected her better.

But I didn't.

And now here we were, waiting to know her fate.

I dragged my fingers through my hair, tugged it back, savouring the pain. It grounded me.

"Monsieur St. Germain?"

My head snapped up, and I shot to my feet as Dr. Blanchett came to stand in front of me. His face was void of any expression.

Merde!

I was shaking, and my heart was pounding hard. I clenched my hands into fists at my sides. "How is she?" I asked in a hoarse voice.

"Let's sit down." He motioned to the seat I had vacated just a few seconds ago.

My legs gave way, and I grabbed the chair arm to support myself as I sat down, dropped my head in my hands and squeezed my eyes closed. "God, no."

The couch dipped as a weight settled beside me. "Monsieur St. Germain."

Deep breaths.

Deep fucking breaths.

He cleared his throat. "The surgery went well. We managed to get the swelling under control before any damage was done."

Swallowing past the lump in my throat, I lifted my head from my hands and slowly turned to look at the doctor. "So, she's going to be all right?"

He nodded, smiling faintly. "Right now, we have everything under control."

I exhaled loudly. "*Dieu merci.* Is she… Can we see her?"

He leaned forward, lips pursed, frowning. My chest tightened in pain as different kinds of scenarios flashed through my head, each one worse than the next.

God, no. Please don't do this to me. Don't take her away.

"We're keeping her in the ICU to monitor her for a few hours." He steepled his fingers, looked away, then back at me. "There's something you need to know first. She remained unconscious the entire time. She barely reacted to any outward stimulation on the tests we did."

Cold sweat broke out all over my body. "What are you trying to tell me, Doctor?"

He inhaled deeply and said, "She is in a coma."

"Wait, you said she was okay, *oui*? That you have everything under control."

"We do. But that doesn't mean she's out of danger. The next few days are critical, and we will do everything we can to make sure she comes out of this all right."

I blew out a breath, my gaze wandering to my son. "How long will she be in this condition?"

"It's impossible to predict when she will emerge from the coma. We just have to keep an eye on her." He sighed, looking weary. "Why don't you and your son get some rest and come back later to visit your wife? We organized for two policemen to guard her room for the next few days as per your request."

I nodded, eyeing Adrien. He needed a good night's rest and food. He also needed a break from being inside at the hospital. I straightened on my chair. My son deserved better care. I wasn't going to lose it now. Selene and Adrien needed me. "I'll be adding my own security guards to the watch team." I didn't know who to trust anymore.

After he shook my hand, he reassured me he would call if anything came up. He then left. I pulled out my mobile from my pocket and dialled Èric's number. He'd arrived an hour ago in Marseilles by car and had booked us a suite in a hotel not far from the hospital.

After making plans for him to pick us up and add more security for Selene, I scooped Adrien into my arms and left the waiting room that had been our home for the past forty-eight hours.

Chapter Forty-Five

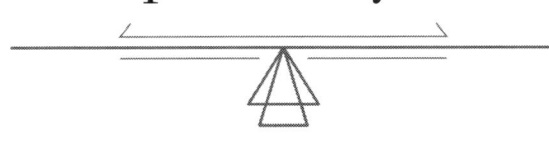

Selene

Wake up, Selene.

Wake up. I want to see your eyes, ma belle.

My eyes blink open in a room with white walls and big windows, but for some reason I can't see the owner of that voice, so familiar. Comforting. Why can't I see him?

Where am I?

I glance around, searching for that voice. The voice urging me to open my eyes in desperate, fervent whispers. But I can't find the face.

Ma belle. I need you to come back to me. I miss you. God, I'm so sorry.

I try to turn my head, but for some reason, I can't.

The voice once again encourages me to open my eyes. But they are open, aren't they? I blink just to make sure. Yes, I'm awake.

Why does the owner of that voice sound so sad? And why is he sorry?

A movement followed by a soft giggle, so soft it feels

as if I imagined it, interrupts me, momentarily distracting me from the man pleading with me to come back to him. I turn my head and gasp. Blink. I scrutinize that face, pert little nose, tiny mouth, smiling at me, a dimple on the chin, blue eyes. I hone in on the nose that's slightly upturned at the tip and the eyes. Very familiar eyes. James's eyes, just like I had imagined they would look like before she was born. The thought of him brings a twinge of pain and nothing more. Nothing like the soul-crushing pain I'd experienced when I found out about him and my best friend.

My sweet baby, Ines, named after my mother. I remember the look on my mother's face when I told her we were naming the baby after her. I had never seen her more happy and proud than that particular moment.

But how—how is my baby here? How is this even possible? She was still not born when I lost her. Am I in a dream? *God, why are you doing this to me?*

The baby smiles, kicks her tiny legs and waves her hands, cooing.

I blink again to make sure what I'm seeing is real. Oh, my God, it *is* real. I shift and turn on my side and slowly reach my hand toward her face. And I touch her. I touch her and she lets me. Her eyes close for a single second as if savouring my touch.

She is real.

"Hey, my beautiful, perfect girl," I whisper, my eyes burning with tears. "I've missed you so, so much." I trace my finger along the soft curve of her cheek. I don't let myself doubt how real her being here is, because the thought of her not being here with me kills me every single time. So I simply smile and stare at her.

"I've thought about you for so many days, months, years.

You sweet baby girl, you. I love you so much, and I've missed you terribly. Stay with me, please." I'm so afraid to touch her again, worried she will disappear, and so I settle in and study her precious face.

Stay with me, please.

Chapter Forty-Six

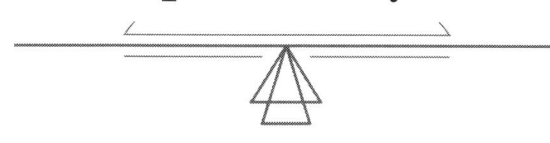

Remington

Yesterday was a trying day for Adrien and me. I returned to the hospital five hours later with a restless Adrien by my side. Once rested, he couldn't settle down until we visited Selene.

Today, Èric took him to a local indoor playground, which seemed to lighten his mood considerably. He's already made a few friends, one of the things he seemed to look forward to during the day.

I glanced at Selene, her expression relaxed. Peaceful. The only sounds filling the room were the beeps from the ECG machine whenever Selene's heart rate went dangerously low or high, the hiss and whoosh of the ventilator and the shuffling feet from the hospital staff outside the door. The doctor mentioned there was a chance she could hear whatever was happening around her, so I continued to caress the back of her hand with my thumb and talk to her as I'd been doing since I walked inside the room.

"You didn't tell me you had a flair for dramatics, *ma belle*." I imagined her laughing at my words. "Andrew and Grace called to check on you. They miss you and send their love. Did I ever tell you how Andrew and I met? I was in a bar in Paris, drowning my troubles in alcohol. He'd walked in just as a woman was about to rob me blind.

"After saving my arse, he put me in a taxi and took me to his home. When I woke up the next day, he gave me an earful, then kicked me out of his house. Damn, even I was impressed. Something that rarely happens. I went back to thank him two days later, looking and feeling more like a human being. I must have poured my heart out to him while I was drunk the night before. He told me to clean up my act. I was not being fair to people who loved me – my family. I had someone who needed and depended on me. Adrien. Those words sobered me up quickly. Do you know he signed me up for therapist sessions, too, even though he knew squat about me?"

I laughed, remembering how stubborn he'd been about that. "I attended three sessions and never went back. I'd learned my lesson well. I'm not one for sharing, especially my life." I lifted her hand to my lips. "I used to wonder what true love was. And I found that kind of love in you. I have my own theory. Yes, you can roll your eyes at me all you want. But I'm going with this, something my mother told me a long time ago. When you find that one person who makes you trip and fall, unable to take your eyes off her, you've found the love of your life. Love is what remains when we let our reservations melt away, when we let our demons come out to play. Please come back to me. I need you."

And I wish I knew who you truly are. Not that it'd stop me from saying yes to you.

The door creaked softly behind me, pulling me away from my thoughts. I turned around and saw my mother, standing on the threshold. Everyone knew Estelle St. Germain for her elegance and stoicism, but she looked nothing like those two words as she left the doorway and walked toward me, her gaze moving from me to Selene and then back to me. Laying Selene's hand back on the bed, I rose and went to her.

"Oh, *mon fils*," she said as she embraced me. "I arrived at the château, and as soon as I heard what happened, I drove here. How are you holding up?"

I shook my head, running my fingers through my hair. "I've never been this terrified in my life," I murmured under my breath. She touched my cheek, and I leaned my head into her palm.

"How is Adrien? Where is he?" she asked as she dropped her hand, stepped around me and walked toward the bed.

"One of my staff took him to a playground." I followed her and stopped beside her, anxious about this meeting between my mother and Selene.

She frowned, her eyes scrutinizing every inch of Selene's face. I heard her breath catch before she turned to look at me with wide eyes. Dropping her handbag on the chair I'd vacated, she motioned for me to follow her out of the room. Once outside, she braced her hands on her hips and took a deep breath as she always did when she was upset and was trying to control herself.

"What in God's name are you doing? Please tell me you haven't gone back to…" She shook her head as if to dispel the words.

I grabbed her hands quickly in mine. "No, no. It's not like that."

She clenched her jaw. "What is it like, then? I thought you stopped this years ago."

"She's different. I know what you are thinking right now, but I assure you that's not the reason why I'm with her." Although my thoughts kept wandering to the last conversation I had with Gilles.

Who are you, Selene?

"Is that the reason you were reluctant to introduce us before?"

"No." I took a deep breath, wondering how I would explain to her that Selene was different from all the women I had dated before. And that I hadn't gone back to how I was after Colette died. "She understands me. She's so good to me and Adrien, and I feel a connection to her I've never felt with anyone else."

"Connection." She repeated that word as if weighing it on her tongue. "What kind of connection?"

"Just trust me, Maman."

Taking another deep breath, she opened the door to Selene's room and entered. I followed her, wondering what she was thinking. She halted in front of Selene. "Do you love her?" she whispered, without looking at me.

"Yes," I said. "I have never been so certain about anything in my life."

At this, she turned around to look at me, her searching gaze filled with disbelief. She scoffed. "You love her? Remington, this isn't love. You probably love the idea of her because she resembles Colette."

"I love her," I repeated firmly. "She's very different from Colette. I've gotten to know her the past few weeks."

"What about Adrien? You have protected him all these years from meeting women you dated. Doesn't he count? I've never seen you this focused on a woman before her."

"I've never seen Adrien so happy. I've never been so sure about anything as much as I am with Selene. It sounds insane, *oui*?"

She strode toward a chair next to the wall and sat down,

burying her head in her hands. "I don't know how I feel about this yet. Please don't think I disapprove of you getting involved with a woman. But we've been through this before. I witnessed what it did to you, and that is something I never want to see you go through again." She dropped her hands and fixed her gaze on mine, eyes riddled with pain and worry. She seemed to have aged ten years between entering the room and seeing Selene.

Merde!

I had brought this on her. She had already dealt with so much shit from me. But I had to make her understand what I felt for Selene was beyond her looks. She had slipped through my defences and carved a place in my heart no other woman ever had. I did not intend to remove her from that place.

"I hope you understand I only want the best for you. May I ask how you two met?"

I pulled over the chair I'd been sitting on before and placed it next to my mother's. God, I loved this woman. She had fought hard for me; she had protected me my entire life. I knew she was looking out for me. But what I felt for Selene, it was primal. Indescribable.

"The first time I met her was at the hotel she was supposed to spend the next three months during her stay in Paris." I proceeded to tell her what happened after that. She continued to stare at me, absorbing my words without a reaction.

"What about her family? Do they know what happened?"

"I called her younger sister yesterday to check on some information the doctor needs. I didn't exactly tell her what happened. I will deal with that when she arrives in a few days."

"*Mon Dieu*, this is a mess. What about her parents? Will they be coming, too?"

I raked a hand down my face. "They will be visiting shortly, as soon as the doctor clears her mother for travel."

"So she'll be going back to the United States," she stated. "How will you handle it when she's gone?"

Fucking good question.

My heart sped up at the thought of never seeing Selene again, but I quickly dismissed those thoughts. I couldn't allow myself to think like that. I needed to stay positive for the sake of Adrien and Selene. And for my sanity, I needed her, and Adrien did as well. I suspected she needed us as much as we needed her, damn it.

"Remember how you told me that everything works out in the end? That all anyone needs is faith? Well, I'm banking on that right now."

She chuckled and shook her head. "I've never seen you so passionate about any other woman. Even Colette. She must be a good person if she has made such an impact on you."

"She is not any other woman." I smiled, something I hadn't done often the last forty-eight hours. "Good is an understatement."

My thoughts automatically went back to the last time I saw her laugh. She had looked fucking beautiful and carefree. Then the memory of Adrien cuddled in her lap as she read him a story replaced it, and the look of utter contentment slammed into me, hard, stealing my breath away. I quickly glanced at the bed, blinking back the tears.

Come back to me, Selene. I can't lose you. I wouldn't know where to begin or what to do if I did. Fight and come back to me.

I cleared my throat as emotion threatened to choke me. The image of Adrien's small face flashed in my head. The pain and heartbreak he'd suffered every time he asked about Selene haunted me relentlessly. This wasn't the time to lose my mind. I had to pull myself together. Right now, he needed me more than ever, and Selene did as well.

I straightened in my chair and faced my mother once again, determined, at least, to change the situation so that Adrien's life didn't solely rotate around hospital visits and the local playground. I also wanted to make sure the best doctors the St. Germain name could afford handled Selene's case.

My mother's face softened. "You are allowed to hurt, too, you know."

I laughed softly, remembering Selene's exact words and the way she went about showing me with her body. When my mother frowned at me, I squirmed on the seat, my body already reacting at the memory of Selene on my lap, coughed twice and said, "Selene said the same thing, too." Her eyes widened briefly as she flicked a gaze at the bed, then back at me. "I'm trying, Mother. Small steps."

She nodded, her shoulders loosening a little. "She is right."

I pushed back the hair off my forehead, realizing how long it had grown. Selene had an obsession about threading her fingers in it. I grew it longer because it made her happy. Quickly shaking my head, I focused again on my mother. "I have to speak to the doctor about transferring her to a hospital in Paris. Adrien needs to go back to his usual routine. At least something to keep his mind off what is going on at the moment."

She frowned. "Do you think it's wise to move her in her current state?"

"I will know more as soon as I talk to the doctor, but if there is a chance to do it, I will. Besides, I will feel safer with Gilles's security personnel close by."

My phone vibrated in my pocket, alerting me to an incoming call. I pulled it out and glanced at the screen.

Speak of the devil…

"I have to take this call first."

She nodded, but her focus was on Selene, her fingers

fiddling with the edge of her sweater as I left the room and went into the hallway.

"St. Germain."

"Remington," Gilles greeted me in his usual calm voice. "How is she faring?"

I rubbed a hand down my face. "Same as yesterday." I sighed. "What's the progress with the case?"

"We have been monitoring your stalker's movements. She's always out on Wednesdays, so my team and I will be checking the apartment in forty-five minutes from now."

I straightened. "I told you I wanted to be there when you made your move," I said.

He sighed. "We spoke about this, Remington. You are not qualified for this operation."

"Bloody hell!"

Silence fell between us following my outburst. I took deep breaths to calm down.

"Listen to me. You take care of Selene and let us handle this. You're not in a position to do this. Not in your current state of mind. You are distracted by what's happening. I will update you as soon as I get back in the office."

Shit.

He was right. I *was* distracted and needed to be there for Selene. But I also wanted to see the person who threatened my family, putting them in jeopardy.

After wrapping up the conversation, I ended the call and shoved my mobile inside my pocket and then tracked down Dr. Blanchett in his office.

"Monsieur St. Germain." He rose from his chair and walked around his desk, his hand outstretched in greeting. I shook it before settling down in the offered chair. Dr. Blanchett's no-nonsense approach to my interruption was something that gave me courage. As he returned to his desk, I could see from the many open files that he was busy. His relaxed posture was not one of frustration, and I believed him to be genuinely interested in how he could help Selene when he asked, "What can I do for you?"

I leaned back in the chair, fixing my gaze on his. "I would like to discuss the possibility of transferring my wife to Paris."

"Are you certain about this?"

I nodded once.

He cleared his throat, then leaned back in his chair. He studied me for a few minutes. "May I ask the reason for this decision?"

"I'll be honest with you, Dr. Blanchett. As we spoke before, Madame Michaels's accident wasn't exactly an accident. Someone has been threatening me—us. I was naïve to think that being in Provence and having a few security guards would provide some kind of safety. As you can see, my thoughts were proven wrong. The only way I feel I can keep her and my son safe while this matter is being sorted out is by traveling back to Paris. One of the best security firms I know is working on this case. Besides, I would like my son to get back to his normal routine, and that can only happen if we return to Paris. So tell me, Doctor," I leaned forward, elbows braced on my thighs, and my fingers steepled, "how can I get my wife into an excellent hospital in Paris?"

He continued staring at me, then chuckled. "You're still sticking to that story? That Madame Michaels is your wife?"

I cocked a brow, but my mouth tugged at the corners, fighting a smile. "Yes, I am."

He shook his head, smiling. "It is possible, but this is not my decision. First, we have to make sure she is in a position to be transferred. But before that, this case has to be discussed by the hospital board, and several neurologists will be involved." The amusement on his face vanished. "Unfortunately, I would still need one member of her family involved in this."

"Not a problem. Her sister will be arriving in a few days."

The stern look on his face eased slightly, and he settled back in his seat. "Let's see what we can do about this."

"But it is possible, *oui*? You've done this before?"

He nodded and began to fill me in on what exactly might be needed to make the transfer possible. When he was done, he folded his arms across his chest, giving me time to take in the information.

I brushed a hand down my face. *Mon Dieu*! I missed her. I missed her cheeky smile and sassy attitude, her shyness. Everything about her. Bloody hell, I wanted a guarantee she'd wake up soon. Feeling impatient, I shot up from my chair and started to pace.

"How is your son taking everything?" he asked.

"Better," I replied. The doctor had referred us to one of the hospital's psychologists after Adrien visited Selene the first day, a woman in her late fifties with a grandmotherly disposition, which proved to be good for my son. He had been hesitant at first, but with a little urging, he'd begun to respond to her. Èric, my mother and I made a point to distract him as much as possible and not spend most of the time in the hospital unless necessary. But the fact he could see Selene every once in a while was good for him. "He seemed quite taken with Dr. Martinez."

He nodded and smiled. "She seems to have that effect on both patients and visitors."

After leaving the doctor's office somewhat satisfied, I

prepared myself for another confrontation: with my mother. I had a feeling my talk with her had in no way eased her mind. I couldn't fault her for assuming I was with Selene because of her resemblance to Colette. I'd been desperate and stupid when she had died.

This was different.

Selene *was* different and the complete opposite of the woman who had dragged me through hell.

Chapter Forty-Seven

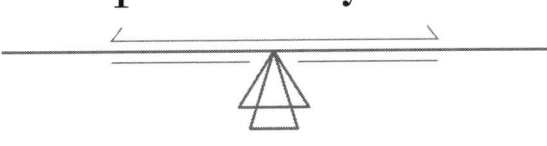

Remington

Three days later ...

The phone on the nightstand startled me, disrupting my concentration. I tossed the pencil and notebook on the table and checked my watch for the time. Three p.m. I had been so caught up drawing Selene; I completely forgot about the time. She had looked so peaceful and beautiful while she slept I couldn't pass up the opportunity, so I grabbed my drawing pad and pen from my bag and started working on the picture while talking to her.

I snatched the mobile from the table and scanned the screen while I left the room to answer the call.

Gilles.

"I've been waiting for your call," I barked into the phone. My patience was wearing thin, and I wasn't in the mood for any kind of civility. "What's happening? You were supposed to call me three days ago after you visited her apartment."

"Unfortunately, the mission didn't go as we expected, but we managed to sneak in on Thursday," he replied calmly. "How fast can you get here? We need you to go through some things for us. It might give a clue of who this person is."

"Can you scan whatever you have and send it to my mobile?"

"Hold on a minute." I heard the sound of a computer mouse click and a whirring sound, the scanner maybe. "Sent."

"I'll get back to you in a few minutes." I disconnected the call and quickly accessed his email with the photos. There were a few crime novels, a pair of scissors, gloves and a diary with a picture. I squinted at the image and shuddered. It was of Adrien and me in the kitchen, wearing pajamas. Selene was standing in the living room, facing us. I couldn't see her face, but I'd know those curves anywhere. An X was drawn with what I could guess was a red pen across her body. This photo must have been taken on the night she slept in my townhouse.

I shot up from the chair and started to pace.

Bloody hell! Who was this person? How did they get so close to the house without anyone taking notice?

I glanced at the picture again. There was nothing that gave away who this woman was. I dialled Gilles's number. "Nothing about the photos you sent gives a clue who we are dealing with. What else do you have for me?"

He exhaled loudly, seemingly frustrated. "We have to do another sweep in the apartment, which means we need you. You might see something we missed. How fast can you fly to Paris?"

"I can be there by nine in the morning."

"Fantastic. Don't worry. We will catch this bitch."

"Good. Because I'm beyond pissed. I'm fucking furious." I dragged my fingers through my hair. "What about the other issue? Did you find any more information about Selene?" I asked casually, hoping to hide the fact that I was still bothered by the blow he'd delivered to me on the night of Selene's incident.

"Yes, I did. But I wanted to give you some time to deal with what happened first." I heard the sound of papers being moved around. "As I mentioned before, according to this report, she was born in Paris. On further investigation, my man found out that Selene did in fact have another sister, other than Marley. Her name was Diane. She is reported to have disappeared twenty-six years ago. The trail had grown cold after she vanished, so no one knew her whereabouts."

I shut my eyes, fighting the feeling of dread twisting inside my gut. "Does it say who Diane's father was?"

He sighed. "*Non*. It is blank."

"All right," I said, massaging my neck to relieve the tension there. "I will see you tomorrow."

After disconnecting the call, I took deep breaths to calm down before walking back inside the room, mulling this new information. And just for a second, the resemblance between Selene and Colette flashed inside my head.

Shit, no. Life couldn't be that coincidental. Could it?

Shaking off those thoughts, I halted next to Selene's bed. My body stilled as I stared down at the woman who was fast becoming a big part of my life.

Tears trickled down the sides of her face, and her fingers twitched on the bed. What was happening? I took her hand and covered it with mine as my mind raced with the possibilities of what might be happening. All of them terrifying. The beeps from the monitor increased as her blood pressure started to rise. I snatched the nurse call button and pressed it repeatedly.

Where are the bloody nurses?

Feeling annoyed and worried, I dropped the call button and stalked out the room.

The two policemen and one security guard positioned outside Selene's room straightened, startled by my sudden appearance.

One of the guards hurried forward. "Monsieur St. Germain, can I…" His words trailed off as he took in my scowl. I stalked down the hallway toward the nurses' station, too impatient to wait.

Four nurses were chatting and laughing. One of them looked up, then quickly gestured to her workmates. One look in my direction had them scrambling up from their chairs and pretending to be organizing files and fuck knows what else, except one short woman with blond hair, who seemed braver.

"That thing is lighting up like a bloody lighthouse, but you're just standing there, talking and laughing?" I snarled.

Her face turned scarlet; she shot up from her chair and darted past me. "*Pardon,* Monsieur St. Germain," she whispered, loudly enough for the words to reach me, her gaze focused on the floor as she dashed toward Selene's room.

I glared at the three women before turning and following the short nurse. Taking a deep breath, I entered the room. She glanced up but quickly averted her eyes as soon as she met mine.

"What's wrong with her?" I snapped, pointing to Selene, lying on the bed.

The nurse wiped her palms on her white uniform. "Nothing seems to be the problem, Monsieur St. Germain. Her vitals seem okay and—"

"That monitor was going ballistic. And my wife is crying." I gritted out the words. The nurse snapped her head back, her eyes widening at my tone. "Why the bloody hell is she crying?"

She moved around the bed and walked toward me. "Her blood pressure seems to have normalized. Sometimes when the patient is experiencing some emotion in her current state, it affects their vitals, especially the blood pressure. It's natural for patients in a coma to show emotion." She raised her hands in a placating gesture. "Look," she pointed toward the bed. I followed her gaze and sucked in a breath as I stared at Selene. "She's smiling."

I stepped around the woman and strode to the bed. "She's *smiling*. But she's also crying." I could hear the wonder in my voice as I watched laughter and sadness play across Selene's face. "What are you dreaming about, *ma belle*?" I murmured, settling down on the chair that had become a permanent fixture next to her bed. I took Selene's hand in mine and weaved our fingers, caressing the soft skin of her knuckles with my thumb. "You have a way of shocking me every time, little minx."

I heard the nurse leave, but I didn't take my eyes off the beautiful woman on the bed. Couldn't take my eyes off her. *Mon Dieu*, I was in love with Selene, and there was no denying that.

"Christ, I love you. I remember the exact moment I fell in love with you, Selene. You'd opened the hotel room door, looking beautiful, while I stood there, fighting myself. Fighting the demons that ruled my mind. You could have walked away, but you put your arms around me, you soothed me. You whispered words and helped me. Please come back to me. I can't live without my home." Did this make me weak, or as Luc would say, pussy-whipped, pouring my heart out like this? I didn't really give a shit how it made me look. I'd be weak for her, drop on my knees and beg if I could see her smile again.

The door opened, admitting my mother, Adrien and Èric. I rose from the chair and strode toward them as Adrien dashed forward. I caught him in my arms, kissed my mother's cheek and we stepped back into the hallway. Èric smiled briefly and nodded in greeting. I could see how difficult it was for him to keep eye contact with me since the incident. We'd finally had a conversation about what happened a few days ago in the château, and it seemed to ease his guilt about this situation.

"Is everything all right?" I asked, forcing him to look at me.

He nodded, then briefly updated me on what had happened after he drove my mother and Adrien to the hotel last night. I let him know what Gilles had found and that I'd be flying to Paris early the next morning. We made arrangements for him to pick up Marley from the airport in three hours, and then I returned to the room with Adrien in my arms. As soon as I was closer to the bed, he squirmed, his usual energetic self, eager as always to see her.

"She is still sleeping, Papa," Adrien whispered, his gaze fixed on Selene in fascination. "Just like the princess in the story Mamie read to me yesterday." He turned his big, innocent eyes to face me. "Maybe if you kiss her, she will wake up."

I chuckled, flicked a look at the bed and exhaled in relief. *Dieu merci.* There was no sign of tears on Selene's face.

"You know that was only a story, my sweet." My mother and I exchanged a glance. He seemed to be taking things easier, now the tube had been removed. "I bet she has been waiting for you. Would you like to talk to her or sing?"

He nodded quickly, smiling and dashed toward the bed.

"Adrien." He jerked around and looked at me. "Remember, no running," I said, softly but firmly. He nodded quickly and pressed his index finger on his lips with a silent "shhh" before tiptoeing toward the bed.

My mother chuckled and then turned to focus on me. "Any changes? What did the doctor say about…her situation?" I heard the hesitation in her voice, as if she wasn't sure to call Selene by her name.

"Her? You mean Selene?" I asked her, raising a brow. She

glanced at the bed, then back at me, giving me a look as if to tell me to stop being cheeky, and nodded.

I updated her on Selene's progress while fighting a smile at the looks she kept sneaking to the bed.

"Take a break, Remington. Go to the hotel, take a bath or shower and change," she said when I was done.

"I'm all right. At least for a few more hours," I said. "Marley will be arriving from Paris soon. I want to be here to meet her."

She rolled her eyes. "I'm sorry to break this to you, but you don't look so great."

"I'm not here to impress anyone," I retorted playfully.

She lifted a brow. "So you're not trying to impress her?" She pointed to the bed with her chin. "What do you think she would say if she saw you looking like this?"

Good point, Mother. "All right." I turned to face Adrien. He was leaning forward with one of his favourite Lego toys, walking it across the bed sheet and speaking in a low voice.

"I'll be back in a few hours, Adrien. Take care of Selene, all right?"

He dropped the toy on the bed, straightened and puffed his chest. "Yes, Papa. Mamie brought a book to read for my mama."

I turned to look at my mother in time to see her drop her face, a soft flush creeping up her cheeks.

"I thought she'd enjoy it," she said.

I smiled, stepped forward and pulled her into my arms. "Thank you, Maman." I kissed her forehead and then pulled back.

"It's nothing, really." She brushed my gratitude aside with her hands.

I cupped her face in my hands, making sure her eyes were on mine. "It's *something*," I said firmly. She nodded, her expression softening as she studied my face. I dropped my hands and grabbed my overnight bag next to the bed. "She is good for him."

I smiled. "He is good for *her*. If anyone can pull her back, it's Adrien." I strode toward the door and spared a look over my shoulder. My mother frowned in concentration as if she was trying to figure something out. I hadn't told her about Selene's loss yet. I wanted her to like Selene without pitying her, before she got to know about her.

Chapter Forty-Eight

Remington

Two hours later, I was dressed and pacing the floor inside the suite we had taken residence in since we arrived in Marseilles. Earlier on when I arrived, I left a message at reception that if Èric arrived, he should be allowed to come upstairs.

After calling my mother to confirm all was well and that they had left the hospital and gone to Adrien's usual indoor playground, I ended the call and picked up my pacing.

The doorbell rang, startling me out of my thoughts. I strode to the door and opened it, my gaze automatically falling on the woman standing next to Èric. I would know she was related to Selene even if I hadn't known who she was. Marley was shorter than Selene, maybe four inches at most, straight hair held in a ponytail at the nape of her neck, brown skin, and wide forehead. The only difference between her and Selene was the missing upward tilt at the tip of her nose. Selene had mentioned Marley was twenty-one years old.

She stared at me, studying me curiously. Her eyes were bloodshot as if she'd been crying during the entire trip to

France. My chest tightened, knowing I had brought this upon her sister.

"Monsieur St. Germain," Èric said, breaking the silence. He lifted a brow, and I cleared my throat.

"Hello, Marley." My voice was hoarse, choking on guilt.

Immediately, her eyes filled with tears. She sobbed my name in a broken voice before she threw herself at me. I caught her, pulling her tight into me as her body shook with sobs. My own eyes burned with tears, so I quickly shut them tightly.

Merde! This wasn't the time to show weakness. Marley needed me.

"How is she?" she whispered against my chest. I opened my eyes and stared down at her lowered head.

I couldn't speak. I wanted to be able to tell her that her sister was doing well, awake, ready to see her. How I hated to disappoint her though.

She pulled back and met my gaze, her eyes so similar to her sister's. "Remington, is she…is she…?" She choked on a sob and covered her mouth with one hand while shaking her head.

"No! No, she is not. She is not—" I couldn't say the word I knew she was thinking. *Dead.* "Please come in so we can talk before I take you to the hospital."

I slid a hand around her shoulders, urging her in and met Èric's sombre stare over her head. He was suffering from his own guilt. I sighed inwardly and guided Marley toward the living room while Èric closed the door behind us. I led her to the couch, grabbed a box of tissues and placed them on the table. Then I squeezed her shoulder in reassurance and asked her if she needed anything. When she shook her head, I excused myself, strode toward the fridge, and took out a bottle of water. Then I grabbed a bottle of Scotch, poured a shot in a glass, and downed it.

"How are you holding up?" Èric asked.

I blew out a breath. "Much better than a few days ago." I glanced where Marley sat, dabbing her eyes with a tissue.

"She didn't break down until she got here. You do have a way with the ladies," Èric said, then quickly looked contrite.

I chuckled, despite feeling as if I was about to jump in a hellish fire, and shook my head. I wasn't going to bite his head off for this. We both needed relief after everything that had happened. "That's me. The Heartbreaker."

He cleared his throat, as was his habit when he wanted to say something. "Let me know if you need anything."

St. Germain didn't have hangar space here in Marseilles, which meant booking a flight. "I might need a lift to the airport to catch a flight to Paris at six in the morning. Did you manage to book a flight for me?"

"*Oui.* I printed out the tickets for you. Your mother placed them on your nightstand."

I nodded. "*Merci beaucoup.*"

After Èric left, I strode back to the living area, carrying a bottle of water and Scotch in a glass, placed them on the table and sat across from Marley.

This is it.

"Thank you so much for flying to France on such short notice," I began, unable to find the right words for this conversation. "I want you to rest assured your sister is being treated by one of the best doctors in the city."

Her lower lip trembled, and she swiped the back of her hand at her face and then straightened in the seat with her chin stuck stubbornly forward and nodded. "Just…tell me what happened to her, okay? I can handle it."

Mon Dieu, Marley was so like her sister. I remembered just weeks ago when Selene challenged me with that look. My chest tightened at the memory, but I quickly shook it off to concentrate on what I was about to tell Marley. I didn't want to lie to her because lies are like ghosts of the past. They have a way of coming back and haunting you at the most unexpected times. Besides, I wanted her to be aware of what was happening—that she might also be in danger.

Taking a deep breath, I told her about Selene's condition. Then launched into the story about the woman stalking us.

One and a half hours later, Marley and I arrived at the hospital and headed to Selene's room. Before we left the hotel, I'd informed her there was a chance Selene could hear everything or most of what was happening around her. We needed to keep everything positive. And if a person was overwhelmed, it was advisable to leave the room. There was no way I'd allow negativity around Selene. She was already locked in a place where God knew what was happening or what she was going through. That was enough.

Marley nodded to let me know she was ready to enter the room. As soon as she saw her sister, she froze mid-step and slapped a hand over her mouth, her eyes wide. "Oh, my God!" Her shoulders started to shake as stifled sobs escaped.

Jesus, just staring brought the pain, searing, destroying me further. I took a step forward and pulled her into my arms wordlessly.

"It's my fault," she said, her voice muffled in my chest.

"What?"

"I encouraged her to come to France. But, God, she had been so happy—"

"Shh. It's not your fault. And I am certain if Selene had a say about it, she would tell you the same thing."

She dug a tissue from her handbag and pulled back, giving

me a wobbly smile. "Crap. She would probably scold me for crying."

"I wouldn't put that beyond your sister," I said, remembering my confident, sassy Selene.

I miss her so much.

The mobile beeped twice in my pocket, announcing an incoming call. "Are you all right doing this on your own?" I asked, digging out my phone.

She nodded and pointed at the mobile with her chin. "Go ahead."

I smiled briefly and answered the call without checking who the caller was.

"St. Germain."

"This is Dr. Hayes, Caleb Newport's doctor," a cool, accented voice said.

I motioned with a finger for Marley to give me a minute. "Is he all right?"

"That's the reason for this call. How fast can you get to London? We need to operate soon."

"How soon?"

"Tomorrow, if possible. He experienced seizures today. His body is quickly shutting down, and I'm afraid of what might happen if we don't operate soon. If you can make it by tonight, it'd be fantastic. We would like to perform a few necessary tests before the surgery."

I raked my hand down my face, shutting my eyes tightly.

His body is quickly shutting down.

Those words reverberated inside my head, causing my heart to beat faster. "I'll catch the next flight out so I can be there as soon as possible."

After wrapping up the conversation, I turned to face Marley. "Is everything okay?" she asked, frowning slightly.

I shook my head. "I'm afraid I have to leave for London as soon as possible. My brother is in need of a kidney transplant, and I'm his donor."

Her eyes widened. "Oh, my God, I'm so sorry." She stepped forward with her arms outstretched toward me and paused, looking uncertain for a second. Then, she put her arms around me, embracing me tightly. Her naturally warm personality made it easy to see why Selene loved her so dearly.

I pulled back and nudged her toward the bed. "Go ahead. I'll be in the hallway." She nodded and walked toward the bed.

Out in the hallway, I called Gilles to let him know of the new developments and that I would fly to Paris after the surgery. Then I called Luc and after that, Dom. They'd called earlier, enquiring about Selene. Both wanted to fly here, and as much as I needed them, Luc was taking part in the Grand Prix in Russia in just a few days and needed to focus. Dom had taken time off and was coordinating what needed to be done at the château. When I was done, I started to pace the hallway, waiting for Marley. I wanted to spend as much time as I could with Selene before leaving for London. God, I was going to miss her. What if she woke up while I was away and needed me?

I dragged my fingers through my hair and closed my eyes. *Deal with one thing at a time, Remington.*

Even after repeating those words inside my head, I was restless.

Chapter Forty-Nine

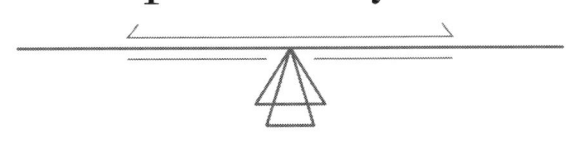

Selene

There was that voice again. So sweet, angelic, singing to me.
Marley.
My sweet little sister, Marley. I've missed you, little sister.

A pair of huge, green eyes on a cute face flashed in my head. That smile…I felt as if I knew him, yet I couldn't remember exactly who he was. He smiled at me and called me 'mama'. I wanted to be his mom so damn badly it hurt.

I turned to face my baby. I couldn't live here in this little world I created for Ines and myself any longer, because I had people waiting for me. People who loved me. Besides, it wasn't healthy. For once, I had people who needed me.

"My sweet baby, Ines. You know I'll always love you. I will always wish you were with me so I could watch you grow." I closed my eyes and took a deep breath. "This is so hard for me to say, but…I have to go. This little boy, whoever he is, needs me. So, baby, I have to go. I won't ever forget you. I love you. I love you so much."

"Bloody hell, she's crying again." The same deep voice that had been urging me to open my eyes announced in a distressed voice.

Someone sighed. "Monsieur St. Germain, we spoke—"

"Yes, I know, I know." The first man—Monsieur St. Germain—cut him off and then exhaled in frustration. Strong fingers wrapped around mine, and then there was the feeling of warm air on the back of my hand followed by soft lips on my skin. It felt thrilling. Comforting. He whispered, "I miss you so bloody much. I love you."

I love you. The words were spoken in reverence, sending a jolt of joy straight into my chest.

I opened my eyes and blinked rapidly to adjust my vision to the bright room.

"Selene?" St. Germain whispered my name, caught between disbelief and relief. I lowered my gaze to his face, and my heart tripled its beating. Black hair, stubbled jaw, green eyes so similar to the little boy's in my dream.

Shit!

The glare from the lights was burning into my eyeballs. I winced and quickly shut my eyes.

What is going on? Where am I?

Another face surfaced in my area of vision. A man with black hair streaked in white and brown eyes. If I could guess his age, I'd say forty-five to fifty-five years.

His smile was kind, friendly. "Madame Michaels? My name is Dr. Blanchett." He paused, leaned back and blinked. "How are you feeling?"

I felt my hands move, hit something, but I couldn't really move. Not really. Every part of my body felt heavy.

"Doctor?" I asked, shifting my gaze to the sides, hoping to catch a familiar face, but found St. Germain's, a confident smile on his lips. It wavered the more I studied him.

"Selene?"

"Who are you?" I whispered.

The smile disappeared, and his eyebrows bunched together. He flicked a look at the doctor. Why did he look so confused?

A pain flashed inside my head and I winced, closing my eyes.

"What's happening to her?" St. Germain asked. His voice had a calming effect, yet I couldn't explain why. I opened my eyes, trying to work out who he was. *Did I know him?*

"I would like to examine Madame Michaels. Could you please excuse us, Monsieur St. Germain?" the man who had introduced himself as the doctor said.

The man—St. Germain—glanced at me with a perplexed, almost hurt look before his face shuttered, leaving a blank expression on his countenance. He turned and walked away without looking back. The doctor turned to face me.

"How are you feeling, Madame?"

How am I feeling? "Where am I? What are you doing here?"

He dipped his hand in the pocket of his white coat and pulled out something that looked like a pen. "Let me examine you. Then I will explain what happened, all right?"

My breath sawed in and out of my chest as panic settled in. "No!" My legs moved on their own accord, and suddenly my body was sliding out of the bed, and before the doctor could catch me, I landed on my knees on the cold floor. The door burst open, admitting St. Germain, a look of pure terror on his face. He glanced down at me, and within a split second, the look morphed to fury.

"What the bloody hell!" He stalked to where I lay, fighting off the doctor's hands, and squatted to my eye level. I whimpered and tried to scoot back, but something was wrong with my body. I couldn't move. "Hey, hey, Selene," St. Germain said, the threatening expression from before falling away, replaced with a tender look. If I knew better, I would say a caring face. But what did I know? I had no idea what I was doing here in the first place. "I'm not going to hurt you. I promise, all right?"

I stared at him, tears rolling down my face, and then dropped my gaze to my lap, catching sight of something from the corner of my eye. A catheter? What the hell? I had one of these when I was hospitalized two years ago after…my baby, Ines. Did something happen?

I clutched my stomach, but I couldn't feel any tell-tale signs of a bump. Christ, why couldn't I remember anything? Maybe these two men could enlighten me. Grabbing the thin blanket on the bed, I glanced up and met St. Germain's pleading gaze as he held up both hands, palms facing me.

"I'm not sure. What's happening? Why am I on this bed?"

"My name is Remington. I would like to assist you. Allow me to do that, okay?" he asked in a calm voice. I nodded.

Gently, he scooped me into his arms and laid me on the bed. He brought his hand toward my face, and I froze, waiting. Watching. Seconds passed before he slowly swept the locks of hair off my forehead, tucking them behind my ear. Then he straightened and from one second to the next, his entire demeanour changed from soft to hard, unyielding, as he faced the doctor.

"What happened?" Remington asked—no, growled—in a clipped tone of voice.

"It's normal for a patient who has been in a coma to wake up confused, panicked."

"I mean, why was she on the floor?" my knight in scowling armour asked, a vein ticking dangerously on his temple.

Forgetting my own confusion, I stared, fascinated. The doctor reminded me of a deer caught between an oncoming truck and a predator.

"I was about to perform a check to make sure everything is okay. I guess she was frightened. I would like to continue, if you don't mind leaving—"

"I do mind," Remington snapped, glaring fiercely at the doctor. He folded his hands across his impressive chest, his feet planted firmly on the ground and jerked his chin stubbornly toward me. "You might as well continue the check-up. I'm not leaving."

The doctor sighed, turned to face me with the pen-like object in his hand. "I would like to do a check-up on you, okay? I want to make sure everything is all right."

I flicked a gaze at my knight. He gave me an encouraging nod. I clutched the starched bed sheets tightly to keep myself from panicking and faced the doctor.

Twenty minutes later, I was tucked back in bed, fiddling with the edge of the sheets as I watched the doctor scribble on a chart in his hands. Then without warning, I burst into tears.

"Bloody hell! What's happening now?" I heard Remington ask. The doctor said something, but I was beyond hearing. I didn't even know why I was crying. When I finally quieted down, Remington told me what happened, and the doctor filled me in whenever he could. My mind was messed up. I could only remember bits and pieces; some scenes came to me clearly but a few were elusive, no matter how much I tried to remember.

In between listening and studying the man sitting next

to me, watching me like a hawk, I lay my head on the pillow, closed my eyes for just a few seconds. I knew I could trust this man, even though I couldn't justify the reason I felt that way. I remember someone kissing my forehead and whispering, "Good night, *ma belle*."

"Good night, Remington," I mumbled as exhaustion pulled me under.

My eyes blinked open. I winced as the bright light hit my eyes and quickly shut them again. The room was quiet.

Where am I?

Taking a deep breath, I opened my eyes carefully and blinked several times to adjust my vision. White walls, tiled ceiling…

I turned my head and winced again. My neck felt stiff, as if I hadn't moved it in a long time. I continued to take in the room, and my eyes rested on the head full of curls with blonde-dyed tips, currently resting next to my hip.

Marley? What is she doing here? And why am I lying on this bed, in this room?

I tried to lift my hand but couldn't; a weight was pinning it down. Glancing to the side, I saw Marley's hand was on mine, her fingers carefully curled around it.

"Marley."

What is wrong with my voice? Why can't I hear myself?

I wiggled my fingers, but they felt heavy, as if I hadn't used them in years. I blinked and suddenly a scene played inside my head, clearly.

I shift on my chair, rubbing my tummy to ease the sudden jabs of pain. Did I eat too much? Admittedly, the food was delicious. Remington hired a chef who specializes in Provençal Cuisine for this evening's dinner. Maybe I need to walk off the food I consumed. I stand up and head out the door to the patio for some fresh air and then exhale in relief as my stomach settles. My thoughts, like every other time, wander back to father and son. Today we had such a wonderful day, something we needed after the fire that burned most of the vineyard. I'm looking forward to spending the evening with him. Maybe tell him I'm thinking of extending my stay in France. The last few days, I've thought of possibilities that leave my head reeling. I've seen how my life would be with Remington and Adrien in it. God, I want that so damn bad. But I also realized I've been selfish, accepting Adrien calling me Mama, yet planning to leave in a little over two months. I need to apologize to Remington, tell him he was right to be angry with me. Tell him I'm staying.

God, I'm about to explode! I need to talk to him and Adrien before the boy falls asleep.

I walk back to the dining room and refill my glass, with water this time, and bring it to my lips. My heart thumps inside my chest, and I have to grip my seat to stop myself from jumping up and heading upstairs to wait for Remington in the hallway. Instead, I laugh as the rest of my nervousness melts away.

"I'm staying," I whisper the words, rolling them on my tongue. They taste like freedom from my past and hope for the future.

I gulp down the water, but suddenly I'm not feeling too good again. I clutch my stomach and push the chair back. Shit! I need to get to the bathroom before I vomit all over the floor.

Something clatters on the stone floor behind me. Startled, I turn around, smiling, hoping that Remington has snuck downstairs wanting to surprise me. But before I can do that, the sick feeling overwhelms me. I heave and vomit.

"Serves you right, you bitch. Did you think I was going to

stand by and let you steal Remington from me? I've watched you for a long time, bided my time, waited."

I groan, raising my head to face this person, and the only thing I see is a face flash in front of me before sharp pain explodes in the back of my head. I fall forward, my forehead hitting the floor. I try to lift myself with my hands, but I can't. My head and stomach ache, my throat is sore, and I vomit again. I close my eyes to clear my vision, and when I open them again, I can't see anything. The darkness that surrounds me is so deep, so terrifying. I think my mouth is open, calling to Remington, but there's no sound.

The tap, tap, tap of high heels grows farther and farther away. The last words I hear are, "Sorry, but this is not personal," before my world goes black.

My breathing came out in pants as the memory faded. Oh, my God, the stalker tried to kill me.

I can't breathe.

God, I can't breathe.

"Hold her down!" someone shouted. Loud beeps filled the room, feet shuffled on the floor.

"Remington!" I called out. "I need to talk to him. Warn him. Oh, God, please. That woman…" I fought against the horde of hands trying to hold me in place.

"A hundred sixty to ninety and rising!" Another voice. "We need to calm her down."

"O2 levels going down fast!"

"Selene!" A familiar voice. Marley. I wanted my sister, but I couldn't get to her.

"Marley! I want my sister. Please don't send her away." I thrashed on the bed in an effort to get to her. "Don't take her away from me, too."

"Get her out of here!" someone yelled.

"*Merde!* Won't do any good. Bring her here." Another voice.

Suddenly, a hand clasped around mine. I turned to find Marley at my side, and I gripped her hand tighter.

"Don't go. Please don't leave me," I said desperately. "I can't lose you, too."

"I'm here, sis. I won't leave you. Ever," she vowed while tears rolled down her face.

"BP still rising."

Then I felt a sharp prick on my arm and seconds later, everything became blurry.

No, I don't want to sleep again. I need to speak to Remington.

Please, no.

Everything went black.

Chapter Fifty

Remington

The flight to London seemed long. My mind was preoccupied the entire time with thoughts of Selene. She couldn't remember me. After we left the room to discuss the final details for the transfer to Paris, the doctor had informed me she was suffering from short-term amnesia caused by the blow to the head. There was no way of knowing how long it would last. A sharp pain dug into my chest and spread all over my body. After leaving the hospital, I had called my mother and informed her of Selene's condition and also asked her to hold off any visits to the hospital for Adrien. I didn't want him to go through heartbreak, especially if Selene couldn't remember who he was.

The airplane touched down at Heathrow Airport at exactly 10:32 a.m. Forty-five minutes later, I strode inside the hospital and was standing in front of Caleb's room, trying to catch my breath. I heard voices drifting through the door.

Merde.

My father was in there. I had planned to spend a few minutes with Caleb alone before surgery. My head was already fucked up with everything that was going on with the stalker and Selene, now awake but agitated and with memory loss; I wasn't about to let my father inflict any more pain on me. I spun around and went in search of Dr. Hayes.

"Remington?" a familiar voice called out.

I looked over my shoulder to see Adele. She smiled widely, hurrying toward me.

"It's so good to see you, big bro." She embraced me, then pulled back. Jesus, it felt incredible to just be held like this. Comforting. "How are you doing?"

I narrowed my eyes at her, studying her face. Black rings surrounded her eyes. "Better than you, I think. What's wrong?"

She shook her head. "It's Caleb. He doesn't look so good."

"Why didn't anyone call me earlier? You know I'd have—"

"Shh…Remington. No," she said, cutting me off. "Selene needed you—needs you, and Adrien as well. You've gone through so much the last few weeks. Caleb…we could wait."

"Adele." She flinched at my tone.

Merde!

I sounded sterner than I had intended. "Adele," I repeated in a gentler tone. "Please don't do that. You of all people know me. Caleb is my blood. I need to know what's happening. I can handle anything, okay?" She nodded. "And I want you to take care of yourself, all right?"

She nodded and quickly wiped her cheeks. "Are you going in to see Caleb?"

I shook my head. "The doctor. I need some information before the surgery."

She narrowed her eyes, reminding myself of me. "Is Dad in Caleb's room?"

I nodded, grimacing. Whatever she saw on my face had her shaking her head, fighting a smile.

"All right. Catch me up on what's happening then. Mum is in Caleb's room as well, so it's like being in a fire and ice storm."

I chuckled and held out my arm. "Come on, walk with me."

She straightened and right there, I saw the Adele I'd known for four years. Cool and confident. We strolled toward the doctor's office while I updated her on what was happening back in France.

Chapter Fifty-One

Remington

It was finally the day where I gave part of me to my brother. I glanced to the bed, watching Caleb. His skin looked pale. Yellow. He seemed worse than when I arrived earlier the previous day.

"Don't look so enthusiastic about this surgery, bro," Caleb said in a hoarse voice, sounding amused. I met his gaze, watching a mischievous smile play on his lips.

"Oh, shut up. You don't look so happy either." He rolled his eyes. "You had better handle my kidney with care."

He laughed, weak and scratchy. "I'll coat it with gold to preserve it."

"Smartarse," I said with a chuckle. "Ready for this?"

He nodded, motioning for me with his hand. "Come here." I dragged my chair next to his bed and clasped his hand in mine. "Thank…you."

"You don't need to thank me. You're my family. Pl—"

"Yes. I…do. Just please shut up and allow me to say this." He closed his eyes; his breathing was heavy. I bit my tongue, waiting. "I am sorry I didn't reply to all the letters you sent.

My father made sure I didn't receive any of them. I only came to know about you after Adele made up her mind to track you down, after I told her who you were. She was very determined to find you." He laughed but immediately started coughing.

"Let's catch up later. Right now, let's focus on this surgery."

He shook his head, becoming more agitated and coughing. The beeps coming from the machine monitoring his vitals increased in frequency. The door burst open, and two nurses came rushing in.

"Sir, please leave the room," one of them said in an urgent voice while the other dashed toward the bed.

I shot to my feet and stumbled backward to give them space.

"Sir, you need to leave now."

I growled under my breath, frustrated, and turned around to leave.

Merde. This can't be happening. I can't lose him. Not when he is this close to getting better.

I pulled the door closed behind me and leaned on it.

Bloody hell!

Unable to stand still, I paced the hallway. It seemed like pacing in hospital hallways was becoming a norm for me. I leaned on the wall, focusing on the conversation I'd had with Adrien thirty minutes earlier to distract me. He'd been excited that Èric was taking him indoor go-karting, which seemed to divert him from thinking about Selene, and worse, that I was heading for surgery, but I knew he'd eventually ask about her. I had to speak to someone before I went insane. Before I even had the chance to call, the familiar buzzing in my pocket changed my direction.

"St. Germain."

As Gilles began talking, my gaze wandered out the window

to the park where a father and son played with their kite. Simple things. Normal.

A lot of things had happened the past few weeks; I couldn't remember what normal felt like anymore.

"Mr. St. Germain?" a voice called out from behind me.

I looked over my shoulder at a female nurse. She'd been in the room when Caleb was seizing. I gripped my mobile tighter. "I need to go. I'll call you as soon as I can."

"Good luck, Remington."

"Gilles," I said quickly before he could disconnect the call. "My family...I trust you to keep them safe."

He was silent for a few seconds and then said, "You know I would die protecting them, *oui*?"

I glanced at the ceiling, blinking hard.

Fucking hell!

I was getting soft in my old age. I disconnected the call without answering Gilles and focused on the nurse in front of me.

"It's time," the nurse said, her expression softening as she scrutinized me. Whatever she saw on my face had hers softening. Or was it pity?

I gave her a curt nod, schooling my features to neutral. Unreadable. I had mastered that art while growing up. Always kept people at arm's length. I flicked my hand, gesturing for her to lead the way.

She smiled, her blue eyes twinkling in what looked like ever-present joyfulness, and started down the hall toward Caleb's room, flicking glances at me every few seconds.

What the hell is she happy about?

When we reached Caleb's room, she stopped at the door and looked up at me.

"It's okay to feel emotional, you know?"

I stared down at her, exasperated.

"You are giving a part of yourself to someone else. Whatever you are feeling is normal. You are brave to do this for him."

"He's my brother," I said, letting those words speak for themselves. I glanced down at her name, patched on her uniform. "Nurse Patricks."

She pursed her lips, handed me a hospital gown.

The phone rang right after I was done changing. I grabbed it from the table and glanced on the screen before answering it.

Mother?

"*Bonjour*, Remington," my mother said as soon as I answered.

"*Bonsoir*, Maman," I greeted her. I glanced up as four nurses walked into the room. "I'm about to go in to the operating room. Is everything all right?"

"She has been asking for you and Adrien," my mother said. I heard her sniff.

My heart was beating fast. "Is she all right? Is everything okay?" I closed my eyes, bracing myself for whatever news she was about to deliver. Yet another thing I couldn't control.

"Her memory is returning in pieces. Most of the things she's talking about don't make sense, but she was agitated, looking for you. She is worried about you and keeps saying the woman is going to hurt you, too. It's just, I have never seen Adrien so happy. He—he loves her." Her voice was filled with wonder.

I breathed out, blinking my eyes open. "*Dieu merci*!" I murmured under my breath. "Yes, he does. And she loves him, too." One of the nurses gestured at the clock on the wall. "I have to go. I will call you later, all right? Tell her I'll be there soon; and Adrien, too."

"I will. Be safe, my son."

After ending the call, I turned to face the medical team,

smiling as hope and relief shot through me. For once since everything started spinning out of control, I felt a tinge of optimism. I could do it. Handle everything and get my life back on track. I pushed aside the looming worries about loving a woman when I had no clue who she was exactly, and the threats of yet another woman who seemed to want Selene dead, and focused on getting my brother better.

"Let's do this."

Chapter Fifty-Two

Selene

A week had passed since I woke up, and my memory was returning in fragments. Emotionally, I was a mess. My moods seemed to change without warning. The doctor diagnosed these changes as post-concussion syndrome. Two days ago, I shouted at Marley because she was urging me to finish my lunch. And the next minute, I was bawling my eyes out. Thank God, she had been so understanding.

Yesterday, I sulked when Estelle told me Remington had called while I was sleeping. I asked her why she didn't wake me up. She explained I needed my rest and her son would call again. Then feeling distressed, I confronted her and asked her why she didn't like me. She'd tried to calm me, but I was inconsolable. Later, she had explained why she hadn't warmed up to me yet. She was terrified her son was slipping back into the state he had been right after Colette's death. She was worried I'd leave her son and grandson in complete chaos when I finally left France. I had assured her I loved both father and son. When I told her about my baby, Ines, she had taken me into her arms, and I'd cried as she held me. Her attitude toward me warmed further, but it didn't stop the unguarded, cautious looks whenever she focused on me.

I slept in fear and woke up screaming every day as my nightmares followed me into waking moments. My only consolation was seeing Adrien walk in with Èric or his grandmother and also speaking to Remington on the phone every day. And Marley. She was my constant and my cornerstone as I continued to recuperate. Dr. Blanchett visited every day to check on my progress. He also informed me of Remington's wish for a transfer to Paris. Sometimes I couldn't remember some details, which was extremely frustrating. At times, I felt as if I was drowning, an onset of a panic attack. Most of the time, when I couldn't calm down fast enough, a shot was administered to calm me.

But today was one of the days I felt invigorated as Adrien sat across from me, his eyebrows pulled down in concentration as he drew a portrait of me in one of my notebooks filled with my lingerie designs. After dropping off Adrien, Estelle left to deal with the company Remington had contracted to work on the château. Marley sprawled on the couch next to the wall, reading a crime novel from one of her favourite authors.

"So, what would you like to be when you grow up?" I asked Adrien.

He paused. Then he lifted his head and wriggled his nose. "A pilot. No. I want to play music." His eyes widened as if he'd remembered something. "I want to be like my papa." He went back to his drawing and mumbled, "I want to be a firefighter, too." He grinned wide, a dimple flashing on his left cheek.

I pressed my lips together to keep from smiling. He

looked happy and so cute. "You can be anything you want, tiger."

After a few minutes, listening to him mumbling in frustration when the drawing didn't go the way he wanted, he announced, "I'm finished." He flipped the book around.

"Whoa, this is really good, Adrien." He beamed at me. The drawing was good for a five-year-old. Other than my hair and my ears, which were extremely out of proportion, he had done a very good job. "Can I keep it?"

He nodded, jumping off the bed. "Toilet." He rushed toward the bathroom.

"How are you feeling, sis?" Marley asked, combing her fingers through my hair.

I smiled. "Better."

She stared at me for a few seconds, her eyes glistening with tears. "Promise me something. Don't you ever scare me like that again, okay?"

"I'm a drama queen, babe. I have to act my part." I grinned at her, as much as the muscles on my face would allow me. It felt strange to smile. She blinked quickly and swiped her fingers under her eyes. *Shit. Why do I always make jokes in dire situations*? "I'm sorry."

I felt a light weight in my hands. Soft hands held mine. Marley's. "Have you spoken to Mom and Dad again?"

She nodded. "They'll be flying to Paris in a few days, as soon as Mom gets clearance from the doctor. He wanted to monitor her sugar levels and make sure the medication he prescribed for her didn't work negatively before giving her an okay."

"I'm so sorry to put you through this. They don't deserve more problems from me, especially after taking care of me the past two years."

She laughed. "As if Mom and Dad would have it any other way." She grinned slyly. "You've been holding out on me. Remington is hot."

I returned my gaze to her, smiling. "He is, isn't he? And he's so good to me."

She squeezed my hand. "It's high time you found someone who adores you for who you are. You deserve that."

I shook my head. "I think it's gone to my head. God, I've been so selfish."

"What are you talking about?"

I took a deep breath. "Adrien asked me if he could call me Mama."

Her eyes widened as realization dawned on her. "Oh. Oh, please tell me you didn't say what I think you did."

I bit my lip and nodded, feeling my eyes burn with tears. "I did. It felt really good. I just…how could I allow him to call me that when I knew I'd be leaving in a few months?"

"Hey, listen to me," she said urgently, her face filled with concern. "Selfish is not a word I'd use to describe you. Not really. You might have answered him in the heat of the moment, but you are nothing if not selfless. You love too much; it colours your judgment. I'm not saying it's a bad thing. It's who you are, and I wouldn't change you. Have you seen how that boy looks at you? Do you know how you look when you see him?"

I stilled, watching her. "How?"

"Like he is your world. Even the mere mention of Remington's name, your face lights up."

I grinned, settling back on the pillows. She studied my face through narrowed eyes, then said, "You had no intention of coming back home, did you?"

How the hell does she know that? "What?"

"You already made up your mind the minute you met Remington and Adrien. You just didn't know it at that time."

I rolled my eyes. "So, I hear psych major is treating you well."

Adrien returned from the bathroom, dragging his feet on the floor. "I'm bored. Aunt Marley, can we go please?"

Marley quickly dropped her magazine and leaped off the couch. I chuckled as I watched her slip her feet inside her shoes hurriedly while Adrien skipped around the room making airplane noises. She was truly and utterly wrapped around his tiny little finger. She snatched her handbag from the table, heading for the door, but Adrien abruptly sprinted toward me and scrambled up the bed and threw his arms around my neck.

"I'm happy you didn't die, Mama."

I blinked back tears. "Me, too, darling." The way he called me 'mama' warmed my heart. Marley was right. I wasn't leaving this boy. Not in a hundred years. But I had to speak to Remington to gauge where he was in this relationship.

Marley gave me a look I couldn't interpret. She quickly swiped the tears in her eyes and smiled. "I'm so happy for you, sis."

Marley, my cheerleader. I love this girl so much.

There was a knock on the door, and seconds later, the physical therapist stepped into the room. He glanced around quickly before beaming at me on the bed. Marley snickered and stood up to leave. Apparently, Remington had made an impression on him the first time they met. According to Marley, my source, Remington had given him one of his looks, a stern look complete with gaze tracking every movement his hands made.

After a wet kiss on my cheek from Adrien and a wave from Marley, they left and my therapy session started.

Last night, I had a problem falling asleep. Every time I tried, the memory of what happened in Provence plagued my dreams. I'd woken up several times in the night and was terrified if the doctor administered a drug to help me sleep, something might happen while I wasn't conscious. So I called Marley earlier today to visit sooner than usual so I could nap for a few hours. Right before I fell asleep, the hospital phone on the nightstand started to ring, startling me.

Marley leaned forward to pick it up and handed me the handset. "Oooh, maybe it's Hot Remington on the phone." She giggled, then stopped when I didn't smile. I felt as if I hadn't slept for years. "I could tell him to call later so you can get some sleep. You really look bad."

I shook my head, and for the first time since yesterday, my heart beat fast in anticipation. I missed him so much. "Hi."

There was silence on the other end of the line, then, "So, it's true. You are still alive."

That voice sent a shiver down my spine. "Looks like your attempts failed. Try harder next time." Marley's eyes widened, and she mouthed 'give me the phone'. I shook my head. If this crazy woman wanted me, then I'd deal with her.

"Those policemen guarding you will not stop me from getting to you, you know. Have you received my gift?"

I glanced around the room, my heart slamming into my chest in fear. "Looks like your delivery failed," I said, hoping

I sounded brave. "Who the hell are you? Why can't you leave us alone?"

"Leave you alone?" She laughed coldly. "You'll know who I am soon enough." The line went dead. I handed the handset back to Marley, my pulse beating fast in my ears. I felt nauseous, hot and cold at the same time.

"Was it her?"

I nodded, pushing the bed sheets away from my body to get some air.

The door opened, admitting a tall nurse with blond hair holding a brown paper bag similar to the ones found in flower shops. She smiled at Marley before sliding me a look. "These came for you." She placed the bag on the nightstand. "Ready for your injection?"

I nodded as Marley shuddered next to me. She'd hated getting shots since she was a child. "How long do I still need these?"

"I'll come back later to draw some blood to run a PTT test. If that has stabilized and your blood clots in the expected time, we can cease administering the Clexane." She pulled the syringe from the pocket of her uniform. "Relax, okay?"

I nodded and concentrated on the sound of crinkling paper, assuming my sister had taken it upon herself to unwrap the brown bag. Leaning back into my pillows, I closed my eyes, gritting my teeth against the sharp pain from the needle. The feeling was gone as suddenly as it came.

"What the fuck!" Marley shouted.

My eyes flipped open to watch a bouquet of irises drop to the floor. I glanced up to find Marley's hand gripped around the nurse's. "What's wrong?" I asked. My voice sounded weird, and my vision was blurry.

"She's trying to kill you! I've sat through most of these treatments, and that's not what they use." She pointed toward the floor. I turned my head and saw the syringe in the corner.

Oh, fuck!

The door burst open, and two policemen and another two men in civilian clothes rushed in. Pandemonium ensued, or maybe it was just me?

"Marley? What is happening? I..." The words trailed off as everything around me dulled in sound and light, then went black.

Chapter Fifty-Three

Remington

Caleb was recovering well, and I was packing my carry-on bag, ready to leave the hospital. I was eager to get to Paris as quickly as possible, then back to Marseilles. The procedure was deemed a success. After the final tests, the doctor assured me I was on the way to recovery and that I'd need at least three weeks before I went back to work. Easy. I would spend those days, every fucking one of them, kissing Selene. My cock stirred in my jeans, sending heat all over my body. I inhaled deeply, dragging my shaking fingers through my hair.

Control yourself, Remington. She is probably not ready for you in her current condition.

True. What I was feeling right now, the relief that at least everything seemed to be working well and the possibility of sinking my cock so deep inside Selene's pussy, had me so hard and panting. I adjusted myself in my jeans and groaned.

"Thinking about her, aren't you? Well, don't stop on my account," Caleb announced himself, jolting me from my lust-filled thoughts. Startled, I spun around to find him smiling wide at me. How the hell didn't I hear him?

"The nurse brought me here." He smirked. "So, when will you bring this goddess you keep raving about for a visit?"

"As soon as your lazy arse is out of the hospital."

He laughed. "Fantastic. I'll make sure to roll out the red carpet and hire a mariachi band."

I chuckled, hoisting my bag over one shoulder. "Call me when you leave this place." I hadn't told him about the drama in my life, and I had asked Adele not to. He didn't need that kind of stress in his current condition.

His gaze dropped to his lap. "My father—our father says he has been calling you, but you keep brushing him off. He wants to thank you for what you did." He lifted his eyes to my face.

"You are alive. That is gratitude enough for me." I took a step forward, making it clear I wasn't in the mood to talk about our father.

"Just hear him out, okay? I know he's an impossible wanker, as you called him, but just give him a few seconds."

I shook my head. "I have a lot of things going on in my life right now. I can't…won't allow him to make my life more difficult. Give me a call sometime, all right?"

He sighed and nodded.

After saying our goodbyes, I left the hospital while pulling my mobile from my jacket to check for missed calls. I froze mid-step while walking toward a waiting taxi and listened to the voice messages.

Bloody fucking hell!

Rage erupted inside me, settling in my veins. The only consolation was knowing the hospital staff had been quick enough to pump whatever was in that injection out of Selene's system. And that the nurse who administered the drug had been apprehended. Enough was enough. I had to identify this culprit before flying to Marseilles.

After calling Gilles to let him know I'd be arriving around one and a half hours later, I stalked my way to the waiting taxi and left for the airport.

Chapter Fifty-Four

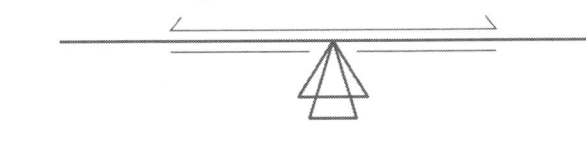

Remington

"Are you sure you're ready to go in there? We don't really need to do this today," Gilles said, turning around from the cupboard filled with what I assumed was surveillance equipment, and faced me.

"I want to get this over and done with. This nightmare has gone on far too long. Besides, if we don't solve this, who knows what else this woman is up to?" I shuddered, remembering how closely Selene had brushed shoulders with death. Because of me.

Fuck.

"She's intent on getting rid of Selene. I'm determined to keep her alive. Let's do this."

Gilles eyebrows shot up. "I'm with you, *mon ami*. Put this on," Gilles handed me a Kevlar vest he had dug from the cupboard.

I cocked a brow. "Don't you think this is going a bit too far?"

"I have no idea what kind of madness we are dealing with. Better safe than sorry, *oui*?"

Touché.

After slipping on the vest, Gilles and I joined Alexei, one

of Gilles's personnel, in the parking lot and drove toward the 10th arrondissement.

Seven minutes later, we were striding down a hallway in an eighteenth-century building. It was quiet, as if no one actually lived here. Alexei halted in front of a brown wooden door, removed a small toolbox from his jacket pocket, and picked a tool from within. Seconds later, the door was open.

I followed Alexei inside, with Gilles pulling up the rear while looking around. The farther we stepped into the interior, the faster my heart pounded in my chest.

Finally. I'm inside the belly of the beast.

I glanced around the living room, taking in the white walls void of any decorations, television or radio. The only thing housed in this godforsaken place was a threadbare couch and a table that looked as if it had seen better days.

I walked from room to room, trying to get a hint, something that I'd recognize, then halted mid-way as I caught a scent. A familiar scent. I followed it through the bedroom door and into what looked like a storeroom of sorts.

"There you go."

I startled and turned, a glare on my face. "Christ, Gilles. Do that again and I'll punch you in the face." My voice echoed in the small room.

He chuckled, shaking his head.

I glanced around for the source of the strong scent as my pulse thudded louder in my head. My mind screamed at me, forcing me to acknowledge the source. But I couldn't. Not until I saw it with my own eyes. I tapped the walls, looking for a way to follow that familiar scent. They sounded hollow, as if there was another room hidden behind the boards. I pushed and shoved but nothing happened.

"Does Alexei have something to open this wall? There's another room behind it."

Gilles squeezed past me and rapped the wall with his knuckles. "Son of a bitch, you're right."

"I'm always right," I said. He snorted and yelled Alexei's name.

Minutes later, he found a way to get in through what looked like an invisible crack in the wall—which was, in fact, a push button.

I scanned the room, nausea rising in my throat.

"What the bloody *fuck* is this?" I asked under my breath. There was a small wooden table decorated with what looked like a thousand pictures of Adrien and me. Three purple candles were placed strategically on the table. At the far end was a CD player. I leaned closer, squinting at the CD case on top of the player, feeling cold sweat break out on my forehead.

"Christ." There it was, my missing CD of *The Nutcracker*.

The walls were covered with more photos, but this time they were of women I'd dated in the past, with the letter X on their faces. And the images that had Adrien and me in them were circled with the words 'My Family' on them.

"Remington?"

I couldn't speak. *Fuck*. I needed air. It couldn't be true. Could God be so cruel that He'd do this to me? Hadn't I suffered enough?

The perfume felt like an invisible hand wrapped around my neck, choking me. I needed to get out of this house, get some fresh air.

"Do you know who this woman is?" Gilles asked.

I shook my head, unable to get the words out, and murmured, "I need some air," and strode out of the small room and the house. I rounded the corner to take the stairwell and froze. My gaze widened as I came face-to-face with my past. The ghost who had been haunting us.

My stalker?

I blinked. No. *NO!* My eyes were playing tricks on me. There was no way in the fucking world this could be happening. Grabbing the wall, I shut my eyes tightly, trying to breathe normally as dizziness threatened to drag me down.

It couldn't be true. The hand at my side formed a fist as my eyes peeled open, slowly. *God, she is still there.*

Her eyes were wide, and her mouth opened and closed, shocked. "Remington?"

"*Colette?*"

Chapter Fifty-Five

Remington

My chest ached. Sweat broke out on my forehead, spreading all over my body. Pain unlike any other punched me hard in my stomach. But above all, shock rendered me immobile. I stared into the face of the woman I had buried five years ago, her eyes wide.

I buried her. I watched the coffin being lowered into the grave. I remembered the day I was notified about her death. I remembered visiting the mortuary after I was informed her body had completely burned in the crash, and instead of identifying her body, they showed me her remains.

I buried you, or did I? This was a nightmare.

The five years hadn't changed her. Not even a bit. She was still beautiful, maybe even more so with her eyes staring at me as if I was the only thing she could see. She smiled, and I sucked in a breath, the exact way I had always responded to her smile, before she cheated on me with another man. Before she pretended she was dead and threatened Selene, the woman who now owned my heart.

"Colette?" Even saying that name again tasted foreign on

my tongue. "You are dead. *Mon Dieu*, I buried you five years ago. You are *dead*."

Her gaze darted up and down the empty hallway, then back at me. "What are you doing here?"

I jerked back, the suddenness of that question slapping me on my face. She'd been alive all this time and all she could ask was what I was doing here? I couldn't believe this woman. Her treachery had gone beyond anything I could ever imagine.

I flexed my hands at my sides and straightened, then schooled my expression, forcing myself to get over the fact she was standing in front of me. *Breathe*. I knew if I warned Gilles, I might spook her, and she'd disappear on us. So I decided to distract her, hoping Gilles would come looking for me.

"What have you been up to, other than threatening the women I've dated?" I asked, in what I hoped was a pleasant voice. Bloody hell, I wanted to stalk forward, grab her, and actually kill her myself.

Her smile disappeared. "Remington, I really want to apologize for what I did. I didn't mean to fake my death, but—"

I inched closer and she moved back two paces, resting her foot on one of the steps. Then she casually rested her shoulder on the wall that managed to hide her body well from anyone walking toward us.

Clever. "Hmm. Are you sorry for neglecting your son, faking your death, or for cheating on me?"

"A-all the above. I was—"

"Remington?" Gilles's voice floated down the hall, and seconds later, his footfalls echoed on the walls.

Colette straightened as panic swept across her face, ready for flight. Fuck, if I was going to let her escape. I leaped forward and attempted to grab her arm. She ducked and I stumbled forward. Pain shot through my lower abdomen, reminding me I wasn't fit enough to tackle her, but damn it if I was about to let her escape. Clutching my stomach to ease some of the pain, I swung forward just as she recovered, shoved her hand inside the handbag on her shoulder and pulled out something resembling a can. She spun around just as Gilles skidded to a stop beside me, and before I knew what was happening, I heard Gilles shout, then curse several times. A clicking sounded followed by "aaargh" from Gilles and a loud thud of a weight dropping on the ground. My head shot up just as she aimed the object at my face and pressed a button. I jerked back, but I was too late. I doubled over as whatever was inside the bottle stung my eyes. I threw my arm over my eyes to shield them from the attack.

"Oh, Remington!" Hands touched my face, pushing the hair away. I gagged as her perfume hit me hard, catching in the back of my throat. "I didn't mean to use the spray on you. I panicked and you wanted—"

"You crazy bitch. Don't. Touch. Me."

She stopped touching me. "I'm so sorry. Please forgive me, my love…I have to leave. I didn't want us to meet again like this. I will see you soon, my love. I still love you, you know. Those women did not deserve you. You and I are meant to be together."

"Stay away from us," I said coldly.

"She doesn't love you like I do. No one can love you like that."

Anger rose in me, overriding the burning sensation from the pepper spray. Where the hell was Alexei?

Eyes closed, I swung my arm toward her voice but came up empty, then winced as pain erupted in my lower abdomen.

"You are mine, Remington. You and I, together. Remember your promise to me? That we will always be together? I'm not about to let that bitch take you and Adrien away from me."

"You never cared for me or Adrien."

"You are wrong," she said. I heard the soft pattering of feet on the stone floor. "I'm never letting you go."

Silence filled the hallway. I trained my ear to the last place I saw Gilles fall and heard soft grunts.

"Alexei!" I yelled, scooting along the floor, my hand searching for Gilles.

Shit, my eyes were on fire. I couldn't believe Colette had bested us.

"Gilles? Remington?" Alexei's heavy footfalls echoed in the hallway.

"Over here." The footsteps drew closer and then a hand gripped my arm to help me up. "No, check on Gilles first. I think he's hurt."

The hand dropped away. I heard another groan, followed by a string of curses.

"I need to get you inside the flat and clean your eyes. Who attacked you?"

"Colette," I mumbled, trying not to vomit from the pain ripping through me. Had I pulled open the stitches? Ignoring my burning eyes, I placed my hand on my lower stomach and exhaled, relieved. It felt dry, so no blood.

"Who?" Alexei asked.

"My dead wife."

Silence followed. The only sounds were laboured breathing and the weight of Alexei's disbelief. I was with him on that one. I wouldn't have believed it if I hadn't seen her with my own eyes.

"Come on, I need to get both of you to the hospital."

"Is Gilles all right?" I asked, using the wall to hoist myself up, grimacing.

Alexei grunted. "I'm not certain, but he doesn't look good."

"Get him to the car. I'll be right behind you." As if I could.

Right now, a feather could knock me over and I wouldn't be able to stand on my own two feet. I despised this feeling.

"Don't move; I'll be right back." He brushed past me, and I listened as his footsteps faded as he descended the stairs, leaving me with the haunting thoughts of my wife alive. I had to warn Èric immediately.

Minutes later, Alexei returned and literally carried me down the stairs and into the waiting car. After safely depositing my arse on the passenger seat, he drove like a maniac to the hospital while I updated him on everything that happened since I left Colette's flat.

She was alive. The woman I despised more than anything on this Earth was alive. And now she wanted us back, after she had betrayed me and lied to us, discarded us like we were nothing more than dog shit under her shoe. What the bloody hell? She was utterly mad.

Chapter Fifty-Six

Remington

I arrived in Marseilles twenty-four hours later, feeling completely humiliated by the fact Gilles and I had been bested by a woman. And not any woman, but someone I thought was dead. Then the humility turned to fury and determination. Now that I knew who the culprit was, it would be easier to put a face behind the attacks. I still couldn't believe she had faked her own death. But for what purpose?

I shook my head, dispersing those thoughts and focused on seeing Selene, Adrien and my mother again. I rubbed my hand down my stomach to ease the discomfort there. The stitches on my stomach were still intact, but the doctor had stressed that I should refrain from any kind of strenuous activity. Gilles had been released from the hospital as well. Colette had used a Taser gun near his armpit where the Kevlar vest hadn't protected him. The doctor argued that he was lucky he hadn't incurred any damage other than being unconscious.

I strode down the hall and toward Selene's room. Taking a deep breath, I gripped the door, my heart racing in my chest at the thought of seeing that beautiful smile and those expressive eyes as they took me in. I could hear voices and laughter, mostly female. Unable to hold on much longer, I pushed the door open and halted in the doorway as I took in the scene before me. She was sitting up on the bed with several pillows propped behind her back, Marley sitting cross-legged across from her.

Mon Dieu! She was alive and even more beautiful than I remembered. My gaze wandered down her body, covered in a gown that did nothing to flatter her curves, and I frowned. She had lost too much weight.

Oh well, I had the rest of my life to bring them back and take care of her.

Merde! I was already building castles in the air, planning my future, yet I had no idea where she stood in regard to our relationship. But I would convince her, even if it took all my strength to do it.

"Remington?"

Chapter Fifty-Seven

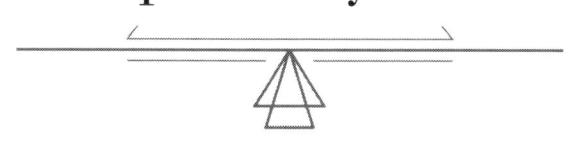

Selene

I had stopped listening to Marley the minute I sensed him behind the door. Remington. There was this energy that always accompanied him. I was pulled to that door as my heart raced and my breathing turned ragged. The minute he crossed the threshold, the hair on my arms rose in awareness.

I watched him, standing there looking hotter than I remembered. Jesus, the look on his face sent heat skittering down my body. I had missed it, that look of pure possession. Then it morphed to a dark scowl as it moved down my body, reminding me that behind that beautiful face was my Mr. Tall, Dark and Brooding, waiting to hop out at any second.

What now?

"Remington?"

He glanced up. The look that flashed across his face was a combination of hunger, relief and desperation. Then it fell away as soon as it had appeared, and he smiled. Sweet Lord, it was wicked, and my body swayed forward on its own accord. Like there were invisible threads that tethered me to him. That right there was the reason I fell in love. One minute he seemed like he couldn't get to me fast enough, and the next he couldn't wait to get his lips on mine, devour me whole.

Shit, I can't believe I'm so turned on.

He dropped the bag he'd been carrying and stalked forward, covering the distance between us in four huge strides. The bed moved, and I assumed Marley was scrambling off it to stay out of the storm that was Remington, bearing down on me.

"Oh, Selene," he murmured right before he cupped my face in his large hands. He stared into my eyes as disbelief and hope fought a war in his. Then he smiled; the smile that had the ability to knock air from my lungs. How could I forget this face? That smile? "You remember who I am?"

I nodded, grinning widely. "I must have been crazy to forget you. Forget your smile and your weapons."

"What?"

"Dimples."

He groaned, the sexiest sound I'd heard since my memory returned, and crushed his lips onto mine. I grabbed his shoulders, pulling him close to me and slid my hands up, holding him in place. His tongue brushed against my lips. "Open for me; I need to taste you. *Mon Dieu*, I've missed you so much," he whispered hoarsely against my lips.

The second his tongue touched mine, I was on fire. I yanked him to me, kissing him desperately and hungrily. When he finally pulled back, we both inhaled deeply to catch our breath, the sound of our laboured breathing filling the room.

"I missed you so much," I said, pressing a kiss on his stubbled jaw.

He leaned back, studying me through narrowed eyes. "You're here. How are you feeling?"

"Yes, and you're here with me. I feel really, really great."

"There is no other place I'd rather be," he said and then chuckled. "We seem to have forced your sister out of the room."

I glanced around and giggled. "We definitely did." Dizziness slammed into me, so I lay back on the pillows, savouring Remington's touch as his thumb caressed my cheek and his other hand my neck.

"You know I would never intentionally hurt you or Adrien, right?" I asked, fiddling with the edge of the thin blanket that covered my body to the waist.

He tucked his thumb under my chin, tugging my face up, and fixed his eyes on mine. Something flashed there. Fear, I think. It quickly vanished, replaced by a shuttered look as though guarding himself from what I was about to say. "I do."

"You were right. I had no right to allow Adrien to call me Mama, especially since I planned to go back home soon. It was wrong of me to put my needs before his. God, how could I have been so stupid. Thoughtless." I dropped the blanket and cupped his face. "I hate myself for doing that. I hate how desperate I feel; it literally clouds my judgment at times. I am a lot of things, and flawed is among them, but know that I'd never hurt you either of you. I would die before that happens. Please forgive me."

He continued to study me, and I couldn't tell what he was thinking.

Damn it, please say something.

Finally, he pressed a kiss on my lips and I leaned forward, eager and desperate for him. "Apology accepted. I know you'd never hurt us. Not intentionally. It's not in you to hurt anyone or take advantage of a situation," he murmured against my lips, then stood up, taking his scent with him, and swept my hair off my forehead with his fingers. "*Tu es belle.*"

Chapter Fifty-Eight

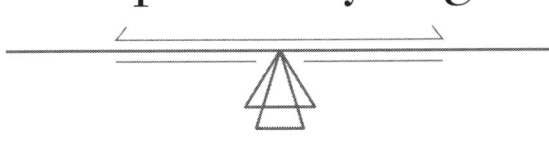

Remington

Straightening, I removed my jacket and tossed it on the nearby chair before turning to watch Selene as she settled back in the pillows, slipping her eyes shut, smiling. The second she said she would never hurt me and Adrien intentionally, I thought she had made the decision that she did not want to have anything to do with me. I wouldn't have blamed her if she did. I hadn't protected her like I'd promised. Then she had left me breathless with her confession and apology, and I still kept waiting for her to say she was leaving me.

She didn't.

Fuck, I didn't know what to do with what I was feeling right now.

"I love you," she said softly.

Every thought came to a screeching halt. "Open those beautiful eyes, Selene. Look at me."

She did. "I love you," she repeated, the expression on her face changing to one of wonder. Her eyes widened and filled with tears.

"What is it?" I asked, scanning her face, worried something

was wrong. I closed the gap between us. "You are scaring me, *ma belle*."

"I love you," she said the words again, louder. "Oh, my God, Remington. I. Love. You." Then she burst into tears.

Caught off guard, I gathered her in my arms, and she pressed her face into my chest, sobbing.

"Are you guys okay?" Marley poked her head around the door, smiling.

I shook my head to let her know I had no idea what was happening.

She grinned wider and said, "Mood swings," then disappeared again, looking very pleased with herself.

Selene pulled back and stared at me through tear-filled eyes and sniffed. I waited, still not comprehending the outburst.

What had they done to her while I was gone?

"I'm so sorry." Before I could ask why she was apologizing, she continued. "I hate that I can't control my feelings. God, I'm trying, but I'm afraid I might push everyone away. I really don't want to hurt anyone. And the nurse tried to kill me. And I missed you. Oh, my God, I love you." Then she started laughing and crying.

She loves me? I didn't realize how much I craved hearing those words until she spoke them. But she continued the confusing display of emotion, and I wasn't sure if she was excited or frustrated. Panic twisted in my chest. I had to calm her down.

I cupped her face, brushed my thumb against her lips, then kissed her deeply and pulled back. "I know, Selene. I know you love me."

"You do?" She gaped at me. At least she wasn't crying anymore. "When…how…?"

I did the only thing I knew would bring back my Selene. "How could you not love me?" I grinned at her.

She narrowed her eyes. "I see your ego has been growing out of proportion while I was lying in here. Well, I'm better now, and I think it's time we worked on getting it back to its right size." She wriggled out of my arms, but I held her tighter. "Let me go before that enlarged ego knocks me off the bed."

I laughed, wrapped my arms around her, and holding her to me, pressed my lips to her jaw in a kiss.

"I love you, too." I trailed a kiss down her neck, nipping the skin there. She shivered and moaned. "God, you are so fucking sexy, and I want you so badly. I've missed you." I jolted as her hand wandered down to my crotch, rubbing my cock through my jeans. "Don't start something you can't finish, you little minx." I grabbed her hand and lightly tethered her wrist with mine on the bed. She batted her lashes at me, and I laughed at her blatant flirting.

Her face quickly fell. "Is it the gown? I know I'm not totally rocking sexy right now—"

What the bloody hell?

"Stop it," I growled. "I. Love. You. You hear me? You." I ducked my head to meet her gaze. "I don't know when it happened, but I knew I loved you, and there was no way I was going to let you go. Could never give you up," I said, staring into hazel eyes. "I'm so addicted to you, I don't know where I end and you begin."

She blinked at me, her eyes gleaming with tears. She pressed her forehead to mine. "That—that was really beautiful. God, I'm so sorry. I'm having a hard time controlling my emotions. The doctor told me it's normal especially after a brain trauma, but I hate this so much. Sometimes I'm terrified I'll scare away the people in my life. One second I'm crying and the next I'm laughing. Or highly turned on. The other night I was watching a movie on TV and started moaning, indecently and uncontrollably aroused. Marley had to take Adrien out of the room." She shook her head. "Be warned, I'm a huge mess right now."

I climbed on the bed and pulled her into me, wanting to comfort her more than anything. "Shh. I don't scare easily. "

She wiped her eyes and laid her head on my chest. These mood changes were giving me whiplash. I needed to talk to the doctor to have an understanding of what was going on.

She looked up at me. "How are you doing? How is Caleb? Did Gilles find the woman?"

Merde!

I wasn't expecting that question. After quickly making sure my expression wasn't displaying the fear and anger rolling inside me, I told her what had happened since I left Marseilles a week and a half ago but left out the details about Colette. I was still absorbing the shock of seeing her. Given Selene's current disposition, I wasn't certain that hearing my wife was still alive and trying to kill her was the best thing right now. Hoping to distract her, I leaned in and kissed her temple, nipped her earlobe.

"Have you spoken to your parents?" I murmured in her ear.

She squealed as I traced my tongue at the sensitive place behind her ear. "Should you be talking about my parents while doing this to me?"

I nipped her earlobe again, my hands finding their way inside her gown and cupping her breast. *Christ, I missed this.* "Tell me." I flicked her nipple, making her suck in a sharp breath.

"Yes!" That word burst out of her lips. "Should be flying to Paris in less than a week. Mom said she'll let us know the exact date."

"Good girl." Before leaving for London, I had asked Èric to organize what they needed for the trip.

The door opened, but my mouth was busy trailing a path down her chest. Someone cleared their throat. I froze while Selene scrambled to cover herself.

"Monsieur St. Germain, I see you're back and apparently very healthy." Dr. Blanchett's voice jolted me upright. Heat filled my cheeks as I tried to regain my poise well enough to face him.

I rearranged the look on my face, replacing it with a scowl before shifting around to face the doctor. Selene pressed her forehead on my back, snickered and whispered, "God, you look so hot, scowling like that. Wanna head to the bathroom and do really dirty things to each other? We can just toss the doctor out of the room."

I quickly shot her a look, fighting a smile. "Behave, insatiable minx." I focused on the good doctor, the look on his face properly chastising me. Obviously, he wasn't amused by me making out with his patient. My lips twitched, fighting a smile as his frown deepened. I coughed once. "Dr. Blanchett."

"Did everything go well?" he asked, referring to Caleb's surgery.

I nodded, shivering as Selene's hand traced my lower back. My cock hardened further in my jeans. I coughed to hide my heightened breathing. How I wished I had my jacket to hide what her touches were doing to me.

Merde! This woman was trouble.

I quickly snatched her hand in mine and linked our fingers, before kissing the back of it. The doctor quickly dropped his gaze to the floor, smiling. "How are you feeling, Madame Michaels?"

"Fantastic," Selene said, kissing my shoulder.

The doctor didn't look disturbed by her words. In fact, he seemed as though he was expecting it. I cocked a brow at him as he sidled closer, pulling a stethoscope from around his neck. I stood up from the bed, and he began his check-up.

"Your recovery is astounding." He sounded surprised. "You should be able to go home in a few days." He turned to face me. "The transfer arrangements have been made. We could release her, but I would like to have our medical team on the flight, just to monitor her until she's checked in at the hospital in Paris."

I frowned. "Do you think she's not well enough to travel?"

He shook his head. "She's fit, but I like taking precautions, especially in cases like Madame Michaels's where the patient was in a coma."

I nodded, relieved.

"The flight is scheduled for two days from now. It gives us enough time to perform final checks to make sure everything is in order."

"What flight?" Selene asked in a chirpy voice.

"To Paris." The doctor smiled at her patiently. "Remember we spoke about the transfer? Your husband and I discussed the possibility of you being treated in Paris. It would also benefit Adrien if he can pick up his normal routine."

At this, Selene looked at me, her eyes wide. She mouthed, "My husband?" and winked at me, grinning. I shook my head, chuckling under my breath.

The doctor watched the entire communication and laughed. "Can I see you outside, monsieur?"

"Remington? Are you leaving again?" she asked, her eyes growing wider. Then she burst into tears.

I glared at the doctor. "What the bloody hell is wrong with her? This is *not* Selene."

"That is the reason I wanted to speak to you." He flicked his gaze in Selene's direction and said, "I'll meet you outside."

Two strides and I was climbing on the bed and pulling her

on my lap. "Shh…I'm not leaving. The doctor would like to finalize the details for this transfer." I kissed her hair and held her tightly against my chest as each sob broke my heart. A few moments later, she raised her head and stared at me, her bottom lip quivering. And even then she was breathtaking. "You have to know I'll never leave you. I've never been able to stay away from you, and I'm not about to start now. You, *ma belle*, are my light. The beacon that calls me home even when I'm a thousand kilometres away from you. I've fallen hard for you, and I'm still falling, but you know what? I don't care because I know you'll always be there to catch me. You won't let me fall, because I'll never, *ever*, let you fall. Do you hear me? We are each other's safety nets."

She gave me a wobbly smile. "Safety nets?"

"Yes. Safety nets." I pressed my thumb on her lush bottom lip, before leaning forward, my gaze fixed on hers. "Now, kiss me and tell me you will be all right when I walk out that door," I ordered, my voice soft.

She lifted her hands to my face, slid them around my neck and yanked me down, kissing me furiously and desperately. My heart was beating hard in my chest, and I've never been turned on so much in my life. Groaning, I slipped my hand between us, rearranged my cock. "Are we good?"

She sucked in a breath and quickly nodded as my fingers caressed her inner thigh.

"*Mon Dieu*, I've missed this. Touching you. I'm so starved for you," I murmured against her mouth as my fingers trailed higher. "Fuck, you are so wet."

"God, I'm so turned on it's not funny. Does that make me some sort of depraved person? We are in a hospital, and someone might come in for God's sake." She sighed in frustration.

"Because you missed me like I missed you. Our bodies follow no rules."

She dropped her hands from my neck and flopped back, grabbed one of the pillows and covered her face, screaming into the fabric.

I stood up from the bed, laughing. „*Je t'aime tellement, ma princesse.*"

"*Moi aussi, je t'aime.*" Her voice was muffled by the pillow. "I love you so much."

With one last look, I stepped into the hallway where the doctor was waiting. I nodded curtly to the police officers, then focused on Blanchett and schooled my expression to passivity to hide my growing panic about Selene's condition.

"Why did someone try to kill my wife? I was assured she would be safe," I snapped, unable to control myself. The thought of Selene missing from my life almost drove me insane.

"The nurse was interrogated by the hospital security guards, as well as the police officers and your guards. It was her first time to work this case. As usual, she collected the injection from a secure box where we placed most of Madame Michaels's medication, following the instructions I had set for the nurses. There must have been someone else who changed the injection with the poison. She swears she had no idea. This particular nurse was arrested for further investigation."

"I hope she is right about that, because God help her if she was out to end Selene's life." I took a deep breath to leash the rage threatening to break through. "What just happened in there?"

"Your wife"—he raised his eyebrows to let me know he didn't believe that association—"is currently having some difficulty controlling her emotions. Post-concussion syndrome. It's normal for patients who have had head injury to experience these mood swings. She has also been having headaches and experiencing dizzy spells and at times nausea. She can't seem to remember some things, but she will regain those memories over time.

"She is also having separation anxiety. The therapist seems to think there are a few things that could contribute to this disorder, mainly the attack, losing her child and the thought of losing the people she loves. If you would like to discuss her case, I would advise you to speak to him. He will be able to tell you more." I nodded once, processing the information.

"How long will it take before she's back to her old self?"

He shook his head. "It might take months or years. There is no way to tell. We are doing everything we can to ease some of those symptoms, which includes medication. And given her history with depression, she has to be monitored very closely. The therapist has been visiting her twice a week since she woke up from the coma, as we agreed, just to make sure everything is progressing well."

"What do I have to do to make it easier for her?"

"I would suggest surrounding her with familiar faces or things she did before the incident. And patience. She has been working on what she calls her 'baby project'. Her designs, I think? It seems to calm her. Maybe she feels it's something she can control." He pursed his lips thoughtfully. "And your son. He is good for her. Did she tell you about the dream?"

"What dream?"

He shifted on his feet. "She saw and touched Ines. The baby she lost a few years ago."

She did? My chest tightened at this information. "What do you make of that?"

"According to the therapist, Madame Michaels had unresolved issues running in her subconscious. She never had a chance to say goodbye to the baby. This was a way for her to do that."

Jesus! What else had she gone through in the time she was in a coma? "Please tell me what I can do to help her."

He smiled, and for the first time since I walked out of the room with my heart in my throat, the panic eased away.

"Keep doing what you are doing, and she will be fine. We still have a few major tests before everything is wrapped up. I will see you both tomorrow morning. If anything comes up, ask the nurse on duty to page me."

After our chat, he excused himself and left as I turned to walk back inside the room, but stopped when I heard, "Papa!"

I spun around and saw my son dashing down the hallway toward me, and my mother walking leisurely. Grinning, I strode toward him and snatched him in my arms, embracing him tight.

"I missed you so much, my little fighter," I said, burying my face in his hair. He wiggled in my arms, and I lifted my head to look into his eyes.

He cupped his tiny hands on either side of my face and pressed his forehead to mine. "I missed you, too, Papa. Did you bring me a gift from London?"

"Yes, I did. A big hug from Adele." He stared at me incredulously then scowled, reminding me of myself. I laughed. "Come on, I have something for you in my bag." I winced as one of his little feet caught me on my wound, and I quickly slid him to the floor.

"How are you, my son?" my mother greeted me, leaning to kiss both my cheeks.

"Now that I've seen everyone who matters, bloody fantastic."

"Watch your language around your son," she chastised

me, as she always did when I cursed. I laughed as we entered Selene's room.

"How is everything?" I asked her, trying to gauge her reaction as she watched Adrien scramble on the bed and into Selene's lap. He threw his arms around her neck and kissed her cheek loudly.

"You mean, how am I warming up to your 'wife'?" She faced me, her lips twitching as if fighting a smile.

I laughed. "Your opinion matters to me."

She pursed her lips. "What if I told you I didn't like her? That you were over your head in this case?" Her expression softened even as she spoke those harsh words that had my heart beating wildly in my chest.

"But you like her," I challenged her. "And you think she is good for me."

She rolled her eyes playfully, then turned to watch the scene before us. Adrien was talking a mile-a-minute. Apparently, he had forgotten his gift from London.

"She is growing on me." She looked up at me, sympathy shining in her eyes. "She told me about her baby."

"Oh? And it made you change your mind about her?"

She shook her head. "No. Selene did that on her own. She is very different from…you know. Anyway, she is so kind, funny and sometimes shy. Although sometimes very frustrating with the mood swings. Not that I blame her. She is trying so hard to keep them at bay, which I think frustrates her even more when she realizes she can't help it."

I smiled. "She needs time. I'm glad you like her because I'm not letting her go. Not without a fight."

Chapter Fifty-Nine

Remington

The last two days had been everything I'd dreamed about since I left London, although I still couldn't get the thought of Colette out of my mind. Eventually, I updated Èric and my mother and asked them not to mention it to Selene. She was already dealing with so much. She seemed content, if you didn't count the spurts of mood swings that sent her bawling her heart out or the abrupt laughter at nothing in particular.

Everything was packed, and we were just waiting for the medical report from Dr. Blanchett. Selene was experiencing separation anxiety, which I completely understood, especially after one of the hospital staff tried to kill her. We decided Adrien, Èric and I would travel with her, while my mother, Marley and Gilles's security men would fly to Paris together. Adrien had been restless, waiting, so I asked Èric to take him to a nearby playground. I would call him as soon as the doctor was done.

My father chose that moment to call. I answered the call, readying myself for the onslaught of righteousness and pompousness that was Mr. Remington Newport.

"Son," he greeted me as he always did. I rolled my eyes, which sent Selene into fits of giggles.

"Father."

"You haven't been returning my calls," he said, sounding irritated.

"I'm busy right now. Is there anything specific you wanted to tell me?"

He sighed, and I could imagine a cloud of smoke billowing out of his ears. "I wanted to thank you in person, for what you did for Caleb. For *me*."

This time, I sighed just as the door opened, letting in the doctor. "I can't do this right now. Listen, I just can't talk at the moment. Call me when you think of another way to thank me, other than with money."

I disconnected the call and quickly shoved aside the murderous thoughts I had going on inside my head from speaking to my father and then stood up to acknowledge the doctor.

"Ready to do this?" he asked, a smile playing on his lips.

Selene and I exchanged a look and grinned. I clasped her hand and gave it a gentle squeeze, then kissed her parted lips and whispered, "I'm here." Ignoring the doctor hovering at the door, I dropped to my knees and her eyes grew wide.

"Remington? Wh—What are you doing?"

"I'll always be here no matter what. Marry me." I should have been surprised by the spontaneity and recklessness of this situation. But I wasn't. Asking Selene to marry me felt natural. "I've always been the kind of man who plans everything meticulously. But with you, you make me do things I never thought I would. I want to be spontaneous with you, reckless with you and always honest with you. I promised to always tell you the truth. This is me, on my knees asking you to marry me, because I can't see myself spending the next hundred years without you by my side. Marry me, Selene Michaels."

She slapped a hand over her mouth, covering it as tears filled her eyes. She flicked her gaze to where the doctor stood, then back at me and quickly wiped her cheeks. "Remington, you don't even know if I'm ever going to be all right. I love you. I love you so much. A few months ago, if anyone had told me that a man, and not any other man, but you, would be on your knees asking me to marry you, I would have told them they were crazy. But here you are." She leaned forward and pressed a kiss on my lips. "What if something is wrong with me? I can't do that to you. I just can't."

"Haven't you gotten the memo yet? I will take you any way I can get you. It's not what is here"—I pressed a finger against her head "—what matters is what is here." I pressed my palm to her chest, feeling her heart beat fast against my hand.

"Oh, come on, sis. Just say yes and put the poor man out of his misery!" Marley yelled from the door. I darted a look at the door and saw her and my mother standing next to the doctor, who looked rather pleased with himself. My mother dabbed her eyes before clasping her hands together.

Selene bit her trembling bottom lip, her eyes scrutinizing my face as fear filled her features.

I pressed a kiss on her knuckles, and she shivered.

God, I love how she reacts to my touch.

"I'm possessive, jealous and there is a very good chance I will shackle your wrist to mine. I may even growl when any man dares to stare at you for longer than three seconds. Your life will be heaven or hell, depending on how you look at it, if you say yes. But, one thing I know for sure is that I love you.

I will love you like no man has ever loved you. I will cherish you and spoil you and do things that will only make you love me harder. You'll forget about my Neanderthal tendencies." I halted my words, watching as her eyes grew wider at my confession. "This is me. This is who I am. This is all of me."

She bit her bottom lip as she continued to study me. I fought the urge to lean in and suck it into my mouth, torturing her until she agreed to marry me.

"Hell, yeah!" Selene yelled, and I cocked my eyebrow at her enthusiasm. I was still trying to find my footing where this new Selene was concerned. She beamed at me, and that smile dug deeper into my heart, warming me.

Clapping erupted, filling the air. I shot to my feet and hoisted her onto my lap. "Can I kiss my fiancée now?" I asked, cocking my head to the side.

"Never trust a man when he says he just wants to kiss you," she whispered against my lips in that breathy voice I loved, reminding me of my words, spoken what felt like ages ago.

"Including me. Because I won't just kiss you. I will fuck you and do some very naughty things to you," I murmured against her lips in a low voice and kissed her, then proceeded to kiss the tears away.

Dr. Blanchett cleared his throat. I was beginning to wonder if he had a problem with it. I tore myself away from Selene and looked over my shoulder. He tapped the white envelope in his hand against his palm, his lips twitching. "So, I would like to give you the results from the last test we did."

God, please let everything be all right.

"Most of the brain tissue has healed. Just take it easy the next few months." He gave her a fatherly smile. "We also have a second lot of test results which may or may not be the cause of the headaches and nausea." I fixed my gaze on him, unable to look away. Unable to breathe. "Are you ready to welcome an additional member to your family?"

I blinked, as the words echoed inside my head. Selene's hand tightened in mine.

"What did you just say?" My voice was a whisper.

"I'm…I'm pregnant?"

The doctor nodded, his gaze bouncing between the adorable woman at my side and me.

"Are you sure?" I asked the doctor, hoping with all my strength that he was right.

He nodded.

"Remington?" Selene called my name, uncertainty in her voice.

My eyes burned with tears. I blinked rapidly before turning to face her. "We are pregnant," I whispered. "We are bloody pregnant!" I shouted, sweeping her into my arms and kissing her. "*Mon Dieu*, this—" I slid my hands to her stomach, staring into her eyes. "We made a baby."

I cupped her face with my hands and wiped the tears trailing down her cheeks. Then I realized she hadn't said anything. Her bottom lip trembled, and her eyes were wide. My heart stuttered in my chest.

"Selene?"

She didn't look at me. Instead, she turned to face the doctor. My chest tightened, and the hope I'd been feeling seconds ago turned to uncertainty.

"I was on birth control pills when we did…er…" Her gaze shifted nervously to where my mother stood. She excused herself and left, but Marley stood, grinning. Apparently, she was still in seventh heaven. "Marley," Selene said, jerking her chin toward the door.

With an "Oh!" Marley disappeared around the door. I chuckled under my breath. Selene was such a tigress in bed, yet here she was being shy. I slid my hand around her arse and gave her a playful squeeze.

"Behave yourself, St. Germain." She turned to face the doctor and explained the situation. The last time we had sex was the time of the incident. She had missed taking the pill that day. The doctor explained that sperm could live inside the woman's body for up to five days. She murmured, "I knew that," her cheeks turning red.

"But, will the baby be okay? I mean, I wasn't conscious for almost a week and…"

"As long as you take care of yourself, everything should be okay."

"Are you all right?" I asked.

She pivoted in my arms. I could see how hard she was fighting not to break down. "I'm just so afraid of getting my hopes high, if something happens…"

"Don't even think about it, okay? Let's take the news for what it is and go with it," I told her, completely understanding her reaction now.

Dr. Blanchett walked toward us. "As your attending doctor, I signed up to escort you to Paris."

I nodded, taking the envelope he was offering me. "Thank you for everything, doctor," I said.

He nodded, smiling. "Congratulations to both of you. I've arranged for an ultrasound in thirty minutes. I'll send in a wheelchair for Madame Michaels. I am sure you'd like to accompany her, Monsieur St. Germain?" His eyes twinkled with amusement.

I nodded and kissed Selene's forehead.

Mon Dieu, we were about to see our baby. When I

looked up, the doctor had already left. I was so absorbed watching Selene's animated face as she told me how excited, scared and happy she was.

"Are you ready for this?" I asked her as soon as one of the staff delivered the wheelchair. "Ready to see our baby?

She nodded, tears now running freely down her face. "Our little miracle."

Chapter Sixty

Remington

A week had gone by, and Selene was leaving the hospital here in Paris today. And I was feeling better. I had an appointment scheduled in two weeks to visit the doctor in London. I had planned to pick Selene up later on from the hospital after her release and bring her home. But first I wanted to be the one to pick up her parents from the airport. Gilles was feeling better after the Taser and pepper spray attack, although his pride, just like mine, was slowly recovering from the blow. Alexei had been watching the flat the past weeks, but Colette never showed up again. It was as if the ground had opened and swallowed her up. After what she did in Provence, I wasn't about to lower my guard. She was a dangerous woman who felt no remorse for her actions. I still couldn't understand how she wasn't dead. I had buried her bones.

Unless they hadn't belonged to her.

I shuddered at the thought and quickly shoved those thoughts away, focusing on meeting my future in-laws. I smiled at the thought, parked the car in the available parking spot and quickly pulled out my mobile. I opened up the text messages and typed,

How is my beautiful fiancée and mother of my baby doing?

I grinned and pressed send.

Moments later, an image of Selene's face, pretend-pouting, popped on my screen. Her eyes shone with mischief, giving the pout a comical look. My gaze fell on the words below the photo.

Missing you like crazy.

I typed, **I can't wait to hold you in my arms.**

Another text message appeared on my screen. **Just hold me?**

I grinned and murmured, "Naughty, naughty girl."

No. First I will undress you—no—rip those tiny shorts you wear in bed. Then kiss you from head to toe, touch you until your body aches. And finally, ma belle, I will shackle your wrists with my cuffs right before I slide my cock inside you. When you can't take it anymore, when you are shaking beneath me, I will let you touch me. Then I will fuck you hard. Mon Dieu, I can't wait to hear my name from your lips. It's been too long.

I paused, shifting on the seat, my breathing laboured.

I will make you come over and over until you beg me to stop. But even then, I might not give you the mercy you beg for. Not until I'm good and ready.

I pressed send and took deep breaths to even out my breathing.

Merde! I was about to meet Selene's parents, and I was turned on like I've never been before. In the airport.

I quickly read her reply. **Fuck, Remington. That's hot. I'm so wet. Wanna know what I'm doing? Touching myself.**

Oops, the nurse just walked in. I stared at the screen, breathing harder and harder.

Another message popped up. **I came. You are a god, Remington.**

I quickly typed, **Remember that when I have your beautiful body beneath mine.**

I spent the next ten minutes calming down and fighting not to look at the messages.

Fifteen minutes later, I walked through the door to arrivals and went to wait for Ines and Anthony.

Chapter Sixty-One

Remington

I watched the arrivals gate, eager but at the same time apprehensive, about meeting Selene's parents. I never met Colette's relatives, so this was really the first time to meet the in-laws.

The minute Anthony walked out, I knew he was Selene's father. Maybe it was the way his eyes, so like his daughter's, scanned the room filled with people, before looking over his shoulder as if searching for someone. Then a woman stepped forward, and his face lit up as he slid his arm along her shoulders, pulling her to him.

I lifted my hand to wave them over, my gaze shifting to the woman at his side, and I froze. My heart raced faster and the pulse thudded louder in my ears.

Colette?

I blinked, the pain in my chest spreading to every part of my body. Then I let out a breath and scanned the face in front of me. Brown eyes, hair more white than black.

No. Not Colette.

And then I knew without a doubt. This was Colette's mother.

They looked around, searching the crowd, and our gazes collided. Ines's face broke into a big smile, and she waved at me. She seemed to be pulling her husband, asking him to hurry up. But I couldn't move. My throat ached, and I felt as if I was about to lose it. I couldn't get air to my lungs.

"Remington St. Germain?" Ines asked, the smile on her face wavering the more I stood there, gaping.

They exchanged a look and shifted on their feet uneasily. "Maybe he's not the one," Anthony said.

"But...look at the photo. It's him." Ines shoved the photo Èric had sent them to help in identifying who I was in her husband's face.

Finally, I blinked, closed my mouth. "*Pardon,* you just caught me off guard," I murmured. How was I going to hold it together until, until what? I confirmed the truth, which was staring me in the face. If I was to really be truthful to myself, the possibility of Colette and Selene being related had always lingered in the back of my mind. A fact I always ignored. Even after Gilles's report about Selene being born in France, I still refused to accept the truth, because the mere thought that two people living in different parts of the world, two people fate seemed intent on throwing in my path, could be related, was just pure insanity. I remember when Selene and I dined at the restaurant weeks ago; she had mentioned she was born in New York, which completely contradicted Gilles's report.

I held my hand in their general direction awkwardly.

Merde. I had to pull myself together, at least for this introduction.

Ines bridged the space between us and pulled me into

her arms, embracing me. I wasn't used to strangers or almost-strangers welcoming me with such abundance. I sank into her embrace, and when she released me, Selene's father shook my hand, sizing me up carefully. He grabbed his luggage and jerked his head. I offered to take Ines's, and then I guided them through the throng of people. When we reached outside, I led them to the car, feeling Anthony's eyes burning into my back the entire way. This was one angry father. I could imagine all the ways he was thinking of toasting me over an open fire.

Well, at least that was what I'd be doing if some bloke dated my daughter, then put her in danger.

"How is my daughter doing?" Anthony asked as I hoisted the luggage inside the car boot.

"Very well. She will be leaving the hospital today, and she can't wait to see you." He narrowed his eyes at me.

And now I need to stop babbling.

Fucking hell! This wasn't me. *Nothing fazes me*. I've been in worse situations than this and pulled through.

After loading the luggage and everyone was securely seated, I backed out of the parking spot, paid for my ticket and drove away toward the city centre. I stared ahead, unable to face them. I was fighting not to blurt out what was bothering me. Worse, I was never good at small talk.

We arrived at the townhouse and quickly unloaded the car, taking everything inside. The minute my mother laid eyes on Ines, I knew that she knew. Her eyes grew wide, and her bottom lip quivered as she turned to face me. After introductions, I asked my mother to take Adrien for a walk, with Èric as their security detail. There was no way I could keep everything in. I had to speak to them before I brought Selene back from the hospital. So, as soon as the luggage was taken to their room downstairs, I approached them.

"I would like to speak to you before Selene comes home."

"Why? Is anything wrong with her?"

Everything was perfect. *And she's carrying my baby.* I stopped myself from focusing on that detail, because I had a feeling I might break into a dance.

They exchanged a look I could only interpret as cautious, but I wanted to know. Selene deserved to know, but she wasn't in a position to be burdened with everything that was happening. Above all, Colette was still at large, which in itself was dangerous. If there was a way to save my Selene, protect her, maybe this was it.

After checking to make sure they were comfortably settled on the couch and refreshments were on the table, I lowered myself on the seat across from them. I leaned forward, my elbows braced on the table, and stared at the two people whose lives I was about to disrupt. Bring some sort of apocalypse that would end the peace that had reigned in their lives.

I cleared my throat. "*Monsieur et Madame* Michaels," I started. Stopped. *Shit.* "Anthony and Ines. I have strong feelings toward your daughter, which is why this is going to be difficult." Ines's expression looked worried as her husband wrapped a hand around her shoulder, pulling her into him.

Good. She needed it.

She laughed nervously. "You are making me nervous."

"I apologize. It's not my intention." Time to rip the security blanket. "I once again apologize for putting your daughter in danger. Numerous events happened recently that have brought some issues into the light. So I will go ahead and ask; where was Selene born?"

Ines gasped, her face paling fast. "What?"

"What is this about, Remington?" Anthony asked, frowning.

I clenched my jaw, shut my eyes tightly and when I opened them again, two pairs of eyes were fixed on me. "I came across some information about Selene. And your other daughter. Not Marley."

Anthony shot from his seat. He charged toward me, his eyes bulging in shock and anger. He pointed his finger at my face, glaring at me. "What the hell are you—" He halted. Jabbed his finger at me several times without a word, swallowing hard. Then, he pulled his hand back, rifled his fingers through his hair before resting them on the back of his neck, rubbing it.

I waited, my heart beating fast.

"You have no right digging into other people's lives," Anthony said bitterly, looking at his wife. "You should have let sleeping dogs lie."

My gaze automatically followed his.

Bloody fucking hell.

I rose from my chair and rounded the table, crouching in front of Ines. "I am so sorry. I have hurt you, but this wasn't my intention."

"She's fine." Anthony snapped at me, pulling his wife into his arms as if to protect her from me. I poured water in a glass and handed it to Ines. Anthony took it with a fierce glare before turning to speak to his wife in soft whispers.

I sat back on my chair to wait for Anthony and Ines to collect themselves. "I'm fine," Ines finally said, straightening. "It's okay, Anthony. I think it's time. But first I need to know what information you have."

Anthony shook his head vehemently, rubbing his hands soothingly along his wife's arms and kissing her forehead.

"I can't keep this inside me any longer. Please, my love. Just…" She turned to face me and squared her shoulders, a determined look on her face. Right there, I saw where my woman got that spunky quality.

My woman.

My Selene.

My heart squeezed in my chest.

Damn right. Selene is mine. And I swore to protect her any way I could. Even if it meant getting to the bottom of this.

This declaration strengthened my resolve. Steepling my fingers, I tried to appear patient and calm, when all I wanted was to shake the information out of them.

"I'm ready. Please tell me," Ines announced, staring at me.

I took a deep breath and then started the tale from the second I met Selene at the hotel, omitting the details that would make me look like a lusty devil. When I was done, I went on and told them about Colette, the girl I met, married and lost in a span of five years.

"What do Selene and Colette have to do with each other?" Anthony asked.

"It turns out that Colette isn't dead, as I thought. She is the same woman who attacked Selene."

"Where is she? Why hasn't she been apprehended?"

I rubbed my forehead to ease the tension building there and told them what happened the last time Gilles, Alexei and I visited the flat.

"Jesus, she sounds dangerous! Who is this woman?"

I fixed my gaze on Ines and for the first time, wished I

had kept some of Colette's photos for this purpose. "That's what I'd been wondering until I saw you, Ines. Colette is a copy of you."

"Oh, God, no. No. It can't be." Anthony pulled her tighter into his arms and kissed her forehead, murmuring words of comfort. Eventually, she pulled back and dabbed her eyes with the handkerchief her husband had passed her before giving me a wobbly smile. "I guess I had better start from the beginning." She took a deep, shuddering breath and gripped her husband's hand as if she needed every iota of energy she could get.

"Twenty-six years ago, we, Anthony and I and…my baby girl…packed and moved from Paris to New York."

My breathing stuttered. Waited. My hands formed fists.

Anthony cleared his throat. "Ines…my wife, had just had Selene." He paused, his face contorted with pain, and this time he took longer before he spoke. Ines leaned into her husband, sobbing quietly.

"I had two daughters," Ines took over. "The first girl was four years old. I had her from my previous relationship, before I met Anthony. Her name was Diane."

"*Was?*"

She nodded. "Was. Is. One autumn morning, Diane was restless, and I took them out for a walk, hoping a little bit of fresh air would do them good. We ended up in a nearby park. They were having a children's festival, and it was completely packed. I turned for just a few seconds, ten seconds at most, to pull the baby blanket to protect Selene from the cool breeze, and when I turned around, my baby Diane was gone. Gone as if she never existed. No one saw her or who took her. Or even if she wandered off. The police searched for her for months and eventually declared it a cold case. God, she was only four years old."

I slumped back on the chair and dropped my head into my hands.

Jesus Christ! "How long did you search for your daughter?"

"Long enough. Eventually, we left. I couldn't stay here. There were too many memories…"

I rose from my seat and started to pace. My legs felt weak and sweat trickled down my back.

Mon Dieu! I was married to one sister and now I was about to marry the other? I tried to compute that in my head, but I came up blank. What were the odds, really?

"Where is…Colette, now?" Ines asked.

I shook my head. "My friend who owns the security firm hasn't been able to find her." I glanced at my watch and then back to Ines. "I have to pick Selene up from the hospital, but I would like to ask you not to talk about this with her. I'm not certain how strong she is at the moment. And God help me, I intend to protect her as much as I can."

"But, it's her sister," Ines said.

"Who is trying to kill her. Selene is going through some changes right now." I exhaled in exasperation. "I will let her tell you herself." There was no way I would take this from Selene. She had been agitated at first, wondering how her parents would take it now that she was pregnant after what she had gone through the past two years. Then she'd perked up and informed me she would deliver the news herself.

After showing them to their room, I left the townhouse and headed for the hospital but ended up driving around. Fifteen minutes later, I pulled into a parking spot, unable to drive anymore. The details of what happened to Diane/

Colette haunted my mind, and for the first time since meeting Selene, I questioned myself. Had I been drawn to her simply because of the minute resemblance to Colette? But how could that be, when I hated Colette with all my being and loved Selene with everything that I was? There was nothing to indicate any relation, and the only thing that would prove they were related was a DNA test.

Shit. I dropped my head onto my arms on the steering wheel. I had to make a decision fast. Selene would notice how shaken I was, which in turn would cause her stress, something she didn't need in her current condition. I was going to protect her, even if it meant going against my own rules.

I was about to lie to my fiancée.

I jolted upright as the impact of those words hit hard. I'd broken several of my rules since I met her.

I love her.

I restarted the car and sped toward the hospital, the craving to see her heightened by the distance between us.

Chapter Sixty-Two

Remington

I sat back with my fiancée's hand in mine, watching while she chatted with her sister and her parents. I caressed the back of her hand with my thumb, unable to keep my hands to myself. She seemed calmer these days, and her mood swings had lessened with the help of the cognitive behavioural therapy she had been receiving since she woke up from the coma. On the night I brought her home from the hospital, Ines and Anthony sat me down for a talk. They expressed their worry about Selene and the baby and that I had proposed too soon given that we hadn't known each other for long. They had a right to worry. I could imagine what they had gone through after Selene lost her child and husband. Even though I was determined to show them that she meant more to me than a three-month fling, I wanted the decision to be hers. Which she explained to her parents yesterday when they had the same talk. I met her, and somehow I knew she would change my life. I hadn't foreseen the proposal though. It just showed how much she affected me.

Lifting her hand to my lips, I kissed her knuckles. I was never one to shy away from public displays of affection. I loved her, and I wanted everyone to know she belonged to me. My heart picked up several beats whenever she turned around to smile at me as if she knew I needed that.

I did.

Somehow I felt needed when she turned to acknowledge me at her side. I didn't want to intrude on the reunion. Besides, my mind was still grappling with the Colette situation. Every time I thought about her—which was quite often—terror ripped through me. What if Selene left after learning the truth? Time was running out. I had to look for a way to tell her, but right now, I needed to focus on what was going on around me before Selene noticed something was wrong. She had asked me several times since leaving Marseilles if everything was all right, and I had told her yes. I loathed lying, especially to her. But this time, I had to go against my own rules.

We had held off telling Adrien about the baby because Selene had been worried something might happen and wanted to wait until she was discharged from the hospital here in Paris before we said anything.

The minute he walked through the door, he came rushing toward us and gave me a kiss before rushing to Selene's side and hopping on her lap. He hugged her fiercely.

"I missed you, tiger," Selene said, grinning hard as Adrien's small arms rounded her neck in a hug. My heart squeezed as I watched them together.

My fiancée and my son.

Selene and I exchanged a look. I nodded at her to break the news to him. At this point, I had no idea how he would react to having a brother or sister.

"We have something to tell you, Adrien," Selene said, and he focused his gaze on her.

"Are we going to Euro Disney?" he asked, his eyes huge and glimmering with hope.

I chuckled softly, as did everyone else in the room.

"No. Something smaller," Selene said, pushing his hair off his forehead. "You know your papa and I will be getting married."

He nodded, grinning. "I will carry the ring, remember?"

Selene laughed. "Yes, I do. So, how would you feel about having a little sister or brother?"

"How little?" he asked, frowning.

"Baby little."

"Baby." He wiggled his nose and glanced at Selene's stomach. As soon as he opened his mouth, question after question shot from his lips. He asked what the baby's name would be, if he would be allowed to sleep in the baby's room, if he or she could eat normal food like everyone else. The last question slammed hard in my stomach. He'd dropped his gaze and whispered, "Will you and Mama and my mamie still love me even after the baby comes?"

"Always. Nothing will change after the baby."

"I could share my toys with him." He smiled shyly and right there, I heard the longing for companionship, for siblings, in those words.

By eight o'clock, Selene was yawning. After saying goodnight to everyone, I followed her upstairs with Adrien leading the way.

"Can I sleep in your bed tonight?" Adrien asked, already kicking off his shoes and socks, and hopping on the bed.

I quickly tackled him, tickling him.

Within minutes, Selene had changed and was softly

snoring, and Adrien was shifting restlessly at my side while I attempted to read him a story. I sighed, content, enjoying this moment. I opted to push Colette to the back of my mind for now.

Chapter Sixty-Three

Remington

Gilles stopped by while Selene was taking a nap and delivered the documents that proved Colette was in fact Diane. Right after Alexei had dropped us at the hospital the first time I visited Colette's flat, Gilles had instructed him to go back and check if he could find something they could use for a DNA test. Watching Ines coming to terms with the fact her long-lost daughter was still alive and trying to harm Selene was exceedingly painful. It hit me all over again. Two women, half-sisters, both played a role in my life. I had loved the first one, lost her and now despised her for everything she had done to my son and me. Then the second one; we had found each other and I loved her. I wasn't about to let her go. Fate had a twisted sense of humour.

"So what do you think of this one?" Selene asked, effectively dragging me out of my sombre thoughts.

I glanced up from the ledgers on my desk to the notebook she held up from across the room on the couch. "Sexy. What is it?"

She rolled her eyes. "A bra," she said proudly and proceeded to tell me she had made a few calls, searching for a seamstress for her designs.

My mobile vibrated on the table, interrupting the conversation. I frowned at the words 'unknown number' flashing on the screen.

"St. Germain."

"It's good to hear your voice."

I froze, flexing my hand on the table.

Merde! Colette. I had so many questions, and I wanted to know the answers. But I couldn't interrogate Colette with Selene in the room.

"All right. Could you please hold on a minute? I will check if she is available to speak with you."

"She's there, isn't she? The bitch trying to take you and Adrien from me." I could imagine her sneering as she said those words.

My sight blurred with rage. I clenched the mobile in my hand as I pressed a quick kiss on Selene's lips and left the room, pretending the caller wanted to speak to my mother.

"Where are you?" I asked when I was upstairs and out of earshot.

She laughed. "Do you think I'm stupid? Anyway, how are you, my love? Did you love the irises? Remember you loved to send them to me as a promise to our love?"

Bile rose in my throat. "You don't have the right to ask me that and never will." I took deep breaths to calm myself. Yes, irises were my flower of choice when Colette and I were dating. I had also sent irises to the women I had dated after her presumed death. I had watched the coffin being lowered into her grave, for Christ's sake. I wasn't going to allow her to distract me with the flowers. "Where were you all these years?"

There was a long pause. "I want to come home."

"Tell me everything first." I tried not to show my impatience, or she might end the call.

She sighed. "Buying time for forgiveness. After I arrived in Paris a week after the crash, I came straight home, eager to let you know I hadn't died in the accident. Then I saw that woman…Madame Girard, leave the house and I knew she told you about me and her husband. Remington, it didn't mean anything. I've always loved you…"

Anger roared in my ears, blocking her plea. "Stop! Just fucking stop," I snarled into the phone. She did as I ordered. "How did you get inside the château?"

She laughed. I grunted, irritated.

What is so funny about my question?

"I sneaked in while Adrien and that man you had guarding him and the bitch," she took deep breaths as if trying not to lose control, "were in the pool and took the CD."

I shut my eyes tightly, hoping to ease the dull headache gathering a storm in the back of my head. Then I opened my eyes and stared at the ceiling. "Didn't you realize Adrien could have been hurt? Your own son?"

She sniffed. "I'm so sorry. My only intention was to scare that woman enough for her to leave. I didn't mean to hurt anyone. But she wouldn't go and that only made me angrier." She said the last words in a cold voice.

Mon Dieu, the woman is insane. Didn't she feel any remorse for what she had done?

"You never think about your actions and never have." I gritted out the words. To hell with being patient. "I almost lost two people I love because of what you'd done. Jesus, you are sick. You need help." I halted, taking in deep breaths. "How did you get past the guards? You almost killed Selene." I gripped the chair arm as that thought crashed into my head. *I almost lost Selene.*

I shot from my seat and started to pace as fury threatened to rip me in two. I heard nothing other than the pounding of my pulse in my ears.

Calm down. At least until you coax more information from her, like where she is living or something to help Gilles track her down.

"Why, Colette? Why did you fake your own death?" I asked the question that had been nagging me from the moment I knew she was the problem plaguing my life. "How could you do that to your own son?"

"My work gave me the freedom I wanted. When I left Paris, I felt free. No attachments. And then the airplane crashed, and I knew I would lose whatever freedom I had if I returned home."

"So you faked your own death. What I don't understand is, if you wanted to be free, why didn't you ask for a divorce? I wouldn't have stopped you."

"Look, I made a mistake, okay? Remember how you said that you loved me so much you would follow me to the ends of the Earth? That you would always wait for me no matter how long it took for me to come back home?" she asked, the words jumbled up in her hurry to get them out. She went on spouting words, and I couldn't make heads or tails of what she was talking about.

Gone was the coherent moment of less than five minutes ago, replaced by what I now believed was madness.

"We were young. And this was before I found out you were in the habit of wrecking homes. I wasn't enough for you. I never was."

She was quiet for a long time. Had she disconnected the call?

"So it's true that you love her. Is it because she looks like me?"

I gritted my teeth. "No. It's because she is the complete opposite of you."

"If I can't have you, then no one else will." Her voice was cold, final. Then, the line went dead.

Chapter Sixty-Four

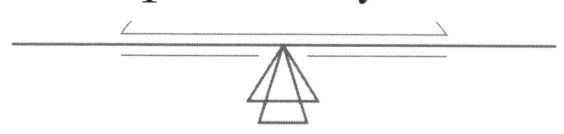

Selene

The car pulled to a stop outside the townhouse. After turning off the ignition, Remington laid his hand on my knee and gave it a squeeze. Commanding. Possessive. And my body fired up as it always did when he touched me. I shivered, leaned my head back, turning to look at him.

Jesus. That look on his face.

He continued to look at me, his hungry gaze roving all over my face. He ran his tongue along his lower lip before biting it.

Holy shit! I couldn't take it anymore. I glanced out the window to make sure no one was around. His closest neighbour was farther down the street. It helped that trees surrounded the place so no one could actually see us. Then I unbuckled my seat belt, slipped out of my coat and scrambled across the console, crawling onto his lap. I threaded my fingers into his hair, giving it a gentle tug, just the way he loved it. His eyes slipped shut as he shuddered, rumbling deep in his throat.

God, I love that sound. "Thank you for being so patient with me." His eyes slowly opened and he watched me lazily, his bottom lip snagged between his teeth. "I know I've been difficult and moody and probably a new level of challenge—"

He pressed a finger on my lips, cutting me off. "You are not a challenge. Your body needs time to adjust to the baby. How is your head today? Any dizzy spells?"

"Just earlier today, but I'm fine now. The doctor gave me something for the pain." I shifted on his lap, readjusting my centre on the bulge in his jeans. "You and I are inevitable. We always were. It took me a knock to the head to realize that."

"It did." His hands skimmed my legs, slipping under my dress and halting on my thighs. "I knew it the second I met you in Hotel L'Arc. What I felt at that time completely terrified me. It turns out I had no reason to fear anything."

I scrutinized his face. What was going on behind those green eyes? He had been distracted and secretive for a while now. I had cornered him several times, but somehow, he had managed to sidetrack me. My squirrel mind wasn't helping much either because I'd completely forget why we had an argument in the first place. I didn't doubt his feelings toward me. This man took every chance he had to spoil me, taking the doctor's instructions seriously, which was quite sweet.

No. Something else was going on, and I hated not knowing what it was that bothered the man known for his attentiveness.

"What's really going on, baby?"

Immediately his expression shuttered. "What do you mean?"

I chuckled. "Your acting sucks. Not Oscar-worthy, really. Why can't you tell me what's going on?"

He sighed, removing his hands from under my dress and placing them on my hips. He dropped his gaze to my boobs and licked his bottom lip. "I'll be fine now that you're home where you belong."

"I've been home for the past five days."

His jaw clenched. I knew that look. He wasn't going to talk anytime soon. I'd done so much worrying the past couple of weeks. I had to take the doctor's advice for the sake of the baby.

"I hope you'll feel comfortable enough to talk to me soon." I tugged my dress, rearranging it around my hips.

"What are you doing, *ma belle*?" he asked in a hoarse voice, caught between amusement and desire, staring at me through hooded eyes while his hands gripped my hips, squeezing gently.

"It depends. What do you want me to do to you, St. Germain?" I wiggled on his lap until I felt his huge cock right where I wanted him.

He cocked a brow. "Feeling a bit feisty, aren't we?"

"Feisty and extremely horny."

"Bloody hell! I want to do some very dirty things to you right now."

"Yeah? Like what?"

He shifted on the seat, pushing his hips up at the same time bearing me down on the bulge on his jeans. "Like fuck you hard. God, I've missed this. And I think I will punish you for teasing me on the phone." He slid his hand to my front, pressing the heel to my pussy and rubbing insistently. "This sweet pussy." He removed his hand from me, brought it around my neck and pulled me to him. He crushed his mouth to mine, and he kissed me hungrily. He nipped my bottom lip and I responded, wanting him, his tongue, his cock in me. He grunted in approval, pushing his hips up, rolling them. I ground into him, wanting the friction, the satisfaction only he could give me.

"You're going to have my baby. *Our* baby," he murmured against my lips. I could feel the smile pressing on mine. "You're going to look so bloody beautiful, so fucking perfect. Not that you don't take my breath away now, but *mon Dieu!* I already see the potential."

"Potential for what?"

"Driving me insane with your curves and everything else."

"Holy hell, Remington. I want your big cock filling me right now. Do you know how long it has been since I've had my Remington fix? Centuries."

His shoulders shook before he threw his head back and this deep, rich sound rolled out of his mouth. God, his laughter was a thing of beauty. An aphrodisiac, because I was completely turned on.

"You're losing points, St. Germain."

He chuckled. "I thought the points system was over."

"You wish. How do you think I'd get you to do what I want?" I asked, leaning down and kissing his jaw, moaning as his scruff tickled my face. Then I nipped his chin.

He took my face into his hands, making sure my eyes were on his. Fierce. Passionate. "I will always fulfill your every need. Points or no points." And as if to stress his point, he brought his hand where it was before, slipped a finger underneath my underwear and entered me as he watched me closely.

"Harder. Deeper."

His fingers froze. "I don't want to hurt you."

"You won't. I promise."

His thrusts seemed hesitant at first, then they became bolder. He brought his lips to my neck, trailing kisses, and murmured, "Aren't you afraid someone will see us?" I shook my head, the idea of doing something this naughty exciting me even more. "When did you become so naughty, *ma belle*?"

"The moment you promised me three months of debauchery and hedonistic pleasure. Come on, St. Germain."

"I love how responsive you are."

I leaned forward, nipping his jaw. "I have a surprise for you."

He cocked a brow. "Which means you won't tell me."

I nodded. "Later. Now I just want you to make me come. God, I love how you fill me."

He grunted, working his fingers faster and fucking me harder and harder. His mouth connected with my neck, and he trailed kisses down my throat. He paused on my shoulder and gently bit down.

I screamed and came right before those wicked lips of his crushed on mine, swallowing the rest of my scream as he kissed me.

"Are you all right?" he asked, his voice hoarse, concerned.

I nodded, smiling. Breathless. "You earned some major bonus points."

He pulled his fingers out of me and licked them, his green eyes gleaming sinfully. "Hmm, you taste incredible."

I squirmed on his lap, feeling turned on again. But before I could do anything about it, the sound of a car door slamming shut startled me. I scanned our surroundings outside the car.

He chuckled. "I thought you weren't afraid of being caught having sex in a car."

"What I want to do is for your eyes only." I winked at him and shrugged into my coat, rearranging my clothing before opening the driver's door and slipping out, shivering at the biting cold.

He followed suit while pulling the collar of his peacoat to his chin and quickly snagged me around my waist, pulling me to his side as he swung the door shut and activated the lock using the key remote control.

"I have a feeling I'm not on your father's birthday invitation list."

She laughed. "He needs a little warming up before he finally graces you with a smile. He doesn't know you like I do."

His hand stiffened on my back, and a soft growl came from the back of his throat.

"What do you want?" He gritted out the words.

I whipped my head around toward the driveway, searching for the source of Remington's shift of mood. His father was walking up the small drive in our direction. He halted before us, his eyes moving from his son and back to me.

"Son," he said by way of greeting.

"What do you want?" Remington asked again, and I swear the temperature dropped twenty degrees.

Oh, wow.

Remington had the power to make a person feel like shit. Subtly, I took his hand in mine and linked our fingers. He flicked a gaze at me, his eyes softening a notch and his body loosening at my side.

"You haven't been answering my calls," Remington Sr. announced, his hands clasped in front of him, his head tilted to the side. He reminded me of a mafia boss.

"I see you can't take a hint," Remington said. "I don't have time for this." He turned me around, ready to leave.

"Son." His father took a step forward and onto the path that led to the townhouse. "Remington."

Remington halted, the grip on my hand tightening. He cursed in French before dropping my hand and turning around to face his father.

"Is Caleb doing all right?"

His father nodded.

"Good. I have nothing further to say to you. We said our goodbyes in London. I don't remember asking or inviting you to my home."

Remington Sr. stared at his son for a few seconds, before frowning and quickly dropping his gaze to his shoes.

I slid a hand up my man's lower back, pressing lightly. I leaned into him and kissed his shoulder. "Give him a chance, baby," I whispered into his ear. He turned and scowled at me. "And stop scowling at me. I told you it turns me on. You don't want me to unleash my skills in front of your father, do you?" I winked at him. His lips twitched as he fought a smile in the midst of that fierce scowl.

The sound of a door opening interrupted us. I shifted around just as Adrien darted out the door.

"Papa! Mama!" he shouted as he barrelled toward us. Remington stepped around me and grabbed Adrien before he could slam his tiny body into me. Remington seemed eager to protect me from anything. But watching them like this made my chest tighten. *God, I love them.*

"Is that…my…grandson?"

Remington shook his head. "We're not going to do this here in the presence of my son."

Chapter Sixty-Five

Remington

Merde! I couldn't do this here. What the hell did he want now? The last time we saw each other in London, he had been his usual pompous arse. He'd hardly spoken to me, not that I cared. I had been there for Caleb, and that was all that mattered.

"Remington?" I followed the shocked sound to find my mother standing in the doorway. Her eyes were wide as they moved from me to my father. She seemed to recover fast, straightened her shoulders and strode toward us in short, purposeful steps. "Remington Newport. What are you doing here?"

"I was hoping for a chance to speak with our son." My father switched his gaze to me, then looked at Adrien and finally to Selene. "Look, I just need to say something, then I will leave you. I'll never bother you again after this."

"Who's that, Papa?" Adrien asked in a small voice, his gaze on my father.

Fucking hell! This wasn't how I wanted him to know he

had a grandfather. I slid Adrien to the floor and nudged him in Selene's direction. "Take him inside, please."

"I don't think so."

I froze, shifted around, searching for the source of that voice, so familiar.

"Colette?" My voice sounded shocked even to my ears. I shouldn't be surprised that she was here, yet, I was. I stood there, watching helplessly as my past collided with my present. She rounded the corner of the house and strolled confidently toward us, but her eyes said differently. They were bloodshot and possessed a wild look that had me inching closer to Selene. Her lips were painted in red lipstick that made her face appear paler. A knee-length dark jacket that hid her thin frame completed the haggard appearance. "What are you doing here?" I took two steps to make sure my body acted as a shield for Adrien and Selene. I glanced at my mother, hoping she would take my cue and return inside the house. But her gaze never left Colette.

"Hmm, let me see. What am I doing here," Colette drawled. "I'm here because I want to be with you and Adrien. Remington, my love, I've been waiting so long to be with you. Be a family again."

I heard Selene suck in a breath. Shit. Where were Gilles's men? The one day I asked them to meet me at the house, this happens.

"Don't bother, Remington. Your security isn't here at the moment."

I looked over my shoulder. "Mother, Selene. Get inside the house and take Adrien with you."

"No, no one is leaving. We have to sort this out now, and I need witnesses to when you finally agree to be with me. Hello, Adrien, remember me?"

Adrien whimpered from somewhere behind me.

"Get inside the house *now*!"

"I just said fucking no!" I heard something click and quickly turned around. Colette stood barely five meters away with a gun pointed in our direction.

"Put that gun away, Colette. You and I will go somewhere and talk, all right? We don't need them," I said, hoping to placate her with my words.

"Remington, *no*," Selene's pleading voice, filled with anguish, reached me. "Colette? Your *dead* wife? What's going on? And…oh, my God, her face…I remember her…that voice. She attacked me in Provence. She—she looks like…my mother."

"Selene?" Ines called out from the door, her voice so similar to Selene's. "Is that you? We heard a commotion out here and thought we'd check what's going on."

"Mom? Oh, Mom." She sounded as though she was about to burst into tears, but then she asked angrily, "Why does that woman look like you?"

I heard a sharp intake of breath, but I couldn't turn. There was no way I would take my eyes off Colette. She was done hurting people around me.

"Diane?" Ines and Anthony's voices called out in unison.

"She is the woman you told us about, Remington?" Ines asked, hope and longing clear in her voice.

"What? Remington, you knew who she was? How long have you known about this?"

Everything was getting out of control. Pulling my mobile out of my pocket, I made sure Colette was distracted by the drama unfolding in front of us before dialling Gilles's number and then hastily slipped it inside my shirt's front pocket, praying he'd pick up the call.

"SHUT THE HELL UP!" Colette shouted, her face red and eyes bulging. I couldn't believe this was the woman I had fallen in love with many years ago. "Now, can someone tell me who the hell these people are, other than the cow trying to steal my husband?"

Was she so blind she couldn't see the resemblance between Ines and herself? Or was she locked so deep in madness she couldn't see anything beyond her selfishness?

"Colette. My name is Ines. I'm positive you're my daughter, Diane."

"Oh, my God, Colette…*she* is my sister?" Selene asked. "So…you were married…to my half-sister?" Her breaths were coming out fast, and I was worried she was going to pass out. All this stress straight after leaving the hospital especially after the doctor warned us to try to avoid situations that would heighten her anxiety wasn't good. I had to get her inside. Colette had shown what heinous acts she was capable of. Selene shocked me with what came out of her mouth next. "Was it why you chose me?" The words were so softly spoken.

Surely, she can't believe this again. I love her.

"No. *Mon Dieu,* where are you getting this notion from?"

"The evidence is right here in front of us, Remington!" Selene's voice trembled. "This is so messed up."

This seemed to distract Colette. She frowned, her gaze focused over my shoulder, then her mouth dropped open. "What kind of treachery is this?" she yelled. "Who are you?" She pointed in my general vicinity with the hand holding the gun.

"Hear me out, please," Ines said. From the corner of my eye, I saw Anthony inch closer, half of his body protecting his wife. "I had a daughter, and her name was Diane. She disappeared when she was four years old. The police looked for her for so many years, to no avail. I hadn't seen you since that day until today. You are Diane; I can feel it in my blood. You're the spitting image of *me*."

Colette narrowed her eyes, seeming to mull the words in her head. "So you gave up on this Diane after what…a few years searching for her? Where have you been all these years? Definitely not in France. After my mother told me I was adopted and that they took me in after a woman handed me to her for a special price," she sneered, "I hired a private detective to look for my real parents. He couldn't find you, but he said he had information that you were no longer in the country. And since I didn't have enough money, I halted the investigation. Did I mean that little to you?"

"Please understand, we left information with the police to contact us if—"

Colette waved the gun in the air. "Stop, stop. Too late. Too fucking late." She shifted her gaze to me. "Hmm, husband. I see you and my *sister* are a couple now, hmm? Were you looking to replace me?" She took a step forward. "You don't need her now. I'm here."

"Well, for someone who claims to love her husband, you have a funny way of showing it," Selene said, stepping in front of me.

I grabbed her arm and pushed her behind me, growling under my breath. "Christ, Selene. Are you trying to get yourself killed?"

She ignored me and ducked around me so that only her head was poking out. "You left him. You cheated on him. You lied to him and faked your own death. What kind of woman does that to the man she loves, huh? Well, listen to me, sister," she jabbed a finger in the air toward Colette, "you treated him like he was worth shit. But guess what? You were blind enough to turn away from this special man. And now, he has me. He has Adrien, he has a whole fucking family that loves him. If you want him and Adrien, you will have to go through me."

Silence followed. I was sure everyone could hear my heart pounding in my chest.

"Selene," I said, unable to get any more words out of my throat. "That was the most incredible bloody speech I've ever heard."

"Shut up. I'll deal with you later."

I couldn't believe even after shutting me down, I was still turned on and that I loved her even more.

"Well, well. Why don't you stop hiding behind 'your man' and come out. Tell me that to my face."

"Like hell she will," I snarled. "You want me. You got me." I took a step forward, ignoring the shocked gasps behind me.

"Don't do this, Remington." *My mother.*

"Papa, stay here with us. She will hurt you. She has a gun." *Adrien.*

"I didn't give that speech for you to offer yourself as the sacrificial lamb, baby. If you go, I go too."

"Don't be stupid, Selene," I growled over my shoulder. She gasped, her eyes widening in shock. I hope she understood what I was doing. If there was a way to convince Colette, I had to at least show I didn't really care about Selene. It might be too late after I spent the first half of this standoff defending her.

But I had to try.

I ignored the pleas. I had to; otherwise, this woman trying to take away my family would do something drastic.

Colette studied me, obviously weighing my words in her head.

"Come, Colette." I stepped away, making sure my body blocked her aim. As soon as she whipped out that gun, I knew she wasn't here for me, but to finish what she'd started years ago when she began sending those anonymous text messages and letters. "Just you and me."

I fixed my gaze on hers, smiled and inched forward. Then I was standing in front of her. "Put that gun away." She shook her head. From the corner of my eye, I saw Gilles's car pull to a stop in a parking lot a few meters away.

It's about damn time.

Two of his men stepped out of the car, followed by Èric and Gilles. As soon as they noticed what was going on, Gilles used different signs with his hands to communicate with his men.

I focused my gaze back on Colette while keeping an eye on Èric and Gilles, now advancing.

"Where would you like for us to go and talk? No distractions, I promise. Do you remember the café we visited on our second date, right after the day we met?"

She nodded, her eyes gleaming and a smile on her lips. I heard a sob from Selene, the sound almost breaking my resolve to take Colette away from my house. My family.

Almost.

"All right. We can drive my car." I had installed a tracker in case of anything untoward happening. I would be traceable.

She quickly looked at the Phantom and back at me. "Get in and start the car."

"Give me the gun first. If you want to go with me, you have to give me the gun."

I didn't trust her with it. The first time Colette and I met, she had told me she had taken shooting and archery classes. We had done a few sessions in a local shooting range before I finally gave up after realizing it wasn't for me, and I knew she had excellent aim. A ten-meter target wouldn't be a problem for her.

She flipped the gun and held it out to me with the butt of it facing my direction. I exhaled and took it.

One step passed. Now, to make sure she was off my property.

I rounded the car to the driver's side, slid into the seat and quickly leaned over the passenger side to open the door for her and froze. She held another gun and was sprinting toward Selene. Everything seemed to slow down as I jumped out of the car. A shot rang through the air, shattering the quiet atmosphere. Selene, Ines and my mother dropped to the ground after the shot went off. Èric, having caught up with Colette, tackled her, wrestling the gun out of her hands, while Gilles and two of his men sprinted toward Selene, Ines and my mother, Anthony and my father. Where was Adrien? Had he gone inside the house like I told him?

Please, God, don't do this to me.

I prayed while sprinting toward Selene, my gaze darting around, searching for Adrien.

"Madame Michaels, are you all right? Madame Michaels!" Gilles asked. My legs weren't working as they should as I rushed toward her.

"Adrien!" I yelled, my heart in my throat. "Adrien!"

But hearing Gilles ask if she was okay hit me with a whole new level of fear. Where was my son?

"Madame Michaels! Open your eyes." Gilles slapped her cheeks softly.

"Someone please help!" My mother's voice drifted through the air. I glanced over my shoulder to where she knelt on the ground beside my father.

"What the hell?" I had to make sure Selene and Adrien were okay first.

I pushed through the huge bodies to get to Selene, lying

on the ground with Adrien tucked safely in her arms. Her back was facing the direction Colette's shot had come from.

"Oh, God." I dropped to my knees and began searching her body for any injuries before moving to Adrien. Her body shivered uncontrollably, but she kept her eyes squeezed tight. I touched her cheek to let her know it was me. "It's over now, Selene. Open your eyes and look at me." Panic twisted in my chest when she didn't respond. "Come on, *ma belle*."

"Papa?" Adrien called out in a small voice. Immediately, Selene's eyes popped open. She blinked rapidly before her eyes found mine.

Mon Dieu! I'd died several times between Colette pulling the gun and hearing Adrien's voice.

"Are you all right?" I asked as I extracted Adrien from her secure hold and quickly scanned his body for injuries while asking if he felt any pain. After confirming he was okay, I hugged him tightly, praising him for being brave, then told my mother to keep an eye on him before I turned to help Selene up.

"But, Colette fired her gun, *oui*?" I asked no one in particular, still puzzled.

"We need help over here!" Èric yelled. I turned around quickly to find him kneeling next to my father. Colette was lying on the ground unconscious with a pair of shackles around her wrists.

"Monsieur Newport needs urgent medical care," Èric said, his hand on my father's shoulder. "Call the ambulance."

"What happened—" *Fuck, no*! I stared in horror at the growing red patch on his shoulder to the blood darkening the tarmac, then quickly pulled the mobile from my pocket to call the ambulance but shoved it back in. I would probably get to the hospital faster than it would take them to drive here.

"Get him in the car, and keep pressure on the wound." Èric nodded. I turned to Selene; her eyes were staring into space.

"Colette is my *sister*?" she whispered. "Colette was your wife?"

"Let's talk about that later, all right?" When she didn't answer, I grabbed her chin and forced her to focus her eyes on mine as I tried to keep the mounting fear from my voice. "We have to get you to the hospital."

"I feel fine," she said, running a hand over her stomach.

"I can't risk you and the baby. We are leaving now." I wasn't sure how much force she had used when she dropped to the ground to protect Adrien.

She nodded, allowing me to help her to her feet.

"Is Adrien okay? What about everyone else? Mom and Dad?" she asked, scanning around in panic as soon as she was settled in the car. After reassuring her everyone was safe and Gilles let me know he was driving Colette to the police station, I informed my mother which hospital we were going to and drove away.

"Are you okay back there?"

I heard a grunt of pain.

A few moments into the trip, I glanced at Selene. She lay with her head back, her eyes closed and her hands curled loosely into fists on her lap. I wanted to reassure her, touch her. Because that was the only way I knew to comfort her. I slid my hand to touch hers, but she flinched and jerked back her hand as if my touch repelled her. I couldn't blame her if it did. I hadn't told her the truth, and I didn't regret my decision. Not when I hadn't known how the truth would affect her. The stress of it. Seconds later, her fingers tangled with mine and I exhaled, relieved.

I peered at my father in the rearview mirror. He leaned into Èric, his glazed eyes meeting mine. "You took the bullet meant for Selene. Why did you do that, Father?" I asked.

"Because I had to save someone you loved. For once in my life, I wanted to do something that didn't benefit me. I have been trying to call you to thank you after Caleb's surgery, but you wouldn't answer my calls or emails. Stubborn like your old man—" He chuckled, then stopped and groaned, breathing raggedly. "I found out through Adele about your life, your son. Selene. I was a fool, and I regret the years I spent away from you. I was proud and made mistakes, and I wish I could turn back the clock and do this all over again. Adele told me about Selene's accident and also about the woman causing trouble in your life. Upon further investigation, I found out Selene was pregnant. I wanted to protect you, protect her and everyone else you loved. I've been a bad father to you…" he trailed off, panting. "God, I want to tell you so much…"

My eyes burned with tears. "It's okay. We can talk about this later. Just—save your energy for now."

I darted a look in the mirror and saw him shake his head stubbornly.

"No. I won't rest until—until I know that you forgive me for being—bloody fucking hell!" he yelled, his face contorted in pain. His head fell back; the only sound filling the car was his heavy, uneven breathing.

My foot automatically pressed on the accelerator as I met Èric's gaze in the mirror. He shook his head, panic colouring my vision.

"You saved me the minute you saved her, Father." *I forgive you.*

Ten minutes later, I pulled into the parking lot. Èric leaped out of the car to alert the hospital's staff. Within minutes, my father was loaded on a stretcher and rushed into the ER.

"I could have been on that stretcher right now, Remington," Selene mumbled, her wide eyes staring blindly at the doors.

I shuddered at the thought and quickly grabbed her in a hug. Her body came alive immediately, and she returned my embrace with a fierce one of her own.

"I will go insane if I think like that. You're safe."

She pulled back. "But your father is not. He took a bullet for me." Her eyes filled with tears. "What if he doesn't pull through? I can't—"

I cupped her jaw, forcing her to focus on me. "He is Remington Newport, and he is a fighter. He wouldn't be who he is if he wasn't."

Chapter Sixty-Six

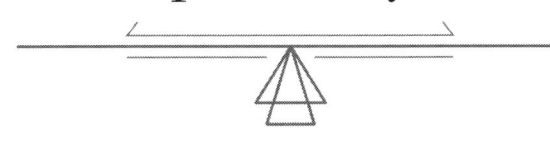

Selene

After answering the nurse's questions at the counter, Remington slid his arm around my waist. I tensed, then relaxed as he led me to one of the chairs facing the TV in the waiting area. He dropped his arm and weaved his fingers with mine, then fixed his worried gaze on me.

"Talk to me," he finally murmured, giving my hand a squeeze. "How are you feeling? How is the baby?"

He looked exhausted. There was no way I was going to burden him with how I was feeling. "Tired. I just want to forget this day ever happened."

"I wish I could take back what transpired today."

Suddenly, I felt tired. Everything was coming down on me, painfully buzzing in the back of my head. I closed my eyes, leaning back on the wall. "I can't do this now."

"Come here." He tugged my hand, but I shook my head. "Allow me to hold you, please. I almost lost you, Selene. Every time the memory of how close…*mon Dieu*. I cannot *not* have you in my arms right now. I need this."

I opened my eyes and met his, sucking in a breath at the

pain there. I scooted into him and lay my head on his shoulder, curling my fingers around a fistful of his shirt as pain flashed inside my head. Taking that as a sign, he literally snatched me up and onto his lap, not caring the room was full of people. I snuggled into him, welcoming his strength and warmth.

"You want the truth?" I mumbled in his shirt. "I'm so mad with you right now, and I'm also really terrified. I love you and I'm angry in equal measures."

"It's over now. Colette will not harm you anymore." He rubbed circles on my back. "You have a right to be angry with me, but please don't shut me out."

"I could never shut you out, even if I wanted to." We fell silent, the sound of machines beeping, the PA blaring to life, feet shuffling on the floor…

"Selene Michaels?"

Both Remington and I shot to our feet and glanced up at a tall, dark-haired nurse. Her eyes lingered a little too long on Remington, colour rising to her cheeks. And he hadn't even unleashed his smile on her. In fact, his jaw was set in grim determination, his beautiful green eyes dark with worry and his lips taut. His hand tightened on my hip, pulling me closer to him as if announcing to the woman and everyone else in the room where he belonged. She turned to face me, eyeing me up and down, and all I could think was, *can you handle these curves?* Despite being angry with Remington, warmth tingled in my blood. He was so irresistible, this man.

The nurse finally looked at me and smiled tightly. I didn't even have the energy to scowl at her. I was still seething at Remington, worried about the little sharp pains twitching inside my belly and battling a killer headache.

"Please follow me. I'll show you the room."

Remington dropped his hand from my hip and grabbed

my hand, following the nurse. We halted in front of room number three.

"I've placed a robe for you on the bed," she announced. "The doctor will be with you shortly." She faced Remington. "Would you like to wait for your wife outside—"

"Not happening," he barked and pushed the door, pulling me inside, but not before I saw the nurse jerk back as if slapped.

Remington was such a Neanderthal, and I loved him even more. Not that I was about to tell him. I needed to hold on to my anger a little longer. Childish, I know, but Jesus, Colette? I still couldn't believe he'd kept that information from me.

As soon as the door slammed shut in the nurse's face, he whirled around and gently pushed me against the door, as though he was afraid I'd break, before sinking his face into the crook of my neck.

He inhaled deeply. "I don't like it when you're angry with me."

"You should have thought about that before you hid that information about your ex-wife from me. We always tell each other the truth, remember?"

He flinched, releasing a trembling breath. "There are some truths that hurt more than help. This one would have hurt you, *ma belle*. Probably destroyed you. I vowed to protect you. I also said I'd always endeavour to tell you the truth. I failed on the first, but I was sure as hell not going to tell you about Colette. I wanted to protect you." His body was coiled tight against mine. He didn't try to kiss me or touch me, other than his chest and thighs brushing mine.

I shut my eyes quickly as dizziness and nausea swept through me, laying my head on his shoulder. Immediately his body loosened, as if that single act of my head on him gave him strength. "I need to use the bathroom."

He lifted his head and cupped my jaw, fixing his tortured gaze on mine. "I know what I did was wrong. I hope you understand that, under different circumstances, I might have told you. But you had just woken up from the coma, and I wasn't going to make things worse by telling you. This was my burden to carry."

Everything he said made sense. But still… "I don't want you to carry that burden alone."

"I know."

Biting my cheek to keep from caving in, I tangled my fingers in his hair, nudging his head down to kiss his forehead. "I need to change."

He dropped his hand and took a step back, watching as I walked away. I sneaked a look over my shoulder. He stood where I had left him, flexing his curled fists at his sides. God, I loved him *so* much, but I was so conflicted about the situation. I just needed some time to come to terms with everything that had happened.

Do you know how it feels to watch you walk away from me?

Those words flashed inside my head, so I knew how difficult it was for him, standing there as I left his side.

I opened my mouth to speak but instead snapped it shut, unable to say anything. I turned and entered the bathroom, locking the door behind me.

After quickly turning the tap on full, I grabbed the sink as nausea rolled in my stomach. I jerked forward and vomited.

Oh, God, I'm going to die. It was like endless torture as my stomach roiled, emptying its contents down the drain.

"Selene?"

Shit. "I'm fine." I rinsed my mouth. "Can you please wait for me in the waiting room?"

I heard footfalls through the door. He was probably pacing,

with his hands gripping his hair. Moments later, he said, "Not until I know you're all right."

"I am."

"I want to see you," he growled from the other side of the door.

I sighed. Stubborn Remington had just made an appearance.

After drying my hands and mouth with the tissues from the dispenser, I slipped down my pants, followed by the panties, and froze. My hand automatically shot out and grabbed the sink for support as dizziness once again threatened to cripple me.

Every snippet of anger and worry I had felt the entire drive to the hospital vanished, replaced by dread. My free hand tightened around the panties.

God, no, no, no! Please don't do this to me.

I continued to stare at the spots of blood on the white material, unable to breathe for several seconds. A sob ripped out of my throat.

"Selene?" Remington called out in a panicked voice. The doorknob rattled forcefully. "Open up, *ma belle*. Please."

I quickly wiped my cheeks and stepped out of the panties. "I'll be out in a minute," I choked out, gathering my clothes in my hands.

There was a long pause. "You're crying. Open this bloody door." The knob rattled again. "*Merde!*"

"I'm not crying," I announced, my voice muffled by the fabric. "Please, I just need a few seconds, okay?" He was already worried about his father; I wasn't about to become baggage as well. I grabbed my sweater and pressed it into my face to drown my sobs.

"Not fucking happening. Open this door, or I'll break it down." He gritted the words from the other side.

"Give me a damn minute, Remington!"

He cursed severely in French but seemed to do as I asked. After splashing water on my face, I dabbed tissues under my eyes to get rid of any signs that I'd been crying. One look in the mirror and I knew Remington would be all over me the second I opened that door.

I could handle this situation. Handle him like I always did. *Easy.*

What if…Jesus, what if I lost the baby?

Suddenly I couldn't breathe, couldn't get air into my lungs. *Breathe.*

Oh, my God, I need to breathe.

Nothing.

Bracing my back on the wall, I slid down to the floor, ignoring the chill racing up my body as my butt connected with the cool floor. I dropped my head between my knees, taking in huge gulps of air.

"Selene!"

I shouldn't have locked the door. I shivered, hyperventilating. "Oh, God," I moaned.

Suddenly, air rushed inside the room, brushing against my bare legs as the sound of the door slamming against a wall echoed through the small bathroom. Seconds later, Remington was sitting on the floor next to me, dragging me into his lap.

"Is she all right?" a female voice asked worriedly in French. "Should I page the doctor?"

"She'll be fine," Remington answered, wrapping his arms around me and hugging me tightly. "Ask the doctor to give us a few minutes. It's okay; I'm here now." He kissed my hair, running a hand down my back repeatedly.

Feet shuffled on the floor, followed by the sound of the door being shut. I didn't have the energy to look up. I curled myself into Remington's chest, my head buried into his shoulder, listening to his soothing voice as he encouraged me to breathe. I did, absorbing some of his warmth and strength into my body.

"Feeling better?" he asked.

I nodded, lifting my head to look at him.

"What's wrong?" he asked as panic filled his features.

My eyes flicked to where my panties lay, and my breath began to leave me again.

I knew the moment he saw the panties. He sucked in a breath, and his body tensed against mine. The hand on my back halted, clenched into a fist, before flexing out and pulling me tightly into his chest. He kissed my forehead, then pulled back and stared at me through red-rimmed eyes. His hair looked dishevelled and his shirt wrinkled. He seemed to have aged between earlier when we made out in the car and now. I'd never seen this look on him, and I hated he had to go through this.

"It's going to be fine," I said, forcing a smile. I swept the hair off his forehead, twining it with my fingers and giving it a gentle tug. "You and I have gone through so much. We can face anything, okay?" Lifting my free hand, I brushed the tears fighting to fall from the corner of his eyes. He took a deep breath and nodded.

"Now kiss me and let's get out of here," I said in what I hoped was a calm voice. I wanted my Remington back. Yes, he was allowed to cry, but worrying about me and his father was just too much. He'd probably be less worried if I perked up a bit, even though I felt like I was dying inside.

He slowly lowered his mouth to mine and kissed me softly, tenderly. A kiss that spoke of so many emotions, it literally stole my breath away. I pulled back, dropping my head to his chest.

"You're my favourite girl in the world," he murmured hoarsely against my ear. "I bloody love you so much, you know that, *oui*?"

I raised my head and grinned at him, knowing I'd effectively lightened up the mood. "Of course I know you love me. How could you not? Besides, I'm made of awesome."

A slow smile spread across his lips, and sweet Jesus, *that smile*, the one that always left me breathless, appeared, chasing away the tired-looking Remington.

"Are you trying to make me come? Because that's what happened the first time you flashed those dimples at me."

He threw his head back and roared in laughter. God, so, so potent. I couldn't believe I was turned on, even under the circumstances. I was such a slut when it came to this man. "You never told me that."

"If I did, you'd add them as weapons to your already overflowing arsenal and unleash them on me when you felt like it," I said, pushing away from him and standing up.

"And now that I do, be very afraid, *ma belle*." He stood up and grabbed the hospital gown, holding it out for me.

"As if that'd scare me. Just don't let it go to your head, baby."

He chuckled and before I knew it, he'd scooped me into his arms and marched out of the bathroom. Stopping at the bed, he laid me down, then stood back to watch me like he always did—as if he was seeing me for the first time. "You're incredible, Selene."

"You're not so bad yourself." I wiggled on the bed to sit properly and watched him as he disappeared back inside the bathroom and returned with my clothes in his hands. "In fact, you and I *go together like rama lamma lamma ka dinga da dinga dong...*" Jesus, I was on a roll. I didn't take anxiety very well.

He grinned, folding the clothes and placing them in a neat pile on a chair next to the wall. "*Grease?*"

I nodded, rubbing my hands along my arms to keep warm. Remington grabbed his sweater from the hook on the wall next to the door and draped it around me. "My mom loves that movie. I know most of the songs off the top of my head." I cleared my throat, lowering my voice.

The expression on his face was a mix of amusement and worry.

I dropped my gaze to my lap, swallowing the ball of anxiety in my throat… "I'm very nervous. You might want to get used to this because it's what I do." I peeked at him through my lashes.

He cocked a brow at me.

God, I love when he does that.

"And you're probably thinking it bothers me? I was seconds away from bawling in there," he points to the bathroom, "but you brought me back. You are…*mon Dieu*…" He shook his head as if he couldn't find the words to convey whatever he wanted to say, then started to pace up and down beside the bed.

"You too," I said, propping my legs on the stirrups and tugging down my gown as it slid around my hips. His eyes flared and darkened as they followed the movement, leaving me hot and flushed. I preferred him like this, better than the broken man of earlier. "Come sit with me."

"I like this view better." He stared pointedly at my legs before grabbing the chair with my clothes on it and dragging it to the bed, just as a doctor with sandy-blond hair, probably in his mid to late thirties, entered the room. He was really hot, if you liked the surfer-type guys.

Remington tensed beside me.

"Don't even think about it," I whispered under my breath.

"Think about what?" he asked innocently, but the overprotective grip on my hip said differently.

"Scaring him off by using one of your patented looks."

"I don't know what you're talking about." His breath was warm on the shell of my ear as he nipped my earlobe.

I sighed, fighting the urge to turn around and mesh his lips with mine. "I love you. I'm still mad at you, but I love you."

His body relaxed, and the growl rumbling in the back of his throat eased.

After the doctor introduced himself and shook our hands, I gave him a short version of what happened and finally the spotting on my underwear. He already knew about my medical history since this was the same hospital I was admitted to five days earlier. He asked me to lie on my back as he pulled the table holding a stainless-steel tray toward him. Remington gave it a look, something between a glare and terror. I pressed my lips shut, fighting a smile even though this wasn't in any way funny. How did he manage that?

When he was done, the doctor pulled over the sonogram machine. My hand tightened around Remington's, and I couldn't look away from his eyes as the doctor continued with his tests.

"There's your baby, Madame Michaels." The doctor's voice broke the tension-filled air, and I jerked my gaze away from my fiancé and blinked at the screen.

The doctor looked at me and then Remington, smiling slightly. "Very healthy and active." He plucked some tissues from a nearby table, and even before his hand could land on my stomach, Remington snatched them from his fingers with a fierce, possessive look on his face.

The poor guy! He obviously didn't know what hit him as he blinked up at my scowling fiancé.

The baby was doing well, but due to my previous medical history and today's fall, the doctor advised that I should be on bed rest, at least for the next couple of weeks. After asking us to make an appointment to see a gynecologist in two days, he rose from his chair. Remington shot to his feet eagerly, and the doctor shoved his hands in his pockets, taking a step back.

"So let me get this straight. My fiancée should be on bed rest for the next couple of weeks. Is that correct?" Did he have to sound so smug about it?

"Yes."

Remington's hand shot out toward the doctor, who slowly relinquished his with caution. "Thank you." He grabbed my clothes, and as soon as the door closed, he locked it and strode toward me. After making a fast job of dressing me while murmuring about doctor's orders, he left the room and returned, pushing a wheelchair.

"Jesus, Remington. I'm not an invalid," I said, standing up from the bed.

He raised his eyebrow, unleashing The Look, willing me into submission. I bowed to the pressure.

"Remind me to use bleach to wipe out the image of him looking down your pussy," he grumbled behind me as he pushed me down the hallway and toward the waiting area.

Heat slapped my face. "Remington, he was just doing his job."

"I have done dirty things to your pussy," he continued, as if he hadn't heard what I said. "Things that have given me a godly status."

"You realize you still have to work very hard to earn the points you lost, right?"

He fell quiet. I looked over my shoulder and saw the haunted look back on his face again.

"I know," he said quietly.

Chapter Sixty-Seven

Selene

We arrived back home at around nine p.m., after Remington's father was wheeled back into the ICU. The bullet had missed his heart by an inch. By the time we left, he was still drowsy, so Remington assured him he'd visit him again tomorrow.

Adrien was already asleep. After letting my parents, sister and Estelle know everything was okay, Remington excused himself and headed to his office, but not before he gave me one of his patented looks. The one that said, *stay put, I'll be back*. He was taking the doctor's advice seriously. As soon as he left, I stood up and went to the kitchen.

"How are you holding up?" my mom asked.

"Good." I shrugged.

"Remington is quite a special man. I had my doubts, but after seeing how he takes care of you, I couldn't ask for a better person for you. He literally worships the ground you walk on. Although he glowers too much for a man so young, it doesn't take away his appeal," Mom said. I smiled tiredly while filling my glass with water from the tap.

"He is."

She sighed. "You're angry with us for not telling you the truth." I looked over my shoulder to find my mother leaning on the island, her brow furrowed as she studied me.

"I'm disappointed." I joined her at the island and sat on one of the seats.

"I would do it all over again if it meant protecting you."

"Funny. He said the same thing."

"Selene." She took my hand in hers, and I met her gaze. "Don't waste time being angry at him. I respect him for what he did, and the fact he didn't tell you, especially in the condition you were in, shows me how much he cares. Sometimes the people who love you do things that seem unfathomable at the time but make sense in the end."

I knew this. Everything she said was true. I had spent the past six years trying to love a man who didn't love me. Yet, here was one who was doing everything he could to protect me, even going to the extent of breaking his own rules. God, why did this have to be so hard?

"Did—what about Diane's father? Is he alive?"

She nodded. "Sit down. We need to talk." I did as I was told. "Your father knows about him. I also told Marley everything when she arrived from town. I was married to Diane's father for three years before I realized he and I didn't have a future. He wasn't good to us. He was always suspicious that I was doing things behind his back. He would come home drunk and hit me. Sometimes he seemed desperate and made me swear I wasn't going to leave him. He would claim some people were following him because he had discovered some government secrets. He was a complete mess."

My heart was beating fast by the time she stopped talking. "He was schizophrenic?"

She shrugged. "I didn't stick around to find out. He terrified me, and I knew if I didn't leave, he would end up hurting us. Last I heard, he was being held in a psychiatric ward. I never looked back after that."

I quickly slid from my chair, rounded the island and hugged her tightly. "I'm so sorry, Mom."

She pulled back and smiled. "There is nothing to be sorry about. I met your father, and everything changed. He made everything better, just like the way Remington makes your eyes light up."

We chatted for a little while until I couldn't keep my eyes open any longer.

I yawned, tired. After saying goodnight to my mom, I excused myself and headed toward the stairs. Suddenly Remington was behind me. I felt his touch as he hooked his pinkie finger with mine, and I shamelessly clutched it like my life depended on it.

Once inside his room, I halted in front of the bed. "You don't need to do this. I'm capable of climbing the stairs without falling, you know."

"I'll carry you up and down the stairs. I'm following the doctor's orders, you know, bed rest and no stress. I'm at your beck and call. Any time of day." The way he was staring at me made my heart soften even more, and the anger I held on to melt a little.

I rolled my eyes and turned away from him, hiding a smile.

He spoiled me, and I really didn't mind. In fact, I craved it. I wanted to be spoiled, and I was beginning to realize what I had been missing. But tonight, I needed space.

I grabbed a T-shirt and shorts, then headed to the bathroom to brush my teeth.

"Where are you going?"

I glanced up to see him frowning at me in the mirror. "I need space to think. I can't sleep in here tonight."

He dug his fingers into his hair, frowning deeper, and then fixed his gaze on mine in the mirror. "All right. Just tonight?"

I dropped my gaze to the toothbrush in my hand. "Just give me time, okay?"

He nodded and leaned against the wall, crossing his arms on his chest, and I knew he wasn't leaving until I was tucked safely in bed.

"Sleep in here," he said when I left the bathroom with him hot on my trail. He grabbed his sexy, black pajama pants and gave me a chaste kiss on my lips before throwing the heavy bedcover aside for me to climb in bed. After making sure I was comfortable, he pulled the cover to my chin, then straightened and watched me.

Christ, did he have to look at me with so much love? So much hope, adoration and longing? The man melted my defences just by being alive and breathing. I knew there was no way I could stay away from him.

"*Bonne nuit, Selene.* I'll be across the hall from you." He turned and headed for the door.

"*Bonne nuit*, Remington."

Once he left, I switched off the lamp on the nightstand. Immediately I missed his warm body. But tonight, I needed some time away from him. I needed to think because my mind was in chaos and I had to come to terms with everything that had happened up to this moment before I could move forward with my life.

He'd already assured me several times that he didn't get involved with me because of the looks. I believed him, at least in the back of my mind. I'd seen how he looked at me with pure, uninhibited love.

I had been trying so hard not to break down until this minute, a huge feat. I'd been doing so well the past weeks. I hadn't let my wayward emotions get the better of me. But I couldn't anymore. My chest ached where my heart beat relentlessly. I wasn't sure what I was feeling anymore; the shock of seeing Colette, the woman who had attempted to kill me turned out to be my half-sister. The memory of seeing the blood on my underwear. The relief I felt during the ultrasound…

I buried my face in the covers and sobbed softly.

There was a soft knock on the door followed by gentle footfalls on the tiled floor.

"Selene? Are you awake?" Marley asked. "I saw Remington go inside the other room, so I wanted to check on you. Don't tell me you threw your future husband out of his own bed?" She chuckled softly.

"Oh, Marley." I pulled the covers off my face and turned the light on.

"Oh, my God, what's wrong?" She climbed on the bed quickly. "You regret tossing him out, right?"

My sister was just like me, deflecting serious situations.

"Aren't you freaked out about this? We have a sister we didn't know about."

"Come here," she said, tugging my arm. I sat up and faced her. "I'm so sorry Colette tried to kill you. And I'm also so sorry I couldn't be with you at the hospital. I was extremely worried about you, but I'm glad everything turned out okay. Yes, I freaked out when Mom told me about Diane and then almost hit the roof when I heard she was Colette.

Remington's supposedly-dead-wife-turned-stalker. But you know what? She will get the help she needs.

"I know you're mad at Remington, but I think this is fate. Otherwise, why would God throw two women who are related in his path?"

I bit my cheek, mulling over her theory. "I guess I had better organize my thoughts by morning. Remington won't stay away. I know him too well."

She hugged me, then kissed my cheek and slid out of the bed. "Damn right, he won't. I love you, sis."

"Right back at you, kid," I said, as I leaned over the nightstand and switched off the light, but not before I saw the fierce scowl on her face. She hated it when I called her kid, but sometimes, I couldn't resist teasing her.

Hours later, as dawn began to creep across the sky, I flipped from my back to my side and stared into the darkness. I hadn't slept a wink. I wanted so badly to traverse the distance between me and where Remington slept, but I didn't.

I heard the door open, then soft footfalls as they headed toward me. Seconds later, I felt the bed dip, followed by a hot, hard body on my back. His scent slammed into me, stealing my breath.

I pretended I was asleep, wanting to see what Remington was up to. He pulled me into him, laying his hand on my stomach, and groaned before pressing a kiss on my shoulder.

"I know I lost points when I lied to you. I intend to earn them back and then some for the rest of our lives." He kissed my neck.

I curled into him, sighing. I hadn't slept since I came in here. My pride had kept me from crawling to the room across the hall. I'd spent my entire life yearning for a man who would love and adore me for me. Craving it. A man who wanted to spoil me without asking for anything in return. I found him in Remington, yet here I was.

"Did she ever tell you her reason for faking her own death?"

He sighed, sounding weary. "Apparently, she thought if she came back to me, she would lose her freedom to live her life."

"I still don't get it."

"Me either. She seems a little…unbalanced. Something is off about this situation."

Remington sounded so defeated, and all I wanted was to turn around and comfort him. I opened my mouth and told him what my mother said about Colette's father. After that, Remington was silent as he mulled my words.

"I wouldn't have guessed," he finally said. "She seemed so normal before all this happened. Sometimes she would get needy, paranoid. She used to beg me to never leave her. I found it to be an endearing quality…Christ!" His body shuddered against mine.

"I'm not going to let her win. She's done so much and almost succeeded. I'm still mad at you, Remington. I know you were trying to protect me. I understand that now, but I still can't help feeling angry. Maybe it's my pride, I don't know, but just let me be mad at you a little longer, okay? It gives me a little control over this situation, even though I had none to begin with. I really hate feeling helpless."

He sighed, and I tilted my head to meet his gaze. "Be mad at me, but at the end of the day, I want you in my arms where you can continue being mad at me while I make love to you." He grinned roguishly. "I don't mind at all. Even scream while I fuck you, pounding my cock inside you and you screaming how angry you are at me."

"God, you say the sexiest things," I said, fighting the heat curling between my legs. Damn him for making me want him, even though my head was in chaos. "I need to start looking after myself, if not for me, then for the baby."

"I will earn back your forgiveness," he swore, his voice hoarse with emotion.

Epilogue

Remington

Early spring

She walked into our room, her hips swaying seductively. She pushed me back with a finger and I fell onto the bed, my eyes narrowed at her. "What are you up to?"

"That's for me to know and for you to find out." She dropped on her knees and quickly undid my belt. The minute her fingers came in contact with my cock, I winced, and this time it wasn't in pain, but the pleasure-pain that comes with having a hard-on the better half of the evening and knowing there was no way to take care of it but bite your cheek and pretend you are having the time of your life.

Today had been the yearly Pets Anonymous Auction. I had spent the night sitting next to Selene, my hands wandering restlessly all over her body, unable to keep them to myself. Then I dragged her into the women's bathroom and gave her the best tongue-fuck she had ever had. She called me a god—a title I humbly accepted—before declaring my tongue was a work of art.

Then, during the dance after the auction, *her* hands had spent four dances slipping inside my trousers, teasing me under the lowered lights. She'd whispered in my ear, daring me to come in her hand. Then she'd withdrawn that wicked hand before I could come and pulled my head down, kissing me, destroying whatever reservations I had left after all that torture.

And now, here she was, wearing tiny pieces of lace. The knickers hardly covered her pussy, and her breasts were so full they were pouring out of the little thing she called a bra.

I could sneak my fingers under the flimsy material, rip it off her body, and fuck her from here to Sunday, but I was curious to see what she was up to.

She leaned over, balancing carefully on the black heels she had been wearing the entire night, grabbed the red lipstick from the nightstand and applied it carefully, teasingly, on her lush lips.

Bloody fuck, fuck, fuck!

"Selene?" My voice was hoarse with need. She had tried several times but always ended up bailing.

"Shh. I have got some moves. I'm about to blow your mind." My brows shot up as my lips fought a smile. "Do you think you're the only one who watches porn?"

"*You* watch porn? No wonder you're not always in bed when I wake up in the middle of the night."

"Yeah, that's the baby keeping me up at night, bouncing on my bladder. Jesus, he or she is quite the kicker."

I laughed, unbelievably turned on. "I want to draw you like this. *Mon Dieu*, you are beautiful." I traced my hands along her full hips.

"I might just let you. I love the first painting you did." She pressed her lips together, and my balls tightened as I watched the crimson lipstick spread seductively.

I had finished working on the painting weeks ago, and now it stood in my art room. I could never get enough of staring at it.

She placed the lipstick back, then cupped the base of my cock and lightly squeezed. Still holding my gaze through her lashes, she lowered her head to the underside of my balls, licking all the way up to the head. My eyes fell shut and my toes curled, my breath coming out in spurts. I threw my head back as that sinful mouth continued its ministrations, and when I opened my eyes, I came face to face with the reflection of us in the mirror on the wardrobe. My gaze wandered down to her arse, and I groaned.

"*Mon Dieu*, you're so beautiful. Just look at that arse." I trailed my hands down her body, and she swatted them away.

"Lie back."

"Oh, Bossy Selene is back, *oui*?"

She didn't reply but expertly licked and sucked me slowly, taking me deeper into her mouth.

"Oh, fuck, Selene!" I shouted. "God, you're going to kill me."

She moaned; I grunted. She murmured, "You taste so damn good. I can't believe I've been missing this," then took me into her mouth, and I lost focus. My hand tangled in her hair, guiding her on. Her hands applied the right pressure. I couldn't take it anymore. My grip tightened, and my hips rose from the bed, jerking my cock into that talented mouth.

"I'm about to come, Selene."

Her hand around my cock squeezed. I tried to pull out, but her hold told me she wasn't letting go. I came hard, and she took it all. Swallowed it and continued to suck me gently as I came down from my orgasm.

When I was able to move without feeling as though my

knees would give way, I pulled her up on the bed and kissed her.

Then I buried my head in my favourite place, at the crook of her neck. "*Je t'aime*, Selene."

"*Moi aussi, je t'aime*, Remington."

And then we fell asleep in each other's arms. Me with my jeans pushed mid-thigh and Selene wearing those pieces of cloth that always teased me, my hand pressed against her left side, slightly below her breast, and the other on her stomach.

Selene

I woke up in the middle of the night with Remington's hot body around me and a heavy leg trapping mine. Remington's hand was on my stomach.

For as long as I could remember, I'd dreamed of having my own happily ever after in a kingdom far, far away from negativity, with my king who loved the shit out of me. I found my king; he wasn't perfect. In fact, I loved the imperfection of him; I loved his possessiveness and jealousy and moody personality. I also adored his laughter.

I turned to my side and slipped my hand under the pillow, hugging it close. Something crinkled under my arm. Curious, I pulled out what felt like paper folded in two. I switched on the bedside lamp and stared at the wrinkled envelope addressed to me in a confident scrawl.

Remington's handwriting.

He wrote me a letter? When?

I quickly removed it from the envelope and glanced over

my shoulder to the handsome, sleeping man on his back, before squinting at the words on the paper.

My dearest Selene,

I woke before dawn so I could watch the rays of the sun worship your sinfully curvy body. Dawn has come and gone, but I still can't make myself leave this chair. Even sitting two feet away from you, I miss you. It sounds insane, oui?

I've been thinking about how to write this letter for a while now, but what I feel for you, Christ, it's impossible to put into words, no matter how much I plan. So I decided to sit and write whatever flows from my head and through my fingers. I've never been one for sentiment or spontaneity. I plan everything meticulously because failure is something I cannot accept. I've always lived and played by my rules. But, ma belle, I've broken several rules since I met you.

I wish you could see yourself the way I see you. Your strength to pick up the pieces of a shattered life, spread your wings and fly, astounds me. You're sexy, confident, shy and brave. And whenever I see you with Adrien, how much he adores you, how your eyes light up, I vow again that I will convince you to stay. The more time I spend with you, the deeper I fall into you, and I'm still falling harder. Mon Dieu! When I try to remember how my life was before you crashed into it, all I remember is a constant dull sound. I'm not certain what happened, but between one breath and the next, I was sinking, drowning in you. I'm scared by what I feel for you. How much I feel for you. But then you look at me with those eyes that seem to see right through me, and I forget to breathe. Forget everything, but you.

Right now I'm torn between watching you sleep and slipping between the sheets, curling my body around yours and sliding my cock inside you. Bite, lick and kiss every inch of you until you wake up, but that would rob me of the pleasure of looking into your eyes as you take me inside you.

I wonder what the future has for us, but if it were up to me, I would chain you to my side and never let you go.

You had my heart even before I had a chance to give it to you.

Ever yours,

RSG

Oh. God. Remington sat down and wrote me a letter? I wiped the tears rolling down my cheeks, smiling. This man was so full of surprises. The letter was dated September twenty-two, a few days before the incident in the château. Taking a deep breath to calm my racing heart, I tucked it back where I'd found it and risked a glance over my shoulder, and my breath caught in my chest. Green sleep eyes stared right back at me, lips slightly parted as he studied me.

I smiled. "It's beautiful, thank you."

His grin was slow to appear. "I'm glad you liked it." His voice was hoarse from sleep. Sexy. I waited for him to say more. "I wanted to give it to you last night, but the evening took a different direction." He winked at me. "I couldn't do it before because the incident. I was afraid how you'd react to those words."

"I'll definitely go shopping to buy a frame for it." I grinned at him, settling back on the bed and pulling him in for a long kiss. Then, I pulled back and buried my head on his chest. "You're amazing. And I'm lucky you are in my life."

"We are lucky to be in each other's lives."

I closed my eyes, feeling his warm breath fan my hair on the nape of my neck until I felt his breathing even out in sleep.

Beneath this twenty-six-year old woman, I was still the seven-year-old girl, a princess, who craved this. Perfection. I had my kingdom, and I wasn't going to let anyone destroy it. I pulled the sheet over our bodies and curled into Remington. He mumbled in his sleep, kissed my hair and his grip tightened, then continued snoring softly in my ear.

Remington

Two months later ...

I watched Selene step through the château's doors, with her father's hand around hers. Adrien stood on her left, beaming proudly. My son and my wife. My treasure. *Mon Dieu*, she was beautiful. Her body had filled out just the way I loved in the past few months. Her breasts were fuller, her hips curvy and rounder. My gaze, unable to absorb her fast enough, narrowed in on her belly, now rounded with child—*my child*.

Utterly breathtaking.

Marley, standing behind her, tapped her shoulder and whispered something in her ear. She nodded and raised her head, her eyes roving the crowd until they found mine. Then she smiled, and I gripped my seat hard to stop myself from doing something insane. Like stalk toward her, haul her over my shoulder and march upstairs to our room.

Right after the Colette debacle, Selene had been angry with me for a full month. Her mood swings didn't help matters. I had so much to make up for. I learned a lesson: a pissed-off Selene was passionate. A turned-on Selene was just as eager, and the Selene who loved me had a heart so big, I was still amazed she forgave me after keeping the truth from her. Colette was now locked away in a psychiatric ward but was charged with attempted murder as well as endangering people's lives. The nurse that had tried to kill Selene at the hospital in Marseilles had been charged as an accomplice to Colette's plans. Colette refused to see anyone, even her own mother, which broke Ines's heart. And Selene's, too, although she seemed to brush it off easily. I could see it in her face, the minute she thought someone wasn't watching. I had finally gotten around to filing for divorce because I wanted to go into my marriage with my fiancée without my past weighing us down.

Life was getting back to normal. My past had collided with my present, causing chaos. I remember wondering briefly if there was a way I could make amends for everything that had happened. But my brave woman, my fiancée, had surpassed my expectations by standing by my side. My father had been released from the hospital and was staying in Hotel Catherine, recovering. Relationships were on the mend, and I couldn't ask for more.

I had caught up with my brothers a few days before and tried to explain as much as I could about what had happened to Colette. According to the therapist handling her case, she seemed to have lost contact with reality given her psychotic behaviour. She hadn't received the help she needed all those years ago, and her condition had worsened. The therapist couldn't exactly pinpoint what triggered this kind of behaviour and still needed to do more tests. But according to Ines, her father had exhibited the same symptoms, so it could be hereditary. I couldn't remember seeing any warning signs of instability. Or maybe I did but was blinded by my feelings for her and ignored any indication that pointed toward her actions.

Other than that, it wasn't my place to extract information from her attending physicians. My wife had died five years before; she was no longer my responsibility. Needless to say, we were still in the dark as to why she had become so unhinged and when it had first occurred. The police had eventually exhumed the bones I had buried five years ago and were investigating who the body belonged to, something they would have done before, especially in this age of technology.

We had decided to tell Adrien the truth that his mother hadn't died but had become very ill; we knew we needed to wait until he was older so he could comprehend something we still had difficulty trying to fathom. Perhaps by then, we might have answers. Perhaps not. Anthony had spent the night with us as we talked and was somewhat an ally and friend to me now. He was a good man.

My beautiful Selene had been incredible as she had resolved the mind-fuck of my prior wife's identity. She knew I loved her for her and not for any likeness to Colette. In many respects, she had enough of Anthony in her that I now wondered how I had ever seen a physical likeness in the first place. Her amazing act of bravery to protect Adrien had forged an even tighter bond between them, and my love for her grew more than I thought possible. And she was about to become my beloved wife, and I couldn't be happier.

I spent the better half of last night with my ear pressed against her stomach, hoping to hear something. A heartbeat, a kick maybe? I just wanted *something*. I had missed most of those moments while Colette was pregnant, because she hated when I did it.

Someone whistled beside me, pulling me out of my thoughts. I turned at the sound in time to see Andrew's wife smack him on his arm and roll her eyes. I glared at him through narrowed eyes. Although my brain shouted at me that he was my best friend and married to an extremely beautiful woman, my heart demanded I set him straight.

Eyes on the prize, Remington. Eyes on the fucking prize.

I shifted my focus to the curvaceous goddess. Her smile widened, and she mouthed, "I love you."

I winked at her and did something I knew would get a rise out of her. "Bloody hell you do," I mouthed back at her, and she rolled her eyes, shaking her head. She raised her hands and motioned then around her head, indicating my head was growing larger. I laughed. Then Grace stepped through the door and handed her a bouquet of red and white roses similar to the ones I had sent to her room the first time she arrived at Hotel Catherine.

"Hey, sunshine," Luc nudged my arm. I turned to face him. "Remember when I told you that you'd find a way? You did it. I am so happy for you; you know that? Fuck, it's good to see you smile often these days."

"Thanks, brother," I said, smiling, my heart swelling at the praise. Lucien thought I was strong. But what he didn't know was that he made me strong. My entire family made me strong, and if it weren't for them, I wouldn't be the person I was today. But I wasn't going to tell him that. At least not today. His ego would steal Selene's thunder.

"When I look at both of you, I know what you mean. You two can't keep your eyes off each other. If I asked you to describe her in one word, what would it be?"

The song chosen for the processional began, and I focused once again on my bride. Adrien held her other hand as she walked down the red-carpeted aisle toward me.

This woman who had gone through so much still managed to get back on her feet with her head held high. The woman who fucked as passionately as she loved. "One word." I narrowed my eyes, studying the woman who drove me insane in a thousand different ways. After her father whispered something in her ear, she tossed her head back and laughed. *Mon Dieu!*

That sound hit me right in my chest as it always did, sending heat and desire rushing all over my body. All I wanted was to drag her upstairs, lock the door and devour every part of her curvy form. To rip off the little, white lace piece of cloth she called underwear and sink my cock so deep inside her. "It's impossible to describe her in just one word. She's my home, crazy beautiful, witty, loveable, sometimes insecure, and a whole lot of confident. She has a big appetite..." for both food and me, but I wasn't going to say that out loud. "But if I was to sum her up in one word, it would be *mine*."

Selene

Late May...

"Stop kicking me," Remington said sleepily, pulling me into him and kissing my shoulder, before drifting back to sleep.

"I didn't do it on purpose—UGH." I squeezed my eyes tight as the pain in my midsection tore through me. I peeled his hand from my middle and dragged myself upright. "Oh God, fuck, damn it."

Remington jolted upright on the bed, any signs of sleep vanishing, and switched on the lamp on the nightstand. "Is it time?" he asked, turning to face me and frowning, touching my forehead. "*Mon Dieu,* are you okay? You are sweating."

The pain faded as fast as it had appeared, and my body relaxed once more. I slumped back on the bed and glared at him. "Am I okay?"

He blinked at me, seeming surprised, then quickly recovered, his face softening. "What are the intervals?"

"Ten minutes," I muttered, feeling guilty for snapping at him. The last twenty-four hours had been a challenge for both of us. The first time they happened, we had just had sex and fallen asleep in a warm mood of love and awoke in a nightmare of pain. Remington had bundled me inside the car and rushed me to the hospital, only to have the doctor tell us I was experiencing Braxton Hicks contractions. The baby was due in three weeks. We drove back home, but the contractions hadn't eased off.

"I'm taking you to the hospital." He slid out of bed and strode to the dresser. He came out moments later with his shirt on and buttoning his jeans. My clothes were slung over one shoulder and he sat on the bed, slipping a hand on my back to help me. "Sit up for me, *my belle*."

I did and winced as pain dug into my lower back. He quickly climbed on the bed and sat behind me, rubbing my back with his hand.

"Better?" he asked, his breath warm on my cheek as he kissed my hair.

I nodded, taking a deep breath, then straightened and put on the clothes. He left the bed and grabbed the bag I had packed a week ago in preparation for this occasion. He slid a hand around my waist, nudging me to stand up.

"I feel like a hippo."

He grinned at me and like always, my knees trembled. "A very beautiful hippo that's about to become the mother of my child."

I stiffened and glared at him again. "Do you want me to sit on you? Because I will and make damn sure I enjoy it. What happened to all the sweet talking and carrying me?"

He dragged his free hand through his hair, his lips twitching as though fighting a smile. "I'm nervous."

"Aw, you big softie. I know you are," I said, as we left the bedroom and started for the stairs.

"I wish I could do something to ease the pain."

He grabbed the coats at the door and held out mine for me. "I'm going to miss seeing you barefoot and pregnant, walking around the house."

I glanced up and saw him staring dreamily in a distance. "You liked that, didn't you?"

He grinned again as we walked out the front door and he guided me toward the car. He actually growled under his breath before sending me a look loaded with want. As soon as he'd tucked me safely in my seat, he rounded the car quickly and slid into his. "I'd keep you pregnant and happy for our entire life, if I could get away with it."

"Please don't force me to kill you. I want our children to grow up with a father, and at this rate, there is a slim chance of that happening."

His snicker started with a soft chuckle followed by a full-bodied laugh. "I just love how this relationship has turned out. You threaten to kill me and I love you even more, despite that."

God, I love this man so much. "Just drive before I—oh shit, fucking pain, pain, pain! Ohhhhh God, Drive, drive, drive darn it!"

The amusement faded, and before long, the car peeled out of the driveway and sped toward the hospital. By the time we arrived, the contractions were about five minutes apart, and Remington's patented look—the one that reminded me of the first time I met him— made an appearance, ready to scare anyone in his way of his baby coming into the world. Behind that look, I saw how worried he was. I knew he hated feeling helpless, but every time I looked at him to let him know that everything would be okay, his face softened and his lips tilted upward in a confident smile.

"I'll be right back, all right?" He leaned forward and kissed my forehead, then straightened. I nodded, breathing in and out like the midwife showed me to do when I started attending Lamaze classes.

He left and came back pushing a wheelchair, made sure I was safely seated and wheeled us toward the reception area, and soon one of the nurses was guiding us to the maternity ward and into a private room.

"Dial down the scowl, baby. I can't be turned on when I'm about to give birth," I teased him while rubbing my stomach and winced as pain ricocheted down my spine. "And you're scaring off the staff," I added as I noticed the nurse circling us as if she was afraid to come closer.

Grabbing the gown the nurse was holding out to me, he met my gaze and the corner of his mouth lifted in a small smile, but it didn't reach his eyes.

Remington

"The doctor will be with you in a moment," the nurse said, smiling at my wife before giving me a nervous look.

"Thank you," I said, attempting to make up for my behaviour. *Merde!*

I'd been extremely nervous ever since I'd taken Selene home from the hospital after the doctor said she wasn't in labour. Just her body preparing itself for our child's birth. But now the contractions were severe. How could I sit here and watch her go through the pain? I couldn't remember the birthing process being excruciating during Adrien's birth. One minute Colette was having pains, and the next, Adrien came out kicking like a champion.

The doctor walked in as soon as Selene was settled on the bed, and after checking her, he grinned wide and told us the baby would be arriving soon.

Two hours later, I was still wiping the sweat off her brow. Selene's breathing was laboured, and the doctor had administered oxygen to help her. He had given her the option of a caesarian, but my beautiful, stubborn wife was determined to have this baby the natural way.

She screamed and cursed severely, making my ears burn as both the dirty words and the fear shot through my veins.

"You're tough, *ma belle*," I murmured in her ear, rubbing my hand down her back in soothing circles as she continued to breathe the way the Lamaze coach had shown her. "I am in awe of you. You are the strongest woman I have ever met." I never wanted to see her go through this pain again.

"I don't feel so strong right now," she said, panting.

"You are, and I love you."

One hour later …

I stared at the adorable wonder in my arms.

"Hope Estelle. A perfect name for my little princess." I leaned down and lay my girl into my wife's waiting arms, then straightened to stare at them both as she breastfed her. We had decided on the first name, because that's what this little fighter gave us. Hope that everything would be all right. "I don't ever want to see you go through that kind of pain again. I felt helpless. I don't like it."

She looked at me through her lashes. "What if I said I wanted more of this?"

I blinked at her. "*What?*"

"Isn't she adorable? Like a little angel."

I tried to catch my breath as panic threatened to bring me down. "Didn't you just hear what I said?" She blinked up innocently at me. I stared down at her with the look she now called The Submission Look. She returned it with a defiant one.

"You wanted to kill me five hours ago at the mere mention of more babies."

She snorted. "Try carrying a baby for what feels like years, craving food, throwing up and peeing every few seconds, then tell me if you wouldn't want to end someone's life."

I glanced down at her and the baby, and my respect for Selene increased ten-fold. I couldn't wait for Adrien to meet his little sister. "You would go through that again?"

Tears rolled down her face. "A million times over."

I wanted more babies. I really did. But I needed time to get over the almost heart-attack I went through as I watched her in pain. The more I stared at how content she looked, the more I knew I would stop at nothing to give her anything she wanted.

Everything that had happened in the past five years had led to this moment. It hadn't been an easy journey, but the ending was everything I could ever want and more. I had my two precious women in the room with me and Adrien not far away. I had love. I felt complete, and the scars that had once plagued my soul were healing, thanks to my incredible wife and family.

"I knew you were trouble the moment we met at the hotel."

She winked at me. "Ditto."

Acknowledgments

There are so many people I would like to thank for being with me throughout this journey, and even way before that. I wouldn't have been where I am without their support and friendship. First and foremost, my two children. Thank you for being patient with me, for making me laugh and for believing in me. I love you so much. My beta readers, K Webster, Amy Bosica, Shilpa Mudiganti, Sarah Kenslee Erinn, Michele Henderson Jami Tamblyn, Nanette Bradford. Thank you for being amazing and your feedback. <3 The Minxes group on Facebook... You ladies rock my world. Thank you for being so incredibly wonderful and supportive and for being my book family. Love you! To the C.O.P.A. girls and Indie Chicks ... you ladies are amazing! I still can't believe how lucky and honored I am to be part of these groups and connect with you. Your support means the world to me. Love you!! Ella Stewart, Karen Ferry, Nanette Del Bradford. I owe you my sanity and I value our friendship a lot. Thank you for being my sounding board and for the midnight chats. Love you, my besties.

I want to thank my amazing editing team – Tricia Harden at Emerald Eyes Editing, Marion at Making Manuscripts and

Becky at Hot Tree Editing. I had such a wonderful time working with you. Thank you for making this story better. Thank you to Stacey Blake from Champagne Formatting for the beautiful work you did on this book. You manage to wow me every single time. And to all the amazing bloggers: Thank you for your support, your patience. Thank you for being a huge part of our publishing journey. Seriously, we wouldn't be here without you. Much love! Lastly to my readers. Thank you for taking a chance on me and getting my books. Every message you sent to me makes me smile. I love getting your emails and reviews. Thank you for accompanying me on this ride.

xoxo Autumn

About the Author

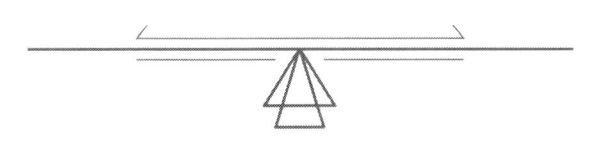

Autumn Grey writes sexy contemporary romances full of drama, steamy kisses and happy ever afters. She loves reading stories with flawed and quirky characters, broody alphas and sassy heroines.

To keep updated with Autumn's work, follow her on:

Facebook:
www.facebook.com/AuthorAutumnGreyAG

Goodreads:
www.goodreads.com/author/show/7337710.Autumn_%20Grey

Sign up for the newsletter: eepurl.com/bZEWzP

Other books

The Fall Back Series

Fall Back Skyward
Breaking Gravity

Grace Trilogy

Desolate (Book One)
Disgraceful (Book Two)
Absolution (Book Three)

What Happens In The End - M/M Romance
(coming May 2022)

Printed in Great Britain
by Amazon

83810272R00276